# The Valt

## Peter Chegwidden

Cover design by Jacqueline Abromeit.

www.publishnation.co.uk

**Other books by Peter Chegwidden**
(those marked # on Kindle only)

*Murder Mysteries based in rural Kent*

- The Chortleford Mystery
- Death at the Oast
- Death comes to Little Scampering

*Other murder mysteries*

- No Shelter for the Wicked
- Deadened Pain #

*Historical Novels*

- Kindale
- The Master of Downsland

*Adventures of Tom the Cat*

- Tom Investigates
- Tom Vanishes #

*Short Story Collections*

- Sheppey Short Stories #
- Souls Down the River

# Chapter One

*Author's Introduction*

This novel starts with two people in love. The second world war drives them apart and the story charts their separate and very different lives, and those of their families and immediate friends in the post-war years. Tragedy and joy, suffering and happiness, achievement and failure lie in wait. But these two people are never quite free of their love for each other. Occasionally their paths cross. Could they ever be re-united?

The tale is based largely in South Woodford (east London/Essex border) where I grew up during the fifties, sixties and seventies, and I have called upon many memories and family recollections, including those related to wartime experiences. Most locations are real including Mersea Island in Essex where my family had a caravan, later a chalet, at Cooper's Beach.

A number of real events is incorporated in the story.

For more detailed information and explanations please see my afterthoughts at the end of the book when you get there.

\*\*\*

*April 1939: Southend, Essex*

"I reckon it'll be war."

Andy was looking over the wide Thames estuary yet not really seeing anything. Nobody had spoken for several minutes and nobody else spoke now. He didn't feel inspired to continue for he reasoned there was no need. The four of them sitting on the beach, sand and shingle, not far from the water's edge, all too aware of the implications of Andy's words.

Micky's left hand was occupied gently tossing stones a couple of feet down the beach. His right arm was in the care of Enid who was hugging it tightly as if she knew war would drive a wedge of separation between them.

"That bloke Hitler," Mary finally intervened, "they're all worried about him, aren't they? They say he'll have to be stopped if he goes too far."

"And that'll mean war, won't it? We'd have to stop him coming here," Andy added, "and he looks like he wants to grab what he can." All four sat in silent contemplation, each musing on what war might mean to them. Then Andy continued in a mischievous manner, "So we ought to make the most of what we've got now," turning to Mary and snatching a kiss before the manoeuvre caused them to unbalance and topple over backwards, much to the amusement of Micky and Enid.

It had been a good day out but the afternoon was getting ready to hand over to the evening and it would soon be time to go home. A day trip to Southend. The pier, fish and chips, the beach, the amusements, beer, many laughs, plenty of chatter.

Micky and Enid had been friends from infancy, childhood sweethearts and now lovers destined for marriage, their recent engagement party a modest affair at her parent's home in Forest Gate. No date had been set for the wedding. There wasn't the money. In contrast Andy employed his boyish charm and good looks to gather up girls at will and was prone to discard them just as easily, Mary being his current success, and he was already tiring of her. As they walked to the station Mary was serious again.

"I mean, that Hitler, I don't like what's going on in Germany...."

"Aw give it a rest," Andy interrupted. "Nobody wants a war, do they?"

"Just saying we should take it a bit seriously. It might just come to it." Silence descended over the quartet, Enid being particularly worried and fearing the worst but feeling unable to speak. And in time they arrived at Chalkwell station where some of the gaiety of the day returned to them, and they were laughing and smiling again as a fussy, puffing but efficient tank engine pulled a long rake of coaches into the platform ready to take them back from whence they came.

\*\*\*

*May 1949: Leytonstone, east London*

Enid looked in the mirror, looked at the black eye, looked at the black eye she'd told everyone was caused by her absent-mindedly walking into an open cupboard door. She was used to lying. Her husband was angry again two nights ago and had lashed out as usual. At least she'd been able to protect her infant children. And that wasn't always possible. A violent man, his worse moods seemed to be when he'd probably spent the evening with another woman, not that Enid knew for sure, it was just feminine intuition. He said he was having a drink with his mates, something he truly did from time to time. But she knew it wasn't always true.

And it had all been so different. He'd wooed her, made her feel special and wanted, been so charming and caring and proved so loving and considerate. He was kind and sympathetic, so feeling, so generous and thoughtful. He'd been everything Enid wanted in a man.

They had married after the war and he'd had enough money to help them get good accommodation, but the happiness had started to evaporate then. The first born, the greatest of joys for Enid, marked the end of her reasonable yet difficult life with her husband as he'd changed and become the man he'd probably been all his young life, not the man she'd fallen in love with, but the man who had deceived her to win her heart. They had deliberately postponed the wedding until after the war in case either should fall victim to the ravages of such an horrendous conflict. Now Enid knew all he had wanted was a wife to show off. It was presently a dark compliment; she had indeed been a most attractive young lady, but one that was spoken-for, the girlfriend of a man who had known her from her youngest days.

As such thoughts cascaded through her mind so the tears fell and she sat and sobbed until little Lorna, precious little Lorna, her eldest, called for her. She dried her eyes and became a loving mother again.

\*\*\*

*1940*
*Michael Reginald Bowen: Gunner, Royal Artillery*

There was little time between receipt of his call-up papers and his departure, and Micky wanted to spend every available second with Enid, their final parting being a sad, tear-sodden and very poignant occasion.

Much of his training was carried out in south-west Scotland, not far from Ecclefechan, Lockerbie and Annan. He'd never been to Scotland but decided it was such a lovely country he'd have to bring Enid there after the war. Make for a lovely holiday; Enid would adore it, he was sure.

Some of the lads, his new mates, were making friends with the local girls but it wasn't for him. Enid was his one and only, he loved her beyond words and to kiss another girl was to be unfaithful so he tried to keep himself to himself in mixed company, yet he attracted unwanted interest from their female companions.

It was in Annan that he was finally undone and unfaithful by his own terms. There had been six of them out on the town and they had conveniently met six young ladies. A very pleasant and enjoyable carefree time ensued, but as night descended and the evening wore on they paired as couples and Micky found himself with Maggie. It was pure friendship, light-hearted fun and nothing more, but when it was time to part they engaged in a warm, passionate kiss. It was meaningless, it could not compare to the beauty of the kisses he'd shared with Enid, but that night, back in barracks, he silently cried himself to sleep.

\*\*\*

*November 1940: Manor Park, east London*

Norman Belham couldn't believe his luck.

He was a lucky boy, a lucky boy. First, he had learned to his pleasure that he was in a reserved occupation and couldn't be sent to fight. Now he was being removed from the terrors of the Blitz and the prime targets of the Luftwaffe, the London docks and the surrounding towns, and packed off to Chesterfield in Derbyshire to continue his work there. Well, it was a rural spot near Chesterfield, but any form of geography was beyond Norman, and frankly he didn't care where it was as long as he was safe. Thanks heavens he'd joined that firm from school. He had initially been dreading being called up; he didn't want to be injured, perhaps maimed for life, and most definitely not killed, so he had quietly celebrated his relief when his manager informed him he would be staying where he was. Of course, he feigned disappointment, being careful not to over-do it.

What he had not anticipated were the nightly bombing raids. The last few months had been horrific. Friends and family had been killed. His parents' home, where he lived, had been destroyed. His grandmother had been taken by surprise by one raid, not been in the shelter, and had been killed as her home took a direct hit. Norman's dad was an air raid warden and he was nearly blown to smithereens one night as a bomb went off a short way behind him. He'd been injured in the blast, but not badly, and had resumed his duties a few evenings later. The young girl he shielded from the explosion was unhurt.

His brother Cedric was in the navy, on some frigate or other, Norman cared not which, and was currently on the Atlantic convoys. He'd volunteered because he wanted to go to sea.

At least Norman was now going to be as safe as safe could be. Away from his rubbishy, basic temporary accommodation, off to the countryside far away. Surely the Germans would not try to bomb him there? He went without a second thought for his parents and for Cedric. And he went without a thought for Annie Greene, his girlfriend who had died in a raid just a month previously.

***

*Singapore: February 1942*

"That's that then." Micky Bowen sat back, his face filled with sadness and resignation. "Bastards," he'd added. It wasn't clear if he meant the British or the Japanese. "Didn't think the Japs'd come down the peninsula, through that jungle. Those politicians and people should've been out here, learned more about the Japs.

5

The one side of Singapore they didn't think worth defending. Stupid bastards." Reg nodded and said nothing; there was nothing to say. They both thought about all their mates who had died defending this British outpost. Hadn't Churchill said surrender couldn't be contemplated? Yet Percival had surrendered.

"Bastards," Micky repeated. Reg nodded again.

*** 

*December 1943: Wanstead, east London*

Ethel Bowen looked once again at the Red Cross notice. The official note had said that her son was missing, presumed dead, the Red Cross unable to find anything to the contrary. Her only son, gone, killed by the Japanese, fighting for her freedom. It wasn't right, it couldn't be. So far from home; Singapore. Whatever was he doing there? Did it really matter? Wasn't Hitler and Germany the real threat?

"Eric where are you?" she asked out loud. Eric was long gone, probably a victim of the Great War, the war to end all wars they'd called it. He'd been a good husband and father but never really recovered from those years in the trenches when he'd witnessed his comrades dying one after the other until his own demise was a mathematical certainty. Yet somehow he'd survived despite being shot to pieces, and returned home without his right arm and two fingers on his left hand. The wound to his right leg meant that he would always walk with a limp. That was what he got for four years fighting for his country and now, Ethel wondered, was it all worth it? War again, war uglier than ever, war that had now claimed their only son, dear Micky.

Eric had died six years ago and in the agony of loss she'd found herself almost clinging to Micky, and her pains had worsened the closer he became to Enid. A lovely girl but one that was sure to take Micky away. Even Ethel had to admit they seemed made for each other and that would mean more heartbreak, but Enid was just so genuine, a beautiful person in every sense, and one that cared about Ethel.

When Micky and Enid announced their engagement Ethel was swamped with joy and sadness all at the same time, but Enid knew how attached her fiancé was to his mother and was most reassuring with Mrs Bowen when it came to planning the future, kindly suggesting they wouldn't live far away and would see much of her, of that she could be certain. Yes, a nice loving daughter-in-law. And Ethel had taken to Enid's parents when they met. She knew she wouldn't be alone, but still felt she was staring a kind of abandonment in the face, and such stark realisation always brought pain.

Then came war. Germany again. Micky and his best mate Andy had thought about volunteering straight away so they could go into the war together, serve together, but Ethel and Andy's parents had dissuaded them. Eventually the call-up papers came anyway and Micky and Andy were separated.

Andy, a gunner on a bomber in the RAF was long gone, his plane shot down over enemy territory. His mother had rung with the sad news. Ethel now had two sad duties to perform, as if her own grief and sorrow was not enough to cope with. She rang Enid first and communication was not easy. Enid was in the ATS and was currently based in Sheffield and it was some hours before they finally spoke. That didn't make the anguish any easier for either of them. Officially Micky was missing and both women clung to the belief he might still be alive even though the Red Cross had been unsuccessful locating him. Yes, there was still hope. A slender dream to hang on to but better than giving in to the devastation ravaging their emotions right now.

Later, Ethel rang Andy's mum with the latest news.

At least, Ethel considered, by putting the wedding off until the end of the war Enid was spared the suffering of being a widow, as if that mattered to Enid. And across the other side of the world her fiancé was indeed still alive, yet only just, already subjected to the harsh regime of his Japanese captors, people who believed surrender was cowardly and should never, ever be a matter of choice, people who believed their prisoners were of little value as human beings. It was a different culture, one the West was unfamiliar with, one that was to lead to a fearsome and seemingly inhuman outcome.

# Chapter Two

*January 1944: Hakodate camp, Japan*

The start of Micky's captivity had left him demoralised and disorientated. His ID tag had gone missing. He was bewildered, unwell, and defeated. Thus began the process by which he vanished from the records.

By now he had borne witness to unimaginable happenings at the hands of the Japanese. He was stick-thin and had seen fearsome beatings handed out for the most minor of offences, he himself having been whipped with a bamboo cane and had no wish to repeat the punishment. There was so little food. Most of them were ill. All of them too physically weak.

"I'm having fried egg tonight," announced Billy Warne to an incredulous audience, most of whom assumed he was losing his mind. Micky smiled. He knew his friend too well. Billy came from Loughton, where Micky went to school, and he had kept their spirits up many a time with his irrepressible good humour and wit, even in times of appalling adversity. The Japanese kept them hard at work but without proper food and rest.

That night, with a small fire in front of where they slept, or tried to, Billy brought out his shovel, warmed it over the fire and then produced the tiniest birds egg you had ever seen, cracked it, fried it, and ate it in one mouthful while his comrades laughed and applauded. You could rely on Billy.

Just a few weeks later Billy died of fever having been beaten for not completing some task. Micky had watched, just as they all had; you didn't interfere. That meant death. Billy was already sick, quite delirious with fever, and incapable of work, the flogging leaving him with just hours to live. His passing left them with a terrible emptiness but gave Micky a renewed determination to survive. There was, after all, Enid's love to look forward to.

\*\*\*

*June 1944: Derbyshire*

From his place of employment close to the village of Wadshelf, west of Chesterfield, Norman Belham and his colleague and close friend Charlie Grimes would often go cycling in the glorious Derbyshire countryside, land untouched by the conflict being suffered throughout much of the world. And it was not far from Bakewell that they found company in the form of two ATS girls, also cycling during a break from their duties. Norman was at once struck by the simple beauty of one of them, although the other lacked, in his opinion, any attractiveness whatsoever. Never mind; Charlie could have her!

Friendly though the girls proved to be, the less attractive one appearing to be quite keen, there didn't seem to be any immediate progress to be made which was a disappointment to ladies-man Norman Belham, for he was quite taken with the lovelier one. Even more so when he learned she came from Forest Gate, right next door to Manor Park where he'd lived. Charlie was surprisingly shy but Dorothy, sensing Norman's interest in Enid, was concentrating her efforts with him, occasionally snuggling up to him and giggling a lot.

After their first meeting they started going out as a foursome at the rare times such a venture could be arranged, and could be found cycling the prettiest parts of the Dales, taking lunch together, and talking generally about the war when conversation was possible. Thus it was that Norman learned about Enid's lost love, Micky.

This is grand, he thought to himself, and if I play my cards right I can step in and fill the gap in her life. I just need to share her sorrow, be a shoulder to cry on, be kind and gentle, and bide my time. No point rushing. That won't work. And this beauty is worth the effort and worth waiting for.

Charlie had no intention of rushing anything, whereas Dorothy had other plans for him. He was actually starting to dread the foursome meeting up and made his feelings known to Norman, whereupon it was decided they'd say that, for the time being, they couldn't be spared from their work together. As an excuse it was successful from Charlie's point of view and worked to Norman's advantage into the bargain, for within a month he met Enid alone for a pleasant ride through the area surrounding the Chatsworth estate.

He was proceeding with caution and was not going to make any sudden and rash moves. Only when Enid showed signs of warmth towards him would he cunningly play upon her sadness and reach out to her. For the time being he would concentrate on being the perfect gentleman, her rock and support, her friend-in-need, her confidante.

It was in October that year that the long-awaited chance finally presented itself. Enid took a local bus which Norman joined on its way into the Dales, and they alighted at a chosen rural spot for a walk in the wonderful scenery that abounded in profusion. It made a good change from cycling. They'd brought picnics which they enjoyed on a stone where the footpath presented them with delightful views, and afterwards Enid spoke quite openly about what Micky's loss meant to her, the first time she had done so. Norman seized on this and put a comforting arm around her shoulder, carefully ensuring it was the lightest of touches so not to alarm her, and was surprised and thrilled when she nestled into his chest and the tears fell, the first tears she had shed in front of him.

He knew that at this very moment he must control himself, for the wrong words, the wrong action, and he could throw all his hard work away. And he still wanted his prize.

Soon the tears dried but her arms were still around him, her head just below his chin, and he could make out her fragrance which only served to intoxicate him more. Slowly she moved her head and they were looking deep into each other's eyes. He had to chance it. He had to. Gently he lowered his lips to hers and his feelings exploded as her lips responded to his and they were lost in a wealth of glorious splendour, this most fabulous of kisses, this tender surrender, this enchanting moment of truth. And Enid knew she had indeed surrendered, just as Norman knew he had won.

That night Enid lay awake in the darkness, happy again at last. She would never forget Micky, never ever, but she couldn't have Micky. He was dead. She hoped Micky's soul would be pleased for her, for hadn't she found this very special man with whom to share happiness and contentment and a future she thought she'd lost? Surely Micky would want nothing but her happiness. She had found love with Norman and that was where her life now lay.

Norman didn't lie awake. He'd been boasting to Charlie that he'd won his proud beauty and that he intended marrying her lest he should lose her, and after all his efforts to secure her love and devotion he could not now contemplate that. He went to bed a satisfied man and promptly fell into the arms of Morpheus, a deep sleep, the sleep of one untroubled by conscience or thoughts of wrong-doing.

***

*October 1944: east London-Essex border*

Ethel Bowen cut a sad figure, all the life gone out of her. Husband and son dead, she had no reason to want to live. She and Eric had longed for a second child, a brother or sister for Micky, but none came, and now she was bereft, all emotional feelings having deserted her. She was living temporarily with an elderly couple not far from the site of her destroyed home, a couple who had befriended her and were only too pleased to have her company.

The doodlebugs had brought terrors anew to the London community. Pilotless, they flew until the engine stopped then plummeted to earth regardless of what lay beneath, an indiscriminate killer. To people who had earlier been pummelled by the bombs of the Blitz this new threat seemed to add a new determination not to be defeated, and many adopted a cheerful aggression towards Hitler and his Nazis at a time when it would've been easy to capitulate.

It was a doodlebug that did for Mrs Bowen's home. At least you knew it was coming. It had a noise of its own, instantly recognisable, and it was only when the engine stopped that you knew trouble was imminent and local. Ethel had been returning from the nearby shop when she was alerted to one of these fearsome creations approaching. You always hoped, with some cynicism, it would carry on past you and be someone else's problem. You would've felt sorry for them but you always knew

11

your own turn might yet come. And on this day it was the turn of where Ethel lived.

As the engine cut out she and a dozen others took cover and prayed they might be spared. They were, but the shattering explosion close by finished Ethel's house and ruined many others too.

The doodlebugs gave you some warning, a pathetic warning, but the new V2 rockets did not. They arrived out of nowhere in an instant. You wouldn't have heard it coming and you wouldn't have heard the explosion because by then you'd be dead.

Thus, on this particular Thursday, in thankfully blissful ignorance, Ethel and her elderly couple passed from one life to the next. And unbeknown to him Micky had lost the two most precious women in his life.

***

*May 1945: end of the war in Europe*

Enid Campton was in Sheffield celebrating victory with those she had served alongside and her new fiancé, Norman Belham. Her thoughts occasionally returned to Micky. She knew she would always love him, treasure him, and pine for him, but life must go on. Micky was dead and he would not want her to be unhappy. Norman was the man she believed Micky's soul would've chosen for her, and she readily discarded any negative thoughts about her forthcoming marriage.

She'd heard about Ethel's demise and felt joy that mother and son must be re-united in heaven, not that she was particularly religious, but wanted to believe in God yet without being totally committed to the arrangement.

Micky did not know his mother was dead, anymore than he knew his beloved Enid was about to marry someone else. Having Enid sustained him in his living nightmare. His love for her had kept him going through his darkest hours, and some of those hours had been pitch black.

Norman Belham had proposed on one knee and presented Enid with a single red rose, and her acceptance of both rose and proposal was immediate. In time she returned home to Forest

Gate and to parents grateful they had all survived. Her mother in particular had noted the way her letters mentioning Norman had steadily changed, from the period when he was simply a kind, supportive friend, to the current stage where she wrote glowing prose about the love they shared. Mrs Campton could see that love developing in Enid's letters alone, and knew everything would be alright. There was further confirmation when her daughter came home briefly on leave, and now she was home for good and the wedding could be arranged.

They hadn't met Norman yet but it would not be long now. They had shared their daughter's sorrow at the loss of Micky Bowen but realised she had grieved long enough before embarking very gradually on a relationship, innocent in its inception, that saw love blossom over time. Norman appeared to be a gentleman, one of the old school, who believed in right and wrong and who clearly had never taken any advantage of Enid, least of all with her heart.

Shortly after Enid arrived back Norman was notified that he'd be relocated back to east London within the month so he too could go home. The factory in Whitechapel had been destroyed in the Blitz but new premises had been secured at Ilford, close to Manor Park. Ideal. His friend Charlie was also engaged but not to Enid's colleague Dorothy. He'd found good company with a shy lass who lived in Matlock and had been working as a nurse locally. In his case he'd decided he'd like to live in Derbyshire, which delighted Louise, and so he gave up his post and set about seeking employment in the area. In due course Norman would lose contact with him, a not unusual state of affairs for Mr Belham who treated all friendships as fickle arrangements.

\*\*\*

*Hiroshima and Nagasaki*

The Japanese looked all around hoping to find an ally somewhere, a country they could produce a favourable pact with, rather than surrender and suffer the dishonour of such a submission. The USA made it clear: all or nothing. Unconditional surrender. The allies did not really want a prolonged fight to the finish with countless deaths to be inflicted on the armed services, and so finally decided with reluctance to turn to a new and terrible weapon, the atomic bomb. Two had to be dropped before Japan would surrender.

Later Micky came to feel it was a kind of justice for the murderous Blitz, the doodlebugs and rocket bombs that had killed and maimed women, children and infants in his own country. A dreadful justice, an abominable price to be paid for eventual peace, a price negotiated by war and all its attendant distresses. That was, after all, war pure and simple. He hated it all; years of fighting, years of death, how he longed for it to be over.

And the more he longed for release the more he yearned for his Enid. He and the others scavenged for food, anything remotely edible, often discarded scraps, perhaps dropped by birds, and ate it ravenously regardless of how soiled it might be. He had suffered awful fevers from time to time, been delirious, and had never really recovered.

August may have brought the atomic bombs but it brought the end of the war and Micky began to dream of going home.

And at long last officialdom found him and his presence was made known; he gave two addresses, for mum and for Enid. The first address no longer existed, just as the lady who had lived there no longer existed, and what happened to the notification remained unknown. But the information despatched to Enid's parents caused shock, considerable distress and heartbreak when it was eventually delivered.

\*\*\*

*January 1946: Leytonstone*

Christmas passed in a blur for Enid Belham. The first peace-time Christmas for years, a Christmas that should've been so full of joy, was for her smothered in clouds of sadness, regret, disbelief and emotional agony. She'd spent it with her new husband and his parents, and then seen the new year in at her own parents where Norman had been the epitome of a kind, courteous gentleman, playing out the role of the perfect guest. Her mum

14

and dad lapped it up, just as she had been taken in by his graceful charm and good manners before they married.

Only a week had passed after the wedding when Micky's brief letter arrived. Even then they thought it was somebody's idea of a sick joke for the handwriting was unrecognisable scrawl. But they checked with the authorities and the sad truth was laid before them. Enid was still too shocked to react with any emotional outburst, making an excuse to go out, and then walking to the City of London Cemetery, a short distance away, seeking peace and quiet amongst the dead. It was a good place to walk alone surrounded by trees and shrubs and was the closest they had to an extensive woodland in this part of the world. Wanstead Flats lay opposite but these sprawling green open spaces were too open for Enid's purpose. She needed to lose herself.

Her homecoming that day was anything but sympathetic, understanding and supportive. While Norman sorted out the purchase of a house in Leytonstone they were living with his parents who themselves were coming to terms with a loss. Their other son, Cedric, had lost his life on an Arctic convoy earlier in the war, not that it bothered Norman much.

His frigate, on escort duties, and in common with all the ships, Royal Navy and merchantmen alike, was having to withstand an almost continuous bombardment from the air and the sea. An indescribable hell. Then Cedric's warship was torpedoed by a U-boat and blew up moments later taking all hands with it. At least they were spared an icy death in the freezing waters, the lot of many seamen whose ships sank there.

"Where have you *been*?" her unfeeling husband yelled at her.

"Just out for a walk, Norman, needed a leg-stretch….."

"Don't think so. It's bloody Micky, isn't it? You can't have him. Just forget him. You'll mess up our marriage if you carry on like that. You didn't want him when you found you could have me, so just remember that."

"Norman, for heaven's sake, it's not like that, I've had a shock…."

"Well, get over it now Enid. You're married to me and that's an end to it."

But it wasn't an end to it. It wasn't an end to her suffering over her loss, and it wasn't an end to the aggressive way her husband handled the situation. They moved to their new home in November, a pleasant enough terraced property, and Enid tried to make the most of her new condition. They had been lucky to get such a house just after the war and with all the devastation it had wreaked across east London. Enid thought Norman, or perhaps his employers, had been able to exercise some power somewhere, perhaps in manner that was not morally sound in the circumstances.

Naturally house-proud she'd looked after the place, keeping it clean and tidy, hopefully to Norman's liking, and had tried to please him by ensuring she cooked his favourite meals to his satisfaction. But it was still a time of rationing so she was not always successful, not that her husband demonstrated an ounce of understanding. So there were rows. He was neither threatening nor violent at this stage; that was yet to come.

He repeatedly made it clear that she had wanted him, not Micky, and that was that. Her choice, he reminded her time and again. Her great sadness was that there was much truth in it. Her other sadness was that, quite clearly, he'd deceived her to win her, and now he would treat her as he saw fit. A fine young woman, a handsome girl, just what he needed to show off.

Norman had denied her the opportunity to meet Micky, an act of insensitivity over something that might have helped her find some degree of peace. Maybe she didn't deserve such peace. Hadn't she deserted her fiancé? But she believed him dead, didn't that make it alright? Her head swirled now as it often did as she sought to justify her actions and come to terms with this dreadful state of affairs. No, perhaps she deserved no peace at all.

In the event she met Micky surreptitiously, but all too briefly. "Enid, you thought I was dead and gone. You've married him. There's nothing we can do about it now, is there?" It was quite the wrong response. She wanted him to come up with a plan to bring about their togetherness, a plan to end her marriage, a plan to bring her the happiness she craved with the man who had been her everything. And Micky had no such plan. It wasn't his fault. He could see the harsh reality and she could not.

Now she was working as a shorthand-typist down the road, her true love lost, and she felt she had no purpose in life. Her marriage possessed no real love on either side. Norman had his

16

trophy to show off to the world, and all Enid's efforts to please him and make him agreeable were failing daily. It was a horrible existence.

# Chapter Three

In due course Micky was on his way home from the other side of the world. Transported across the Pacific to Canada he now faced a train journey from west to east, and thence a sailing over the Atlantic. A protracted journey indeed.

He'd never seen such a long train! The carriages stretched out forever, so it seemed. They gave him a map so he could plot the course, and he became utterly fascinated by it all. Of course, he had his mum and his Enid to look forward to, and how he longed, *longed* to see Enid again. That longing was now his driving force and it warmed him, cheered him and gave him a new lease of life. Not so long ago he had all but given up, clinging to the love of his life, desperately, all but hopelessly, yearning for something disappearing with sickening rapidity, and believing he might yet die in this far off land.

They knew about the bombs. Some prisoners had been deliberately moved into the target areas, so they were told. Micky knew the Japanese would never surrender. It was dishonourable. So the bombs came and only then did the war end, and suddenly came the realisation survival was a possibility, and with that realisation came the chance of dreams coming true. And here he was on the train, this immense leviathan of travel, the medium by which he might return home. It was all so …. well, yes, it was all so exciting, he had to admit it.

At a station along the way he purchased some nylons for his beloved, but when he returned to his compartment a fellow soldier offered to buy them from him and was prepared to pay much more than the initial outlay. Thus was born a new enterprise. Micky found, to his astonishment, he could buy different things in one part of the train and sell them at a profit in another! Had he laid the foundations of a new career? Perhaps he had.

The final leg of his journey was on one of the converted peace-time liners, the size of the vessel completely astounding him, but everything he had witnessed so far was of nought compared to the shocks that awaited him back home.

His mother was dead. His fiancée married to someone else. Andy, his best mate, killed in action. He sat in his temporary accommodation bewildered and shattered. He wished he had died in Japan. His close companion Reg had succumbed to fever and died after a beating. He had left a wife and two young children. Micky sought them out and visited them hoping to bring them some solace, but left knowing his call had merely inflamed the pain. If only Reg had been spared and Micky had died in his place.

For now there was no future, no hope for Micky Bowen, and then one day the picture changed.

"Damn it all," he exclaimed, sitting up on his bed, and speaking to nobody but himself, "I'm blowed if this is the end. This is just the start. Get yourself going, Micky boy, and build a new life. You've been spared for a good reason, boy, now pick y'self up and let's get going." It wasn't much of an inspiring speech but it did the trick.

There was his mum's money, of course, but he needed that to seek a property to call home, and so he applied himself to earning a living.

He tried his hand at various jobs and then thought back to his Canadian rail journey. Buying and selling. Was that the way forward? He was working for a shop that sold various accessories and essentials for cars and just happened to enquire what happened to the dead batteries customers brought in.

"We just give them to some totter," his boss informed him, "but nothing else we can do. Shame really, those batteries got a lot of lead in them, and the price of lead's good at the mo. Well, most metal's riding high right now, what with wartime shortages and so on." It was food for thought. Micky investigated and discovered metal was indeed a saleable commodity, and swiftly realised there was much scrap metal out there, such as in those car batteries, that could have a value. Making enquiries he learned that some foundries simply gave away, or sold at a ridiculously low price, the metal borings (metal equivalent of sawdust), the waste material created when they manufactured metallic items, and he realised people were actually making a success of selling this waste.

He bought an old van and started buying up this waste. He had a head start. Hitherto the material was given away or sold cheaply. He was prepared to pay a reasonable price for it and that put him in a strong position. In a couple of rented garages in Wanstead he set up a steamer so that he could dismantle the car batteries and retrieve the lead contained therein. He went round the foundries and other metal works and bought the waste. Car radiators too had a value. And in due course his business flourished. He found a good and reliable dealer to sell his material to and made appreciable profits.

Enid was never far from his thoughts. It was an impossible dream but he clung to it. One day, maybe one day they would find each other again.

In time he moved from his rented home to a small property in South Woodford, thanks to an appreciable mortgage from his bank who could see that his enterprise was thriving and had promise. He had cards and letterheads printed. A true man of business.

## M.R. Bowen
## Non-Ferrous Metal Merchant

Micky Bowen had arrived. His reputation and business were growing a-plenty, but he never stopped thinking about Enid and cheered himself by thinking that he was building for her future as well as his own.

News of her first-born knocked him for six. The arrival of her second child destroyed most of his hopes and dreams. Surely this was the end? He couldn't countenance it, and did not do so. In truth it provided an extraordinary impetus. He would be there for her whenever she might need him. His spirit was undaunted, his love unchallenged, and in the times ahead it became his salvation from destruction, his reason for living, and it gave him strength and the will to succeed.

Always in his mind was that one short meeting with her, and how the intense misery tore at his heart as the distress ripped through his very being. He had kept a stiff-upper-lip, for her sake he believed, held on to his tears (not the time to cry), spoken words of wisdom or such as he thought them to be. He barely knew he had said anything; he was 'saying the right thing' to try and comfort her, but they were not the words he wanted to speak, not the words he wished he could say.

How he wanted her. How he longed to hold her, to kiss her, to run away with her, and he could do none of this. She was married to another man and she must honour her marriage vows. She thought, with good reason, Micky was long gone, and had wed a man who loved her. That had to be the end of the story. He felt his heart destroy itself as he'd walked away that night. Her muted voice, her pitiful cries, followed him into the darkness.

"Micky, Micky, I love you. I love you Micky. Micky, come back to me, come back to me...." But he left her where they had met and resolutely carried on walking, quickening his step hoping distance would blot out her pleas. He hadn't looked back. He'd wanted to, he'd wanted to run to her, gather her up and take her to their own paradise. He had turned his back on his dream, this most wonderful woman and deserted her in her hour of need.

But he had 'done the right thing'.

\*\*\*

*Norman Belham*

Doing 'the right thing' was not the sort of terminology Norman Belham bothered with. Quite the reverse, if truth be told. A man who was used to pleasing himself, without a care in the world for anyone else. The war had been a blessing in disguise. Reserved occupation, working in rural Derbyshire while others fought and died for his freedom. Fools, he considered them. He'd had a gay old time and met this gorgeous woman into the bargain. Married her and his mates were jealous. Boy, were they jealous! She was beautiful, lovely, radiant and all woman.

He'd had some times in his youth. That Elsie Braise, his first conquest, she knew what it was all about. Experienced woman. She'd improved his education ten times over. Edna Parry, nothing to look at, but raring to go. And what about Dilys Coulton? Had that Alvis (or rather her father did) and it was as sporty as she was. Even allowed him to drive it occasionally! Then there was that Phyllis McDonald, gave him a few good games of tennis, and he'd cheated so that she won every time without realising she would win anyway. But he could believe what he wanted! She was good fun after each match, that was for sure.

But Enid was extra special, worth all the effort just to make everyone envious. They could be married, she could have his children and look after them, and he could seek other pleasures.

The Twenty's and Thirty's were good years, when the young started taking control and doing as they saw fit, and Norman was at the forefront. At first the arrival of world war two left him dreading what lay ahead, just as he'd really started enjoying himself, but in time he reaped dividends thanks mainly to the job he'd landed, and that was indirectly responsible for him meeting Enid.

In his youth brother Cedric had been an absolute nuisance. Mr prim-and-proper. Cedric thought there should only be one woman in your life, the one you loved and eventually married, and that you should be true and faithful no matter what. He despised Norman's antics and told him so, often, in his younger days, reporting him to their parents who would signal their disapproval.

When war came Cedric volunteered for the navy at once. Typical, Norman decided. Well, let him go and fight for King and Country and die if he must. He won't be a good sailor, Norman reasoned, as he won't have a girl in each port!

Norman's school years had been difficult. Not one for learning and concentration he had played up, been beaten often, yet somehow avoided expulsion. It might have been due to the fact that he was a good sportsman, an excellent cricketer and footballer, a slightly poorer tennis player, and often represented the school successfully, that saved him in the end.

How he managed to land his job, well, God knows, for he had precious few qualifications. Friends were for the here and now, and were dumped whenever the fancy took him elsewhere. So unsurprisingly women were treated the same, his only concession being when he met Enid, an outstanding beauty, a girl to be shown off. He decided he would marry her, become respectable, and enjoy the fruits of marriage whilst indulging in the pleasures of playing the field.

Now here he was, post-war, married to a gem, enjoying a position of power and wealth in business, a doting father, and able to sample the pleasures of Maud Jolley when the opportunity presented itself. His boss, Charles Greatham, had arranged his home by greasing the right palms. Cut from the same cloth, he and Charles were.

# Chapter Four

*Enid Belham (nee Campton)*

Enid's world had been built on love. Born in East Ham after the first world war she enjoyed an idyllic childhood, loved by her parents and adored by her family. An only child she had many aunts and uncles in an extensive family that was closely knit, and in due time had many cousins to appreciate in this pleasing existence. They moved up the road to Forest Gate when she was four. War was gone and, it was assumed, never to return, but as time progressed it proved a false dawn.

But at first there was peace to be enjoyed. Enid did well in her studies especially when she moved on to the Girls' Grammar School. A Girl Guide she loved the camping holidays taken with her troupe as well as those experienced with her family. At Junior School she had formed a close friendship with a fellow pupil, Micky Bowen, who declared his love and found it returned. He wrote her childish love letters illustrated with drawings of the sun, of birds, and all things delightful as well as red hearts.

Overjoyed, Enid had taken some to school to show the teacher who then embarrassed Micky by holding the drawings up in class for all to see. It didn't dampen his enthusiasm, nor hers.

1929 arrived with the educational parting of the ways, Micky going to the secondary school where he nonetheless proved himself to be quite talented at maths, history and, of course, art. English Language was, oddly enough, not a strong point, but he persisted.

Although they were now at different schools the pair were inseparable friends, meeting after school some afternoons, and at each other's homes at the weekend, their principal sadness being the holidays when they went away with their own parents. After much badgering Enid's parents were eventually persuaded to bring Micky along on one trip, a camping holiday in Dorset. It was the boy's first time under canvas and it was an eye opener and a shock for a lad used to going to seaside bed and breakfast establishments. He shared a tent with Enid's father and took a while to get used to the overnight outdoor life, with its weird attendant nightime noises such as the hooting of owls, a new phenomenon in his young life.

Both were fourteen and becoming acutely aware that there was more depth to their relationship than mere enduring friendship, and at the same time they were seeing beyond the simple concept of being close mates as they came to notice new feelings within them, feelings they perhaps could not understand at that age, but an acknowledgement they were of different sexes. New sensations indeed.

Walking alone on a footpath near the campsite Enid stopped in her tracks.

"Have you ever wanted to kiss me, Micky? Y'know. Properly. Lips and that?" He blushed, and looked at his feet, then everywhere except her.

"Yes, s'pose I have, really, Enid." Finally he looked up and saw a smiling face full of mischief.

"Well, go on then. Let's have a kiss." He was hesitant.

"Mmmm …. Yes, but suppose someone sees us?"

"So what, you silly boy. Come on, kiss me." And she puckered up and closed her eyes.

Yes, he wanted to find out what kissing was all about, and there was nobody else he would ever want to kiss, but he was struck motionless by nervousness. She opened one eye.

"Micky, kiss me, come on." And the eye closed. He took a deep breath and stepped forward, and then suddenly their lips were touching. She threw her arms around his neck and pulled him closer and he instinctively put his arms around her waist and held on tight. As a juvenile experiment it could be classed as a success. As a passionate display of heartfelt love erupting in glorious colours and unbelievable sensations it was a failure. The kiss lasted about two minutes but left them engulfed in happiness. They walked on hand in hand.

"See, Micky, we're really in love now. We can be married."

"Yes, I see that. I liked the kiss. Can we do it again?" They did. Longer this time and with rather more gusto and determination.

"Are we even more in love, Enid?"

"Yes, 'course we are, Micky. You do want to marry me?"

25

"Of course. I love you."

"Love you too, Micky. Shall we have another kiss?"

And so this young, adolescent and pleasantly childish relationship blossomed, and was nonetheless very beautiful for all that. Who can say that love was not involved?

\*\*\*

Enid had her life mapped out, carefully planned from a young age. Despite her tender years her marriage was now taken care of, and she decided she would work as a secretary until she started her family. She harboured a dream of being at Wimbledon, not as a spectator, but as a star player, for she was noticeably good at the sport, though not to the sort of standard her dream would've required. Enid acknowledged the fact. She was very level headed and a clear thinker. A secretary she would be.

The threat of war did not enter into this thinking during her early teen years. Always a thoughtful, caring person, her time as a Girl Guide saw her appreciate the help and support she could actively give to the less fortunate, so consequently took to Micky's father, Eric, who in turn took to her. In 1937 she was as devastated as Micky and his mum when Mr Bowen passed away. Here was one of life's true heroes; badly maimed during the war, he never complained, yet suffered his pains lightly, remained cheerful and content, making his loss all the more poignant to Enid.

Otherwise her life had been one of splendid yet simple pleasure. Utter contentment. She finished her school years as a proud prefect, obtained suitable employment as a clerk to a shipping firm with promotion to the role of manager's secretary in her sights, and had Micky to look forward to.

Her parents supported her at every turn, so dedicated were they to their only child. They did not truly pamper her but ensured she was sufficiently cosseted and given all she needed to succeed in her plans. Enid repaid their kindness and devotion by being diligent in her studies and generally making them proud of her. Overall, this had the effect of making her appear rather aloof and superior which counted against her amongst her peers, although this may also have had something to do with her blossoming into an extremely beautiful young woman, the envy of her girl friends.

She liked social events, and the annual tennis club dinner-dance was viewed with excited anticipation, always thoroughly enjoyed by Enid and her guest, the faithful Micky Bowen. His best mate Andy was a good friend to both and fun to be with, and they often had days out as a foursome which included Andy's latest girlfriend. He changed them quite frequently, not having any desire to fall in love and marry one this early in life.

Promotion to the MD's secretary came, together with a reasonable pay rise, and a small party was arranged at home to celebrate the success. This would do, she resolved, until she became a mother. It was only the advent of war that started to dampen things. And in September 1939 it all became a reality and dreams began to turn into nightmares.

\*\*\*

After Micky's call-up Enid decided she would do her bit and volunteered for the ATS and was eventually sent to Sheffield where she often worked as a spotter for the anti-aircraft fire. Her neat, tidy mind, devoid of panic, able to absorb no end of information, made her ideally suited to such vital work. It was where she met fellow ATS girl Dorothy Leonard.

The two struck up a keen friendship, allied by their circumstances rather than their backgrounds. Dorothy, who was a little older, came from Shrewsbury. A university graduate in literature she had still not decided the direction her career should follow and therefore had not yet enjoyed any form of fixed employment related to her qualification. She was one of four children born to a wealthy Shropshire family, had her own horse, and had usually holidayed abroad with the outbreak of war putting paid to that. In most respects then, Dorothy and Enid were socially poles apart yet they formed a healthy alliance and a sound relationship that was at its best when they cycled into the Derbyshire countryside together, for they found much common ground for discussion and a common love of fresh air and beautiful scenery.

Dorothy also proved to be the perfect friend in need when the terrible news of Micky Bowen arrived. Gently comforting when necessary, solidly supportive, but not overbearing, she gradually nursed the heartbroken Enid into a better state where she could have a more positive outlook. And with time the smiles returned, tender smiles, sometimes sad smiles, but smiles that were signs of recovery. Miss Leonard had another purpose for this attention as she was concerned Enid might lose her concentration at a crucial moment, which could have catastrophic results given the vital work the ATS girls did.

Later Enid was to return the favour when her friend heard of the loss of her brother, Arnold, in the north African desert campaign, doing her comforting very well. These were true friends, bound together in life and loss at a time of national crisis. Thus they also made a success of their jobs to the benefit of the country.

*** 

"Forest Gate, Manor Park," Dorothy said softly and meaningfully, "sound quite idyllic but I assume they are not." Enid leaned back in her chair in the room they shared and pondered how best to reply.

"Well, not really, Dorothy, but it's all about home, isn't it, and we're not far from Wanstead Flats, green open land, small lakes with beautiful swans, somewhere to relax. Tell me about Shrewsbury."

"Nice town where the Severn turns almost back on itself. We have an English Bridge to the east and a Welsh Bridge to the west, and pleasant riverside walks. I was born near Meole Brace, close to Rea Brook, a quiet little stream to the south-west of the town, but moved further out to a house in the country not far from the village of Arscott when I was quite young. Shropshire's a lovely unspoilt county, Enid, and we're called Salopians, by the way. Never known why." And they shared a gentle laugh.

They chatted amiably about their home towns and their childhoods as they often did. And then they discussed the progress of the war, and then, on this particular evening, they discussed love.

"I envy you your love for Micky in a way. I've never looked at love like that. Y'know, to have a one and only. You're very lucky, Enid."

"And how have you looked at love?"

"That it'll find me one day, probably when I'm least expecting it, but in the meantime I am too gay and carefree to go searching for it! I live for the moment my dearest Enid. I find some men so very interesting, but I've often run into rotters and types who have turned out to be absolute bores, I can tell you."

"Dorothy! You sound as if you have quite a collection! Have you really known so many?" They laughed again, this time more heartily.

"If you don't take them seriously, Enid, you can simply get to know so many, and know them as friends and little more. And if you get more than friendly with two or three, well, why not? Life's for living, and I think war has made it more so, don't you?"

Enid looked suddenly pale and sad.

"Oh my dear Enid, I'm so sorry, that was so thoughtless of me, please forgive. Knowing Micky's away at war I don't know how could be so insensitive….."

"No, no Dorothy. Nothing to apologise for. It's good to be able to talk about all these things, and speak just as we feel. Don't worry about me….."

"Oh Enid, Enid, thank you, but it was thoughtless. Here, I'll make us a cuppa, the cup that cheers eh?" Her room-mate nodded, "and then we can decide where we shall cycle to on Friday." Enid instantly looked happier if just as reflective. Her fears for Micky seized her and dominated her mood, and it would take more than a cup of tea to change that.

*** 

There was always something alluring and enchanting about the Derbyshire peaks and dales. There certainly was after a few days and nights in Sheffield, especially when the Luftwaffe had been too close for comfort. Out here the air was fresh, the stiff breeze quite stimulating, the clouds strangely reassuring despite the fact they were hiding the sun, and the only accompaniment

29

was birdsong not the throb of bomber engines, the screech of fighters and the rattle and thud of anti-aircraft guns.

Indeed, out here, today, it was difficult to imagine a continent gripped by war, where life expectancy for those at home was a daily lottery, and where life for those fighting was a precious device that could be lost in a second at any time. You could blot out the worst for the most part and you could gather up peaceful periods to soothe your concerns, but the war was always there.

Somehow Enid and Dorothy could not let go of the situation because their work in the ATS set war right on their front doorstep and there was no moving it. But there were escapes, and this particular Friday was all the more poignant.

They had cycled out through Hathersage and shortly turned south across moorland towards Monsal Head. They placed their cycles against the stone wall and looked down upon the river as it curled southwards away from where they stood, under the railway viaduct, over which thundered a train hauled by a mighty locomotive. They could make out people in the carriages. There were troops, perhaps on longed-for leave, or maybe heading for their barracks and the end of their respite.

There were women and children. How many stories were there to be told on that one train? Enid's vivid imagination considered the prospect that every carriage possessed a wealth of tales that could be told, tales of happiness, of sadness, of despair, of resignation, of fear, of loss. Dorothy simply saw a packed passenger train and was pleased she was not on it.

They sat on the grass and opened their picnic lunches. They were ready to eat. The ride had made them hungry and thirsty. It was a favourite viewpoint for them, overlooking spectacular Monsal Dale, and from where you could gaze right down this magnificent valley with its verdant slopes and free-flowing river. The railway was an integral part with trains from the south bursting out of the tunnel and thrusting their way over that viaduct often in a cloud of smoke.

"Makes you think," Dorothy started, speaking in a most serious and philosophical style, "that there are two quite distinct aspects to war. I mean, we can come here into this loveliest of countryside and be completely removed from it. Tonight we'll be in the thick of it. Then there are our troops, like Micky, who can rarely escape the horrors. Do you mind me talking like this?"

"No Dorothy, not at all. I think it's a good thing we can look at how it affects us all, and I know Micky's fighting for our freedom and that makes me feel proud and fearful all at the same time. Then there's my parents back home, powerless against the enemy, almost in the front line you could call it. Your dad's in the home guard, isn't he Dorothy?"

"Yes, and mum's busy digging for victory. Every spare bit of land back home is a vegetable patch. Dad was in the artillery last war, on the continent, surviving four years of seemingly endless assault. Invalided out right at the end. Unfit for call up this time round, thank God. Had to get badly injured to achieve that. But he's okay, he's fine, and he feels he's doing his bit in the home guard. Still very active, my dad, and right now he's looking after my pony. I hope! Have you ever ridden, Enid?"

"No, not for me...."

"You should try it. Great fun."

"I would be frightened of falling off or the horse bolting...."

"If you went to a riding school they would make sure you had the right horse and, believe me, you'd soon conquer your fears."

"Well, perhaps after the war....."

"After the war, my pet, you're invited to Shrewsbury and you can try my horse." Both girls smiled, Enid remembering that she wasn't Dorothy's social equal, Dorothy genuinely pleased to have suggested, indirectly, they remain friends when it was all over. Involuntarily Enid put her arm around Dorothy's shoulders and hugged her, an event her friend found particularly touching. Yes they would always be friends. And soon news was to arrive to challenge their closeness.

\*\*\*

The tears had dried. Dorothy continued cuddling her friend as they sat on Enid's bed both feeling bereft, totally empty, now beyond the sadness that had swamped them at first. Dorothy seemed as badly affected as Enid was. Micky, missing, presumed dead. Through the tears she'd pleaded with a God she didn't really believe in to make her dream come true, that Micky might

31

be spared and be found alive. Dorothy kept her own counsel knowing that Singapore had been a notably bloody affair, with huge casualties, not wishing to add to her friend's woes.

"I suppose it's better than being told your man's dead, isn't it? I mean, there's hope Dorothy, there's hope isn't there?"

"Yes my sweet, and it's worth recalling that Singapore must've been in quite a mess after all that fighting, a lot of confusion and all that, so I wouldn't mind betting Micky'll turn up, you wait and see." She didn't believe her own words and hoped Enid didn't realise. But somehow her words proved comforting and Enid managed a watery smile, just for a couple of seconds, no more, before her face once again reflected her heartbreak. "Why don't you think about trying to get permission on compassionate grounds to skip tonight's duty?" The look on Enid's face as she turned sharply to look her friend right in the eyes told Dorothy something about the inner strength Enid must possess.

"I could never do that. Never. And I would be letting Micky down if I tried. I owe it to him anyway. He would never have shirked his duties and I shall not do it Dorothy." Miss Leonard felt a warmth inside and knew in that instant Miss Campton would pull through, and was inspired to gently slap her back.

"God Enid, that's the spirit. That's what we need to defeat the Hun. Tonight you'll be better than ever. Show 'em good and proper." And the smiles glowed between the girls as they dissolved into a strong embrace, hugging as if there was no tomorrow. "Micky is alive Enid, he'll be back. Believe me. Let's give them Nazis what for tonight!"

Dorothy continued to support her friend in the days ahead, cajoling, comforting, praising and occasionally admonishing as each situation required and gradually Enid found herself again and was strong and determined. It was not long before she had to be the comforter herself.

The letter from Dorothy's mother was brief. Her brother, Arnold, had perished in North Africa and, unlike Micky, there was no hope, no slender thread to cling to. She'd always been close to her brother and his loss hit her very hard, but Enid was there and proved just the tonic Dorothy needed, for they were both strong women, united now by adversity, their friendship being a bond of such intensity that recovery was an inevitable outcome.

*\*\*

And so they went back to war.
And into Enid's life came the cunning, deceitful Norman.

# Chapter Five

*Micky Bowen and Rita Grant*

With more and more business success Micky was in a position to buy his own property, thanks to a mortgage, and secured a bungalow in Malford Grove in a different part of South Woodford from where he'd been living. A nice neighbourhood, he'd concluded.

He traded in his small van and bought one of the fairly new Standard Vanguard vehicles, a very sleek design, positively American in looks he felt, not that he had much knowledge about such a subject. To offset this lack of information he'd learned much about his chosen trade to his advantage and found his services to be in increasing demand. He'd also learned the hard way that when loading car batteries onto his van catching your fingers between two such items was excruciating!

By the same medium he learned that metal borings in your fingers were as painful as their wooden counterparts, and sometimes as difficult to extract as splinters.

He worked long hours but approached everything in good cheer. He'd gone off alcohol and rarely touched a drop these days. It wasn't unusual to find him in one of his garages using the steamer he'd made to extract the lead from the batteries or carefully sorting out the materials ready to make up a load for a specific destination. Most went to a metal merchant in Plaistow who dealt in bulk and paid reasonable prices.

The world seemed a good place. His efforts were being rewarded in almost every direction, but in the evenings, after a simple meal, he would normally sit and read a book looking occasionally at the photo of Enid he kept on the mantlepiece. To Mr Bowen television was something that lay in the future and was seen as one of those new-fangled devices that the world could probably do without.

He possessed a radiogram and enjoyed the broadcasts, but was happier listening to his records. His favourite was a recording of the third and fourth movements of Mozart's 39th symphony, which occupied two sides of a twelve-inch 78 r.p.m. record. Beyond all that he had little social life, persuading himself he had no time for it. So it should be no surprise that Micky had little idea that he had an admirer.

The young woman who handled the accounts at Williams and Co (Metal Merchants) always enjoyed his visits and found him attractive physically and in personality. He made her laugh; he could see the funny side of almost anything, and was usually in a good humour even when the foreman, Syd, was in one of his bad moods. Syd was unpleasant with everyone in these circumstances and that included Micky. All and sundry took Syd's apparent nastiness in their stride and either avoided him, if they could, or kept quiet and let him have his rants.

And he could rant, yet strangely there was never the hint of bad language and most definitely not in the company of women. Micky had witnessed him tearing one of his workers off a strip and then been on the receiving end of a tirade such as when his van lingered on the weighbridge a couple of seconds too long. But not one bad word. Syd had been in the RAF during the war, ground crew out at Debden, and had rather regretted not being allowed to get his hands on the Germans directly. He had been constantly reassured his efforts contributed to the RAF's successes in dealing with the enemy, but he remained resentful. Perhaps he carried that resentment into later life. Perhaps.

He had a lovely wife, Moira, whom Micky had met, and now four young children that he was known to be a caring, kind father to, a dad who always had time for the kids especially when they wanted to play. For Micky it was a reminder not to always take people at face value. Syd was an excellent foreman, ruthless but efficient, and clearly a wonderful husband and father. Everyone appeared to like him despite his propensity to ranting, and certainly Rita Grant had a soft spot for her gentle giant as she termed him.

But Rita had a softer spot for Micky Bowen. They often found time for a quick chat and a laugh while she prepared his account and paid him his money, and over time had gently probed his past. In these conversations Micky discovered she came from Ilford, had lost her father and brother in the war, served in the women's land army herself, and lived with her mother in

35

something approaching contentment. She was not in the first flush of youth but had a lovely round, slightly chubby face which was often decorated with a smile, and which made her very appealing. Like Micky she had no obvious social life, her evenings and weekends spent pleasurably with mum and they felt the better for it.

It was because of mum that Rita had avoided any sort of relationship with men, for she knew she would never leave her mother's side, but that did not stop her looking kindly on Micky. It was in one of her light-hearted chats with him that she learned about his lost love and at once felt the pangs of sorrow.

"Oh Micky, I'm so very sorry. And you both being childhood sweethearts and that. And there's been nobody else?"

"No Rita, faithful to Enid I am. Always will be. She was my one and only; nobody could replace her." Rita's heart sank and sadness came upon her. "Anyway, Rita, what about you? Lovely young lass still unwed." She rallied and smiled coyly.

"Away with you, Micky. Young lass? Old maid more like…."

"Not a bit of it, Rita. A lovely, lovely young lass. There must be men queuing for you!"

"Never, not me. I thought I might've found the one for me on the farm where I worked during the war, but I discovered he was after all the girls. Not been out with a man since and my day's passed."

"No it isn't Rita, especially if you still have your hopes and dreams…."

"Oh you romantic fool, Micky. Give over. Anyway, here's your money if you'd like to count it and then you can be on your way before Syd gets here, and he's on his way." Both laughed. But it was an encounter that sowed tiny seeds, and time would tell.

\*\*\*

There was now something new and fascinating in Micky's life. For the first time he had a garden, rather more at the rear than the front, but had little idea about gardening although he appreciated the beauty of the trees, shrubs and plants. He needed a gardener to help and guide him, and thus it was he came upon a retired gentleman called Albert Coombes who lived with his disabled wife Emily in a ground floor flat with no garden.

Both had been keen gardeners in their time but as Emily's condition deteriorated they'd had to sell up their house in Wanstead and settle into the convenience of their flat. However, Albert missed his gardening and in due course a concerned Emily persuaded him to look for some part-time work, saying she would be more than happy for him to do so, and they could enjoy the added advantage of additional income.

So it was that he put a card in a newsagent's window that was seen by Micky who quickly engaged his services and came to be as delighted with the results as he was with a new friendship.

From the small verandah to the rear of his bungalow an array of flower beds spread away towards the three lawns and a rockery beyond. There were five quite tall trees but he didn't really know what they were. Brick paths twisted around the beds and between the lawns was a concrete fountain that had no connection to a water supply or for that matter a power source of any sort, so it remained purely ornamental. The front garden had beds and plants surrounded by low hedges.

When he first set eyes on it Albert Coombes gleamed with pleasure and expressed his eager desire to get cracking. A deal was arranged there and then with immediate effect. Thus on at least three days a week he would pedal over on his cycle for a day's work, occasionally popping in on a Saturday or Sunday so he and Micky could work together, for the owner had discovered a new love, one he welcomed as a joy and as an escape. He and Albert became firm friends. He soon heard about Emily and on one Sunday invited the pair for Sunday lunch so that she too could share the beauty of the garden.

The Vanguard had a bench seat at the front which actually made it easy for Mrs Coombes to climb in, followed by her husband, her wheelchair stowed away in the back, and the three of them sat side by side as Micky drove them the short distance home. After a delicious roast dinner the three explored the back garden and the men explained to Emily their plans and current work, and she added some bright ideas. It was the first time Micky had met Emily and she was such a lovely lady, one clearly determined not to be done down by her worsening condition.

"I was very sorry to hear about you son, Mrs Coombes," Micky said with formality when they were taking tea in the lounge. He always called them Mr and Mrs as he believed that was right and proper, and for the same reason they called him Mr Bowen. Thomas Coombes had been in the Navy during the war and had lost his life when the *Bismarck* blew his ship, *HMS Hood*, out of the water.

"Yes, thank you Mr Bowen, we still miss him very much, especially with Sylvia now in America." Their daughter had been a WAAF and had married a British-based American airman after the war, emigrating to his home in Michigan where, apparently, she was extremely happy and had raised four children, grandchildren the Coombes were yet to see.

Both garden and friendship blossomed and Micky came to realise the true meaning of the word beauty, and equally so the words happiness and contentment.

*** 

There was still something missing in his life, other than Enid of course.

He did his best but housework was not his forte, so he concluded he needed help around the house as well, and a neighbour put him in touch with reputedly reliable Mrs Harris, a stout, generally cheerful soul from Leyton who, in due course, came in twice a week and did his washing and ironing and completed various other tasks appertaining to cleaning. There were three downstairs bedrooms, one converted into his office, one more upstairs (it was a chalet-bungalow), a lounge and a dining room as well as a kitchen and bathroom, and there was plenty to keep Mrs Harris busy.

She worked with gusto. Normally Micky would let her in, leave her to it, and set off to work, his housekeeper letting herself out later in the day. There were odd occasions when they shared a cup of tea and when Mrs Harris invariably let forth on her family woes. Her main worry, as ever, was her teenage daughter Sybil who was frequently in trouble at school, and who had once been humiliated in front of everyone at Assembly one morning, leaving her in fits of tears for days.

"She's not really a bad girl, Mr Bowen, just gets into mischief, if you know what I mean, and I don't think the headmistress always handles it right, and I've been up there several times to see her, and she's a right stickler for discipline, and she wants to blame me and Mr Harris for her bad behaviour. Well, did you ever, I ask you? Well, Mr Bowen, I know she's always had this mischievous streak and, well I mean, I never liked to smack her, well, not hard, and Mr Harris left it all up to me, and I know he was too kind really, but you know how it is, and now for the headmistress to blame us! Well, I don't know….."

Mrs H hardly ever drew breath when expounding on the latest trials and tribulations of Sybil so Micky was only required to sit, listen, drink his tea, and nod or shake his head as dictated by the progress of the saga.

"And she's messing about with boys now….."

Thankfully these discourses lasted just as long as the cup of tea. He would relate the stories of the unruly Sybil to Rita who would chuckle merrily at his humorous way of telling the tales, interspersed, as they were, by his own light-hearted interpretation of events. He also regaled her with tales of developments in his garden, a place he was incredibly proud of. Finally Rita decided to chance her arm with this man she viewed with such growing affection.

"Don't have much of a garden myself. Love to see yours Micky. It sounds so lovely. But I don't drive…." He took the bait.

"Oh … oh … oh, well, what say I fetch you over one weekend. Tell you what, you could bring mum as well and I'll do you one of my special roast dinners. Good at that I am."

"Thank you Micky, but I couldn't put you to the trouble, of course I couldn't."

"No trouble at all, least of all for you Rita." She blushed at the words. "How about this Saturday? Love to meet your mum too."

"I'll ask mum tonight and ring you. Give me your number. But I think we'd be imposing…."

"Nonsense, nonsense! It's at my invitation, so just come! Do you like roast beef?"

"Oh Micky, there's no need to do a meal….."

"Roast beef, yes or no?" She giggled almost uncontrollably.

"Yes, alright, roast beef. And I'm sure mum will be overjoyed. Hey, watch out, I see Syd approaching with a face like thunder….."

"Right, here's my number. Give me a ring. We can always have a jaw over the phone if you like." Rita liked but didn't say so, instead making a shoo-ing noise and waving him towards the door as Syd walked in.

\*\*\*

When Rita saw the size of Micky's property her heart sank. Surely she would have no chance with a man of such position and wealth. She consoled herself by remembering mum, and knowing that she had promised never to leave her, so an attachment was pointless anyway.

Micky took to Mrs Grant at first sight and in due time she came to remind him of his own dear mother, now long gone. Having toured the garden and partaken of their host's superb dinner they sat and chatted in the lounge before Mrs Grant diplomatically suggested she would like a rest, perhaps a little doze, so why didn't Micky and Rita go for a walk, it being a pleasant enough afternoon?

They set off down Malford Grove, into Hermitage Walk, past the flats and into the woods, part of Epping Forest, where they came upon a herd of cows.

"Crumbs, have they escaped, Micky?"

"No, no, they have grazing rights. And, believe it or not, they occasionally wander off around the local streets, like mine, and if you haven't got y'gates closed they come in and eat your plants!

"Now you're having me on, Micky Bowen…."

"Not a bit of it, just ask around. Seriously."

"I don't think I really believe you." She tugged at his arm, looked at him sideways, and they both laughed as they continued their stroll. In fact, they were nearly two hours gone before arriving back, but mum was quite at ease having made herself a cup of tea when she awoke. They had walked right across to the Hollow Ponds near Whipps Cross. Once Micky had nearly taken Rita's hand, an almost unconscious moment, but stopped himself

40

feeling it wasn't the done thing, and was all the sadder for it. He didn't want to say or do anything to spoil a lovely day, least of all to spoil it for Rita for whom he acknowledged a growing affection, little realising in his innocence she had harboured hopes for him. Those hopes had taken a knock today, but she found she loved being with him, talking and laughing together, and wanted it to go on forever, just as he did had she but known it.

When he left them at their home in Ilford later he was aware of an emptiness, and then he knew he was becoming quite attached to her. Unfortunately, she had told him of her devotion to her mum and he guessed she would not leave her mother, so it was purposeless pursuing her. Rita was just as empty emotionally, sensing she could never aspire to such a gentleman, that he would only ever see her as a friend, and she would make a fool of herself if she made her attentions obvious. Besides there was Enid, even if she was lost to him.

For his part Micky did not want to look foolish by declaring his interest and decided that friendship was all he could wish for.

And so these would-be lovers kept their distance until fate played its hand a few weeks later.

# Chapter Six

Enid Belham looked out of her kitchen window and saw her young children at play in the garden she had worked so hard in. How pretty it now looked. Neglected when they moved here a year ago she'd transformed it with all her efforts, gaining knowledge as she went, experiencing success and failure in equal measures, and now her plan was bearing its fruits with plenty more still to be done. Gardening, as she knew, was year-round, and something that could be absorbing and rewarding. A garden can constantly evolve, developing as the seasons and the gardener's moods dictate. It was her pride and joy after Lorna and little Patricia. And they all had become her reason for living.

Norman had wangled himself a management post, Enid wondered how but didn't ask, and they moved from Leytonstone to Cheyne Avenue, South Woodford, ironically less than a mile from where Micky resided, not that she knew that. She had resolved that she would make the most of her life and her dreadful marriage, devoting herself to her children to ensure they enjoyed the best opportunities at every turn. She would win her own war by being strong and determined, and not be afeared of anything her husband might do to her.

Having a new home, a spacious semi-detached property with a long-ish back garden, was a fresh start, commensurate with the new Enid. Norman could do what he liked away from home; if he wanted to see other women, so be it, she would not let it bother her as long as she wasn't dumped by the wayside, and that was unlikely all the time she as at home to rear the children.

He was a violent man and she wished to shield the girls, which wasn't easy, for just a word out of place could bring his wrath down upon them all, and she'd seen enough of it. So she tried her hardest to maintain calm about the house when he was around, and happily her daughters appeared to sense the need not to upset daddy, so peace usually reigned. But there were odd occasions when he would strike out and hit her with considerable force. She

42

never cried out or sobbed lest it disturb Lorna and Patricia, and so she bore her beatings with fortitude and made excuses to the children when they asked after her latest cuts and bruises. She'd decided; he'd never win. She would.

Her appearance was important to her these days, whereas initially she'd let herself go as her marriage disintegrated, but now she'd learned how to use make-up to disguise or lessen the visual effect of any marks. Hair always neat and tidy. Smart clothes. As least he gave her a good allowance which also covered their food and had enabled her to learn to drive. He'd laughed at that but said if she passed her test he'd buy her a small car.

She passed. First go.

But it would be another year before she saw a car.

*\*\**

Lorna had started school and was walked there and back every school day by her proud mother with Patricia in the pushchair. It was a fair journey and took some time which may have given Enid extra impetus to pass her test and hold Norman to his promise. Now she had the opportunity to meet other mothers and at last she started to make new friends, as did Lorna.

Her daughter proved very popular and was frequently invited to birthday parties, but the best party of all was for her own birthday and Enid made absolutely sure it was special.

Being a Saturday this year dad was home and was a keen participant in the celebrations, helping to organise the childrens' games, making them laugh and generally shining as an excellent host. Enid hated it. It wasn't the real him, and here he was ingratiating himself with children and parents alike, all of whom would've considered him a wonderful father.

And when the party was over and the last guest had departed he reverted to his usual self. He shouted aggressively at Lorna over some minor misdemeanour which left her in tears and running to her room.

"On her birthday, Norman, how could you?"

"She'll do as she's told, Enid. It's only 'cos it's her birthday I didn't wallop her."

"Don't you ever dare...."

"I'm her father, I'll punish her as I see fit, don't stand in my way."

"I *will* stand in your way. Like all bullies you only take on the young and weak." She stood with her hands on her hips, eyes blazing, knowing what was coming. He was bright red, shaking with rage as he advanced upon her. She was still, unmoved, trembling with fear inside but determined not to show it. His right hand thrashed into her face but somehow she managed not to wince or to make any sound despite the extreme pain. It was a slap rather than a punch but it was bad enough.

"You're a bully, Norman," she repeated. He grabbed hold of her but no more blows came; he merely thrust her aside where she fell into an armchair, and then he was gone.

"I'm going out," he bellowed over his retreating shoulder, "and you better be more amiable when I get home. An apology wouldn't go amiss." With that he gathered up his things, went out slamming the front door behind him, and she heard the car start and set off. She breathed a sigh of relief, fought back the tears and went in search of Lorna whom she found with her sister.

"I'm sorry mummy, I didn't mean to do wrong...."

"You didn't my love, it's just daddy's a bit wound-up at the moment, very busy at work, and he didn't mean it either. Please forgive him my darling." And she sat and hugged her two daughters.

"Mummy, why is your face red?" It was the inevitable question.

"Oh my pet, is it red? Well, it's been quite a day, hasn't it? And mummy's been rushed off her feet. I expect I'm a bit tired and worn out, but I'll be alright in a minute or two. Have you had a lovely day my darling? Been a good party, hasn't it?"

"Yes, until daddy shouted at me."

"Well, you must forgive daddy. After all he did so much to make it a special day, didn't he?"

"'spose so."

"Yes he did. Now did you have lovely party? Tell me." Lorna cheered up and the pair started reminiscing about the event and finding more and more to chuckle about. Thus Lorna revived and the day was saved.

44

After Lorna and Patricia had gone to bed, happy at last, Enid made a cup of tea and tried to relax in the lounge while she nursed her cheek where it felt as if her teeth had been shaken free. She was confident no damage was done and as she contemplated the terrible row and the slap she found her resolve strengthening. Yes, she would prevent Norman hitting her precious girls. He could do his worst to her but she would defend them.

Her husband came home just before midnight about an hour after she'd retired to bed, and he behaved kindly and as if nothing had happened. That suited her. There was no mention of the violence and no enquiry as to whether she had recovered from it. And so they went to sleep and Saturday rolled into Sunday, the end of another day in Enid's life, a day that would've sore tested all but the brave, but she had come through it, just as she always did, just as she always would.

\*\*\*

There was one more brief drama for Enid and Norman to cope with. Patricia became very unwell and Enid summoned the doctor who examined her and then took her parents to one side.

"I don't want to alarm you but I'm concerned it could be polio." There was no chance the news would not alarm them. They had seen all too many stricken by the disease and the sad results. The young doctor continued, "But I'll get Dr Whitworth to come out as I'd like a second opinion."

They fretted their way through the night and waited impatiently for the senior doctor to come.

And in time their minds were put to rest. Dr Whitworth concluded that Patricia probably had nothing wrong with her other than a bad attack of severe constipation and he would send the district nurse to administer an enema, the application of which did the trick and the girl recovered, just as Enid and Norman recovered from their shock.

\*\*\*

The country was in mourning. George VI had recently died and Micky Bowen was filled with concern for the king's daughter, Princess Elizabeth. She would be taking the throne and at a relatively young age, and he hoped she'd be up to it. At least she had the extremely handsome Philip as her husband ready to be by her side. It was all quite fitting to Micky, for surely Elizabeth was a very beautiful woman who deserved such a man. He fretted that Philip might not realise how lucky he was, and then he knew luck did not come into it. Love did. And that was what mattered.

Love, what a strange creature it was, he thought. Then he recalled it was war that tore him and Enid apart, not a lack of love. She was married to Norman when she learned the truth, so there was no going back. That didn't stop him wondering where she was, and how she was coping with life. He hoped she was happy and was successful, not knowing that she lived a couple of streets away and was in a horrible mess of a marriage.

It was Sunday and he was going to Rita's for Sunday dinner, pork chops she'd promised him, and he was looking forward to it all. Her mum, whom he adored, hadn't been too good of late but was keen to entertain him, for she could see her daughter and this rather lovely man had the look of love in their eyes when they gazed at each other. And she was equally keen to bring them together.

Mrs Grant knew about Enid and also knew Rita had said she'd never leave her mum. So were they the reasons they were reticent about becoming a couple? How to make it happen, that was the conundrum she faced. She appreciated she had to release Rita from her promise, but how to do that?

The three of them had a splendid dinner and were relaxing afterwards when Mrs Grant suggested, as she often did, that they go for walk while she had a nod. As they prepared to leave Mrs Grant mischievously told them to hold hands.

"Mum! For heaven's sake…."

"About time you two held hands…."

"Mum, it's not like that…"

46

"You're two friends. What's wrong with holding hands? Only friendship. Two friends holding hands." Rita was quite embarrassed and Micky came to her rescue.

"We'll hold hands later, if we get up to Valentine's Park, Mrs G. Promise." Rita's blushes did not vanish until they were on their way and going at a brisk pace as if to escape her mother's recommendation. But suddenly Micky grabbed her hand and she felt no inclination to prise it away. Eventually they arrived at the park. In a quiet corner as they strolled around, deep in conversation, Micky took Rita completely by surprise.

"May I kiss you, Rita? Please. I'd so love to." She took a step back, clearly shocked.

"oh ... oh ... oh, well, yes I suppose so..."

"No need to be so enthusiastic," he laughed.

"Micky, I'm sorry, but, yes please, I'd love a kiss. I just didn't feel you thought of me like that, that way, you know."

"Well I do. Tell the truth I think I love you, Rita." She stood open-mouthed, rooted to the spot. This couldn't be so, she knew she stood no chance, she'd convinced herself there was no chance, not this remarkable man.

"Love me, Micky? What makes you think that?"

"Let's share a kiss and talk afterwards." He had such a sparkling look about his face, full of fun and joy and she found him irresistible. She knew she loved him, wanted him. There was no further discussion, just a warm embrace and a kiss that sent them into orbit. Nothing else existed, nobody else existed, they were entwined in love, real love and their first kiss was all the more passionate for it.

They returned home different people from the couple that had set out. But already Rita was worrying about mum and her promise. Had she but known it Micky had a solution. And a problem.

\*\*\*

*1953 Cheyne Avenue, South Woodford*

Enid had her car, an Austin A30. Although two doors it was perfectly adequate for her needs. Compact yet adequate. The

47

journeys to and from Churchfields School easily managed. And she was a chauffeur for two of Lorna's friends, Yvonne and Nola, who lived nearby but whose mothers were without transport. She'd widened her circle of friends amongst the young mothers and that suited her fine.

The situation at home had improved. Norman left discipline to her so there had been no unpleasant issues with their daughters, and furthermore the violence had ceased, this being in some way due to Norman spreading his wings and engaging with willing women, most married but easily charmed by the same skills he had applied to Enid during the war. It was nonetheless a dangerous activity, husbands unlikely to take kindly to being cuckolded.

He had also bought his family a holiday caravan which was towed to Cooper's Beach, East Mersea, an island in Essex south of Colchester, so they now had a place to enjoy leisure together at weekends and school holidays. And the girls loved it, despite the sea retreating a long way out over the mud flats at low tide!

The coronation of Queen Elizabeth had been in June and there was an air of celebration everywhere. Patricia had started school, also Churchfields, last autumn, and appeared to love it. Both girls were able to invite friends to Mersea and the caravan. Happiness looked unassailable but, of course, it rarely is.

Norman became a director of his company and his head swelled. He had a string of lady friends and could see no end to his life of success and pleasure. Enid looked after his children and that was all he required of her. In this she was aided by her mother and father who were well loved grandparents. Norman's parents hardly bothered now and that was completely acceptable.

Most importantly, from Enid's perspective, she had a good life now, the life she decided she would make for herself, and that included ensuring the girls' had enjoyable childhoods and could look forward to future successes. She had plenty of friends, good friends, just as the children did, and she had much to be grateful for, not least that there had been an end to Norman's violence following the vicious face slap two years prior. He controlled his temper and as long as Enid didn't ask any questions, such as what he was up to when away from home, a degree of stability had come into their relationship. Likewise there was no further threat of disciplinary action against the girls, Enid able to work her magic with Lorna and Patricia to keep them quiet and well-behaved if she sensed Norman was getting ruffled.

During the school holidays, and when Cooper's Beach was open, they would go to the caravan leaving Norman at home to concentrate on his work. Enid didn't doubt this gave him all the scope necessary to enjoy the company of other women, and had even found evidence on one occasion that someone else had been in their bed. But she kept silent on the subject.

Another pleasure had been her friendship with Dorothy Leonard. After the war she'd returned to Shropshire, qualified as a teacher and was now at a Girls' Grammar, English her subject, her degree in English literature finding a home at last. Then a year ago she'd married an accountant, Maxwell Hawcress, and Enid and family had been invited to the event, in truth a rather ostentatious affair with very little expense spared. Dorothy came to Enid's wedding just after the war but needless to say that was a rather more modest occasion.

But as the storm clouds had gathered in 1939, so darkness was now approaching Enid's new life in the early fifties, for Norman was not the sort of person to take kindly to being humiliated by a woman, least of all his wife who, he considered, should be obedient and subservient in all things. A housewife and mother, looking after his kids, that was his philosophy. She didn't need to be anything else. He would resolve this issue, have no doubt about it.

A cunning, conniving person, even now he was plotting how he might achieve his ends, and bask in revenge taken at Enid's expense. She was still a damn good-looking woman with an exquisite figure, one to be seen and admired on his arm, one to make other men jealous, and he used her for show and to his advantage. It was handy to have her around, such as when he entertained potential business associates, for she could make good conversation, knew how to behave properly, and clients were easily taken in by this or so he assumed. He had landed a contract on the basis of an excellent dinner at a top restaurant where his wife charmed the two appreciative men until they were itching to sign on the dotted line. That was his interpretation, but it was a very poor assessment, the summation of a man of limited intelligence who believes what he wants to believe. Enid's presence made no difference to Norman's success that night, but he thought it did.

And it wasn't only in business and marriage that Norman was presently plotting.

\*\*\*

*Malford Grove, South Woodford*

Micky was in a quandary. He'd been unfaithful to Enid that time in Scotland, and his conscience was getting the better of him. His beloved was wed to someone else and that was an end to it. Now there was Rita, yet it still seemed to him he was going behind Enid's back, indeed cheating on her, and he found it hard to bear with equanimity.

It just didn't seem right. On the one hand he could ask Rita to marry him and she and her mother could move into his home, thus eliminating a problem, for he was quite taken with Mrs Grant and knew he would get on well with her if they all lived together. On the other hand Enid might need him at any moment and he knew it was a forlorn hope, but one he curiously held on to, just in case. Now, which way to turn?

He had nobody to confide in, few friends, no close relatives and certainly not the garrulous Mrs Harris. Albert Coombes, perhaps? A fine gentleman, but in advancing years. He possessed wisdom, yes, but experience in matters of the heart, probably not. Besides, how could he begin to explain his dilemma, that he loved a woman we wished to marry but also loved a woman married to another man? No, the gardener would not understand and not be able to help. He'd have to sort it out himself.

This morning in particular things were not going well and he was allowing thoughts of Rita and Enid to spread across his mind too easily. Out first thing he'd narrowly avoided an accident when his mind wandered while he was driving. Then he dropped a car battery on his toes; happily it was a small battery and the distance it was dropped was very short, so no damage was effected although it was a mighty painful occurrence. And now, having come home for a drink and to let Mrs Harris in the wretched woman was giving him all the ins-and-outs of Sybil's latest catalogue of misconduct, and not drawing breath in the telling.

He set off and went round-the-corner, his expression for going to his rented garages, a misleadingly employed expression as there were several corners, one set of traffic lights and about a mile of distance. But round-the-corner it always was! He loaded his van with metal he'd sorted the day before and drove off to Williams and Co. where he was in for a shock.

Rita was not there. Her mother had been taken ill and she'd stayed at home. Micky finished his business and sought out a telephone box only to discover he had insufficient loose change to make the call. He stopped at a café for a bite to eat and made sure he received the right coinage in his change. On then to another call box.

"Hello Rita, heard about mum, what's happened pet?"

"Well, I've got the doctor coming. Not running a temperature but she's not herself at all and I'm very worried. She's in bed looking very pale and her breathing's poor. Can't imagine what's wrong Micky."

"I can be over later Rita. Be there by late afternoon...."

"There's really no need Micky….."

"It's no trouble Rita. Give your mum my regards and I'll be there as soon as I can."

"Micky, that's so kind of you, but it isn't necessary and I can ring you this evening."

"No, my mind's made up. See you later pet."

"Oh dear," she sighed, "well alright then. Be pleased to see you."

"Good, be pleased to see you as well. Bye for now Rita."

"Bye Micky, Bye."

***

*The Plough at Navestock, Essex*

"Like country pubs, Eric, but good job you gave me directions or I wouldn't have found this one."

"Not far from the Roding. Here, you know all the Roding villages? Well, I was told the river was named after them, not them named after the river."

"Get-away Eric. Who told you that?"

"Blowed if I can remember. Anyways, this is a good place for a private chat. Nobody knows us here, nobody'll recall us. Gawd, this beer's good, right tasty."

"Never mind the beer; just enjoy it. And tell me more, like what's in it for me Eric."

"You know darned well me old son. About three grand. And if this is the success it's going to be the next one will mean a whole lot more. Very little risk. Well-planned operation. You're a good salesman if you know what I mean; could sell anything to anyone, you could."

"Three grand? That's a hell of a lot, Eric."

"Well, we'll have to see how it works out. Might be a bit less. Expect less then you won't be disappointed, and you'll be delighted if it's more."

The two men hunched over their beers at a table in front of the pub and discussed their plan in more detail free from ears that might hear too much. Nobody else was sitting outside. Smartly dressed in their suits they could simply have been businessmen concluding a deal, or colleagues relaxing over lunch, or just friends meeting at a quiet pub. They could've been anything other than what they really were, two men discussing a shady deal that meant defrauding innocent people while they and their other associates in crime pocketed the profits. And Eric was determined to ensure the other man was convinced it would appear all above board so no question of police involvement. An investment opportunity that would sadly go wrong …. for some.

"I like it Eric. You've thought of everything."

"That's because we've got the right people where we need 'em. No square pegs in round holes. Plenty of brains been put together for this job. People who think of the problems and make sure they're ironed out. People who can plan with precision. And that's why we want you, Norman. The right brains, the right approach, your expertise shall we call it."

"Yes, I can see that, and I won't let you down…."

"I know that Norman. That's why we're sitting here now, planning. I've got the best man for your role, believe me. You're ideal, Norman." It might have been a cold day but the two were so intent on their conversation that neither noticed the weather and it was only when he was back in his car that Norman Belham shivered and looked forward to the heater warming up on the journey to his office. Must remember my coat, he muttered to himself as he set off along the country lanes.

And so this quiet, picturesque and unspoilt corner of Essex played an unwitting host to the planning of a heinous scheme unbefitting the beauty of the countryside, a project more suited to a dark city back street than a lush, scenic pastoral landscape. Navestock did not ask for it and would've frowned upon it, but Navestock had no choice any more than the pub did. The evil intruders left soon enough, never to return.

# Chapter Seven

*Mid-Nineteen-Fifties, South Woodford*

Life has changed again for Enid Belham. Despite her inner strength sustaining her through the early years of her marriage when her husband exposed his cold, ruthless side, probably his real self, she now realises she has not won at all, for the violence has returned although thankfully not aimed at the children. There have been other changes too.

More and more she is asked to accompany him to social and business events where he can show her off and rely on her to enhance his standing. To facilitate this he has enlisted the help of his own parents for baby-sitting, Enid's parents being repeatedly sidelined. It has been pointless arguing especially as too much confrontation inevitably leads to painful retribution. She can cope with that particularly as he now hits her where the marks will not show, but that doesn't lessen the pain and the anguish.

In another development he has taken to hitting her when the children misbehave, which is fortunately rare, because, as he points out, she does not want him punishing the girls himself. It happens late at night, after the girls are asleep, and he takes a morbid pleasure in it knowing Enid will not make a sound or resist. He is utterly controlling and enjoying himself, Enid's humiliation complete.

Happily she has her precious daughters, her parents, her friends and the redoubtable Dorothy. As yet she has confided in nobody as she does not consider that anyone should discuss private matters with another, and that as she is married there is no alternative to her lot in life.

Meanwhile, in business, Norman has gone from strength to strength as the company expands and he is contemplating a move to a better house, something that will help demonstrate his success and wealth. A suitable detached property is on the market nearby, in Broadwalk, and he will make an offer. He now drives a new Vauxhall Cresta. They have exchanged their holiday caravan for a larger version and it is one place Enid can often relax with her daughters, as her husband rarely accompanies her and she can take her parents there as well.

Norman has become a devoted father on the surface and Enid acknowledges that in his cunning manner he is trying to pull Lorna and Patricia away from their mother's love, another way of getting at his wife, but she is determined he will not succeed.

Unbeknown to Enid he has also enjoyed dabbling in the realms of fraud, and profitably so, but he is proceeding cautiously anxious to keep clear of the law. In this he has become wary of those he has associated with as it is clear they are up to their necks in other criminal activities and he does not want to be involved. However, he may have little choice.

\*\*\*

As the months have passed Rita's mother has deteriorated in health at every turn. Mrs Grant is not an old woman but the years are catching up with her, and she is further pained by arthritis in her feet and hands.

It is a long time since Micky dashed to Rita's side when her mother first showed signs of what was to be prolonged ill-health, but the situation has not improved.

Eventually Micky proposed to Rita saying that her mother could come and live with them at Malford Grove but Rita rejected him with gentleness and kindness. Nonetheless Micky was badly hurt. Rita knew her mother would not leave the family home, for various reasons, and would release her daughter from her obligation to remain with her, but Rita would not countenance it, and she explained this to Micky as best she could. What she didn't add, but which worried her rather more, was that she felt he still yearned for his lost love and that might place an intolerable burden on their marriage in years to come.

Micky is still doing well in his trade and has taken on two more lock-up garages, round-the-corner as he calls it, but tends towards being morose since Rita turned him down. They still meet, spend time together, but it is an awkward friendship both being in love with each other yet unable to be lovers.

Meanwhile there's business to be done and Micky's catchment area is expanding, and he enjoys his occasional visits to Holloway Road in north London where a car accessory shop always has plenty of batteries for him. But his immediate interest is not work related. For some reason he loves seeing the trolleybuses thundering down the road, always sitting in his van for a few moments to revel in the spectacle, and wonders if cars will ever be driven by electricity. To him the trolleybuses represent the future, yet he knows, deep down, they will be doomed. Perhaps one day they'll make a come-back, he considers, when they realise how lethal the London smogs are, when you can barely see a hand in front of your face.

It'll have to be cleaned up one day, he supposes, and trolleybuses will help, you wait and see! But electric cars? They belong in the realms of science-fiction, he chuckles to himself, as he heads for Williams and Co.

It is there that Rita has been saddened by unpleasant news.

The foreman, Syd Berry, has lost a great deal of money on an unwise investment, money he could ill-afford to lose, and he and his wife are in danger of losing their home. His wife, Moira, rightly holds him responsible and what was once a stable, loving marriage has become very strained and unhappy. There are four children. Rita wishes she could help and in her anguish turns to Micky.

Neither is aware Syd has been a victim of the scheme Norman was involved in.

***

Enid was very proud of Lorna, her eldest, who was doing well at school and seemingly enjoying her time at Churchfields. Lorna was not only good at her school work, she was also something of an athlete being successful in sport as well. Her younger sister, Patricia, showed no interest in sport whatsoever, was hopeless at anything physical, and was frankly not very good at learning anything either. She was also prone to getting into trouble, coming home in tears on one occasion having been smacked by a teacher. Enid soothed her but secretly harboured concerns.

She resolved to dedicate more time with Patricia in the hope of improving the girl's knowledge, and in the hope she might find something that would truly interest her daughter. It was worth exploring all kinds of subjects, for there had to be an area where the girl could shine. It also occurred to her that perhaps Patricia felt Lorna was always in receipt of praise whereas she was not, and that had a negative impact on her. Enid had consciously tried to ensure she treated both equally in all things, but inevitably with the elder sister doing so well in both studies and sport she was bound to have acclaim heaped upon her. Did Patricia resent that? Did she feel a failure? Time for Enid to step in.

She'd been to the school and approached one of the teachers, a woman renowned for her no-nonsense attitude to learning and one her youngest daughter seemed afraid of.

"Her mind wanders too easily, Mrs Belham," Mrs Munton pronounced, "and I've had to tell her off for humming in class. She goes into a world of her own. She's been seen singing and skipping along the corridors on her way into class, as if she's not with us at all. And she hasn't made many friends either, Mrs Belham. She could probably do with a parental guiding hand helping her at home because otherwise she'll be left behind. I think she's capable of taking more in but chooses not to do so. If you could gently help her along it might be to her benefit."

"I did wonder if the fact Lorna is doing so well has left her feeling, well, second best, not that I've favoured one over the other...."

"If you don't mind me saying so, Mrs Belham, it has been my experience in such circumstances that parents do quite often favour the more successful child, unwittingly, unintentionally, but it can happen. You've asked me about Patricia so I hope you won't be offended," Enid shook her head, "but I think it necessary to be blunt with mums and dads where a child's education is concerned. And you do want her to do well, don't you?" Enid nodded.

Back in the car Enid was surrounded by noise as Lorna, Yvonne and Nola chattered away endlessly. The A30 was a small car, Noman had promised a bigger one soon, and conditions were cramped to say the least, with Patricia squeezed between Yvonne, who was quite rotund anyway, and Nola on the back seat. In the mirror she could see her youngest looking all around her but not taking part in the conversation. She'd never really looked before partly because she was concentrating on her driving.

Pulling onto the main road they came to halt where other children had gathered, outside Downey's, the sweetshop, and her passengers disembarked enthusiastically to go and buy some treats. Even Patricia approached this with a smile and signs of pleasure. Enid decided it was time for her to take a closer interest in her daughter's development and an idea was forming in her fertile mind.

After tea, with Lorna buried in a school book, Enid looked across to Patricia who was sitting and staring into space. She realised she was humming, something she'd never really noticed before.

"That's a nice tune, Patricia," she tried.

"Like it, that's all," came the disinterested reply.

"Do you sing at school, in Assembly perhaps?"

"Yes, but I have to sing the hymns and I don't like them."

"Do you sing in class, I mean, are there singing lessons?"

"No." Enid ignored this terse one word response and ploughed on. Patricia did not look as if she cared at all.

"Shall we put some music on? Perhaps you could sing to it, darling?" Now her daughter just looked away but had a surprising remark to make.

"Wish we had a piano. Yvonne's got a piano. Could make my own music then, not have to listen to somebody else's."

"Have you tried Yvonne's piano?"

"Yes. Yvonne's good playing and she showed me how to do scales, I think they're called."

"So you'd like a piano, darling?" Patricia looked at the floor.

"Spose so," she muttered.

"Alright. I'll ask daddy shall I?"

"You mean he might get us a piano?" Her expression did not match the warmth of her words, as if she doubted her mother but was keen on the idea.

"I'll ask him, darling. Now I'm going to put a record on."

She selected the *Mazurka* from Delibes' Coppelia, a rather scratched record, but one that she felt was cheerful and rousing. Patricia was looking at nothing in particular, just swinging her legs where she was sitting. Enid started singing, hoping her la-la-

58

la was tuneful, and was rewarded when her daughter did the same. Lorna gathered up her book and stomped off to her bedroom muttering something about there being no peace.

Enid took a chance, right out of the blue, and began dancing, certainly not a mazurka nor anything like it, but it was obviously inspiring enough for Patricia rose and joined in, a huge smile now decorating her face. When the record ended she pleaded to have it again; in fact, it was played four times over. Afterwards Enid explained the story of Coppelia, the mechanical doll, and the ballet dedicated to the tale, and Patricia sat utterly spellbound, face afire with excitement.

Was music to be where her young daughter's forte lay? It was worth exploring. Meanwhile Patricia spent much of the evening humming the tune and occasionally dancing, later providing a brief show for an impressed father who applauded wildly. The question of the piano was yet to be raised, but Enid had high hopes. Norman was, after all, trying to overly ingratiate himself with the girls at Enid's expense, but she could play him at his own game, yes she could.

\*\*\*

*Williams & Co (Metal Merchants)*

"How's Syd, Rita?"

"He's just so ordinary, Micky. Not grumpy, hardly speaks, just not himself."

"He's not really talked about it?"

"No. Doesn't think people should talk about their problems, but perhaps he doesn't want everyone knowing. Maybe that's it."

"I wonder who talked him into that mess, Rita?"

"Sounded like a good investment, he told me. Paid a good dividend to start….."

"And the firm went bust. Isn't anyone responsible?"

"Limited company, apparently. You lose your investment. Nobody carries the can."

"God, that's awful. Pleased my business isn't like that."

"Yes, but Micky, you know if your business failed they can take your home, car, anything that can raise money to pay off your creditors."

"If I went bust I'd expect to suffer that. What's right is right. I'd want my creditors paid."

"Oh Micky, you're my hero! Such a perfect gentleman. A perfect everything, even in business. Perhaps you're too honest, there's lots that aren't, especially in this game."

"You got to be honest in life, Rita. That's the way I was brought up and the way I shall stay. And you won't catch me being talked into an unsound investment. Poor old Syd, four kids as well. Is he in debt, do you know?"

"He was telling Lenny he might move a bit nearer to work. Mean getting a smaller place, but handier. I think he might have to sell his place in Loughton, Micky, so I'm guessing he put a lot of money into that firm. He was so pleased with his divi, thought he'd done the right thing. Then came the collapse. More than that I do not know."

"Wish we could do something to help…."

"Well, we can't. He's a bit like you, wouldn't want it, wouldn't accept it. Principled, he is. Just like you. And talking about you mum wants to know if you'll come and have a Sunday roast this week."

"Love to. What's on the menu?"

"Pork joint and then a walk with me."

"Both of those sound good to me. Count me in! Now seriously, about Syd."

"I can't think of anything, but you're clever, let me turn to you, you'll think of something. But nothing approaching charity, mind, he won't stand for it."

"Okay, I'll put my thinking cap on. Have you heard from Moira?"

"Yes, she popped in but talked generally about other things and I didn't like to mention it. But I get the feeling things are a bit strained at home. Sad really. They seemed such a happy couple and this has put them under pressure, especially with the kids and all."

"Right," Micky sighed, "I'll have a good think. And I'll look forward to Sunday." They smiled at each other, Rita made up his ticket and gave him his money and he set off on his next job with a cheery 'goodbye' and a wave which was returned.

\*\*\*

*Malford Grove, South Woodford*

It was one of the days, rapidly becoming rarer, when Micky took tea with Mrs Harris and today, as usual, he was being treated to the latest chronicle of mischief in life of the wayward Sybil.

"Gave her the slipper, the headmistress did. Thought that a bit harsh. Sybil said it didn't half hurt and I bet it did, poor dear." What had started out as an amusing interlude when Mrs H began working there was now, quite frankly, getting boring, so Micky was reducing the occasions when they talked together over refreshments. He wondered if there was anything else in Mrs Harris's life or whether Sybil was the only thing that was ever worth mentioning. Today he pondered the possibility that a little more parental discipline earlier in the miscreant's childhood might have borne fruit, and that mother's slipper could have been the medium for bringing her to heel.

"Poor love, she was so sore, Mr Bowen," she droned on while Micky considered how sore his ears were getting, "and she's seeing all the wrong boys, y'know." *All* the wrong boys, Micky mused silently, be they ever so many!

"Well, I'd better get going, Mrs Harris, if you're okay."

"I am indeed, Mr Bowen, thank you." He rose, put his mug in the sink, gathered up his keys and other items and walked from the kitchen, sighing heavily once free of her earshot. He was going first to look at a Bedford van as he realised it was high time he had a larger vehicle, and it looked as if it ought to fit the bill. Within the hour the deal was done, and he could collect it next week. The sliding front doors were ideal, much easier for getting in and out, and he didn't need to bend double in the back, the roof being a little higher than the one in the Vanguard. There were windows right down the sides, and there were wooden bench seats in the back, also running down the sides, although they were simple and narrow affairs. They wouldn't get in the way, might even be useful. He hoped Mrs Grant would manage the climb into the front seat but was confident she could. Work had to come first, but he could not bear the thought of not being able to transport Rita's mum to Malford Grove for her frequent visits. No, she'd manage alright, he was sure.

\*\*\*

*High Beach, Epping Forest, Essex*

"Now look here, old son, you're one of us, you've done well for us, and done very well for yourself into the bargain. We need you. You can't walk out on your old mates, now can you?"

"I'm not walking out, Eric. It's not like that. I've done what was asked of me and the job's complete and I've assessed the situation and I've decided that'll do. I'm too busy to do any more."

"Ah now, Norman, that's not like you, not like you at all. You knew that once the heat had died down after the first job we'd be going for something bigger and better…."

"Yes Eric, but I don't think what we did was really legal. I've got my family to consider and I don't want any trouble from the law….."

"There won't be any trouble, Norman, as long as you just do what we ask. That's all. Let's go and have a pint and drink to our success….."

"No, my mind's made up. Count me out."

"Can't do that, old son. Can't be done. You start messing us about and the law will be the least of your worries."

"You threatening me?" Norman was snarling, clenching his fists, not that he intended to use them on Eric, and was growing red in the face. Once again they had met at a beauty spot and were talking well away from the other visitors. Eric raised his hat, wiped his brow and replaced the hat further back on his head. He'd have to play this carefully, so he elected to smile and nod as if to suggest he accepted Norman's decision, then tapped Norman's shoulder.

"Look, tell you what, let's have that pint. If you want out that's fine, but we don't have to fall out, now do we? Tell you what, we'll meet up again and I'll outline the whole plan. You

62

can think it through, have all the time you need, see if you have any real concerns, and if it's not for you, well, we call it a day. Norman me old son, you can't deny me that, can you?" Norman calmed.

"Okay, let's have that pint. Your shout, *old son*. But don't keep your hopes up." Eric chuckled at his response, and led the way down the hill, having defiled another piece of delightfully pleasant countryside with plans of evil deeds.

***

*Valentine's Park, Ilford, Essex*

A wet day in Ilford did not deter Rita and Micky from going for their post-dinner walk, and so, wrapped up against wind and rain, they strolled up the park holding hands as they always did. There was love, but it was kept imprisoned by both parties, for they knew it was love without a future, without hope, and it was Enid and Mrs Grant that made it so. That did not prevent them holding hands but nowadays there were no kisses other than gentle pecks of greeting or departure. Their sorrows they kept to themselves. The stiff upper-lip.

Micky explained all about his new van and did so with great enthusiasm while Rita smiled kindly and shared his joy. And then the conversation turned to Syd.

"No clever ideas there, Rita, can't think of anything."

"I'm not sure he'd want us to, Micky." They walked on slowly and in silence. There was nothing left to say. Then seeking to cheer the mood he told her all about Mrs Harris and her daughter and did so in a humorous way that left Rita laughing out loud.

"Micky, that poor woman…."

"Poor woman? And Sybil's going out with all the wrong boys! I think she's just growing up and not the way Mrs Harris envisaged. Could be it's her way of rebelling against her parents. All the wrong boys, I ask you!"

"Do you think she really gets into so much trouble at school?"

"No reason to doubt it. But maybe it's not as bad as I hear."

"Well, I hope not. Poor Sybil, always in trouble and then got a mother like that!" This time they both laughed, hardly noticing the rain was falling much harder than before, and it was only when they did that they quickened their step and headed back home.

They had not resolved Syd's problem, had offered scant sympathy for Mrs and Miss Harris, and kept their love for each other tightly locked away where it was in no danger of escaping. Their time together was thus empty, joyless and exhilarating all at once, a most unpleasurable and frustrating experience.

*** 

*Dorothy's telephone call*

One weekend Enid was enjoying a call to Dorothy that was to add another dimension to her life. Norman had taken to walking up and down in front of her, constantly looking at his watch to indicate that the time she was spending on the 'phone was expensive. It made her all the more determined to keep chatting. Eventually her husband abandoned the exercise and went in search of the children.

"Oh Dorothy," she sighed, "sometimes my dear friend I really do wish you were here. I have my lovely children and my friends, mostly the mothers of other girls attending the same school, but there are times during the day when it's just me and I'm inclined to wallow although I can't think why."

"I suspect it is because you do indeed have such a full and rewarding life, and when there is a lull you lapse into a kind of boredom and restlessness." Enid couldn't help wishing that was the case when she knew it was her loveless marriage and her enduring affection for Micky that laid her low. "Couldn't you get some part-time work?" Dorothy continued.

"Norman isn't keen. You know the sort of thing – no wife of mine is going to work – he believes he should provide, and I should stay at home and look after his children." Both laughed, but for Enid it was a hollow laugh reflecting her inner despair. "If I did anything at all it would have to be something of class, not just any old job."

"Mmmm, given me an idea you have. Won't tell you now. I'll look into it and let you know."

"Dorothy, you're teasing, how dare you?" They laughed, Enid with humour this time. "Alright, let me know when you're ready. How's Max?"

"He's grand. Playing golf as we speak. Do you play still play tennis, my dear?" The question took Enid by surprise and she blustered in response.

"Oh … well ….well …. no, not any more. Norman doesn't think it seemly for me to be playing sport nowadays, y'know, having the children and all that."

"Good grief, darling. I hope he's not the controlling sort," and she cackled at what she assumed was just a light-hearted comment made in jest, but when no laughter emanated from the receiver she became instantly concerned. "Sorry Enid, have I spoken out of order?" There was silence for a moment.

"Please wait," came her friend's quietly uttered words. Enid checked Norman was nowhere nearby; in fact he was in the garden playing with the girls.

"Dorothy, I'm sorry but that's exactly what he is. And he beats me, and I've never told anyone, and I don't know what to do. Oh God, I miss Micky, I really do…." And her words dissolved into tears Dorothy could only listen to, tears that turned into a mighty flood as the pitiful cries swamped the 'phone line. Dorothy was helpless and in terrible pain as Enid's distress burned into her heart, but she made an instant decision.

"Right, I'm coming over. I'll be on the first train tomorrow. Just tell him I've got a problem and I need to talk to you. I'll sort things out at work, don't you worry, I'll be there. Count on me. And between us we'll get you right, believe me, my pet."

"Oh Dorothy, Dorothy ….. I'm in such a state …."

"I know you are. And to think you've never mentioned this to me or to anyone. You must be bursting at the seams."

"Dorothy, Dorothy," she whimpered through the tears, "please, you mustn't confront him. Please…… "

"I won't, don't you worry. We are going to have some time together, that's all. But I can't leave you like this. Glory be, I had no idea, no idea at all. Now, be strong for me, be strong for Lorna and Patricia and get through to tomorrow. I'll get there as quick as I can."

"Let me know when you arrive in London and I'll wait at Snaresbrook station for you...."

"No you won't, my girl. I'll get a taxi. I've done it before."

"Dorothy, Dorothy, I want to beg you not to come, you know, do the right thing, but now I need you more than ever...." And once again the raging tears overtook her.

"Appreciated pet. I'll be there. Now dry your eyes and be strong or Norman'll catch you and want to know what it's all about." Yes, thought Enid, she's right. Trust her to be right. Full of good advice and common sense. And she began to control the flood.

"There's a good girl," Dorothy called when she realised Enid was pulling herself together.

But Enid could do nothing about her sad red eyes when she had finished the conversation and Norman appeared. She had to think quickly.

"Oh Norman, poor Dorothy. She's got problems. Couldn't talk about it over the 'phone but it's so very upsetting. I've told her to come over tomorrow and stay a couple of days. Hope you don't mind."

"No, of course not," he replied without sincerity, for he minded very much.

# Chapter Eight

Dorothy arrived just after lunchtime having endured a trying journey from Shrewsbury. Norman, playing the role of the perfect host and perfect gentleman, was there to greet her, much to Enid's annoyance. It was typical of the man. He should've been at work and came home late morning saying he had some documents to study and had decided to undertake the task in his own house. Enid didn't doubt his real motives.

Her friend had her story prepared, a pack of lies that astounded Enid, and had no qualms about telling Norman brief details when she arrived. He appeared convinced. But that didn't mean he was going to leave them alone. It led to an uneasy period when the ladies simply could not begin to discuss Enid's plight.

Mid-afternoon, there being insufficient room in the Austin A30 for Dorothy and the girls, Enid went alone to pick them up from school leaving Mrs Hawcress to read the paper in the lounge in the hope Norman would leave her be. But he didn't and what happened next took her by surprise.

"Well, well, Dorothy. That was a little story wasn't it? Sorry, but it was all rubbish, wasn't it? You're here for another purpose, aren't you? What's Enid been telling you? That I'm a bad husband and father? That's her usual ruse these days. Don't take too much notice, Dorothy. In fact, I've been worried about her for some time now, so I'm very pleased you're here. You're the one person she'll listen to, and I think she's far from well. I love her very much, and we have lovely daughters, this rather nice property, and I'm in a position to fully support my wife and family. I've worked bloody hard to get to the top so that Enid and the girls can have the best of everything. But it's come to my notice she's started talking about me derogatively, if you know what I mean." Dorothy looked shocked as well she might. Norman continued.

"The thing is, she still misses that other bloke. You know all about that business. She married me and came to regret it and she's letting her feelings for him ruin her life. It eats into her and it's chewing her up, if you ask me. Add to that the stresses and strains of being a hard-working mum and, well, I'm sure you understand. Me? I care for her, am concerned about her, and so I've started giving a hand with the girls, a hand around the house and all that. I take Lorna and Patricia off her hands from time to time to give her a break. Does that make me a bad husband?

"Dorothy, stay as long as you wish but be careful what you counsel, and bear in mind what I've told you. Encourage her to let me help her, share the load as it were, as I know she'll pay attention to what you say. It'd be a real help, it really would."

Dorothy felt dumbstruck, which was unusual, but in much the same way Norman had seen through her tale she could tell he was being less than truthful, and it made her very uneasy. She needed another plan and had to think quick.

"Norman, thank you for your candour. I too care for Enid and I will do all in my power to help both of you. I trust then, if you genuinely wish to engage my assistance, you will allow me time alone with Enid, perhaps tomorrow when you have gone to work?" Norman nodded. Come bedtime and he'd have a quiet word with his wife, remind her of her duty and that she should not undermine the marriage as Lorna and Patricia would suffer if things turned nasty. Yes, that was the way to work it.

***

The next day, with Norman safely out of the way and the girls at school, Dorothy revealed the chat she'd had with him. Enid sat passively. She was as pale as a sheet and listless, wringing her hands in her lap as she studied the floor in front of her. In a way Dorothy had expected the tears, the emotional outburst, to manifest itself as soon as they were free and was astonished Enid looked so calm and was so quietly spoken. She sat next to her and put her arm around her shoulder, pulling Enid towards her and trying to cuddle her, her own tears welling up in her eyes.

Suddenly Enid rose and stood in front of her and slowly lifted her skirt until the livid bruise on her upper thigh came clearly into view. Then, before her friend could react, she lifted her blouse to show another, lighter, smaller bruise just below her breast.

Dorothy threw her hands to her face, squealed with horror and leaped to her feet to grab Enid and hug her and hug her and hug her. Only now did Enid succumb to the terrible emotions roaring through her heart, her mind and her soul, and break down, weeping copious tears, crying out in agony, while a shattered Dorothy hugged and caressed her as furiously as she could while her own tears fell.

The storm was a long time passing. The fury was not yet ready to abate.

But then the howling and sobbing elapsed. There were no more tears left to cry. Enid felt relief at last, as if so much suffering, pent up deep inside, had been released and a weight lifted from her shoulders. No longer did she have to carry the burden alone.

Later they sat in the kitchen with their coffees and Enid experienced a calmness she had never known before.

"Would you leave him?" Dorothy enquired.

"Out of the question. I've little money anyway, but my girls mean everything to me, and I want them to have happy childhoods. As far as they know mummy and daddy are loving parents. I just want them to know the love of a beautiful family and to see them grow up to be successful and have enjoyable lives. I wouldn't want them to know anything else. I've heard of families that have broken up and it hurts me to try and imagine the effect it has on the children. Lorna and Patricia must never know such sadness."

"How good a father is he?"

"That's the trouble. He's been doing his best to be a good dad, but it's his way of getting at me, and he wants to wean them away from me, don't you see, Dorothy? He gives them whatever they want, never tells them off, plays with them ….. he's going to get a piano so Patricia can learn to play because I think she might have some musical talent. That's what I mean, that sort of thing, and they love him all the more for it. And it's distressing me because I can't do anything about it. If they only knew what he was up to. He's a perfect dad, just a rotten husband."

"My heart goes out to you, my lovely, but you can call on me when you need to. Sorry I'm so far away, I feel so guilty about it. I can't always drop everything; I am a teacher, after all. But please rely on me. I'll do what I can, you know that."

"Yes I do, Dorothy, and you mustn't jeopardise your job."

"I think a good start would be something to occupy you when you're alone. You did say Norman wouldn't wear you doing a part-time job, but what if it was something a bit special?"

"Such as?"

"Well, I have an idea and I'll make some enquiries. Leave it to me. I'm not going to say any more now until I've looked into it. Trust me please." Enid laughed in response.

"Oh alright, if you must. But why the great secret?"

"Wait until I let you know. I think you may be surprised. Possibly shocked."

"Shocked? Oh, I hope not….."

"Not in that way, actually. You want something that Norman will smile upon and I may just have the answer."

*\*\*\**

They went for a walk around the block, down Bushey Avenue and Malford Grove (unknowingly passing Micky's bungalow) to Hermitage Walk, returning along The Drive where they admired the large properties lying back from the road.

"Phew, they're expensive, I bet," Dorothy commented.

"Yes they are. Norman did look into it when he wanted to move but had to settle for where we are. Not sure I'd actually like to live here. Yes, there's the small greensward at the front with all those lovely big trees, and they've probably got big rear gardens but it's too close to the main road for me. That's a lot of traffic." She pointed generally in the direction of the traffic, flowing past parallel to The Drive the other side of the green. Dorothy stopped for a moment, looked at the main road where something caught her attention, then spoke.

"Mmm … always thought London buses were red. What's that green one?"

"Oh, that's a Green Line coach, a kind of express I suppose you could say. Just call at certain stops and I think the fares are a bit higher."

70

They turned up Broadwalk and headed for home, unaware Micky had driven past a few minutes earlier on his way to Malford Grove.

"Norman once took the girls down to that green to get conkers. They haven't the strength to throw a stick into the trees, so big, strong *daddy* went and did it for them. That's what I mean. He'll do anything for them just to win them away from me." Dorothy was beginning to wonder if Enid was imagining the whole issue and then remembered the bruises. "I know, I know, I expect you think I'm making a mountain out of a molehill, but I'm just so sure what he's up to and I can't stop him…."

"Yes, but Enid, think about all the things you do for the girls, and you don't want to spoil them, do you?"

"No, of course not, but *he* is, and I can't tell him and warn him because he'll beat me. That's the wretched man he is." Dorothy felt that perhaps Enid did indeed need something to keep her mind occupied when she was alone, and she'd had that bright idea, and hoped it would be the answer. But in the meantime she wanted to reassure her.

"Enid, you are doing a splendid job with the girls. They love you and appreciate you, but, if you'll forgive me saying so, you have become obsessed with that dreadful, brutal man and cannot see the good you are doing. Maybe you cannot see how much Lorna and Patricia love you and need you and appreciate you. Please, please, take a step back and try and ignore Norman and enjoy your time with the girls."

"Oh, Dorothy," she sighed, "I know you're right, and you're so full of common sense of course I must listen to you, but it won't be easy." They walked on in silence with Dorothy contemplating the possibility that her friend was over-reacting and was probably rather worn out, and therefore appearing as unwell to Norman. It could be the truth lay somewhere in-between. Norman had managed to sound quite rational when he was alone with Dorothy last night, in fact, quite sensible, but then there were those bruises, especially that horrid bruise on her leg, that left Dorothy thinking Enid was right to be worried.

"How long can you stay?" Enid cut right across Dorothy's deep thinking.

71

"Ah, well, I've told the school a couple of days, and they've been most understanding, as has Max of course."

"Oh Dorothy, there's Max. I'm keeping you from your husband, not just your work....."

"Wouldn't have it any other way, my pet, not when you were so distressed." They reached the house and walked up the drive arm in arm, Enid knowing that if she'd had to turn to anyone she'd chosen exactly the right person. And Dorothy wouldn't be intimidated by Norman, that she was sure of.

***

Enid collected her own brood as well as Yvonne and Nola and brought them home, dropping the other two girls on the way. Dorothy made observations throughout the rest of the day, especially after Norman came home, and reached the conclusion Enid had nothing to fear as far as Lorna and Patricia were concerned, both truly loved their mum. She was further encouraged when she realised the sisters appeared slightly wary of their father. She couldn't put her finger on it, but it was there, and she explained this to Enid later that evening when they were alone.

To Dorothy it was clear Norman was a horrible man and the girls were, in some way, aware that he was not so nice as he seemed. People can pick up on these things, she reasoned, and children are wide awake to anything that's not quite right. As a philosopher Dorothy had limited experience of children apart from being a teacher and having been a child herself once.

She stayed another day and went home Wednesday.

"I'm going to treat myself to a first-class ticket! About time I wallowed in some luxury." Enid was reaching for her purse and Dorothy knew she was going to offer her money for her fare. "Put that away, don't you dare!" Both women smiled, and then hugged for the last time. Enid ran her to Snaresbrook station where they said their farewells. "Keep your husband to his word. Let him get you a bigger car, and right now! The wife of such a well-to-do company director should be seen in something more appropriate. Tell him that. I already have!" Dorothy had to run as the train was already rattling over the road bridge into the station, but she was fit and agile and over the footbridge in no time. The ladies caught a brief glimpse of each other as the red Central Line train pulled away towards Leytonstone, and Enid shed the tiniest tear as she watched it run away with her dearest friend.

\*\*\*

## Half-Term

Lorna was staring out of the window at the lorry. She was fascinated by it. It came to clean the drains in the road, and she was absolutely intrigued by the long counter-weight arm that went up and down at the rear while the driver plunged the other end of the device, at the front, into the drain itself. It was just one of any number of amusements and pleasures the sisters enjoyed when they were home.

The baker came round with his basket on his arm. They loved the smell of the fresh bread and were allowed to choose a treat apiece which, in truth, the baker had anticipated, ensuring his basket contained some goodies.

Arthur, the milkman, arrived in his horse-drawn cart and the girls were permitted to pat the horse which was more interested in the food in its nose-bag. Arthur was reaching retirement age and was a bit of a problem for United Dairies, being apt to stop for a cuppa and a jaw with all too many housewives, and by which medium he was often last back at the depot to the consternation of the other milkmen. They had to wait until everyone was back before being paid!

The coalmen came and carried their sacks on their shoulders, and looked as dirty as the coal they carried. The dustmen also carried the dustbins on their shoulders yet, peculiarly, looked marginally cleaner than the coalmen.

And occasionally a rag-and-bone man would go past on his horse-drawn cart. Lorna could never work out what he was calling, for it appeared to be a higgledy-piggledy mess of words that sounded a bit like 'a-yee-aw-ron'.

Then there were the door-to-door salesmen, often ex-servicemen who could find no other worthwhile employment. Enid always bought what she could knowing what many of these men must've been through, her thoughts turning readily to Micky's plight. One man would turn up with a suitcase of various polishes and other cleaning items and he'd give the girls small sample tins of polish which delighted them no end.

Enid had a brand new four-door Hillman Minx, which Lorna and Patricia loved, and they had an upright piano which was of no interest to the elder sister but of great joy to the younger. Lessons had been booked with a teacher in the road they used to live in, Cheyne Avenue. Enid had followed Dorothy's advice and was more relaxed these days, and all the better for it. And, thanks to Dorothy's enquiries, had a part-time job Norman thoroughly approved of.

She'd become a Spirella Corsetiere.

Arranging fittings for wealthy ladies in their own homes.

Yes, she'd had to demonstrate the corsets, but her husband took a perverse pleasure in her stripping for the benefit of other ladies as long as she remembered to give him a show in the privacy of their bedroom late evening. It was better than being beaten. She'd show ladies how supple the corsets were. And ladies of all ages and shapes lapped it up. A Spirella corset was the one to wear; it set you aside from the ordinary people, even though you could hardly advertise the fact.

The bonus for Enid was the income on sales, which she was authorized to keep by her husband. So once again Enid found the inner strength she needed and was re-born. She was strong again and was no longer threatened by Norman's attempts to win the girls over.

# Chapter Nine

Her mother was shocked, but then so were her teachers. Lorna had failed the eleven-plus, although success and failure was measured by the number of grammar school places likely to be available. Faced with this surprising situation Enid turned to private education and managed to get her daughter into Gowan Lea, not far down the main road, and hoped that it's exceptional reputation would lead Lorna to greater success. There was always the thirteen-plus to come so maybe she would have another chance.

Patricia could play simple tunes on the piano and practised often. But her mother had also enlisted her in ballet lessons and it looked as if dancing might be where her better interest and opportunities lay. She loved the lessons. Sadly it seemed that the more studious and academically bright Lorna was slipping behind and Enid could not get at any possible reason. Perhaps Gowan Lea would make the difference. Patricia was altogether a happier child these days, full of fun and harmless mischief, and much more amiable than she had ever been. She had new friends from the ballet school and since they shared a common interest in dancing the friendships were all the more rewarding and deeper.

With this development Patricia's school work was showing signs of improving. Norman's behaviour is not. He uses violence against his wife, but by and large she is kept busy and altercations are increasingly rare. Dorothy keeps in touch and the family stayed with her in Shropshire during the Easter holidays this year, Dorothy visiting the family during the next half term break. Norman doesn't like her (the feeling is mutual) and she is very conscious of the fact. Put simply, he sees her as a threat to his well-ordered life in which exercising control over Enid is of primary concern.

Dorothy has, on occasions, asked Enid to be frank about her feelings for Micky but her friend is usually evasive, leading

Dorothy to believe those affections still run very deep, more so when she considers the miserable marriage Enid is suffering. Just how much has that affection influenced Enid's approach to her relationship with Norman? She can only guess.

Micky's business continues to flourish, but Mrs Grant's health is deteriorating to the point where Rita thinks she might have to give up full-time work to care for her.

On a happier note matters are improving for Syd Berry after he lost a great deal of money in an unwise investment, coincidently one Norman Belham was involved in, and has not had to sell the family home. They are struggling financially, but he's patched things up with his wife, Moira, and she has provided additional income by obtaining a good job.

***

"What on earth's happened to you?"

"Tripped on the pavement outside the office. It's nothing, don't worry. Fell over, landed face down, that's all. I'm a big brave boy. Nothing to worry about." But Enid *was* worried. Norman had a cut lip, badly bruised chin, a cut on his nose and a black eye. He'd had a nose-bleed as well, apparently. She might not love him, or care for him, but she was still concerned that he'd had an accident and hurt himself, and worried for him. "They patched me up at the office. We've got a first-aider, she looked after me." He was keen to dismiss his troubles as trivial and hoped his wife would leave him alone.

But Norman was hiding a sinister truth that had nothing to do with the pavement and everything to do with making money by nefarious means. He changed the subject.

"Patricia's doing better at school. I'm pleased about that. She's a good lass and she likes that dancing, doesn't she?"

"And you'll be pleased to know she's in the school country-dancing team. Quite the shining star, y'know." Enid's pride and enthusiasm shone through her words. There was added warmth from the knowledge she had been largely responsible for discovering where her daughter's talents might lie. Norman was speaking again.

"Pity Lorna's fallen behind a bit, but that new school'll set her right. Good job you got her in there."

"Yes, I'll keep a watchful eye on her, Norman. Early signs are that she's enjoying it and making new friends so maybe things will pick up of their own accord. How's the bonfire coming along?"

"Great. Hope we don't get any rain, mind. I've built it up nicely, give a good blaze, that will. And those girls have put a lot into their Guy, haven't they?" Enid nodded. "Really loved it and that's good. I like to see 'em happy. Anyway, I've got them plenty of fireworks including a special treat. An expensive rocket. Big thing it is, separate stick. We'll have colour everywhere up in the sky. Light up the whole of Woodford!"

"I hope you haven't got any bangers....."

"No, promised I wouldn't, and I haven't. Some jumping crackers, mind."

"Well you just be careful, Norman. You're a bit of a show-off with the girls." They shared a gentle laugh, Enid's possessing less humour. She fretted about occasions like this and hoped they would all stay safe. Perhaps Norman's accident might make him more careful.

\*\*\*

*Guy Fawkes Night*

It had remained dry but very cold, and now Norman had lit the bonfire which was already radiating heat. He added a little paraffin to the flames and Enid wished he wouldn't.

They were all wrapped up against the cold this freezing November evening, but the joy of the occasion was keeping them warm, the girls dancing around, thrilled by the array of fireworks they were seeing. Enid had prepared bowls of hot tomato soup which they scoffed with vigour as Noman hurled the Guy into the flames where it was rapidly devoured amid cheers all round.

The jumping crackers produced mirth, screams and frantic dances. Lorna particularly liked the Traffic Lights which changed colour just like the real thing, but the favourite for all of them was the Chrysanthemum Fountain with its star-studded

77

display. Patricia was charmed by the Catherine Wheels which Norman nailed to the trellis and not always successfully. It didn't matter, it was all good fun and treated as such.

Eventually they decided it was time for the highlight of the evening, daddy's huge rocket. He secured the long stick in the side of the rocket and for launching purposes used one of the handles on the dustbin, sliding the stick down so that the whole affair was close to vertical. It had a long fuse.

Once lit they all retired a very safe distance and waited and waited. And then it happened. Lift off. With a roar and a jet of sparks the rocket was away. Unfortunately it left the stick behind and set off horizontally across the gardens where it disappeared from view until they witnessed a vivid display of multi-coloured light from a neighbouring property. Patricia looked close to tears and was hugged by her mother. Norman tried to be philosophical, and true to the man he was tried to blame everybody but himself.

"I don't know. They don't make things like they used to. Obviously something wrong with the bit you put the stick in. Could be the stick was the wrong size. Never mind, we've still got some more fireworks, let's have a display." Spirits were down but the remaining pyrotechnics cheered them a little, especially when Enid arranged a game of chase around the garden lit only by the sparklers they carried.

The fire had died down, and it was time to go in, the girls much happier but still sad the mighty rocket had not worked properly. They were also sad it was over for another year. But was it? Just as they were about to take their coats off Norman stopped them in their tracks.

"Well, hold on, what on earth's this?" he exclaimed as he made a fuss of examining his pockets. "Well I never. Did you ever. What's this I've got in here?" And he produced four more fireworks that he'd concealed especially for this purpose while the girls jumped around with glee. But minutes later it really was all over and they were back indoors where Enid had prepared another hot snack. It was fair to say that a good time was enjoyed by all, and once in bed the girls were asleep within seconds!

At the end of this most pleasant of family evenings Enid and Norman settled down together on the sofa to reminisce about the event. He'd poured himself a bottle of beer and for Enid a glass of her favourite sherry. There was jollity; the loss of the large rocket was a keen source of humour. There were plenty of smiles and chuckles, particularly when discussing their daughters' fun and frolics. Norman was mildly, perhaps light-heartedly, admonished for his antics with the paraffin and with one of two of the fireworks, not least the ones he'd had in his coat pocket all the time! He praised her for the refreshments she'd made which, he claimed, had made it all rather special.

Enid felt a glow. Here they were, two parents revelling in a family affair of great happiness and bliss, and it all felt right, all as it should be. Now mum and dad were sitting together recounting the entertainment and the pleasure it had all brought them. In that moment Enid found it hard to realise that a beast of a man was sitting next to her. Why couldn't it always be like this? He was personable, jolly and seemingly content, exactly as a loving husband should be. And she wondered when it would all go wrong again. He hadn't changed, not one bit, and she didn't love him. Did she?

No, of course not. But he was being so sweet and, well, normal and it hurt her. If only he was different and tonight was typical of their marriage, not an exception.

When he'd finished his drink he nestled up to her. She felt revulsion at first, just as she did every time he sought what he believed was his by right. But this was odd. She found herself immersed in feelings that were strange to her, feelings of comfort and warmth, feelings of elation, feelings of safety. Yes, safety. Safety and security, and she couldn't comprehend it. Yet she automatically snuggled up to him. It wasn't the sherry; she'd only had one glass. Maybe it was a longing for something she'd yearned for and had been eternally absent. She just didn't know.

And that night, when they retired, they shared a tender lover's kiss, a kiss of wonder that became passionate in all its splendour. Finding no resistance Norman was transformed into an appealing, thoughtful lover who was gentle, kind and pleasing. It was a bewildering and exciting night for Enid Belham.

Later, as he slept, Enid lay awake simply basking in dreamy sensations and joyous memories. For tonight they were a true family. And she prayed that it would last forever. For tonight she would believe, believe it could be so, for she could not bring herself to think otherwise after such a magical and enchanting evening. It was only when she turned over to sleep that she had a silent thought as she drifted into the arms of Morpheus: 'I am so sorry, Micky. I am so sorry.'

\*\*\*

*Malford Grove*

"Look Rita, I've done some research and I think I could get planning permission. If I make my office the main bedroom, and move the office into the small bedroom next to the verandah, I could convert this back room and the large alcove there into a self-contained home for mum. The alcove could be where the bed goes and this would be her sitting room, with those large windows to look out over the garden. She'd be right next to the bathroom." Rita was stunned and positively overcome. She struggled to keep the tears under control. She'd not let go this time, it would do no good. Micky had looked into all this just for her and her mother.

"Micky, Micky, where's the money coming from……?" she squealed.

"I've had it costed and I've got the money. Just forget that side of things, Rita."

"Forget it? How can I? Oh Micky ….."

"Call it a wedding gift then. We can all live here, just as we planned originally and mum can have both of us to look after her. Now how simple is that?"

Rita knew it wasn't simple at all. Mrs Grant would not leave her own home. And there was the added worry about Micky's feelings for Enid which were far from dormant, Rita was so sure of that.

"Micky, mum just won't leave her home; she's so secure there, it's what she knows and now she's not well she feels she needs that security even more. I'm so sorry." He put a consoling arm around her shoulder and gave her a couple of gentle pats.

"I know. Just thought I'd try, that's all…."

"Micky, it's so lovely of you, truly it is, and I'd love it for all the world, but I can't help how mum feels and I can't leave her...."

"No, of course not, and I'm not asking you to." He sighed deeply and Rita was vexed that she'd hurt him. "Well, the offer's always there, never hesitate to ask." Rita tried to smile but she was too upset to manage one.

"Thanks Micky, you're an angel. Thanks again."

It was Sunday and Micky had fetched Rita and her mother over for their Sunday roast, chicken today, and while Mrs Grant slept afterwards the would-be lovers took a turn around the garden as was their wont. Micky was acutely aware Mrs G was not finding it easy to climb into his van, even though he now had a strong, portable step he carried with him.

"I'm going to learn to drive. Micky. Then get a small but suitable car so that I can take mum out now and then, and it'll be easier to bring her over to see you. She said last week I should come over alone to you, but I can't do it. She's only saying it to be nice to me, dear old mum she is. But apart from anything else we're like a threesome anyway and it wouldn't seem right without her."

"No, it wouldn't, and I'm pleased to hear you have some plans. I adore having you both here as you know and I never want it to be different." They hugged for a few moments before continuing their stroll, past the redundant fountain and around the flower beds, Rita knowing her heart was breaking and she mustn't show it.

***

*"The Fir Trees" Hermon Hill, South Woodford*

The men looked just like two friends having a quiet drink together. The pub wasn't busy but there was the soft thrumb of pleasant conversation hanging in the air, ideal for the two casually dressed men sitting near the window.

"Your bloke still okay, Les? Heard there was a bit of a to-do."

81

"Yep, he got nasty with Eric, said he wanted to get out and when Eric warned him, so to speak, he got all shirty and lashed out."

"Phew! Bit dangerous taking on Eric!" Both men smiled and nodded.

"He went a bit easy, so he said, just duffed him up a bit, gave him a split lip and a black eye for his trouble, and a few well chosen words of warning and encouragement apparently." The smiles developed into laughter.

"Anyway Alf, he understood alright. He won't be any bother. Got a family to worry about. He's with us. And he's very good as he's proved already."

\*\*\*

*Malford Grove*

It had been an easy mistake to make. Micky Bowen let Mrs Harris in and, as he was gasping for a cuppa, agreed to her making one which they shared at the kitchen table. Overall he liked her. She was good at her job, worked well and hard enough, paid great attention to detail and was reasonably likeable. He'd often wondered about her husband, what sort of man he was and so on. She spoke about him with affection but gave the impression that he actually did very little when he was home, and definitely did not get involved in raising the children of which there were two.

The other one, Jackie, was hardly ever mentioned. But Sybil was a thorn in Mrs Harris's side, and today she was letting forth on the latest misdemeanours of her unruly daughter who would be leaving school next summer.

"I don't know what she gets up to with those boys, Mr Bowen, and I've no idea what she's going to do when she leaves school. I don't think she'll pass any exams. I'm really worried that she won't get a job and will get into trouble with the law." Micky only half-listened to this diatribe and his mind was wandering in various other directions. "She's useless, Mr Bowen, utterly useless. No good at school and she'll be no good in life, you mark my words." At which point Albert Coombes arrived ready for some work in the garden and Micky invited him to sit down and have a cup of tea.

Mrs Harris eagerly poured him a cup while Micky swiftly finished his and made good his escape, having neatly passed the cleaner onto the gardener who could now have his ears bent on the problematic subject of Sybil. Poor Sybil, he mused with a smirk as he went into his office for some paperwork. Can she really be so useless? She's a teenage girl, of course she's interested in boys! And inevitably his thoughts turned to Enid.

No, Enid hadn't been like that. He was her one and only from their youngest years, and now he managed to sadden himself wondering where she was and if she was content, totally unaware that she resided less than a mile away and was anything but happy. He was now climbing into his van.

"I hope it's all worked out for you, darling Enid. God, I miss you," he said out loud to himself, "and I wish it had all been so different. But then it isn't, so, Michael Reginald Bowen, get on with your life, there's work to be done." He cheered up a little and tried to think of Rita and then remembered she was another lost love, well, all but lost. As he reversed down the drive he had to wait for a Hillman Minx to pass. They're nice little jobs, he concluded, observing it gliding up the road.

It was not to be the only time he and Enid would be within a few yards of each other and not know it. As he set off he found himself considering the plight of Sybil Harris, and then laughed out loud. Poor love. So useless!

\*\*\*

*Broadwalk, South Woodford*

Having successfully applied her skills as a corsetiere to a lady in Wanstead Enid hurried along to Churchfields School to collect Patricia who was outside the gates wondering what had happened to mum. Patricia gabbled away once in the car, explaining what she'd done at school today, what she'd enjoyed, what had pleased her most while her mother tried to concentrate on her driving. She also said she'd invited her friend Rosemary round the following evening, straight from school, and was that alright? Yes, it was.

For a teenage girl Gowan Lea was easy walking distance from home so no transport was required for Lorna who turned up later in the company of Donna Curtis and Margaret Swain, neither being to Enid's liking. Her view was that Lorna was being too easily led and that the two girls were not the sort of companions she wanted her daughter to have. Perhaps she could very carefully talk her out of a closer relationship, but knew only too well she might risk pushing Lorna away and into a world of secrecy. Better by far to know what she was up to and who with.

Enid knew Donna and Margaret had a bad reputation for misbehaviour at school, and from her own experiences when the two came home with Lorna their behaviour out of it left a lot to be desired. There was one other friend, Cathy, who Enid infinitely preferred, but who was rarely invited, the reason being that Donna didn't like her and Lorna did not want to upset Donna. She was a lovely girl, Enid felt, kind and studious and therefore an ideal schoolmate for her daughter. She knew Cathy's mother and decided she'd contact her and invite the girl that way, and hoped Lorna would not mind. But it might be a difficult route, fraught with problems. Worth a try, though.

The sisters were Enid's reason for living. She would make any sacrifice for them, do whatever she could for them, and put up with the abuse from her husband and his occasional beatings to ensure they grew up in a happy, loving family, having the best of everything. As long as that was their perception, and they believed that mummy and daddy loved each other, even if it was not the truth, Enid was satisfied. Sadly she didn't realise that Lorna was sub-consciously sensing that all was not well and that was the basis for the changes to her temperament which in turn was affecting her school-work and choice of friends.

However, Enid was about to be faced with a more immediate personal problem that had the potential for untold woes.

\*\*\*

Norman, good as ever with the girls, was annoying his wife on a daily basis by being critical of almost everything she did, and grumbling about all manner of things such as the government, the weather, the trade unions, even football. It was all very wearing but then it was supposed to be. He even maintained this moaning drivel when they went to bed. She could've strangled him. But, of course, she could say nothing for to ask him to desist or to argue about any viewpoint was to entice anger and violence.

Discipline was a double-edged sword in which, thankfully, Patricia was proving to be no trouble at all, whereas Enid was finding Lorna increasingly challenging. It was left to her to reprimand and withdraw pocket money when necessary and if she failed in her parental duties Norman would take her to task in the bedroom. Recently he had held her down on the bed and used his belt on her, punishment for not being more severe with their eldest daughter. It was becoming a fearsome struggle but Enid was determined not to capitulate completely.

Into this mix was added her husband's infidelity. Since she didn't love him she could put up with his wanderings as long as they didn't threaten the childrens' contentment and well-being. There had never been any suggestion of him leaving her, let alone taking the girls, so while Lorna and Patricia enjoyed being reared in a loving family environment, even if it was a façade, Enid would cope. But Norman, in his evil, cunning way, had to deliberately apply additional pressure to make her life more miserable.

From her point of view the fact the feckless Norman 'played the field' had the advantage of not presenting her with a serious rival. Nowadays he made no secret of his conquests, actually boasting about them when he wanted to turn the screw even harder. However, Enid was aware that one name in particular flitted in and out of these revelations: Maud Jolley.

Mrs Jolley was one of the parents she befriended at Churchfields, her daughter Gwen being close to Patricia in the early days. It was during a childrens' party at their Cheyne Avenue home that Norman, playing the good host, had taken a shine to the woman, a fact that didn't go unnoticed by Enid. It was weeks later that he revealed he'd had a fling with Maud. But now, years later, her name still cropped up and it was distressing Enid. Of course, there might be nothing in it, and no relationship, the whole business could be dead but mentioning it as if it was alive would be bound to raise Enid hackles.

Then came black Wednesday.

Back from dropping Patricia at school Enid was setting about some washing when the doorbell rang. She recognised Maud Jolley at once.

"Can I come in, Enid? It's important." Enid felt shock and distaste rising within her but, gathering her wits, stepped back and invited her caller in.

"It's alright, I won't stay, just not something for the doorstep." Maud remained in the hall by the now closed front door. Enid decided to try and be friendly and welcoming.

"Would you prefer to come into the lounge and sit down, Maud….."

"Here'll do nicely. Put simply, Enid, your husband is having an affair with me, and he tells me you know anyway, so not a surprise, eh?" Enid could feel her blood boil but she took some deep breaths to control herself. How dare this woman come here like this! Maud continued. "My husband knows so no good you thinking you can tell him. Norman regrets marrying you, did you know that? He'd like me but he can't have me so that's an end to it. Best for the sake of all our children, don't you agree, if nobody makes a fuss and it's all kept quiet? But Norman and I want to see more of each other and for the sake of the family my husband has no objection. I'm just coming to ask if you're going to cause trouble for our kids, mine and yours, or if we can have an agreement to let sleeping dogs lie."

Enid wanted to sit down, fall down if truth be told. She was shaking and struggling to control her emotions and a seething rage that was building to a crescendo. She must, *must* calm down. The two women stared at each other. Maud was looking contemptuously at Enid and the makings of a sly smile was appearing on her face. Finally Enid spoke, softly and slowly, carefully uttering each word separately.

"I will not lower myself to your level to discuss this."

"Suit yourself, little miss high-and-mighty, but it'll be your girls that suffer if you make a fuss. Goodbye." And she was through the door and away. Enid went into her lounge, fully enraged and plopped down in an armchair, knowing a horrible truth was upon her. It was not a time for tears, and she must reduce her anger, think this through quietly and logically when she felt better. It took a while before the storm eased. The tragedy of the situation was that she was helpless. Maud was right and she couldn't afford to make a noise, let alone confront Norman and object. Just mentioning Maud's visit might inflame him and bring him to violence.

Now another woman had a grip on her to add to Norman's controlling ways. Had he arranged for her to call? Had he told her what to say? It was always possible. And the fury rose up again. Knowing it was all so futile, she closed her eyes and sank back into the comfort of the chair to allow her temper to subside. She would have to find a way to forget this dreadful encounter and all it meant to her. And then the 'phone rang.

*** 

"You poor darling." Dorothy had listened to the tale and was aching for Enid and feeling just as helpless. "But I admire the way you handled it. No shouting, no rage, few words that, believe me, did more damage than anything else you could've said. You didn't even order her out!"

"No, but that I would've done if she said much more!"

"Best left as you did it. Probably hurt her a bit. I expect she's the sort of woman who loves a good row. She may've rehearsed all she could hurl at you and you didn't give her the chance. Well done, my precious."

"I won't mention it to Norman unless he brings it up. He's callous enough to ask me how my meeting with Mrs Jolley went if he knows she was coming here, and I bet he does, the wretched man."

"I quite understand and agree. Oh Enid, what a terrible life for you...."

"But I keep telling myself I'm strong enough to see this through. But do you know what? I've started dreading what's going to happen when the girls grow up and leave home. Will I just be thrown out?"

87

"No, he can't just do that. As far as I know after all these years you'd have some claim on the home, but see a solicitor soon, my darling, and ask….."

"Yes, but suppose he brings her here, moves her in….."

"That's what a good solicitor will tell you, Enid. Know your rights. And don't forget your girls are not going to desert their mother."

"Oh Dorothy, I hope you're right there. You know, I keep thinking about Micky and how different it might've all been ….."

"Sorry pet, but you mustn't think like that. Sorry, but you'll just drag yourself down. By the way, have you ever heard from him or know where he is? Because I wouldn't mind betting that he's married now, you must consider that."

"Yes I know. Dear Dorothy, you're an angel and my saviour, crammed full of common sense and sound reasoning." Both ladies laughed. "No, no idea where he is. Suppose it's best not to know and I've never gone looking."

"Pleased to hear it. Look on him with affection but keep him out of your thoughts when you're bothered by Norman's behaviour."

It had been just the 'phone call Enid needed. Afterwards she made a coffee and continued with the washing her strength renewed. I will overcome this latest dire development, she decided, and I will be a better person for it. My children come first and I will be strong for them and not give in to this nonsense. It will not affect me, for I shall not let it. Dorothy, as ever, is right. I am going to succeed, nothing can stop me.

She went to the back door, threw it open, and took in some deep breaths as she stared at the blue sky and fluffy white clouds. Then she smiled, knowing she felt good about herself again. No, she resolved, I shall not lower myself to Norman's level either. There's a new me emerging and I like the look of it!

# Chapter Ten

*1960*

There have been some changes as the years have rolled by. Against all the odds Patricia passed the eleven-plus and has secured a place at Woodford County High School, Woodford Green, leaving Enid awash with pride and glowing with satisfaction. It is scant consolation Maud Jolley's daughter, Patricia's classmate at Churchfields, failed the exam, for Enid would not have wished ill-fortune on any child. However, Lorna, once full of promise, is giving serious cause for concern and has been in trouble at Gowan Lea school, Enid believing Donna is leading her astray. Certainly Lorna is not doing well in her studies and Enid has recently been summoned to see the Headmistress for a discussion on the subject.

Enid tries to help with the girl's homework but it is an uphill struggle, for there is a lack of interest. She has not yet realised that her daughter senses all is not well at home and it is affecting her life quite badly. The tension between mother and father, despite their best efforts to keep it from their children, hangs in the air and Lorna is noticing the fact without yet understanding what she is witness to.

To make matters worse Norman's father has died and he is moving his mother in with them at Broadwalk. Enid knows that whenever she goes out there will be someone at home, a woman with her son's best interests at heart, and it is a sore point, a constant worry. It is also a further source of unhappiness for Lorna who has never taken to her grandmother.

Rita passed her driving test and has a second-hand Ford Anglia which Micky helped choose for her, but Mrs Grant is in very poor health and becoming less active so her journeys in the car are few and far between. Rita has now asked about going part-time and her bosses are looking for someone to assist her who can cover adequately when she's not in the office.

\*\*\*

The summer holidays had been glorious for Enid and the girls. They spent nearly four weeks at their caravan and for once the weather was mostly kind, although there had been a couple of thunder storms with torrential rain. Norman joined them for two weekends, all the time he could spare, but Enid noted the sisters were not too bothered.

Interesting.

The three had some enjoyable days out. Abberton reservoir proved an instant success on account of its wildlife, including the hungry ducks that ate everything that could be thrown to them. They loved Clacton especially the pier with its many attractions, and of course Butlins where they took advantage of day tickets to sample the rides. Yes, and there were donkey rides on the beach too, so unsurprisingly they visited the resort five times during their stay!

Colchester Castle fascinated Lorna in particular, and Colchester was another favourite for a different reason. There were evenings when they drove into town, bought fish and chips, and enjoyed them on Hythe Quay where they could also feed the swans. Enid could not have been happier.

Mersea Island lay to the south of Colchester and was truly an island when tidal waters covered the only access road, the Strood, when most traffic was brought to a halt. The girls adored going to see the spectacle. West Mersea was the busier part where the shops were located. Patricia's joy was a call at the ironmonger's, Digby's, which she viewed as a kind of Aladdin's cave, packed high with all kinds of items. They usually went there when they needed gas mantles for the caravan lights which, like the cooker, ran off cylinders of Calor Gas.

The older gentleman who ran the store always spoke pleasantly and respectfully to the sisters who liked him all the more for it. He was ahead of his time in some ways. It amazed Patricia that he could find whatever you wanted in what might otherwise have been regarded as a complete mess. And that having acquired what you went in for you went out with even more. He would always ask you about other items, such as matches, "Such a shame when you get home and find you've run out and could've bought some here." This salesmanship usually worked; at least it did on Enid with prompting from Patricia.

The eastern end of the island was quieter away from the holiday camps. You could see across the river Colne estuary to Brightlingsea, which they visited once, and a walk around the north-eastern side of the island at this point would take you past pill-boxes and other wartime defence buildings, the use of which Enid explained at length.

Mrs Northwood, and her daughter Cathy, came down to stay for a few nights, but Lorna was unkind and largely ignored the girl, the situation being saved by Patricia who made her very welcome, despite the few years age difference. Enid's plan to encourage friendship with Cathy was unravelling, Lorna even asking in front of Cathy why Donna couldn't have been invited.

One of Patricia's friends from ballet school stayed for a while with her sister and mother, and a gay old time was had by all, except by Lorna who sulked and often went out for walks by herself. Enid even tried taking her elder daughter to the tennis courts for a game, but Lorna's heart wasn't in it, and they packed up after a quarter of an hour. That was day Enid resolved to have a quiet chat with the girl, an event that was to have serious repercussions.

It happened after they had popped down to West Mersea and the far west of the island to see the wonderful array of houseboats, and to take a trip across the River Blackwater to Bradwell on the 'Pedro'. The estuary was dotted with moored tankers, laid up when there was no work or awaiting the final trip to the breaker's yard. The little vessel bobbed up and down as it worked its way across the waves and poor Patricia felt seasick. But the sight of the tankers, rising like mighty cliffs above their heads, was utterly absorbing. They'd only ever seen the ships at a distance from Cooper's Beach, but to see them close up, these massive sea-going workhorses, was a staggering vision and Patricia quite forgot her mal-de-mer. Even Lorna was thrilled.

Pedro's owner, also their skipper, explained about Bradwell Power Station and the wall that had been erected in the estuary where the hot water was fed back into the sea, water used to cool the nuclear innards of the station. Not that any of them understood nuclear power, but it all sounded very important.

That evening they went for fish and chips, enjoyed them on the quay just outside Colchester as usual. It was a quite delightful August day, and they'd had a smashing time. Back at the caravan Patricia's friend Brenda came and asked if she could go over to her chalet for some games and Enid readily agreed. Brenda's family were lovely people and she knew her daughter would come to no harm.

"Don't be late back, darling, please," she'd called out as the girls skipped off towards the chalet park.

"No mummy, promise," came the answer. Enid knew it was the right moment to tackle Lorna. It had to be done. They'd had a lovely day; it might encourage her daughter to open up. And it was to achieve that aim, it certainly was.

\*\*\*

Lorna was sitting quietly looking at nothing in particular. Her mother came and sat opposite. Lorna glanced across and spoke.

"Mum, please leave me alone. I don't want to do anything. Please." And her head sank, her eyes falling into her lap. Enid responded at once.

"I want to help, but you must let me in. While there's just the two of us I'd like to ask you once and for all why you're like this. You can say what you like, Lorna. Say whatever you like. Please. Say anything at all as long as it's the truth. Say anything. You won't be in trouble I promise you." She gazed at her seemingly careworn daughter, then added softly, "Please Lorna, please." Lorna looked up, with pleading eyes which Enid recognised at once, and she repeated her request. "Please Lorna, please."

"Say anything? Anything? Bet you'd wallop me if I did."

"No Lorna. Say anything as long as it's the truth. I promise you faithfully, I just want to help, no punishments, nothing." Lorna considered this and Enid noticed the first tears forming in her daughter's eyes. She almost moved to Lorna's side but decided against it. She was driven by a mother's desire to love her child, to support her, to comfort her, but she had, just *had* to encourage her to speak freely.

"You'll tell daddy….."

"No I won't, and if it's about daddy then all the more reason to tell me. You have nothing to fear my darling. I won't tell anyone what you tell me. Promise. Please trust me." Enid was absorbed in feelings of tension and fear, but desperately wanted to know the full story, especially as there was a suggestion in Lorna's manner that Norman was playing a part in all this. Lorna leaned back in a resigned fashion.

"Oh, let's get it over with, then you or daddy can do what you like with me, see if I care."

"Lorna darling, nobody is going to touch you, but I can't help you if you won't let me in." Lorna appeared to ponder this, then sat back and spoke, her voice quiet and shaky, sad and resigned. What she had to say was a shock, a terrible shock.

\*\*\*

"I don't love daddy. I just don't. He frightens me. He's always doing nice things for us but he frightens me. He's too kind. It's like he expects something in return, I don't know, I can't explain. I expect you love him, but I don't, and I wish you didn't love him, but for all I know you don't. I wish you didn't, then we could be a happy family, a proper family. I love you, mummy, and I love Patricia; why can't it be just the three of us? We've been so happy here except when daddy came to stay. It's like he's doing it because he should, not because he loves us. Does he love you, mummy? How can he love you when he hits you?"

These final words tore through Enid's heart and bored into her mind, destroying her senses and all good reason. Suddenly she was almost afraid, afeared of what might be coming.

"Hits me? What do you mean….?" She stammered, clutching at her chest and throat with the disbelief of it all, the shock thrusting its way mercilessly into every inch of her being.

"I've crept across to your bedroom late at night and I hear him grumbling at you, and then he hits you, I know he does. Not seen it, but I know what's happening, and it's happening to my mummy….." Her words slipped quietly away to be replaced by tears, and now Enid did go to her side to hug and cuddle and kiss.

93

"I love you mummy, I love you…." Once again the words died on her lips as tears cascaded down her cheeks, and Enid hugged her tight all the more. The truth was in front of her, out at last, and what she'd denied to herself privately was now the reality. Lorna knew, knew her parents were at odds constantly and, worse still, realised her beloved mother was beaten.

"I love Patricia but she gets everything. Daddy looks after her, doesn't he?" It was a new tack and a direction Enid had never contemplated, the question of sibling jealousy. "She got a piano and ballet lessons. Nobody, not even you, asked me what I wanted. What did I get for being a good girl at school? Learned lots and I liked it, but then I was ignored. I know I can't have a horse like auntie Dorothy, but I could've had riding lessons. There's a stables right near where we live and they go in the forest. Donna goes. Whenever we go to auntie Dorothy's we're always too busy for me to ride her horse. But we have to listen while Patricia plays the piano, and watch her dance."

Enid was bursting inside. Her emotions had been given a torrid ride as she'd listened attentively and in gathering despair to a tale that had dimensions she hadn't anticipated.

"I love my sister, but I love Donna too," Lorna continued, "and I wish she was my sister as well. She gets to go riding and do other things, but I can't. Patricia gets everything…." and her voice trailed away into nothingness as her head sank and she turned her face away from her mother, but not to hide tears for there were none. Enid hugged her close. "Daddy looks after Patricia. He used to hit me but he never hit her. It wasn't fair. She wasn't as good as I was but I was the one getting into trouble." Could this revelation be true? She could barely remember Norman smacking the girls at all, even when they were very young. Discipline was left to her and she always tried to treat them as kindly as possible, rarely administering a slap.

Enid was churning, her insides, her mind, her heart, all churning in the most dreadful fashion and she felt so wretched. She'd heard things to turn the stomach, and if there was truth in Lorna's words the situation was worse than she could've imagined. What could she do? Try to bluster her way through? Say that she and Norman had stayed together for them? It was true but it wasn't what Lorna needed to hear especially as the girl seemed horribly aware of the fact. But she had to say something, and now wasn't the time to simply apologise and offer to put things right. She felt so empty and devoid of ideas. How she wished Dorothy was there to advise! It was no good making excuses or being less than honest. Lorna would know. Face it head-on, she decided.

"Daddy's hit you? Is this recent?"

"Some time ago, more than once. Told me never to tell anyone or I'd get worse. If he thought I'd been bad he'd do things like slap me round the face, and that hurt. He boxed my ears and I couldn't hear properly for the rest of the day. He walloped me with his belt once when you and Patricia weren't home. But he's not done it for a long time." Enid was shaking, the words having cut through her like a knife. Was Lorna lying, perhaps because she didn't like her father? "And he hits you mummy. I don't know why you put up with it. It makes me cry. I wish we could be a proper family, I just wish we could, then I could be happy….."

"Lorna, I've promised not to tell anyone what you've told me…."

"But you will, won't you? You'll tell daddy…."

"No I won't. But I must know if what you have told me is the truth. You must be honest, darling."

"I *am* being honest. Now you be honest and tell me why you let him hit you. It must hurt."

"Alright. Alright, I'll tell you. I've let him hit me to protect you both. There, that's the truth of it. I've taken beatings when either of you misbehave and he thinks I haven't done enough to discipline you. I would rather him beat me black and blue than lay a finger on you." Lorna had turned to face her mother, her eyes red and pleading, as if she was searching for something better, when it was something she knew didn't exist. "That was the arrangement, horrible though it sounds. He should never have touched you. You have no idea how I feel now, darling, no idea at all. The blows do not hurt because I have suffered them for the girls I love with all my heart. And what will you do now? Tell daddy what I've just said?"

"No, no, no, mummy, no." she squealed in a pathetic voice, suddenly full of fear and dread. "No, I won't. You can't love daddy, you just can't, and neither do I. Oh mummy, what are we to do?" Enid hugged her even closer if that was possible, and tried to pull herself together. She must be strong, more so than ever before.

"We're on holiday, and I thought we were enjoying ourselves. Let's do that. Not a word to Patricia, mind. I assume she doesn't know how you feel?" Lorna shook her head. "I will put things right for us, I promise I will, and the three of us can make the most of being us. Please promise me you will tell me if daddy does anything you don't like. And in the meantime I will do all I can to make life good for us, and that includes being more considerate to you, my precious. I am truly sorry for my shortcomings where you are concerned, but give me chance to put things right. We all have to live with daddy just as he is, and if we're strong we'll cope. Can you be strong like me, my darling?" Lorna nodded again and this time they hugged each other with furious passion as gentle tears made good their escape at last. The tempest was dying, and Enid was thinking more clearly. She'd make this work, just as she'd vowed all those years ago.

They were playing snap when Patricia came home, and for all the younger girl knew they had passed their evening as pleasantly as she had, which was how they both wanted it to appear.

*** 

Enid slept in fits and starts. Her breathing wasn't steady. She was, in some respects, still numb and yet her emotions were running riot. She was going to have to handle this alone, virtually the same burden she'd carried since the wedding day. Norman was evil. She was nervous; she couldn't confront him, and there was always the chance Lorna had made some of it up. Against that was all that she knew about him and it made her cringe. Naturally she would consult Dorothy, and soon. Lorna had also let slip that she wasn't keen on her paternal grandparents either, but that could be down to the dislike of her father. Of course, Norman's dad was dead and now the grandmother was set to move in with them and neither Enid nor Lorna welcomed the idea.

Now she lay awake, trying to hear any sound that might suggest Lorna was having a nightmare, or was not asleep and unhappy, perhaps crying quietly to herself. No sound came and eventually she dozed off and slept untroubled until about 7 a.m. when Patricia awoke and noisily roused the other two. Enid had made her mind up; today was going to be a special day, she would make it so. Nothing elaborate, but a very enjoyable day.

*\*\*\**

*Williams & Co (Metal Merchants)*

"Rita?"

"Yes Mr Gaffney?"

"I've got a young lady coming for interview and I'd like you to meet her, join me for the interview itself, maybe. I don't know if she'll be any good. No qualifications, but I spoke briefly to her mother, Mrs Harris, and apparently she's very enthusiastic but not been able to find a job since leaving school. Reckon I'd like to give her a chance but I need your honest opinion, Rita. After all, you've got to work with her, and she'll be doing some of your work when you're not here."

"Thank you, Mr Gaffney. I'm sorry to have put you to this trouble….."

"No, no, no, it isn't any trouble at all, don't be so silly. Anyway, she'll be here at three this afternoon."

"Oh .. er .. Mr Gaffney, do you know the girl's first name?"

"Yes, let me see …. yes, it's Sybil."

*\*\*\**

Micky couldn't believe his ears when Rita rang that evening.

"Well, anyway, she came over well enough, very polite, nicely spoken. Keen, and quite honestly, I don't think she's going to be asked to do anything difficult, anything that's beyond her. The boss gave her the job there and then after he'd got the nod from me. She starts next week, so we'll see. But if nothing else I'm anxious to find out what she's really like after all you've told me! You haven't actually met her, have you Micky?"

97

"No, although I feel as if I've known her for years, y'know, lived through every episode of her life with her!"

"I might be able to get some inside gen on her mum, you never know. Could be mum's been the problem." Both chuckled. "We'll see. I expect you'll be looking forward to making her acquaintance!"

"In a way I suppose I am. What's she look like?"

"Smartly dressed, curly black hair, very nice face, smiles came easily, that sort of thing. Good figure, not that you'd be interested in that!"

"Now, now! I've only got eyes for you, Rita."

"Then make sure you keep them on me!" They laughed freely, as they so often did, while they felt the pain of their situation scratching at them. But keeping his eyes on Rita when he met Sybil was to prove difficult as he soon discovered.

\*\*\*

*Canning Town, east London*

Norman shuffled nervously from foot to foot, but not because he was cold. He knew the man approaching him, arm outstretched ready for a handshake. They'd only met once before and although it had been a convivial meeting Norman found him intimidating. Why had he ever become involved with this outfit? No way out now, he was in too deep, and the only exit was the road to painful retribution, he'd been made only too aware of that.

He'd tried to kid himself, in those early days, that there wasn't much illegal about their operation and the thought of all that money, lovely, lovely lolly, was too much of an encouragement. But that was the way they'd hooked him and he realised now that they needed him for something far more important, far more rewarding, and far more illegal, and he couldn't simply turn his back on them. He didn't fancy prison one bit, but he'd be going down for a long time if it all went wrong and he was caught.

That first scheme, he recalled, so straightforward and easy, was just the teaser, the appetiser, and it seemed so innocent when it was nothing of the kind. People like Norman could close their minds to the seedier side of such shenanigans, and he'd done so quite conveniently, without appreciating where it might lead. Eric had given him the money afterwards and he'd been so pleased he was enthusiastic about the next job. That is, until he started to think about what he'd done, the money innocent folk had lost, and at this moment what it all might come to cost him. And there was no going back.

"Mr Belham, good to see you again." There was a gleam in the speaker's eyes as he took Norman's hand firmly, a pleasant enough smile on his face which Norman saw for the façade it was. The man was well-dressed and well-groomed but the overall picture was let down by his portly physique and the fact he was sweating.

"Mr Faulkener. How do y'do." As a greeting it sounded every bit as insincere as it was intended.

"Mr Belham, here's your envelope. Instructions inside. Burn them when you know them but don't make notes anywhere else. Understand?" Norman nodded once as he took the proffered brown foolscap envelope. Mr Faulkener continued. "You know what to do so get cracking and let's all make some more money, eh?" Norman nodded again. He hadn't removed his eyes from the man's face where all he saw was menace and evil. "Right, I'll be on my way. Good-day to you." And he was gone leaving Norman to study the plain envelope now in his possession.

He made his way to the station and sat on the platform awaiting his train, wishing he could return home, burn the wretched thing unread, and simply walk away. He wasn't a man for regrets, but this regret hung over him like the grim reaper ready to claim his next victim, and it was a darkness from which there was no escape. If this plan worked, and, he consoled himself, it should, they'd want him again for another project. For the first time in his life he felt anything but secure. It was probably the first time he hadn't felt in control of his life. And he knew fear, just as he'd known it back in 1939 until salvation presented itself.

As the train slid noisily into the station he came to a conclusion. Doing the job and getting paid was infinitely better than prison, so he'd just have to leave any conscience behind and do his absolute best and trust none of his colleagues let the show down, not that he had any good reason to imagine any would fail.

He changed at Stratford to the Central Line but was so deep in thought he caught a Hainault train by mistake and ended up at Wanstead, silently cursing and blaming, as usual, everyone bar himself, before rectifying the error by taking the bus to Snaresbrook station where he'd left his car.

And later that night he exercised control in the only arena open to him, beating Enid mercilessly in the bedroom, leaving her in a heap on the floor, sobbing silently while the unbearable pain in her stomach and abdomen gradually receded. She had no idea what was wrong; he'd said nothing, the girls had behaved impeccably all evening, and after she and her husband had changed into their bedclothes he suddenly and inexplicably starting thumping her.

All she could do as she slowly rose and climbed into bed with him was to pray Lorna had not been outside. Her prayer went unanswered. Lorna was back in her own bed weeping copiously. How long could this go on? She'd only just stopped herself throwing the door open to try and rescue mum, a mission doomed to failure with the most fearful consequences awaiting her.

In that moment of despair, anguish, frustration and helplessness she resolved to write to auntie Dorothy and pour out all she knew and all her worries, and hope Dorothy would come to their rescue. Lying in bed other concerns swept through her mind.

She'd been untruthful when telling her mother Norman had beaten her. She'd only said it to make her mother hate him, or hate him more. But she'd lied. That was the worst part. And if she wrote to Dorothy would she be believed? Would the lovely lady she called her aunt telephone Norman? What would the price be? She dared not think on it. No, she could not write, it was too dangerous. But surely she had nothing to fear if she talked privately to Donna? Her friend could not help her, obviously, but having a loyal friend she could speak to in confidence, no harm could arise from such a liaison, could it?

On Saturday she was going to the stables for another ride (thanks to mum) and perhaps afterwards she and Donna could find somewhere for a quiet chat. Yes, that was the place to start.

***

*Williams and Co (Metal Merchants)*

"Sybil, this is Mr Bowen, the gentleman I told you about. This is Miss Harris." Rita made the formal introductions as Sybil rose and shook hands with the visitor. For his benefit Rita added: "Miss Harris started this week and she'll be assisting me and will be here when I'm not. I'm sure she'll look after you." The girl blushed.

"Hello Miss Harris, and please call me Micky. Good to meet you. I hope you'll look after Miss Grant as well." All three shared a brief chuckle.

"You can be sure of that Mr Bowen, I mean, Micky. And I'm Sybil."

"Yes," Rita joined in, "and I'm Rita. Best not to be too formal. When I mentioned you to Sybil she told me you might know her mother, Micky." Out of sight behind the girl Rita gave him a mischievous wink and a saucy smile to go with it.

"Oh yes Micky. Do you live in Malford Grove?"

"That's me."

"I think my mother's your cleaner."

"Of course. Mrs Harris. Yes she is. I've heard a lot about you Sybil," she blushed again, "your mother's often spoken of you."

"I do hope she's said nothing unpleasant about me."

"Good heavens, no. It's fair to say you mean a lot to her, if I'm any judge."

"That's nice to know, thank you."

"Well, sorry to interrupt, but we must press on," Rita insisted. She was becoming concerned by the way he was looking at Sybil and Rita didn't like it at all.

The reason Micky was looking so closely at the girl was that he was stunned by what he was seeing. She bore a stark resemblance to Enid at that age, an incredible likeness, and he couldn't get over it. He was at once hurting for Enid, and admiring the lass who looked so similar to his lost love. Sybil looked away, no doubt some sixth sense advising her of his intense interest which was making her uncomfortable. But then it was back to work. He concluded his business with Rita as

101

cheerfully as always, occasionally glancing at Sybil, and then Syd walked in. Back to his normal self, much to everyone's pleasure, his troubles sorted, he was grumbling fit to bust, so Micky said his farewells and departed in haste!

Back home that evening he brought out a pre-war photo of him and Enid and shook his head in disbelief. Sybil Harris was uncannily like her, so much so that he experienced a mixture of pain, pleasure and fear, but for reasons he couldn't readily explain. And it left him longing to see Miss Harris again. She had all Enid's beauty, the same loveliness that had come to attract so much attention back then, and which ultimately led her into Norman's lair.

Rita was also feeling discomfort. She didn't like the way Micky had been almost staring at Sybil for, in her opinion, he was doing it in a lascivious manner and should not be doing so in front of a young woman. She too was pained; she loved Micky even though they had no future, but was hurt by the way he studied Sybil especially as he was far too old for her. Of course, Rita had no idea why Micky was struck, and managed to dismiss the encounter as an expected male response to being presented with a fetching female. Yes, that had to be it.

\*\*\*

*Eagle Pond, Snaresbrook, South Woodford*

After an enjoyable ride Lorna was pleased that Donna was only too happy to go for a walk, and they decided to find a quiet spot in the fringes of Epping Forest that lay close by. They saw to their horses and went up the lane to the main road, close to Snaresbrook station, crossed over opposite the Eagle pub and made their way along Snaresbrook Road, alongside the Eagle Pond, actually a small lake overlooked by the majestic buildings of the Royal Wanstead School on the opposite bank. At the far end of the Pond they walked into a comparatively small remnant of the Forest, intending to go towards the Hollow Ponds, but their progress was arrested by a suitable log and Lorna's overwhelming desire to want to talk.

102

There they sat while Lorna poured out her woes, that is, those that she wanted Donna to know about, while her friend remained silent, shocked by what she was hearing, too shocked to cry. Donna put an arm around her and hugged her tight. Later she vowed that she would always be there for her friend and could be relied upon, she could count on it. Arm in arm they walked slowly back the way they'd come, Donna escorting Lorna all the way home, declining to come in before returning to her own home in Eagle Lane.

And within the week most of the class at Gowan Lea knew about Lorna's troubles, and Lorna had learned a lesson about friendship that cut through her like a knife. How could Donna? It was only a question of time before parents became aware of the situation and Lorna was acquainted with darkness anew, and knew she faced terrors as yet unencountered. Donna, her friend, had betrayed her. How *could* she?

But out of this frightful darkness an angel of light emerged. Cathy Northwood came to Lorna's rescue. At first Lorna rejected her, believing everyone was as bad as Donna had proved to be, but Cathy slowly and purposefully pursued her aim, and in time was accepted. Suspicious at first Lorna came to appreciate what turned out to be true and enduring friendship at a time she needed someone more than ever.

# Chapter Eleven

*The early Sixties*

Enid fretted for Lorna, worried sick that her daughter was going to be seriously ill in the times ahead. Her school work was suffering badly. She engaged a private tutor but Lorna's response to learning was poor and there was every chance she'd leave school with no academic qualifications whatsoever.

After her horrific beating Norman's attitude towards his wife has changed and he even brought her a delightful bunch of flowers by way of apology, not that Enid was interested. She told him if he was truly sorry he would stop beating her. To date he has not laid a finger on her. But that beating has further soured their relationship.

Lorna's friendship with Cathy has deepened and the two are now inseparable, and gradually her schoolwork has improved, vital as the serious exams lie ahead. Lorna is closer than ever to her mother and is aware her father no longer hits her. She confessed to her mother that she lied about Norman beating her, and Enid simply hugged her and told her it was alright, she understood.

Norman's mother has moved in with them at Broadwalk and is a constant nuisance, an untrustworthy person who picks holes in Enid at every opportunity. Norman has bought a chalet at Cooper's Beach to replace the caravan, and it brings mixed blessings. Much more spacious, better equipped, but his mother now accompanies them on holiday there, an unpleasant development.

Norman seems pre-occupied. Enid assumes it is his relationship with Maud Jolley whereas it is in fact his involuntary involvement in criminal activities. The police have called once and Enid is beginning to suspect there is something wrong.

After collapsing in agony Patricia was rushed to hospital to have her appendix removed and is recovering easily. She's doing commendably well at school and has become, for her age, an accomplished pianist, even writing some music of her own.

Unsurprisingly for a teenager she is taking an interest in a new pop group, the Beatles, and loves the dancing associated with pop music.

In a funny sort of way Micky dreads seeing Sybil at Williams and Co., yet he yearns for it, but knows it can only lead to greater heartache. He has told Rita about the similarity and she despairs, knowing he will only take himself to appalling grief if he continues to pursue a lost cause. She is hoping he will not make an unwelcome approach to Sybil. To forestall this she considers accepting his proposal knowing only too well nothing can come of it, unless her mama should perish and she does not want that. It is a dilemma.

Lorna still rides and often helps out at the stables, hoping to secure employment there when she leaves school. It may not be the sort of work her mother had in mind for her, but she has found happiness with the horses, the only creatures she felt she could trust at one stage. Enid is afraid her experiences may have damaged her beloved daughter who could carry the scars into adult life, and where they could affect her relationships. It is heartrending.

Albert Coombes, Micky's friend and gardener, has passed away after a brief illness. Micky attended the funeral and often sees his widow, also a good friend, and he brings her over to Malford Grove on odd occasions for a meal and a good chinwag, and she returns the compliment at her flat. Micky hasn't had a holiday since the war and is considering a few days away, wishing he could take Rita and her mother, but knowing he can't. Rita herself used to take short breaks with her mum in the early days but that is now impossible, Mrs Grant being too ill.

Micky hasn't just lost his gardening pal, he is about to lose his cleaner. The redoubtable Mrs Harris has said she's going to pack it in soon now that her daughters are at work and the family income is improved. She's very proud of Sybil, at last!

\*\*\*

Rita couldn't believe it. She was utterly astonished. Micky had popped in one evening for coffee with the Grants, and Mrs G was dozing peacefully in her favourite armchair when he showed the daughter his pre-war photo of Enid Campton, as she then was.

"Micky, Micky, that's nothing like Sybil, now is it?"

"Well, I think so." Rita could barely see any similarities whatsoever and shook her head in despair.

"Micky, you're seeing something you want to see, not what's actually there, for heaven's sake. Oh Micky, Enid's gone, my love. She's married and away. You'll wreck your life like this. It'll eat away at you and destroy you. Supposing we'd married? This would've been the spectre at my shoulder. We'd both be haunted by it, don't you see?" It was getting frustrating. After all this time he needed to be moving on but he was weighed down by the past and couldn't let go. And now he was looking at a girl half his age. Frustration was only part of Rita's problem, and the annoyance and hopeless despondency was showing in her face as she shook her head again.

"No ……. You're right," he finally agreed, sighing as his eyes studied the floor, his own face a picture of resignation and solemness. "Sorry Rita, you're quite right. I suppose I wanted you to confirm my feelings about the similarity when I knew all along it wasn't there." Rita moved to his side and, sitting on the armrest, put a consoling arm around his shoulder and hugged him. If only she could lift this burden, if only she could.

However, a couple of weeks later a catalyst for trouble raised its ugly head. It was a Wednesday afternoon, Rita was off-duty and Sybil was alone in the office when Micky came in for his paperwork and money. From the outset the girl had liked the way he looked at her, almost spellbound she reckoned, and her mother had always said what a lovely gentleman he was, one of the old school. And he was wealthy. He had a large bungalow with a glorious garden. With all this in mind Sybil began thinking: she was tired of boys her age, strutting peacocks, all full of their own entitlement, and some had hurt her badly.

This kind man, twice her age, was very different. Rita had praised him to the heavens. He was handsome despite being in his early forties. He always had time for her, chatted to her, listened to her answers and seemed genuinely interested, and made her laugh. Today she had a plan. After a brief light-hearted natter she was ready to try her luck.

"Mum says you have such a lovely place, Micky, shame I shan't see it."

"Mmmm …. perhaps one day when you're not working you could come over with Mrs H. But she'll be leaving me soon, as you know, so don't waste any time!" His eyes were glowing. She'd not noticed how blue they were before, but today she convinced herself they were shining for her. He liked her, liked her very much, she was certain.

He was suddenly aware of her own eyes, her radiant smile, her loveliness, and in that moment could only see Enid. It *was* her. Never had Sybil replicated that appearance as she did now, and he wanted to reach out to her, take her in his arms, reassure everything was going to be alright after all. At that precise point Syd came bustling in, full of the grumps, and broke the spell. Nonetheless, as he drove out of the yard a few minutes later, Micky hoped Sybil *would* come over with her mum. He was yearning for her, but a voice in his head told him he was yearning for Enid and no good could come of this situation.

But that evening he couldn't get Sybil out of his thoughts, and he knew now he wasn't seeing Enid at all but a delightfully beautiful young lady. Could she be the one to help him bury the past? And then common sense struck him. She was in her late teens, that was all, and she was just flirting with him. Didn't Mrs Harris say she was always mixing with the wrong boys? She was a danger, but fortunately he hadn't made a fool of himself yet, and he must avoid that at all costs.

With such considerations came a horrible realisation: if she did visit him she would be bound to tell Rita and all hell would be let loose. Now his difficulties had become manifold and he fretted, unable to see a way out of his predicament. He needed to mention his invitation to Rita and do so in a light vein so that she might dismiss it as just an act of friendship, typical of the man, and not be bothered by it. And he knew it wouldn't work.

He saw Rita and Sybil in the office twice that week and nothing was mentioned. And on the Monday Sybil arrived with Mrs Harris, his worst fears made flesh.

*** 

*Broadwalk*

Having devoted herself to her children, they being her salvation in a bleak and disturbing marriage, Enid is feeling stronger in spirits despite the presence of the awful Mrs Belham, her mother-in-law. Norman no longer hits her, but is less attentive and often distant, clearly having something permanently on his mind. She dare not ask.

Tomorrow is Patricia's birthday and preparations for the party are well under way. The teenager has written a special piano piece for the occasion. Norman has been to the record shop and bought a selection of singles, mostly top twenty hits, all being suitable for dancing as his daughter has advised. Enid and the girls are preparing the food but Mrs Belham *will* stick her nose in where it is not wanted and, with Norman about, Enid decides against saying anything, so there is tension in the air as usual.

Lorna picks up on this and it is making her wonder if it is all worthwhile, indeed, if anything is worthwhile anymore. She is becoming increasingly despondent, her solace being the time spent with the horses, animals she sees as being preferrable to unreliable humans.

However, Friday promises much, and it will indeed be a party to remember, thoroughly enjoyed by almost everyone, Lorna included. But for Enid it will bring a shock that will rock her.

Norman, at his best and, from Enid's point of view, his worst all at the same time, is playing the perfect host, initially welcoming everyone at the door. Happily the weather is good as they will need to spill out into the back garden so that everyone can be accommodated, especially as the patio has been set aside for dancing and games. Patricia's friends are there, as are some of the parents, Lorna has Cathy for company, Enid's parents have arrived as have some of Enid's cousins and their offspring. Even Dorothy has come over from Shropshire but has come alone.

108

The party is going with a swing and Patricia is awash with presents. Norman is organising everything and doing it all very well. He seems to be everywhere and is clearly well liked for being such an hospitable host. The patio, a packed dance floor, is heaving with teenagers carrying out all kinds of outlandish moves, or so it appears to the older guests! The cake cutting ceremony goes particularly well, with Patricia subsequently treating them all to a rendition of her "Broadwalk Cakewalk", a lively piano piece which is received with rapturous applause.

As the hectic and noisy evening progresses things do die down a little, and most of the adults are in agreeable conversation while the youngsters continue dancing and engaging in teen banter which often dissolves into little screams and much laughter. Enid is talking to Millie Stevens, the mother of one of Patricia's friends, a woman she knows well and is very friendly with.

"You've done brilliantly here, Enid. And your Norman! Anyone would think he was a teenager! I don't know where he gets all his energy from. Must be good having a husband like that. I bet he's a dab hand with the housework." Both women were giggling cheerfully. "Wish mine was as good as that. Still, Ed's good in other ways, mustn't run him down too much!" Enid kept her thoughts and her sadness to herself.

"Yes, Norman's always good at things like this. Don't know so much about the housework, Millie!" They laughed together. "By the way, any luck finding a part-time job?"

"Yes indeed. I envied you being a corsetiere but I could never do that. I admire you so much, Enid, finding something like that to do. Not me. Found something much more basic. Got a part-time job as a cleaner. Sounds awful, doesn't it?" More shared chuckling. "No, this is alright I assure you; a touch of class, I think. I am going to do some domestic cleaning for an absolute gentleman. He's so lovely. You can tell with people, can't you? Anyway, he's got this gorgeous bungalow in Malford Grove, lovely big back garden and so on. I was introduced by one of his neighbours I know. I gather he's well to do. Doesn't appear to be a lady in his life and his present cleaner is leaving. Suits me fine."

"Oh Millie I'm so pleased for you, and as you say, a touch of class." They smiled at each other. "Any idea what he does then?"

"A metal merchant apparently, Mr Bowen his name, Michael Bowen ………. Enid, are you alright, you look quite pale? Come outside, perhaps it's stuffy in here." If Enid looked to Millie as if she had seen a ghost it was probably because it was almost true. Abruptly the party vanished from Enid's existence and was replaced by a wild nothingness where only one thing stood in her field of imagination. Micky, as she remembered him the last time they met all those years ago. Without realising she had done so she allowed Millie to lead her outside, past the patio, right down the garden to where they located two unoccupied camping chairs. Enid flopped down staring straight ahead.

"Wait there dear, I'll get you a glass of water." When Millie had dashed off Enid murmured quietly.

"Micky, my Micky. And you haven't married. Have you been true to me, is that it? True to me when I deserted you? Perhaps it isn't you at all. Maybe someone with the same name. Oh God, I feel quite ill ……" Shortly Millie returned with the water which Enid drank swiftly, handing the glass back as her friend took the other seat. She became aware that somebody else was standing in front of her.

"Enid, you're deathly pale, are you alright? Has it been too much for you? Don't worry, we'll take you upstairs and you can lie down for a bit. It's alright. Come and have a lie down, pet, come on." Dorothy was holding out her arm ready to provide escort and Enid was so pleased to see her that she instinctively rose and gave herself wholly to Dorothy's guidance.

"I'll take care of her. She just needs a short break and a rest, Millie," she called back over her shoulder as she took her charge towards the house and respite.

In the comparative peace of the bedroom Enid lay in the dark, feeling cold inside herself, frightened to confront her emotions, while Dorothy drew the curtains and sat on the bed alongside her.

"What is it love?" her friend whispered. After a couple of minutes Enid stopped gazing blankly at the ceiling, and turned on her side. Her voice when she spoke was broken, flat and devoid of sentiment and expression.

"It's Micky. I've learned he's living close by and that he's probably not married and I feel disgusted and ashamed that I didn't wait for him. I've betrayed him, Dorothy, I've ruined his life while he's been true to me ……."

"Hush, my precious, hush. You have no idea what's happened to him. I doubt you've ruined his life. Perhaps he's already a widower, you just don't know. Tell me what you *do* know." Enid related all that Millie had told her and then turned over on her back. Dorothy spoke at once. "First of all you don't know for sure it's your Micky and secondly it doesn't matter where he lives, my pet, he's living his own life. He might've been living hundreds of miles away. Listen to me. Don't go looking for him, Enid. Leave well alone….."

"I must know it's him, I must, don't try and stop me. I won't do anything, I just want to know."

"Enid, I know you better than that. You won't be able to stop yourself….."

"Dorothy, my dear friend, please don't lecture me. I give you my word. I only want to know for sure, then I'll leave it at that. I swear I'll leave him alone." And as she turned away from her friend the tears came, a violent outpouring, a deluge, her whole body shaking uncontrollably. Dorothy decided to sit quietly and motionless, helpless in these circumstances, not knowing what comfort was needed or would be appreciated, and believing whatever she did would be wrong.

There was a knock at the door. Dorothy rose and opened it slightly to find Millie outside.

"Is she okay? People are asking for her. Thought I'd better tell you. Shall I get Norman?"

"She's fine, thanks Millie, and she'll be down when she's had a brief rest. Just a few minutes, and please don't worry Norman, he'll only fuss. Better he looks after the guests, eh?" Millie nodded and set off downstairs while Dorothy gently closed the door.

"I don't want to go down. I don't want to. I want nothing more to do with it ……"

"Yes you do. Now just listen to me. It's your daughter's birthday and you won't spoil it for her, now will you?"

"I don't care…"

"You *do* care. It's Patricia's birthday. Everything you've done, all the strength you've had to find, all the suffering you've been through, it's all been for those girls. You won't let them down now. Pull yourself together, and come downstairs. Do you hear me?" Dorothy's sharp words bit home.

"Okay," Enid whimpered, "let me go to the bathroom, clean my face, deal with my make-up and I'll be down when I feel better. Go now, I'm okay." And she rolled over face down on the bed. For all that Dorothy was worried for her she knew better than to wait, knew better than to go to her and put an arm round her, so she slipped out and made her own way back to the gaiety of the party.

***

*Malford Grove, Monday morning*

Micky had just reversed his van out of the garage and down the drive when a Mini pulled up outside. He paid no attention to it at first and his thoughts were on Mrs Harris who was due to arrive shortly; he'd see her in as usual and make good his escape! He was also thinking about a leaving present for her, and, having no experience in that direction, decided he would ask Rita.

He was suddenly conscious of a portly figure trying, no, *struggling* to extricate itself from the Mini's passenger seat and wondered if he should go and offer help when he realised it was none other than Mrs Harris herself. At that moment Sybil emerged from the driver's door and waved. She went round to help her mother while Micky pondered his next move.

"Hello Micky," Sybil called out cheerfully, "I've come to help mum and you did say I could come over with her and see your home. Hope that's alright."

"Yes, of course. You're welcome. Hello Mrs Harris, good to see you again." He wasn't sure he meant either comment and managed to look insincere, not that his facial expression bothered his visitors.

"Morning Mr Bowen. Brought Sybil over for a hand. Is it okay? She's been dying to see your home but she can go and do something else if it's not convenient."

112

"No, no, no, it's absolutely fine. And you can show her around house and garden at your leisure Mrs Harris. Unfortunately I've got to dash."

"Oh that's a shame, but I know how busy you are. Did hope we'd all have a cuppa." Yes, thought Micky, I guessed that would be foremost in your mind. By now they were in the kitchen and Mrs Harris made one last try.

"Sure you can't have a quick one, Mr Bowen?"

"No thank you, that's kind but I must be away. I like the Mini. Had it long?"

"It's Sybil's. Me and Mr Harris bought it for her so she can get to and from work more easily. It's second-hand but goes well, so I'm told. Bit of a squeeze for me!"

Soon afterwards he was away and pleased to be on the road. Sybil had been smiling continuously and was clearly making eyes at him, and he was finally acknowledging the hazards of the situation, not least that she wasn't a reincarnation of Enid at all. He was also waking up to the fact he could hurt Rita badly and make life very difficult at Williams & Co for both women and for himself.

Having cleared his head of one puzzle he then thought about the Mini. They must've come into money, he concluded, or perhaps the younger daughter was in a very good job. No, must've been something like a bequest in a relative's will. Intriguing for all that. Another puzzle. He'd never met Mr Harris and didn't know what he did for a living as he'd never asked and not been told. Maybe he had the money. Oh well, nothing to worry about, and it was probably for the good that Mrs H was leaving his employ soon. Mrs Stevens was a good prospect, a very different person to his present cleaner, and he found himself hoping she wouldn't regale him with tales of a wayward daughter!

\*\*\*

*Broadwalk, Monday*

With both daughters at girls' schools Enid has not thought about the issue of boys. For one thing Lorna has no obvious inclination, more of an aversion if truth be told, and she thinks Patricia is too young. Patricia if often invited to her friends' for parties and visits, just as some of her school-mates come round to see her from time to time. Enid is therefore blissfully unaware that her younger daughter has a boyfriend, the brother of one of the girls she spends much time with. It is a closely guarded secret as she thinks mum will not smile upon the arrangement. She has discovered the joys of kissing and the pleasure of having strong arms holding her securely while practising her new skills with her lips. Mum would not approve, she's certain!

Friday's party was a great success and, after taking Patricia to school, Enid takes Dorothy to the station via The Drive. Here they stop for a private chat, Enid grateful for all her friend has done and for her wise counsel. With Mrs Belham close by at home the chance of a private conversation is virtually non-existent, and the two women have been for walks together over the weekend to overcome this problem.

"Do you know the address?" Dorothy enquired. She had ensured their walks had avoided Malford Grove but was confident Enid would go there once alone in the car.

"No, but it's a big bungalow and I don't think there are that many."

"Even so you can't pinpoint it, can you? So you'd be counting on seeing him. Good heavens, Enid, you don't even know what car he drives. It might be in the garage if his home has one. And you can't go knocking on doors. Promise me you'll leave it be."

"Dorothy, I'll be alright now, and no, I am not going searching for him. Promise." But it was a promise she was destined to break and all thanks to an idea planted in her mind by Dorothy's comments.

After waving her guest off at Snaresbrook station Enid went on her quest. She located two large detached bungalows side by side and decided on a simple ruse. She went to one of the adjacent houses and knocked there. A well-dressed middle-aged woman answered the door.

"I'm so sorry to trouble but I'm looking for Mr Bowen, Mr Michael Bowen, and I've lost his address. I thought perhaps he lived here but I presume not. I'm sorry to have bothered you."

"Not at all, please don't worry. He lives next door so you were very close."

"Oh, that's so kind of you. Thank you so very much. Thank you." Now she had the information she required. She looked at the Mini parked outside and wondered if there was any connection, for there were no cars in the drive. But it was a big place, no question about that. Micky, Micky, she thought to herself, you've done well and I'm so sorry I wasn't by your side. That's where I'd have wanted to be even if we had ended up in poverty, nothing would've mattered but us. I wonder what you look like, I wonder if there have been any other ladies in your life, I wonder if you are happy? Taking a deep breath and sighing she turned and went to her car knowing she would go home and put it all in the back of her mind. At least that was the plan.

\*\*\*

*Wanstead Flats*

He'd parked here and walked across the grass away from the sound of the main road traffic. It was easy walking, fairly flat, but his mind was not on his surroundings or the noises. He'd found it easy to ignore any slightly dodgy aspects about that first job, and had convinced himself it was just the right side of legal. After all, the law hadn't got involved so it had to be okay. But they were all getting greedy and he knew what they were doing now was illegal, no arguments. They were blatantly defrauding people and you could go inside for that.

He sat on the grass and looked around him. Just a few short years ago they'd demolished the prefabs here that had been built to house people after the war, and he began to wonder what his life might've been like had it been so different. What if he'd gone to war? Why, he might be dead! What if he hadn't met Enid? Who might he have married? Supposing he hadn't been able to wangle his way to a directorship in his ever-expanding company? Cor, he thought, might've been very, very different.

If only Enid had forgotten Micky and not let it affect their marriage how different it might have been. No, that's not right, he reasoned. Would've been just the same! Bloody woman. I detest people I can't control. Even when I hit her she just used to take it, not a bloody sound, never made a fuss, God I loathe strong-willed people like that.

And with that his mind turned to those others he couldn't control, those who got him to work with them and who now wouldn't let him get out. Bastards! That Eric had pasted him once, and that was only a warning! He didn't doubt full retribution would not be to his liking. There was no way out of their schemes, well, none that didn't involve pain or worse, and he'd heard about one of the gang who'd been found floating face down in Barking Creek. That man had wanted out, but not that way.

With that Norman Belham rose to his feet, dusted the back of his trousers, and made his weary way back to his car, unsure of his future and prospects. Bloody woman, he silently cursed his wife again, couldn't even turn the kids against her could I?

*** 

*Williams & Co, Monday afternoon*

Micky quickly appraised Rita of developments where Sybil was concerned, and did so in a very light-hearted manner hoping the issue would be glossed over and confined to history.

"Fancy inviting her over, Micky. Still, no harm done I suppose." Rita's comment left him wondering whether he'd succeeded or failed. "And Micky, are you still seeing Enid in her?"

"No of course not," he laughed, "I've got over that, and I've only got eyes for you. Go on, give us a kiss."

"Oh you fool, Micky," she admonished amongst much mirth, waving him away. Not that he was about to leap over the desk! Yes, he did love Rita, loved her very much, and in different circumstances he would marry her if it was possible. For her sake he would put Enid out of his mind forever, or at least he thought he could.

"Any joy finding a gardener, Micky?"

"To be honest I've not really been trying. I did ask a lady over the road who has a gardener but apparently he's got all the work he wants. Trouble is, after Mr Coombes, well, I reckon I'm looking for someone to be as much a mate as a gardener! I felt so close to Mr C. But I'll have to do some serious looking soon or it'll all get away from me."

"When does your new lady start?"

"Mrs Stevens? Week after next. Mrs Harris finishes Friday. Was thinking about having a break, a few days away as you know, but I'll not bother. Very busy at the mo, and it wouldn't be the same without you, Rita."

"If course it would. Do you the power of good to get away. You talked about going down to Kent or up to Suffolk. Now, why don't you do it? See something else of the world. You don't need me…"

"Wouldn't be right without you, Rita, don't you see?"

"No, I do not see. You were going all lovey-dovey over Sybil, you fool, so don't tell me you'd miss me." They shared mild laughter at what was a harmless humorous remark whereas Rita felt a pang of pain as soon as she spoke. She would've loved a few days away with Micky, and she knew she loved him and wanted him desperately. But it was no good. Mum was too ill, and that was that. "And I bet you're still pining for Enid."

"Not a bit of it, love. You put me wise and that nonsense over Sybil taught me a valuable lesson, for which I am very grateful to you, Rita. You are my heart's desire…."

"Oh yes, of course I am, but isn't that a song from an operetta or something? You are my heart's desire?"

"Blowed if I know, but you're my one and only, Rita, and I'd marry you tomorrow if we could."

"Well you can't, so there." They chuckled again, both understanding marriage was what they wanted but was a pleasure denied them, and cold humour was all they had left at the present time.

\*\*\*

*The Stables, late Monday afternoon*

"I know you'll never betray my secrets, Monty. I thought Donna was my best friend but she let me down badly, told

117

everyone my secrets, and the next thing I know people are talking about my troubles. I heard some of the nasty things people said, sometimes I heard because they spoke out loud so I could hear. One mother said that we get what we deserve in life so my mum must've been bad and was getting her just desserts, so she said. Another said I was a wretched girl, ungrateful for all my parents had done for me, and wasn't I awful to them."

Monty gave Lorna such a kindly look of care and love that she kissed his cheek again and gave him another quick hug.

"Oh Monty, I wish I could take you home, but I don't think mum would like it. I'd like you to meet her, you'll love her, she's so kind, and she's had to put up with so much. Perhaps you can meet her soon, I do hope so. There! I think you're done for another day."

She stood back to admire Monty's beautiful black coat that she had taken such care over to ensure it shone brightly and was immaculately groomed.

"Best horse in the stables, you are Monty. Wish I could get to ride you. Keep my secrets safe, won't you Monty? You're the only person I can trust apart from mum. I want to trust Cathy but supposing she turned out to be like Donna? She's a lovely friend and I like her so much, but I'm afraid of trusting her." Monty gave her a look that she felt was saying 'at least give her a chance'. Perhaps the horse was right. Maybe she should try.

Close by, also grooming a horse and keeping out of Lorna's line of sight, Philip Cullen, the owner's son, stood and watched the girl who had captured his imagination and much more besides.

# Chapter Twelve

For some 1963 turned out to be a special year. Against all the odds, it appeared to Enid, Lorna passed six GCE O-levels, left school and secured employment at the stables much to her mother's regret. The wages were not good, the hours were long but her daughter was in heaven and happier than she'd been for years. Her friend Cathy managed seven O-levels and moved on to higher education with the hope of attending art college, her aim being a career in advertising.

Patricia had also been thinking about her future and wanted to study music, but was already looking forward to her own O-levels in the next couple of years, and the A-levels to follow. It was possible university might be on the cards depending on the career she might set her heart on.

Norman pulled off a master-stroke, managing to buy three tickets for the Beatles Christmas Eve concert at the Finsbury Park Astoria at a time when such tickets sold out almost instantly. He would drive Enid and the girls over to the concert.

Patricia struggled to keep her boyfriend secret from mum but failed simply because mums are more wide awake than their children realise! Challenged, she admitted her friendship and found her mother surprisingly supportive, Enid suggesting she brought the young man round for what proved to be the first of many visits. Enid's motive is to keep the situation in the open where it can be more readily seen and monitored! To that end she has become good friends with the boy's parents.

Enid has never returned to Malford Grove but still yearns for Micky, or perhaps she is yearning for the life she might have enjoyed had things been different. She isn't sure. In her own way she feels she had kept her promise to Dorothy, and funnily enough has come to think that she has found peace of mind as far as her relationship with Micky is concerned.

Micky continues to thrive in business, his new cleaner, Mrs Stevens, has settled in and is excellent, and he has a new gardener, Mrs Stevens father! Mr Connaught is a retired policeman and proves to be just the sort of person Micky wanted.

Rita's mum is virtually housebound but thankfully not bedridden, but Rita, working part-time at Williams and Co, has to get someone to come in when she's not at home, and has been delighted to obtain the services of a middle-aged woman, Iris Coffey, who has become a good friend too. However, the finances are not in a good state and there is concern about the long-term. Rita would not dream of her mother having to go into a home.

Sybil is doing well in the office and now works full-time, handy as the company is expanding thanks to increased business. They may well be moving premises to the Hainault area. She quickly realised she was wasting her time pursuing Micky and has started going out with a man at the works, one of the senior employees, second-in-command behind Syd. Peter Collis is single, thirty-three, drives an impressive looking Ford Zodiac and lives alone in a semi-detached house in Debden. An ideal target! He's flattered by the young woman's attentions and is touched that she should be interested in an older man.

Micky is worried about Rita as clearly her mother's condition is weighing heavily on the woman and she is not the happy-go-lucky person she once was. He has put Enid from his mind, or so he believes, and his love for Rita is so great that he wants to always be there for her, and is aching that he cannot be closer in any sense.

1963 was the year Norman changed becoming quite bearable at times, and is quite considerate to Enid. It wasn't much of a change, but he stopped being domineering with his wife, never being threatening again, and appeared quite an ordinary family man, a fact Enid could not come to terms with. Surely he could not have changed that much?

In truth Maud Jolley has ended their affair but Enid does not know this. And the company he is a director of is not doing well, suffering a bad year, and he thinks his position might be in jeopardy if things do not improve. At present his income from his criminal activities is more than useful but the operation is now giving him nightmares. Nemesis may be just around the corner.

***

*Cooper's Beach, August 1963*

The weather was dreadful, and Mrs Belham senior was worse than that. Nonetheless, the family was having a pleasant fortnight at the chalet. Norman was due for the last weekend, otherwise his absence was welcome, despite the presence of his mother who was troublesome in the extreme.

Patricia and a couple of friends had engaged themselves with the group who ran 'Sunshine Corner' on the beach, a religious concern run by the Baptist church for the youngsters, and this met with Enid's wholehearted approval although neither she nor her family were in any way God-fearing. Lorna's friend Cathy was also staying with them and the two shared the bunks at the rear of the property where there was often late-night conversation, away from adults who might not commend the subject matter.

Their GCE O-level results were awaited, Cathy full of optimism, Lorna not bothered either way, Enid dreading a poor showing. Norman had been philosophical before they came away, saying Lorna would make a success of her life whatever happened. He seemed so calm and reasonable that Enid was at a loss to explain his behaviour, but frightened that he might explode at any given time.

Lorna eschewed the idea of going to 'Sunshine Corner' and went on long walks with Cathy, the pair finding great depth in their discussions. On this particular day they had strolled right along the sea wall path in the direction of West Mersea when their tête-à-tête turned surprisingly to love. Both were unconscious of the fact the rain was now falling and they were getting soaked.

"I don't know, Lorna, it doesn't make sense. Love seems so black and white, doesn't it? I've never been kissed, have you?" Lorna shook her head. "I love my mum and dad and I love my brother, but that's got to be different to, well, being in love with a boy. Do you know what I mean?"

"Never had time for boys, Cathy. No interest. Give me a faithful horse any day!"

121

"Well, I mean, it's like I love you, Lorna, but not like I love mum, not how I think I should love a boy."

"And I love you, Cathy, but what good does it do us? I mean, I love my sister but I love you in a different way. Can't explain."

"Now isn't that love, Lorna? Something you can't explain?" The conversation continued in much the same vein until they both realised they were wet through and it was time to turn back. They arrived at the chalet, two drowned rats, welcomed with open arms by Enid who led them into one of the bedrooms to towel down and change while Patricia tactfully kept Mrs Belham occupied with pointless questions, a surprisingly alert and perceptive piece of work from one so young.

There were days when the weather relented, but they were few and far between. They all went to Clacton for a day and managed to enjoy themselves despite the light rain that persisted much of the time. But it dried up for the evening. And Lorna and Cathy took advantage of the drier conditions to take another walk, and it was during this time together that they shared a kiss, an exploratory kiss, a kiss that threw up more questions than answers, but a kiss that bound them closer than ever before, a kiss Enid remained in complete ignorance of.

Norman's Vauxhall Cresta arrived on the second Friday night, but its driver appeared anything but happy. However, Norman being Norman, pretended to be full of bonhomie and good cheer although Enid recognised he was not. She was beginning to loathe his mother, but, she had to admit, Norman seemed distant to her, not taking sides as he'd often done, and bluntly ignoring her on occasions. Was there a rift?

Norman was not one for regrets but he was starting to feel a certain sadness about his marriage and family life. When all was said and done, it wasn't a bad life. His wife had been attentive in the first years, his daughters liked all he did for them, surely he could've put up with everything else and enjoyed a simple life at home? Why had he wasted it all? Why had he thrown away what might have been a good life? He was full of regrets and that wasn't Norman. It wasn't Norman to think about other people, least of all his family. It could've been so nice, a good family, a loving family, but he'd messed about with Maud Jolley because she let him do as he pleased, and it hadn't worked out well at all.

If he'd been faithful to Enid it might've been so different. But he was not a man to suffer pangs of conscience. No, he had no regrets he concluded. Save the one thing he did regret, namely getting involved with that gang.

*** 

"Rita, this time I'm not taking no for an answer." Micky felt less sure of himself than he sounded, but it had to be done. "You know your poor mum is one step away from a home. She's got to give it up, her home Rita, you know it. She knows it. It's over. For Pete's sake come and move into Malford Grove, both of you, and you can have your people to look after her, Iris will come I'm sure, and I'll pay and that'll be an end to it. For God's sake, persuade her my darling."

Rita sat in tears. Micky was a man in a million, God how she loved him.

"Micky, it's quite impossible….." she whispered through the tears.

"No, it's not. Let me speak to her. Come with me by all means. But let me do the talking." And Micky did the talking. Rita was distressed at first but Micky won the day, Mrs Grant agreeing to the measure at long last. It had been a hard fight but he'd won the battle and probably won a bride into the bargain.

In the autumn of '63 Mrs Grant and her daughter moved into Malford Grove and nobody could've been happier than Rita. The wedding would have to wait. For now she had the best of all worlds. Iris Coffey did indeed come to help out and Millie Stevens, the cleaner gave a hand with mum as well, enabling Rita to continue her part-time work.

She had an easier journey now that Williams & Co had moved premises.

Come November Micky, Rita and Mrs Grant watched the Remembrance Sunday service on the television, and Rita was aware that tiny, soft tears were running down Micky's cheeks, not that she'd mention it or try to comfort him because she understood. Her father and brother perished fighting for their country and their freedom, and Micky had lost his mum and close friends and bore witness to horrible events in Japan, incidents he

123

never spoke of. His own father had fought in the First War and come home with terrible physical and mental scars, dying before his time in 1937. It was a poignant occasion for all of them sitting there in mum's lounge, her new and final home. At least she would see her daughter wed. Best of all she would not lose her daughter to a husband, and she would gain a son.

It had taken a while to settle in but she now loved her 'little flat' as she called it, the room Micky had converted into a lounge and bedroom with views across the gardens. And her failing health actually showed signs of moderate if temporary respite. So far, so good.

*** 

It was only a question of time before Enid heard the news, and the intelligence came when she asked Millie Stevens how she was getting on at Mr Bowen's place.

"I don't see much of him, Enid, with him being at work mostly, but I'm really enjoying it. Of course he's moved his fiancé and her mother in now, the poor woman, Mrs Grant, is very unwell and I can help with her, so that's good. Her daughter, Rita, has a part-time job so she's not always there, but they are such lovely ladies, really lovely ladies. So friendly and charming. Another lady comes in from time to time to help with dear Mrs Grant, and we all get on so well together, it's hardly like being at work at all.

"All very right, proper and correct as you'd expect. They won't get married until the spring, so I'm told, so they have separate bedrooms in the meantime. I'm pleased about that, if you know what I mean......"

Millie continued her discourse but her words went unheard. There was no comfort, only pain in what Enid had taken in, yet she took a strange heartening pleasure in knowing they hadn't tied the knot and were not sharing a bedroom. Alone later Enid's emotions ran riot in an indescribable melee as she tried to come to terms with the situation. She had nothing to reproach Micky for as she herself had gone off and married, and that gave her no scope for anger and bitterness, yet that is how she felt and she couldn't control it. She wanted to cry out and scream with anguish. Since Millie first told her he was unwed and there was no woman she'd clung to some extraordinary belief that there was still hope despite her own marriage.

Now it was clear Micky must've been in love with this Rita for some time and had done a wonderful thing bringing her and her sick mother to live together. She shook her head; wasn't that typical of the Micky she'd known and loved? A special man, a precious man. Oh why had she thrown it all away? But then she hadn't. She thought he was long gone, a victim of the war. Surely she had a right to happiness? And Norman appeared so lovely, so sympathetic, wasn't he the man she hoped Micky would approve of from beyond the grave?

It wasn't until she spoke to Dorothy, sensible Dorothy, that she pulled herself together.

"It was such a shock, I can't tell you how bad it was ……"

"I know, I know my pet, but you can't go on like this. I always end up saying the same thing to you, don't I? You live for your children and nothing else matters. Whatever had happened to Micky, whatever happens now, he's out of your life, but your girls need you. You've been so strong for them, be strong for them now, and be strong for yourself, my precious. Have a little corner of your heart reserved for Micky but keep him and your happy memories there to be cherished, don't let them interfere with your life now."

"Oh Dorothy, I don't know what I'd do without you. Go to pieces probably."

"No you wouldn't. You've been plenty strong enough. You'll always have sad moments. Life's like that for all of us. But we have to brush those moments aside and get on with it. Just as we all had to during the war." Enid found her friend's words stirring and uplifting and inspiring, and knew then she'd put this latest episode out of her mind, or at least, at Dorothy's suggestion, put it in that little corner of her heart. What a lovely idea that was. Trust Dorothy.

\*\*\*

Norman had been so, well, so *normal* that it was almost unnerving. And this Saturday he took the girls off to George Lane where their local shops were to buy a Christmas tree, and they returned with a beauty. It was quite the largest and tallest tree they'd ever had, and the girls had great fun helping to carry it home longways. Enid didn't think it would fit in the lounge but somehow it did, and then there was all the fun decorating it. Inevitably, after a year in the attic, the tree lights didn't work but Norman corrected that without fuss.

The family spent the rest of the day decorating the lounge, hall and one or two other places, and Norman had them laughing when they discovered he'd hung a sprig of mistletoe over the toilet! That sprig didn't last long where it was and it was relocated in the kitchen.

Christmas was going to be extra special. Norman had managed to obtain three tickets for the Beatles concert at the Finsbury Park Astoria Christmas Eve and he was going to drive Enid and the girls. Needless there was much envy amongst the girls' friends! In the event it was a spectacular way to see in the festivities. Enid had much trouble preventing Patricia from joining in the screaming that was particularly prevalent as they were leaving the concert, but the common view was that they'd witnessed something very special, been part of something phenomenal. The girls sang all the way home in the car, Enid and Norman chuckling and trying to join in with mixed results.

Wednesday brought with it Christmas Day. While mum prepared their family dinner, with help and hindrance from Mrs Belham senior, Norman took the girls to the forest for a walk where they met, by prior arrangement, Cathy Northwood and her father. Lorna and Cathy exchanged small gifts, pecks on the cheeks, and the five walked on in good spirits and seasonal cheer until it was time to part.

The sisters had done well for presents at home. Norman always made sure they were spoiled, not that Enid approved. The slap-up dinner was a grand affair, savoured amidst mirth and jollity, but Norman rather over-did the brandy on the Christmas Pudding resulting in a more than decent blaze!

There were various 'phone calls, one being from Cathy, this one producing a look of gloom on Lorna's face, and Enid felt she might be close to tears.

"Everything alright?" she asked her daughter after the call. "Thought you'd had some bad news."

"Oh no, mum, Cathy's alright. Nothing's wrong." But Enid knew there was without being able to imagine what.

Following a quiet afternoon other family members started to arrive for the evening's party which was anything but quiet. There was a mid-evening serve-yourself buffet, and then more dancing and games, but by now Enid was conscious that Lorna was not herself and took her to one side.

"What is it, love. Tell me."

"Wish Cathy was here," her daughter murmured while studying the floor.

"I'm sorry she isn't but she's with her family just as you are with yours." Enid was going for firmness still not quite realising the truth of the matter, and Lorna wasn't going to tell her.

Not far away in Malford Grove Micky was experiencing an altogether different and quieter Christmas and he and the ladies were happier for it. They had a simple breakfast, exchanged gifts, found something to enjoy on the television, and then he helped Rita with the dinner, a chicken roast but with all the trimmings (they weren't ones for turkey), followed by warm homemade mince pies. There was the Queen's speech to be watched and then it was time for a peaceful doze, a lengthy one for Mrs Grant as usual.

Later Micky and Rita had a short stroll, hand in hand, and returned for a light tea. There was a film on the telly that left them rocking with laughter but after that they partook of their nightcaps and an early night. Having seen Mrs Grant safely tucked up in bed Micky and Rita shared a lingering and passionate kiss in the kitchen before retiring, he to his bed, she to hers. Mrs Grant had had a good day by her own standards, had been happy and content but there was no doubting she was unwell and suffering, although she tried to keep the worst of it from her daughter and did not succeed.

"Thanks for everything, darling," Rita whispered as she parted from Micky at her bedroom door, "thanks so very much.

And mum loves you too." And the tiniest tear slipped down her left cheek. He gave her one last hug, one last kiss, and she was gone.

***

*New Year's Eve 1963*

Patricia was going to a friend's for a New Year party. Her boyfriend would be there but Enid knew the parents who were giving the do, and was happy there would be no nonsense as she termed it. Norman would pick her up about 12.30. Lorna was going to Cathy's and was going to stay over, this presenting no difficulties as there was no party or gathering to worry about. Enid would see in the New Year with her husband and his mother and was not looking forward to it.

As it turned out it was a lovely evening and even her mother-in-law made an effort to be pleasant. They had a delicious buffet both women had prepared quite amiably together in the kitchen, and made do with a couple of glasses of sherry before settling down to a game of whist and then watching a film on television. With the approach of midnight they refilled their glasses and tuned into Big Ben and then the Scottish celebrations on the BBC, but it wasn't long before Mrs Belham was asleep in her chair and had to be woken to go to bed. Norman and Enid spent some time in light-hearted and pleasurable conversation prior to his departure to collect Patricia.

In Malford Grove Micky had been persuaded to be the first-footer and he set off from the back door and around the verandah to the front complete with a lump of coal and mince pie. Having gained admittance, and been given a kiss by his fiancé, he came into Mrs Grant's lounge where the three shared drinks, watched the same programme on the television as the Belhams, and then retired.

In the general mayhem at the party Patricia and her boyfriend managed to find a remote corner at midnight away from prying eyes, and indulged in what Patricia herself would've regarded as a 'jolly good snog'. At Cathy's things had been much quieter; there were a couple of relatives there and a couple who knew the

128

Northwoods who had brought their son, Vidvuds. They were Belgians but had moved to Britain when Vidvuds was six as the father's work had brought him to England, and so the family settled here. Cathy had met the son before and seemed quite taken with him. Eventually the opportunity presented itself for Cathy, Lorna and Vidvuds to have a quiet chat together and they got on famously, discussing all manner on things in the way of adolescents debating serious issues with all the seriousness they could muster. Cathy, in particular, was clearly impressed with his philosophical and political views believing him to be truly knowledgeable, whereas Lorna was rather more sceptical and questioning of his opinions and statements, although she chose not to interrogate him too closely. He had an answer for everything, and frankly Lorna thought he was preaching without any grip on reality, especially when expounding his understandings of the benefits of true socialism, which he did in a way that suggested he was fully supportive of such measures without actually comprehending the implications.

While Cathy was enthralled by the idealism, Lorna decided he'd been easily led by Utopian promises and didn't have the sort of enquiring mind to query what he'd heard and read. The three were permitted alcoholic drinks at midnight, the first time Lorna had tasted white wine, and then, after a rendition of 'Auld Lang Syne', they retired to their bedrooms, one and all. The girls were sharing a bed and they remained awake for some while, peering into the darkness, and talking quietly about a range of subjects, including some of the views Vidvuds had expressed. They snuggled up tightly together, Lorna thrilled by the warmth of their closeness, while they chatted and discussed their hopes and dreams for the new year.

But in time tiredness overtook them and they fell asleep.

*** 

*January 1964*

The new year brought optimism and hope, the feeling of a fresh start. Rita and Micky looked forward to a spring wedding, and even Enid was drawing some benefits from the

129

improvements in Norman's disposition. But for some it heralded tragedy, sadness and heartbreak, and for poor Lorna a final act of betrayal.

# Chapter Thirteen

*1964*
*Williams & Co*

Sybil had proved herself to be a useful acquisition and was very successfully handling all aspects of office business, much to the pride of her mother, Rita and, of course, Peter Collis, the latter enjoying a very close relationship with the younger girl. In her turn Sybil had discovered that Peter had appeal beyond his material attributes, and they had thus formed a partnership based on real love and affection. Time will tell.

After his near-disastrous financial losses Syd's position has recovered, as has his marriage, and he's happy with the firm's new location.

"Better? I'll say so, Micky. Got room to move, plenty of space for storage, room for the vehicles, especially getting on and off the weighbridge …. gor, do you remember the old one? We had some fun there at times, did we ever!" Micky laughed recalling only too well the cramped conditions of the old site and how Syd used to rant at him when he struggled to manoeuvre round the weighbridge area.

Rita and Sybil are the best of friends and their efforts well appreciated by the boss, Mr Gaffney, who knows how hard they work, and how efficiently they perform their duties.

Before Christmas Mr Gaffney ('call me Des') took Micky out for a meal as a thank-you.

"Do y'know, Micky, I always kind of wondered if you and Rita might make a go of it, not that it's any of my business, but she's a lovely lass and deserves a decent bloke. Think you fit the bill there. Have another glass of wine."

"Thanks Des, and thanks for your words. She's very special to me and, well, I'm getting another mum out of it." Des poured the wine while both chuckled before Micky continued. "And that was a good move coming out of town like that. Your site's tailor-made."

"Just what I thought, Micky, knew it was right soon as I set eyes on it. And a lot cheaper despite being bigger. London's getting dear now the war's long gone, and there's more demand of course."

"Yes, I expect that's true. I've got five lock-up garages in Wanstead but it's a sprawling place and I bet it'll be sold for development before long, so I'm keeping a look-out, ears to the ground, as I may have to move on."

"Good luck with that. But why not move out of town like us?"

"Might come to it, I suppose, but it's handy for bringing my stuff in, it's sort of central if you know what I mean, but then again if I was nearer to you it'd save costs that way, so maybe it's a good idea, Des."

"That's the spirit, Micky, and I'll keep my ears open too, just in case I hear of anything coming up. And in the meantime take good care of that woman. Worth her weight in gold." Micky smiled and nodded as they raised their glasses and toasted Rita.

And sure enough, in January 1964, Micky learned that the garages were going up for sale and he'd be out, so his hunt intensified.

While Williams & Co were going from strength to strength the company Norman Belham was a director of was heading in the opposite direction. There'd been some shady dealings and several where, in order to be competitive to win contracts, profit margins had been very tight resulting in losses. Now they had pulled out of one deal and were likely to be sued for breach of contract. The writing was on the wall and Norman could see his own future diving down the same drain.

To add to his discomfiture his illegitimate operations were causing him sleepless nights. If he pulled out it wouldn't be a case of the gang suing *him* for breach of contract, it would more a case of instant justice on their terms.

*** 

*Lorna and Cathy*

In early February Lorna was looking casually around in a shop and came upon the array of Valentines cards. How she would

132

love to send one to Cathy! It was a dilemma; if she sent one she'd want to write her own words of love and sign it, but then her friend would be in no doubt who sent it. It was normal for such cards to be anonymous but Cathy might then think she had a secret admirer. Of course, Cathy might send *her* one! In the end she selected a very pretty card with a few brief but moving words and decided she would use her left hand to add a few more fitting words of her own, and leave it unsigned. Yes, that was for the best.

About a week before Valentines Day Lorna invited Cathy to spend the occasion with her at Broadwalk.

"Sorry Lorna, got something else on that evening, but perhaps the next day? Saturday would be great as I can be over earlier and we can have more time together. How about that? Is that convenient?"

"Yes Cathy, that's fine." Her face betrayed her disappointment and sadness, but her friend didn't notice or, if she did, she chose to ignore it.

A couple of nights later Lorna carefully wrote her words in her card, kissed it several times, and got her mum to write the envelope which Enid did quite unwittingly, not realising it was a Valentine nor questioning why her daughter was writing to her dearest friend.

Lorna kissed the envelope as she popped it into the postbox at the top of Malford Grove as she made her way to the stables as usual the next day.

Cathy had come to mean something precious to her, a true and loyal friend, someone she loved being with, and someone she now knew she loved, but loved in a different way to her mum and sister. The girls often shared hugs and cuddles that meant only the warmth of friendship to Cathy, but which had come to mean something quite different to Lorna. It is doubtful Lorna could've arrested the surge of feelings inside her as love arrived unbid and swamped her heart and soul, and yet she was always cautious with Cathy, never speaking of a closer affection for fear of frightening her away. Better to let her beloved friend develop her own feelings at her own pace.

133

However, Lorna never considered for one moment that Cathy didn't love her and assumed it would come right for them at a later date when Cathy was certain of those emotions.

And so she had a lovely couple of days at the stables her excitement rising and rising as Saturday approached. There was a minor disappointment Friday, Valentine's Day, when no card arrived but, she reasoned, perhaps Cathy would bring one the next day.

Saturday was cold but dry and after an early light breakfast Lorna went off to the stables for a couple of hours work, returning home full of expectation and exhilaration, dying for Cathy's arrival. She'd decided, she'd take a chance. She'd confess her feelings and hope for the best, mainly hoping she wouldn't be rejected. Cathy wasn't like that, was she? Hadn't they occasionally shared gentle little kisses while they cuddled? Cathy must, *must* feel the same, or at least understand how Lorna felt. She'd be kindness itself, of course she would, or their friendship wouldn't have lasted this long or their affection for each other grown so deep.

Later that afternoon she and Cathy went for a brisk walk out into the forest and talked, as they always did, about so many things. Had her card arrived? Obviously Lorna had no way of knowing unless Cathy mentioned it. On the way back, seemingly impatient and full of enthusiasm, Cathy took her arm, eyes glowing with pleasure and made an announcement.

"Come on, let's get back. Can't wait to get back now Lorna. I've something I've been dying to tell you, and I've brought something I'm dying to show you. You'll never guess. Anyway, as soon as we reach your place we'll go up to your room and I'll tell you all. You're going to be so surprised!" Lorna wouldn't have guessed although she did try to imagine what on earth it could be that had so excited her companion.

\*\*\*

Cathy's eagerness was gathering Lorna up in its path and both girls bounded up the stairs removing their coats as they went, and flung themselves on the bed making tiny little squealing noises, their merriment overwhelming them. Cathy reached down for a carrier bag she'd brought with her.

"Been dying, just dying to show you this. Look, look, look, it's a homemade Valentine card from Vidvuds. Have you ever seen anything like it? So beautiful and romantic, don't you think? He spent last evening with me at his place, his parents were out, so it was really romantic. He gave me the card, went down on one knee, and swore undying love," She giggled at the telling, unaware of Lorna's reaction to the news, "and then we got cosy on the settee and had a fantastic kiss. So I told him I loved him but that I didn't think we'd ever marry, or anything like that. Too sensible for that, me. I wish you could've been there to see us! He turned the lights off and we got even cosier in the dark, and kissed and kissed, and it was just so lovely.

"I think it's good to be in love, not that I have any intention of encouraging him further, and I don't suppose it'll last long, but for now I have one beautiful boyfriend and I'm going to make the most of it. That's my news dear Lorna, what do you think? Tell me how lucky I am. He even spoke to me in Flemish at one point, not that I understood a word, he could've been telling me the football results for all I knew, but it added to the romance of a terrific Valentines Day."

The words had gone through Lorna like a knife, her mind was in disarray, her heart was tearing itself apart, her whole world had just shattered in front of her. There were no tears; she was too shocked. Somehow she found the wherewithal to speak.

"Did you have any other cards?"

"Oh yes, six this year, only had two last year, but none so good as Vidvuds. Look at the workmanship Lorna. Isn't he brilliant? Did you get any cards?"

"No ..... no, I've never had one."

"Oh Lorna, you should've told me. I'd have sent you one!" And her laughter screamed into Lorna's head.

"No, it's alright, it wouldn't have been the same." And she turned over on the bed, buried her face in the pillow, allowed the pain to sweep through her body until it produced the tears that brought relief. Cathy still had no understanding of the situation and thought Lorna was sad simply because she'd never had a

Valentines card, so her comforting was as useless as it was pointless and of no value whatsoever.

But in time Lorna pulled herself together, allowed her friend to hug her, shying away from the proffered kiss, determined she would rise above this heartbreak. But it was difficult to look Cathy in the face. She just wanted her to go home but knew she couldn't ask or tell her why. Eventually Lorna regained her composure. It was just another betrayal. This had to be the way people treated each other. Best not to lose Cathy's friendship although it could never be the same again.

Right now she never wanted to see her ever again but hoped such a desire should pass in time. How could Cathy be so flippant? She talked of love in such an abstract manner, so surely she can never have loved Lorna? All the words of love that had passed between them, the cuddles, the kisses, the togetherness, none of it could've meant much to her.

She was torn in two different directions. She found herself desperate for their precious friendship but believed she'd been cast aside and could not countenance closeness any more. God, how it ached. Was this what life was all about? Was this what love was all about? She loathed her father, her mother loathed her father, she loved Patricia. What *was* it all about? The Valentines card had obviously been glanced at but probably little more. If it had been the only one would it have made any difference? Then she remembered she had intended to tell Cathy the truth about her feelings, and was grateful no such opportunity arose, for what a fool she'd have made of herself.

There was a weird atmosphere as the rest of the day played out, Enid sensing it and Cathy remaining ignorant of it, so absorbed was she in her success with Vidvuds. But Lorna had become morose and gloomy, and remained so throughout tea, especially when the card was produced for Patricia's approval. In her turn she raced off to get the card she'd had from her own boyfriend so that Cathy might admire it, and she also revealed she'd had two others and couldn't figure out who they might be from. It was a time of great jollity, but not for the elder sister. In time their guest's father arrived to take her home and Lorna made sure she was nowhere near enough to be kissed, their customary farewell gesture. It was all too raw, too real.

By Sunday afternoon, with Norman out on business, or so he said, and Patricia away at a friend's, Enid decided it was time to tackle her other daughter, and the whole story came out. There were very few tears to accompany the telling, for the well had run dry, and Enid listened and comprehended precisely. She'd tried so hard to make life good for her daughters, but circumstances had changed the picture in a way she couldn't have imagined all those years ago when she made her silent promises. Now she felt a failure.

She thought back to that time at Mersea when Lorna told her about her hatred for her father, and that she had borne witness to the beatings her lovely mum had to endure. Had she done enough from that time forward to help Lorna? Or was she in some way responsible for her daughter's great sadness? Of course, she recognised that what Lorna saw as love for Cathy was an infatuation built on her escape from the betrayals thrust upon her by Norman and Donna.

Lorna had never had a boyfriend, never been out with a boy, and was in her late teens now, so it was hardly surprising that she turned simple close friendship into a kind of love. It was almost childish in a funny sort of way, but had she been like that with Micky? Perhaps she had been. Micky was her first love and it was intense, so obviously Lorna was going to feel the same about her first love. It was a kind of proving ground for teenagers. First love, ah, so beautiful and so delightful, so painful. The more she considered it the more she realised it was time to tell Lorna her own story.

"You don't love dad, do you mum? You don't, do you? Have you ever loved him? I hate him." It was the perfect chance for Enid to speak.

"I loved him once, my darling. If you like I will tell you the whole story, but it is quite a tale and I don't want to bore you." Lorna looked up at her mother with eyes that pleaded and with eyes that spoke volumes of love. Lorna still loved her and that warmed her. It was so priceless and precious and justified all that she had done for her daughter. Maybe her own story would help Lorna through this latest crisis.

"You'll never be boring, mum. Please tell me, I'd like to know." Enid hugged her.

"It starts with something you know nothing about, but believe me, it came to the same pain you're feeling now….."

And Enid began by telling her how she met Micky, whom she referred to as her fiancé rather than by name, and about how their love grew from childhood, right through their teens, to the point where they became engaged.

"I was the happiest woman there'd ever been. When we were about fourteen my parents took me on a camping holiday and kindly invited him. He had to share a tent with my dad. But one day I was walking with him and I asked him if he wanted to kiss me. I knew he did but he was so shy. Nonetheless we did kiss and we agreed we were even more in love, and that we could be married! Two fourteen-year-olds, I ask you. But real love did grow later and I shall never forget our engagement party. But something dreadful was just around the corner."

She went on to describe the coming of war, how they put their wedding off and why, and then told her about the war years and the awful occasion when she learned Micky was missing, and was probably killed in action. She could see in Lorna's eyes that in that moment they were both sharing the pain of that fateful day. She talked of the kind, caring friendship she enjoyed with Norman, the perfect gentleman, and the way he treated her with such generosity of spirit and understanding when she learned of Micky's demise.

"He seemed so lovely and, do you know, I actually thought he was the man my fiancé's soul would've approved of. Shortly after the war we married. And shortly after that my fiancé turned up alive. He'd been a prisoner in Japan. I wanted him to undo my marriage and run away with me, but it was no good. So maybe, just maybe, I wasn't quite the loving wife Norman expected although I did my best for him. Then two of the most wonderful things happened; you were born and Patricia followed. By then your father had revealed himself to be the monster he always had been, and my love, you know the rest of the story."

Lorna threw herself into a tight embrace with her mother and they hugged furiously, united in emotional agony, anxious to relieve each other's pain. At that moment Norman arrived home giving them no more time together.

"I love you mummy, love you always."

"And I love you too. You have saved my life, you and Patricia. You've given me something to live for out of heartbreak and distress. Live your life too, Lorna. Live it well for me my darling. Make a success of it and I will be happy and you will be happy also." They shared a last cuddle then Enid set off downstairs to see her husband.

Enid didn't mention she still held a light for her lost love, and she didn't mention that she knew where he lived and that it was a short distance away. And she didn't mention that she harboured a dream they might yet be re-united, despite knowing he was about to be married.

*** 

"Look, let me be honest with you, straight up, there's no way back. We can't work our way out of this and the creditors are getting itchy feet. I'd love to pay us all a nice little bonus before the outfit goes to the dogs but they'd be down on us like a ton of bricks. Could go inside for that. We've already creamed off too much individually which is one reason we're going down the pan, but according to my solicitor we should get away with those expenses as we called them." He chuckled ruefully, but the man sitting opposite could see no humour in it.

Charles Greatham leaned back in his chair, tapped his fingertips together in front of his face as if in prayer and waited for Norman Belham to comment on his words. A couple of minutes elapsed before he did.

"So we're going to be out of work, that's the lie of the land, isn't it? We're directors, they can't do us for the debts Charles, now can they? Just means no redundancy I suppose."

"That's about it. So any time you want to go, Norman, be on your way. There's no spare for wages, expenses, anything. You've had your last payment. Sorry, but I've kept you in the picture and you knew this was coming."

"Okay, I'll get away in the next few days. Anything you need me to tidy up?"

139

"Thanks Norman, but no. Me, Dave and Barry will get done what we can. Phil's already gone, as you know, and Ron's off tomorrow. We'll close down within a month, or earlier if the creditors want to take us to the cleaners. I suppose we can all look back at the good times, fleecing firms and individuals, making a mint that every one of us pocketed. All thanks to the war I reckon. Gave us a firm footing and an advantage. You've done well Norman, don't forget that, walked off with plenty of dosh."

"Oh no, no, not denying that, and that's why it seems a shame. Like we're not going to finish something we started! What about the staff, Charles?"

"We all keep mum, not a word to anyone. They know we're up the creek, but if we go under they won't get paid and there won't be any redundancy. Don't want them to realise that just yet. Understand?"

"Yep, fine with me. I'm not one for compassion ….."

"One of the reasons you've done so well here Norman, if you don't mind me saying so, you're cold and ruthless, just like me!" The two men shared a disgusting laugh. The meeting was obviously over so Norman rose, shook hands with Charles, and set off for his office. Sally, his shorthand-typist was checking some documents at her desk just outside. His charm hadn't worked on her, which was a shame because she exuded feminine appeal and he'd longed to take her out and work on her. Now she was married to a window-cleaner and about to be out of work, had she but known it. He didn't care a jot. Serve her right for rejecting his advances.

But he had done well out of the business for years now, so he couldn't grumble, and, for the first time in months, he felt pleased he had that other string to his bow. Of course, he'd have to come up with some story for Enid, damn her, perhaps say he'd decided on a change of direction and was expecting to be head-hunted. Yes, that'd do for now.

*\*\*\**

Mrs Grant's health was giving cause for concern, but she was determined to get to her daughter's wedding, and that was planned for May. Rita and Micky had said they'd have a winter wedding, maybe March time, but Mrs Grant had told them not to be so silly, it was too cold and May was a lovely period for such events.

But they were worried about her, knew how much seeing Rita married meant to her, and couldn't help hoping that by naming a May day her dream would come true, despite natural doubts. Her old house had been sold and the money had gone to her daughter who wanted Micky to have it, but he told her to keep hold of it 'for their old age' he'd said.

Micky remained unaware that his cleaner, Mrs Stevens, knew Enid. Her father, Mr Connaught, was proving a champion gardener and, like Mr Coombes before him, worked well with Micky when both were in the garden, and had become a firm friend. At the moment, in the throes of winter, much of their effort went into clearing up and preparing their charges for spring, although there were a few winter blooms about adding a welcome touch of colour.

Snow had come and gone, twice over, a wretched interference with Micky's work as getting about was never easy in such conditions, and he had extra worry on days when Rita had to drive to Hainault, but she managed it without incident. That was more than could be said for the unfortunate Sybil who once slid into a letter-box, happily causing no damage to car or Royal Mail's possession, and also spun right-round when the brakes failed to grip with a main road looming up. But she was learning, that is, learning what you *can't* do on an icy road.

Micky's other worry was finding new garage accommodation and that wasn't proving easy. He'd found some down George Lane but space was the problem, and there was always the chance that, being in a prime location, the site would eventually be sold for development. Maybe that was the same everywhere.

\*\*\*

Lorna went about her work at the stables, diligent as ever, but in a grief-fuelled daze most of the time, only conscious of people around her when they spoke to her. How she loved those horses, loyal, uncomplaining companions, the only creatures other than

141

mum that she trusted. She was inclined to be sullen and off-ish, and her attitude was starting to bother her employer.

"Cheer up Lorna," Mrs Cullen called across to her in a desperate attempt to motivate her, but in all honesty such words were anathema to the girl. The owner advanced on her having decided that perhaps a heart-to-heart was needed. "Look Lorna, come and have a chat. You seem so down and knowing how much you love working with the horses I wouldn't want you to put your job in jeopardy." Lorna spun round, alarmed at what she was hearing.

"Mrs Cullen, my job? Please, I don't want to lose it."

"Then come and have a chat. Come on." She led her to the office, diplomatically asked another girl there to go and perform some lengthy task or other, and when they were alone sat with Lorna and pleaded to know what the matter was. All of a sudden, afraid of being sacked, Lorna opened up and gave Mrs Cullen a brief resume of her lost love without actually mentioning it was another girl involved. Her employer was startled. Yes, such heartbreak in a girl of fourteen or fifteen would not be unusual in her experience, and could be more readily dealt with, but Lorna was that much older. She really didn't have anything useful to say that might have helped the poor girl and in the end treated her as she would've treated a typical lovelorn youngster.

"Well my girl, you've lost your boyfriend, so pull yourself together or you'll be in trouble. You have to get over these things Lorna. We've all had our hearts broken, but there are other fish in the sea and you'll soon find a nice boy. It's all part of growing up, simple as that. Now cheer yourself up, look happy, put a smile on your face and make sure you don't lose your position here."

They were the last words Lorna needed to hear but she couldn't bear the thought of not working at the stables so she resolved she would do her best, and hoped it would be good enough. But such a resolution paid no heed to grief and grief would rule her behaviour yet a while.

\*\*\*

"Well, thank you Mr Belham. Should you remember anything else that might be of interest do please get in touch." Norman

142

showed the sergeant out. It wasn't the first time the police had called at his house, and this time they'd wanted to know about Mr Faulkener. Were they getting closer? He hadn't yet told Enid anything about his job as he was still working on a feasible story and was far from convinced she'd believe any ideas he'd hit on so far. And now, once again, he had to explain the presence of a police officer asking questions.

Enid's intuition told her was involved in something that wasn't right, possibly illegal, but in any case something that had attracted the attention of the law. She couldn't challenge him; to do so might incite violence and it could be more brutal than ever. She noticed he was shaking as he explained the sergeant's visit, and his explanation was so full of holes it wouldn't have needed someone of Enid's intelligence to see through it.

It was Enid's turn to shake. She watched her husband go through to the lounge where he sat and tried to read the paper, and she shook with apprehension and fear, dreading what he might be up to, concerned for the consequences for her and her daughters.

At that point Patricia went into the lounge and started to play the piano.

*"Can't you shut up, for heaven's sake,"* he bellowed at her. Enid came to the lounge frightened for Patricia, but in time to see her gently close the piano lid, rise and walk out, ignoring her mother as she went to her room. Lorna had appeared at the top of the stairs having heard her father shout and went after her sister. Enid decided to leave them alone as Lorna would come to her if she was needed, and then slowly she crept back to the kitchen, angry and enraged, and still shaking. In her mind there was no question of innocence in his demeanour. *Whatever* was he involved in?

\*\*\*

It would be only a couple of days before Norman received his next bombshell: Maud Jolley's husband was divorcing her on the grounds of adultery and Norman was named as co-respondent, the husband having sufficient evidence.

143

# Chapter Fourteen

*Shocks and Surprises*

There had been an air of disagreeable tension in the Belham household. The last thing Enid needed was Patricia falling foul of her father and another rift appearing between father and a daughter. She desperately sought out Lorna after the piano incident and learned that she'd been turfed out of her sister's bedroom, unwanted. Another woe. As if things weren't bad enough as they were she certainly didn't want the two girls falling out, and she knew Lorna would take this rejection very badly in her present state.

But things could get worse and did so. That night Norman took all his frustrations out on Enid as they prepared for bed. No words were spoken, but for the first time in ages he hit her, twice round the face, hard slaps, and then he threw her face down on the bed and beat her with a belt. She bit into the bedcover to ensure she made no sound and hoped and hoped and hoped Lorna was not outside to hear.

Earlier she had tried to talk to her younger daughter but was met with an impenetrable barrier. Oh please God, she thought, please don't let Patricia be caught up in all this, please don't say she's becoming affected by the atmosphere, please don't let her come to hate her father, I couldn't stand it, I really couldn't.

And in her despair and anguish she wished she could phone Dorothy for help and support, but there was no hope of such a course of action. Patricia had obviously taken umbrage at her father's bluntness but was not going to talk about it.

"Look mum, dad didn't need to shout at me. He's always liked me playing, hasn't he? Well, I can't now, can I? And that's all there is to it. I'm okay, just leave me alone." Enid prayed she would come round, that Norman would return to his current affable self, and peace be restored. Thankfully the beating suggested that the matter might be closed from her husband's point of view, yet clearly he was extremely troubled, and he had never been one to discuss things that bothered him. But the situation between the sisters, that needed repairing.

Unfortunately, when Norman was notified of Maud Jolley's divorce and his role in it, he took it out on Enid. Another beating, while being berated on her long-term failings as a wife. His words were softly spoken, almost as if he wanted to make sure the girls didn't hear. He was trying to claim that her failings drove him into Maud's arms.

The next day there was no disguising the black eye and the split lip. Lorna guessed what had happened whereas Patricia, who seemed reconciled with her father, did not. She accepted her mother's explanation that she'd tripped and fallen against the banister on the stairs, and was genuinely concerned that she'd been hurt so badly. Enid was pleased, however, that Lorna had not been on the landing to hear either beating so remained unaware of the first occasion.

It was a weird state to be in, aggrieved by her treatment, worried sick about Lorna's reactions, yet delighted Patricia had not been drawn into this horrid unpleasantness, and relieved her elder daughter had not witnessed either thrashing. Weird indeed, and Enid wondered if she was going mad in some way. It would not be a surprise.

\*\*\*

Micky had found just what he was looking for, and not too far away either. There were two units, side by side, on an old factory site. They were large enough. The whole site had been renovated after factory closure and, he understood, the local council was anxious to keep it as an industrial location in order to ensure employment opportunities. There were reasons why it would be unsuitable for domestic development so Micky was confident he'd be there for as long as he wished.

It wasn't far from where he'd been to school in Loughton, so reasonably close to home and within an easy distance to Hainault. Ideal. Things were going so well for him that he had decided to find someone to work for him once he'd moved his stuff from round-the-corner in Wanstead, but that was for the future right now.

He'd been pondering whether Rita would return to work after their marriage and concluded that she would probably want to anyway, and that if her mother should pass away at any time she might welcome the chance to go back to full-time. Being Micky he worried that such a move could have repercussions for Sybil, but really that should not be his concern. But he worried for her as it was in his nature to do so.

Back at Malford Grove Mrs Grant was doing her best not to be a trouble to anyone while actually lapping up all the attention that came her way.

"I don't want to be a nuisance, dear," she'd said to Rita for the umpteenth time.

"You're not a nuisance, mum. We're all only too happy to look after you. If there's anything you want just ask."

"But I don't like being a nuisance ….."

"You're only a nuisance when you *don't* ask, mum!"

"I don't like to think I'm giving you work …."

"You aren't, mum. Now have you got all you want right now, as I've got some ironing to do?"

"See, I'm keeping you. I'm just an old nuisance …"

"Oh mum, don't be exasperating. You're my mum, I love you, and I'd do anything for you. Now stop this nonsense." A tender smile swept across her face and Mrs Grant returned the gesture.

"Alright my darling. Alright. Now before you go could I have another cushion please? Right here, behind my right shoulder." Rita smiled some more, for this was her mother all over, managing to be precisely what she didn't want to be, when all Rita wanted was her happiness at all times. They were an exceptional pair, bound by love, now rejoicing in the good fortune fate had presented them with. Mother and daughter, united as one, Mrs Grant's autumn years a treasure for both of them, and it was all thanks to Micky. Rita made sure she was comfortable and took a last glance out of the window to where Mr Connaught was busy in the garden, and headed off to the kitchen and the ironing.

\*\*\*

Not far away another mother and daughter were to be engaged in less pleasant conversation later in the day. Enid had gleaned from Patricia that she wanted to leave home. There was no chance of that, of course, but it was difficult trying to ascertain why. Finally Patricia, keen to do some homework and practice the piano, blurted out the truth.

"Look mum, you only love Lorna, don't you? You don't love me and you don't love dad. I love my dad and I'm fed up with the way you treat him. What wrong's he ever done you? Best dad in the world. When I'm old enough and leave school dad'll help me set up home with Daniel." Enid was shattered but had to recover her composure with alacrity.

"I love you both equally. You are the best things that have ever happened to me, you and Lorna, and I care for you and about you more than you can ever know. I would make any sacrifice for both of you ...."

"Lorna's told me terrible things, said that daddy hits you. She's a liar, I know she is. Daddy wouldn't hit anyone." Enid recoiled at this latest intelligence. So Lorna *had* told Patricia. The sibling relationship had fallen apart, and worse than that Patricia believed in her father, thought him to be the perfect dad. How could Enid address the truth when Patricia believed otherwise? Patricia had dashed away to her room leaving Enid crestfallen and weighed down with misery.

Lorna's day had not gone well. She'd been told off by Mrs Cullen and was frightened of losing her job. The latest attack on her mother was a burden upon her young shoulders, her sister's attitude viewed as yet another rejection, a further betrayal, and the world was as gloomy and despondent as she felt.

She left the stables that evening and walked up past the Eagle pub and Gowan Lea school and, full of her own thoughts and emotional instability, she absent-mindedly went to cross the road. She didn't see the vehicle until the last moment when it was only a couple of feet away.

\*\*\*

Work done for the day Micky was heading for home from round-the-corner and looking forward to another of Rita's excellent dinners. The day had gone well. Plenty of business. He was looking forward to moving to new premises and finding someone to do some of the donkey work, like 'pulling' those batteries, and acknowledging that life was good. He'd passed the Eagle pub and was indicating his left turn into Hermitage Walk when he was suddenly aware of the young woman walking into the road from the right. She was looking right ahead, not at him. He slammed on the brakes. At the last second she turned and her horror was etched in her face. Micky pulled up inches from the girl and in that moment realised he was looking at Enid, the Enid he'd remembered from their courting days.

He was utterly bewildered. Was it a ghost? Was he being haunted because he loved someone else and had betrayed Enid? Applying the handbrake he leaped from the van. The girl was motionless, fear written all over her face, but she was Enid.

Gradually Micky pulled himself together. Of course it wasn't Enid. He'd been through all this with Sybil. It was so surely the shock of the incident, that was all.

"Are you alright? What's the matter love?"

"I'm … I'm….I'm sorry. I'm sorry. Didn't think. I'm sorry."

"That's alright love. Look, come and sit in my van till you feel better. Can I take you home?"

"Okay. I need to sit down. I'm sorry, I'm sorry …."

"Come and sit in the van, I'll just pull over, out of the way." And he guided her round to the passenger door and helped her into the seat. He returned to the cab and pulled in at the roadside. He looked across at her and all he could see was Enid. God, it was Enid as he remembered her.

"I'm sorry, I'm sorry. So much on my mind. Wasn't paying attention. I'm sorry."

"It's all okay, as long as you're alright. Tell me where I can take you. What's your name?"

"Lorna. Lorna Belham. I live in Broadwalk, but please, I'm alright. I can walk."

Belham, Belham. It could not be so. Could it? Was this Enid's daughter?

"It's okay, have you home in no time." He risked another glance. Unlike Sybil this really was Enid.

"Thanks. Yes, please, take me home." He drove off towards Broadwalk, Lorna just staring straight ahead. Micky's feelings were all over the place. He was afraid of the truth but daring to hope it was all coincidence. Lorna directed him to her home. "Thanks, and I'm so sorry, I really am. Will you come in, please?" There was nothing Micky wanted more.

"Better be away. I'm expected home. Hope you're okay now Miss Belham."

"Thanks again. Thanks for saving my life. Sorry, I don't know who you are. Please tell me your name." The question left him in a dilemma but he went for the truth.

"Bowen. Micky Bowen. Take care Miss Belham. Hope you're alright now." She alighted, nodded in his direction and walked up to the front door with a simple wave in his direction. But he had already pulled away. No time to stay, just in case his Enid was there.

*** 

Micky returned home, stunned, devoid of any other feelings, cold in his soul, and was a very different man from the one Rita knew and loved. Quiet, withdrawn, and she could place nothing upon it, could discern no reason, just that he had changed, and he would not talk about it.

He really did think he'd put Enid away in his memories where she belonged, but she had made good her escape, and here he was, boats burned, committed to Rita and her mum who had moved into his house. No, he had to conquer this. She might be happy as a wife and mother and might've forgotten him, though he doubted it, and for the sake of his own marriage he had to overcome these feelings and push her away.

Then he tried to puzzle why Lorna had gone into the road in front of him. What on earth could've been on her mind to distract her so? She was so obviously shaken-up, as anyone would've been, and that might've explained her quietness on the way home, but Micky sensed there was something else and it troubled him when it should not have done.

In due course he pulled himself out of his self-inflicted melancholy, determined to send Enid's memory packing, and

149

started being the man his fiancé knew him to be. But Rita remained perturbed by the aberration; something had occurred to disturb him and he was not prepared to reveal it.

Lorna had gone straight to her mother and quietly explained what had happened, and also told her about Mr Bowen's quick reactions that had saved her. Enid was devastated and speechless, and tried not to show her agony in front of her daughter. But thank God Micky had stopped in time, thank God Micky had saved Lorna's life. Eventually she asked if Lorna had the man's address so that she could go round and thank him, not that she had any intention of doing so, and was therefore pleased that Lorna hadn't obtained the information. She knew anyway, but was now excused from further action. That was a relief in one respect.

Patricia was busy at the piano, then took a call from Daniel, and finally went upstairs ostensibly to do some homework. Dinner was nearly ready but there was no sign of Norman. Patricia took little notice of her sister or mother, and had shown scant sympathy for Lorna's plight. Enid decided that Lorna needed to see a doctor and would not be going to work in the morning, not that her daughter would thank her for it, but it had to be done for the sake of her health not to mention her safety, as today's incident had proved.

The three sat down to dinner; Enid would make sure her husband got his meal if and when he turned up, but it was getting late for the girls to eat. Mrs Belham senior ate lunchtime and largely kept out of the way in the evenings, which suited Enid perfectly.

"Dad's really busy at work, isn't he?" Patricia commented.

"Very," replied her mother, "and I wouldn't mind betting he's working on an important project right now, after all, he has a very senior position at the office, and we've come to expect him to be working all hours."

"I just wish he was here. Meals are boring without dad. Just you two miseries for company." Enid held her temper in check. Lorna, who had being doing little more than fiddling with her food, pushed the plate away, said she wasn't hungry, and strode off upstairs, much to Enid's despair. "Can't wait to finish this and

150

get back to the piano. The pair of you hate dad and it's no good denying it." Enid's appetite had vanished altogether.

"Alright, you finish your dinner by yourself. I'll leave you in peace," and she rose smartly, gathered up the unwanted plates and walked off to the kitchen struggling to keep herself in check. Just then the doorbell rang.

The plain-clothes police officer showed his identification and asked if Mr Belham was in.

"I'm sorry, no, and I don't know what time he'll be back. He's at work."

"Mrs Belham, is it?"

"Yes that's right."

"Well, we need to speak with him quite urgently and apparently he's not at his office. They said he'd left mid-afternoon but had assumed he was coming home. You've not heard from him or seen him then?"

"No I haven't. I hope nothing's happened to him." She was visibly shaking but the sergeant wasn't sure if it was concern for her husband's welfare, or anger, perhaps because he might be with another woman. It bothered the sergeant, but he let it ride. He wondered if she knew what else Norman was up to.

"I'll call back later, if you don't' mind …."

"Why are you pursuing him? What's he done wrong?" she squealed at him, exasperation and annoyance getting the better of her.

"He can help us with some enquiries we're making, and I can't say any more. Sorry Mrs Belham." Patricia had appeared behind her mother and waited while she and the officer said their goodbyes and the door was closed. Enid burst into tears, tears of anger and frustration. Patricia ignored her weeping.

"What's going on, mum? Why are they after dad? I want to know. Tell me."

"I don't know and your father's never told me. I don't know and I wish I did. And that's the truth. You must ask him yourself." And she walked briskly away, back to the kitchen, leaving her daughter standing in the hall. Lorna had come down the stairs and stood near the foot.

"What do you know, clever-clogs?" Patricia screamed at her. "You and mum keep everything from me. What's wrong with dad? Why are the police here?"

"We don't know Patricia.... "

"Mum *must* know...."

"She doesn't. She dare not ask. And you know the reason why." Lorna shot back up to her room leaving Patricia to bellow after her.

"You're both liars. You tell lies about my dad, you say horrible things about the best dad a girl could have, and I hate you both....." But Lorna's door was closed and she heard no more. Enid's tears had dried. She had to sort out this wretched business and most importantly re-unite these two sisters. But how? She was at the end of her tether, emotionally, mentally and physically.

*** 

Norman came home after ten that evening and after the sergeant had called a second time. Enid offered to get him some food, anything he wanted, but he declined. She told him about the police and refrained from mentioning that she knew he hadn't been at work; too dangerous. He seemed weary and worn as he flopped down in an armchair, and then Patricia came dashing downstairs. Enid thought about trying to stop her but chose not to, minding out of her way.

"Dad, dad," she cried, "where have you been, daddy? The police are looking for you and they said you weren't in the office? Where were you?" In the hall Enid stiffened, closed her eyes and took a deep breath. In the lounge Norman leaped to his feet and went for his daughter; he caught her completely by surprise. He was enraged, shouting angrily.

"None of your business, none of your business what I do. Mind your own business. Now get out of my way," and he punched her violently round the face with his fist and threw her aside. Enid could stand it no longer and raced into the room to confront him. He punched her full in the mouth and pushed his way past, and made for the front door and was gone.

152

In the immediate aftermath of this act of terror mother and daughter, crying profusely, came together and clasped each other tightly. It had taken one brutal and un-called-for attack to re-unite them, for in this shocking moment Patricia came to know the truth. Lorna stood in the doorway looking horrified. Enid spoke softly.

"Come on girls, let's get ourselves sorted …."

"Mum, you're bleeding," whimpered Patricia.

"Yes, well, let's get the first aid kit, shall we? Are *you* alright, darling? He hit you, didn't he?" Patricia cried even harder and Enid clutched her close to her, and Lorna came and cuddled up to the pair of them. They were a family together in dreadful adversity, but they were a family again, or at least all of a family they needed to be.

Mrs Belham senior slept through it all, or so she claimed. Even she had endured a recent fall-out with her son, but not one that ended in violence.

# Chapter Fifteen

*Nemesis*

They fished Norman's body out of the Eagle Pond where it had been spotted by a couple of schoolboys early morning.

Initially foul play was suspected but there were no other signs of injury or a struggle. It was also established he hadn't been drinking. The post mortem recorded that he had drowned and possibly been in the water several hours before discovery. He may have gone straight from his home to the location.

The net was closing in on the gang and Mr Faulkener was already in custody along with two others. Whether the gang had anything to do with Norman's demise would never be known, but it wouldn't be long before his role was exposed and the other members rounded up.

After the horrors of the evening before Enid had spent the night fearing her husband's return, sleeping fitfully, and hoping she would prove herself a good enough mother to pull the girls through this latest crisis and the times ahead. One thing for sure they would not be going anywhere the next morning. Both sisters had experienced unpleasant reactions to the events of that fateful evening and had not slept well unsurprisingly. School and work could wait. Enid let them sleep on but both arose before 8.30 a.m.

She telephoned the school and then Mrs Cullen at the stables. The last thing she wanted to do was jeopardise Lorna's job and merely said she was unwell after a bad night, but was so looking forward to getting back to work quickly. The owner sounded quite sympathetic.

Within the hour their whole world turned upside-down.

*** 

Police officers brought the news, and imparted it with great sensitivity and kindness, having first asked to see Enid alone. Stunned, Enid did not break down, for there was no love left in her heart for that evil man. The police wanted to know if he'd left

154

a note which might suggest suicide, but at that stage they actually believed he had been killed. When they departed they left Enid with a hundred and one questions she never asked. They also said a senior officer would come and see her later.

She gathered the girls and Mrs Belham together in the lounge and broke the news as best she could, and watched their reactions. Patricia was in fits of tears, Lorna showed no emotion whatsoever, but went to her sister's side to comfort her, and Mrs Belham threw a hand to her mouth as the colour drained from her face, her head shaking from side to side in disbelief.

Patricia soon quietened herself, then hugged Lorna, then dried her eyes and blew her nose. Up until last night she hadn't wanted to believe her father was that bad.

"There is something else," Enid began, "and it is important that you prepare yourselves. The police have hinted your father may have been involved in something he should not have been, and will want to question me later. Not that I know anything about it, but talking to close relatives is apparently quite normal in these circumstances. I am going to ring the school and Mrs Cullen and advise them now. I have been warned that the papers will be interested …. "

"Oh God," cried Patricia, "and the whole world will know."

"Yes, and that is a matter we have to cope with as a family. We must stand firm together. I suggest you let me answer the door and the phone for the time being. We must be strong for each other. That way we will come through this." And indeed Enid felt the strength and resolve rise within her, just as it had done many times over the years. Yes, she'd pull them through, because, in the girls' case, their wellbeing and lives depended on it. She would also ring Dorothy later, hopefully before any news reached Shropshire.

She went and sat next to Mrs Belham and held her hand and the woman placed her other hand on Enid's, and sobbed a little, sniffed and sat up straight.

"Enid, you've not always seen eye to eye with me, but we have all suffered a loss today, and I want you and the girls to know you have my support and affection. To begin with, Enid, I want you to call me Louisa, please. It is time for a fresh start. I've lost my own family and I don't want to lose you all. I'll be here for you, all of you, if you want me."

There was nothing more to be said on the subject and they all sat quietly contemplating the news and their situation. After a while Enid rose.

"I'm going to telephone my parents. They may want to come over."

\*\*\*

Detective Sergeant Morris sat with Enid and asked his questions, struck by how calm she seemed and how unemotional she appeared. He explained what he could, and she listened intently, hearing for the first time what her husband had been caught up in.

"I have to tell you, Mrs Belham, that we have good reason to believe another gang member was killed on the orders of those he worked for, so we have to investigate the possibility your husband was another victim." Somehow this didn't surprise her. "I'm sorry to intrude on your grief but time is of the essence, and another officer may want to come and speak to you." He coughed. "Ahem …. there will also be the question of an identification …."

"I will identify my husband if that's what you're asking." He nodded. The interview was over soon afterwards and Enid went straight to the family to let them know what had happened. The mood was sombre. They had eaten little, no appetite, and had sustained themselves with hot drinks. She was thinking about her mother-in-law: perhaps this new attitude reflected some cunning, concern on the woman's behalf for her future with Norman gone. She now had no backing and was where she was not welcome. Was she feathering her own nest and ensuring some degree of security?

With that thought Enid found herself wondering if he'd left a will, and a ripple of apprehension ran through her mind. What if he'd been devious to the last, and she was about to suffer the ultimate humiliation in some way? No, she would not worry about that just yet. For now, the girls were coming first.

Newspaper reporters did turn up at various times but Enid politely told them she had nothing to say and closed the door on them. One reporter phoned but received the same response. Where did he get the number, she pondered? No matter, press on.

Whatever else occurred the one thing that was missing in the household was any real sense of grief and loss. Lorna felt relief but did not mention it. Patricia was wrestling with the story as she knew it, her father's behaviour last night, and the fact she had loved him as her dad, and that he'd always looked after her. Was he really such an evil man, violent and cruel? If he was worried out of his mind last night might that explain his unacceptable actions? But he hit her so hard, thrust her over and then punched her mum right in the face leaving her with a nose-bleed and cut lips. And that was exactly what Lorna had tried to tell her, that he was a brute without compassion. She had rebelled against that then. Was she now in possession of the truth about his wickedness?

\*\*\*

The story was on the television that night, or at least it was the news that a gang of fraudsters was under arrest and that an alleged one of their number, Norman Belham of South Woodford, had been found dead, drowned, foul play suspected.

Micky, Rita and Mrs Grant stared at the screen in disbelief. Rita was at once frightened of Micky's reaction. Would he rush to Enid's side? No, of course he wouldn't, common sense told her, but she couldn't help the flash of pain or the fear.

She needn't have fretted. Micky had no idea how life had turned out for Enid, but he knew she had a family and might well have been extremely happy. He certainly hoped so, and right now he had the utmost respect for a widow bereaved in such appalling circumstances, but respect was all he had, no emotional feelings at all.

Enid's parents hurried round and their presence added fortitude to her resilience and her determination to hold on and to cope. She'd come this far, she would not let go now, not now she was shot of him.

157

In the days after she wrapped herself in being busy and there was plenty to do. She identified Norman's body without upset. She was blowed if she was going to shed tears. The funeral could be arranged and her father helped there, as he did with many other things. Her mother and mother-in-law found they could get on well together and between them took care of most of the domestic issues, leaving Enid free for the girls and for other matters.

Patricia returned to school, Lorna to the stables, with Mr Campton providing lifts wherever they were needed. Lorna was becoming a changed woman, and was pleasing Mrs Cullen to the point where the owner stopped worrying about her. She was surprisingly cheerful, which Mrs Cullen put down to her way of coping with disaster, whereas it was nothing of the sort, and she was once again efficient in her work. Her job was safe.

Her sister was not coping too well, almost unable to accept that her beloved father was a criminal and a wretched bully who beat her mother, trying to think good of him as a dad she adored, and getting her feelings into a terrible tangle. Although school friends behaved well towards her it was Daniel who proved her salvation being an excellent comforter; Enid permitted him to visit several times and that found the approval of her daughter who was now turning to her mother more than ever.

Happily there were no problems with the will apart from the clause allowing Louisa to remain at the family home, and any future home should the family move. Enid was the principal beneficiary; the house was hers (there was no mortgage) together with his money and the household effects and, of course, the cars. She began to wonder, with some trepidation, whether she was enjoying the benefits of the proceeds of crime, and that increased her uneasiness for a while.

There was nothing she could do about it anyway. If nothing else, he'd left her and the family well provided for.

The coroner's verdict was accidental death since there was no clear evidence he'd wanted to take his own life, and foul play had by then been ruled out. The verdict gave Enid another income as his life insurance paid out. In a moment of twisted madness she actually smiled and thanked her husband, silently, of course. Was she in danger of becoming inhuman? Or of rather liking Norman after death? No, she just needed to pull herself together. She was free of the monster and she was solvent and well-catered for financially. She mustn't let her mind be overwhelmed with strange thoughts!

# Chapter Sixteen

*Aftermath*

Micky sent a brief note of condolence to Enid and she replied with a short message thanking him for his kindness. They wanted to meet but both, for different reasons, knew they could not and made no mention of the fact in their letters. It would not be right so soon after the death.

The national news did not dwell on it, but the local paper ran a thorough front-page story that ran across two other pages. Norman Belham was the only local man caught up in the fraud case. His life and business activities, and his wartime work, were detailed with much being made of him being a company director, and the fact he left a widow and two daughters also received rather more publicity than the family would've liked.

Consequently it was some days before Patricia returned to school, although Lorna did carry out some part-time work at the stables. Enid's parents did the shopping along with other routine duties, which eased the burden on Enid, and her father busied himself with the funeral arrangements. Other family members got in touch and it all seemed rather hectic to the new widow who was keeping herself fully occupied anyway.

That the family felt little pain for their loss was helping them cope, although Patricia had been saddened by the stark realisation that her much loved dad was not the man she had grown up with, and that hurt more than losing him. There were days when her disbelief got the better of her and she cried out with the sheer frustration of having her emotions pulled two ways at once as she rolled up in a ball on her bed sobbing profusely.

The paper, having suggested in its story that Norman had been interviewed in connection with a criminal gang he was allegedly a member of, stated that, at the time of going to press, there was no evidence or proof one way or the other, thus leaving the reader to assume the worst as readers are apt to do.

Genuine friends had rallied round in support and now Enid and the girls learned who their far-less-than-genuine friends were, for they kept their distance and ran down family Belham with great ease. Gossip was in control.

Dorothy could not leave her school but made frequent phone calls. Louisa Belham proved to be a good help and a good listener, always ready when anyone in the house needed to talk.

Lorna threw herself into her work at the stables, much to Mrs Cullen's pleasure, and gradually increased her hours. The owner's son, Philip, went out of his way to be kind, but was incredibly shy, especially where girls were concerned. She accepted his friendship as she had always liked him without realising he had long wished to ask her out but was too coy to do so, and now wasn't the right time.

Patricia was soon off school again and her mother took her to the doctors fearing she might, at worst, be heading for a breakdown. Some unpleasant things had been said at school although most of her fellow pupils had been more sensitive, some very supportive. Enid rang anyway, determined to do whatever she could to stop the problem escalating. Dr Sylvia Ashworth was very good and took plenty of time with the daughter, prescribing some pills for the short term, and telling her to come back in a week's time, adding that help was available elsewhere.

In truth the doctor was concerned about the conflict in Patricia's head; the girl had loved her father dearly until he exposed himself as the absolute animal Lorna had painted him. Then came his death. It was a great deal for a teenage girl to have to come to terms with.

Syd Berry had contacted the police having read the newspapers as he'd been defrauded by the gang and was only too willing to respond to the request for information. He was in the office at Williams & Co telling Rita and Sybil about the statement he'd made when Micky came in from the weighbridge.

"Hello Micky. Just telling these ladies about that organisation that cost me a fortune, and now it's come out that it was a fraud all along. Thought it was genuine, I did, and they convinced me I'd do well out of it. And that bloke that drowned over your way, Micky, he was one of them apparently. Know you can't believe all you read in the papers, but I reckon he topped himself thinking the law was about to catch up with him. Mind you, left a widow and two daughters to grieve; bit cowardly that. They say he might

161

have been murdered but I don't know. What do you think, Micky?"

Micky was thinking about Enid, and Rita knew he was, and he was barely listening to Syd. Sybil sensed something was in the air and broke the spell.

"Well, poor chap, but he'd have gone to prison if he was guilty, so either way I feel sorry for those he's left behind. But I feel specially sorry for you, Syd, knowing how serious it was and how bad it might have been." As diplomacy goes it was a first-class intervention.

"Thanks Sybil. Yes, know you're right. Nasty business, but at least the rest of those devils will be put away and for a long time, so that's some consolation I suppose."

Micky was looking at Rita and no words were necessary. He'd told her he'd sent Enid a note and had a reply, but assured her that was as far as it was going. Rita hoped he meant it. Now she was staring at him, wondering what else was going through his mind. He decided it was best to speak.

"Yes, nasty business, but we're all pleased things have worked out for you Syd, and sorry it had to happen at all. There are some rotten people about. I think fraud should be more than just a major crime. After all, people use vile means to gain your confidence and trust and then run off with your money, like they did to you Syd. Should be a hanging offence." Rita didn't know if he was serious or just saying the right thing in support of the foreman. There was much nodding at his comment but no further discourse on the subject, so Sybil sorted out Micky's notes and money, handed it over and the two men left the office together.

Rita had never told anyone about Micky and Enid and was sworn to never do so.

"Wonder about that bloke's missus," Sybil queried, "and if she knew what was going on or even had a part in it. Can't help wondering, can you? Even so, she's living off the profits, isn't she, Rita? Must've wondered where the money was coming from."

"I don't think we'll ever know, my dear. And I think it's time we got some more work done." Rita successfully diverted her colleague from pursuing her latest theme as she guessed Micky had probably asked himself the same questions and it could be

162

causing him some distress. She'd try and ask him, tactfully of course, later that day.

\*\*\*

The family found themselves shunned or ignored for the most part, not that it bothered them too much. There was enough tittle-tattle doing the rounds amongst those who condemned them to keep the gossip-mongers occupied but that didn't prevent obnoxious moments arising. Several anonymous letters arrived, generally filthy in content, saying such things as they were a family of thieves and lived well on money stolen from others, and one or two making highly offensive personal comments of a hurtful nature.

Mr Campton placed himself in charge of all incoming mail, with everyone's agreement, and opened the official, the pleasant and the unpleasant, and destroyed the latter without drawing it to anyone's attention.

Patricia arranged with Daniel that he should put a small green cross on the back of the envelope, if he should write, so that Mr Campton didn't open it. In fact, he sent several letters of comfort and support, full of love and warmth, that helped cheer the recipient no end. They may have assisted her eventual recovery.

Enid's father also answered the phone, when he was there, and was thus able to keep two horrible calls from his daughter. How *did* they get the number? The phone had always been ex-directory. He couldn't understand it.

Most of the abuse followed Syd's line of reasoning, that Enid must've known, possibly been involved, and that they lived in style because of Norman's illegal activities. The police made extensive enquiries, interviewed Enid at the station, and could find no evidence against her. He had been a company director and was highly paid, this accounting for his lifestyle, his large home in an expensive, sought-after area, and the cars. They didn't take expensive holidays or buy luxury goods, and Enid had worked as a corsetiere for extra income. This was all made crystal clear to a reporter for the local paper when Mr Campton visited their offices. It was a dicey manoeuvre that could backfire. In the event it was a success, for the following week there was a follow-up article in which the other side of the story was presented in a particularly poignant manner, much to Peter Campton's delight. It didn't stop the abuse, of course, but it greatly reduced it, and more and more people came to feel sorry for the family.

The funeral, attended by many on Enid's side of the family, and precious few on Norman's, went ahead without incident, and was also attended by friends and by business colleagues and associates from Norman's firm.

The cortege drove out of Broadwalk, down to the Green Man roundabout at Leytonstone, and thence across Wanstead Flats to the City of London Cemetery where he was to be cremated. Rather surprisingly Patricia did well holding herself together, but as they drove slowly away she happened to glance back at the crematorium and in that instant detected the faintest puff of smoke from the chimney, and with that she exploded into a terrible and agonising flood of tears, thrusting herself into her mother's breast where she found solace and ease, unconditional love and tender peace, comfort and security.

Neither Enid nor Lorna shed much in the way of tears. It was more numbness than a lack of grief, any tears making good their escape doing so out of respect for the solemn situation. Louisa sobbed a little in the chapel but was otherwise restrained. Oddly enough Charles Greatham, the managing director of Norman's firm, was seen with moist eyes but he may have been weeping for the loss of his company which was now only a couple of weeks away.

Refreshments had been laid on at Broadwalk, but Enid's main concern was to get the whole wretched business over and done with, and seeing the back of the multitude of mourners, none of whom appeared sincerely filled with much sorrow. Bearing in mind only Enid, Lorna, Patricia and Louisa knew what a monster Norman had been it could only be assumed that the rest were there to support the close family rather than lament the passing of another soul.

Thankfully relief came and then, tactfully, Louisa, Peter and Maggie retired to Louisa's lounge while Enid and the girls sat quietly together in the main lounge.

"Girls, this is a beginning," Enid said with an affectionate softness, "and we must make the most of our lives from this day forward. What I have to say I can now speak with an openness that has been denied me up until today. You have both been my great love and salvation without whom I could not have survived. I had to fight to keep you from seeing your father as he truly was. I had to fight to make sure you felt you were growing up in a normal, loving family. I had to fight all these years just to make it alright for you. I never gave up that fight.

"I resolved from the outset that I would devote my life to you, to your happiness and to your success, and I would do so no matter what the cost. Without that determination I would've gone under ages ago. I know I haven't always got it right, and I beg your forgiveness, but by God I've tried hard, believe me I have. You were babes in arms when your father first hit me. I've endured it all this time. I am so sorry I haven't been the perfect mum and I so wanted to be, so please, please forgive me, and let us all start afresh. As I swore back then I would do anything for you, so I swear that again now. Forgive me for my failings my darlings, and let us be a truly beautiful family ……" And as her head sunk into her chest and her shoulders heaved her daughters came straight to her side and hugged her, the three lost in a deluge of tears, immersed in glorious love, clinging to each other for dear life, and becoming as one, a family re-born.

That night mum and daughters slept together, bonded by the love that had won through despite the trials and challenges of the years past, and safe in the knowledge they had each other and would prove to be an unbreakable triumvirate, the new family Belham. Enid stayed awake until both Patricia and Lorna were asleep and, as she lay in the dark, thought of Micky for the first time in days. It was in his arms that she surrendered to sleep.

Micky had been giving thought to an entirely different project. The back garden of his bungalow included what he had termed the 'big lawn' – a lawn that could comfortably accommodate a tennis court, although he'd never considered such usage. It was actually located at right angles to the main garden and reached across to the next road, Bushey Avenue, and it was surplus to requirements. With agreement from Rita he was selling it for a property development and in the hopes it would pay off the remaining mortgage. He wasn't one for any sort of debt.

165

Mrs Grant had wanted Micky to benefit from the sale of her house but he wouldn't hear of it, and right now his main interest was marrying Rita debt free. It was almost a matter of honour, being sure he could provide for his bride, not starting married life weighed down by monies owed, and knowing Rita would inherit her mother's money so she would always be financially secure. It was so important to him.

And the May wedding date was drawing ever nearer.

# Chapter Seventeen

*Mid 1960s*

With the passage of time most local people forgot all about the man whose body was removed from the Eagle Pond, and equally ceased to think about his alleged criminal activities and the family left behind. These were the swinging sixties; people were taking inexpensive package holidays abroad, pop music was ushering in an incredible new era, and in 1966 England won football's World Cup. Three years later man walked on the moon for the first time. So much else was happening in these modern and enlightened times. There were new beliefs, new dreams and the black and white past was transforming itself into the all-colour future. It was the advent of flower power, a movement dedicated to peace that came to embrace all aspects of love in the word's widest sense.

If this was the heyday of the Beatles and the Rolling Stones, pop music was given a shake-up by the arrival of the Who, a group with widespread appeal amongst the young, for the young were ready to fight back and put themselves firmly on the map. They wanted to show they could think for themselves, weren't afraid to question authority, and were prepared to put forward and support ideas that in some cases were quite revolutionary. The Who encapsulated the way in which many young folk felt they wanted to break free. This kind of attitude did not appeal to their elders who frowned upon the new order. But, like it or not, the world was changing.

And Enid and her family were part of it, just as Micky, Rita and Mrs Grant were part of it. Enid took her daughters for a fortnight on Spain's Costa Brava and they all had the time of their lives. She paid for Daniel and Cathy to accompany them, and left Louisa Belham to her own devices watched over by her parents. Louisa had been invited but eschewed the idea, grumpily so. Enid ensured Peter and Maggie Campton would be frequent visitors whether her mother-in-law wanted them or not.

Rita and Micky married at Christchurch, Wanstead, and the sun shone brilliantly on their special day, made even more special by the attendance of Rita's mother who loved every moment, and actually took on the role of giving the bride away admittedly with some mobility assistance. Syd Berry was Micky's best man, his speech at the reception bringing the house down. Micky and Rita never knew he had such a delightful and wicked sense of humour.

The mid-Sixties were a time of opportunity, a time of new beginnings, but for some they spelled problems whereas for others they brought joy and success. Micky had sold his 'big lawn' and a house now stood there. His mortgage paid off. But sadness was not far away. For Enid there was the sorrow that Patricia passed only three O-levels and had abandoned any hope of higher education.

*** 

*Lorna*

Lorna settled into her life, a comfortable life at home, her work at the stables, and Enid decided if she was truly happy she should be left alone to enjoy it free from maternal criticism and advice. But she worried about her future.

Her friendship with Cathy appeared to flourish, despite the earlier feelings of betrayal she'd suffered, and the pair of them were inseparable during the Spanish holiday. For one thing Cathy had abandoned Vidvuds and his revolutionary ideals, yet Lorna acknowledged that her friend could be fickle in her heartfelt relationships but had remained a close friend for all that. Perhaps there was more to real friendship than the need to be in love.

Philip Cullen worshipped her from afar, not believing for one moment that he stood any chance, and was as shy as ever. But he kept his distance, did not crowd her, and was there when needed. Finally he struck up the courage to ask her out and was surprised when she accepted, and even more astonished when she said what she'd really like was a walk in the forest with him. In the event they strolled over to the Hollow Ponds on Saturday afternoon and discussed many things, wide ranging things, and found they were kindred spirits in numerous ways. The afternoon raced by and was followed by many further walks as the days went by. And then it happened.

"Philip, our walks together started when you asked me out. I am so sorry, but I realise you were trying to date me and I have perhaps misled you." He almost spluttered in reply.

"No, no, Lorna. Yes I wanted to go out with you, because …. because … well, because you are such a lovely girl, a lovely person, and I wanted to get to know you better. I've loved these walks, just being with you, and you've made me so happy. But …. but, well, yes, I wanted a date I suppose." Her response shook him.

"Philip, I've never kissed a boy and I'd like to kiss you. Have you wanted to kiss me?" It took a while for him to recover. And in that moment he had never seen anyone so beautiful, and he longed for her, wanted her and had no idea how to proceed.

"Oh Lorna," he stumbled, "that would be so nice, but … but … but only if you want to. I wouldn't impose…."

"You've been so nice to me, Philip, and I've needed you, you can have no idea how much I've needed you. I've been betrayed so many times, but all this time you've been there and our walks together have kept me alive. You're a perfect gentleman and I know you won't take advantage of me. I won't be betrayed again, you know. Right now I need you more than ever…" And she grabbed hold of him and thrust her lips against his, and passion engulfed them. It was very different to that kiss with Cathy, very different indeed. She felt overpowered and was enchanted with the feelings, surrendering to the surging force within her, a force she had kept suppressed following her disappointments, a force Philip was unleashing from behind the barrier she had built around her heart.

The magic smothered them both, Lorna amazed by her emotions, Philip astonished at her reactions.

In that moment, by extraordinary coincidence, Lorna had almost replicated her mother's actions with Micky during that pre-war camping holiday.

And in that moment Lorna came of age, emerged from her misery and put the horrors of her past behind her, and gave herself wholly to something so lovely, so irresistible, so desirable. For Philip liked her for herself, liked her as she was,

169

accepted her as such, and hadn't he indeed been there for her when she wanted support at the stables? Yes, every time. Quietly, in the background. Not overbearing, not putting himself in her way. He'd been there nonetheless.

Lorna was learning to trust again. She trusted her mother and sister, and she now trusted Cathy as a friend. Philip seemed so nice and so harmless she trusted him too. She trusted her maternal grandparents but definitely not granny Belham!

\*\*\*

*Patricia*

Patricia had travelled in the opposite direction. At the doctor's suggestion she contacted the Samaritans and at last she could tell the whole story, speak about all her mixed emotions and do so without fear, and found some degree of peace from the turmoil of the past. For all that she suffered badly, the nightmares all too frequent, and she could not cope easily despite Enid and Lorna offering every comfort.

Daniel was a great support, a kinder young man it would be hard to find, but Patricia eventually gave him his marching orders and he reluctantly departed her life, saying she could contact him at any time, even if she just wanted a chat.

She failed most O-levels and lost all interest in improving herself. At the heart of this was her enduring love for her father who had given her so much, just as she knew now he was a brutal man who beat her mother and a man who had achieved wealth through defrauding other people. It was a cross of enormous weight she had to bear, and she could not do it comfortably.

Patricia went to work in a local shop and did not do well at it. Enid feared for her, but her wise counsel was unwanted and largely ignored.

One day, a Sunday, a bored and irritable Patricia decided to ring Daniel and found a willing ear at the other end of the phone. Later that day they met and once again, as with the Samaritans, she poured out her story, lock, stock and barrel. Then she hugged him and he embraced her, carefully, gently, so as not to distress her in any way. It was to be a brief reunion for gradually she pushed him away again and this time, abandoning hope, he simply wished her well and set about living his own life free from expectations where she was concerned. In due course he met another girl and began the process of forgetting his former love.

A frequent customer in her shop asked her out and was given short shrift.

"Okay, let's just have a coffee maybe, and a chat, nothing more. What d'you do in your lunch break?" He was determined not to give up. "Let's go to the café down the road one lunchtime, eat and talk. Honest, not asking any more than that." Without blinking she stared right into his eyes and the experience almost frightened him, she looked so haunted.

"Alright, but I don't eat much, a coffee will do fine, and if I don't ever want to see you again you keep out of my life." Another young man might well have been put off by her words, but not Richard Gregory. She was a beauty, no denying it, and well worth the effort. Patricia had many of Enid's fair features without being quite so lovely as Lorna, but she had appeal, there was no question of it.

Two days later they went for their lunch date. Richard didn't seem quite so kind and caring as Daniel, was often blunt in his observations, and lacked the thoughtfulness of her former boyfriend. And yet she liked him for it, as she realised his approach to life was bringing a surge of excitement into her feelings. He was clearly reckless, detested authority if it prevented him doing whatever he wanted to do, possessed a rebellious nature and could find something funny in almost everything.

Yes, she was warming to him. After a while she realised she had been laughing with him, he was quite funny and amusing and, unbeknown to her, her eyes were glowing brightly which in their turn excited him.

"Life's for living, pussy cat," he'd said, "and there's no point trying to live when you're dead." She was smiling broadly, something she rarely if ever did, and then laughing again, laughter having previously been consigned to history in her miserable life. Daniel was never like this, she reasoned, so why did I ever bother with him when there's blokes like this out there.

171

There was never going to be any question about her accepting his invitation for an evening out. This lunchtime had been a revelation in her sad life and she wanted more, much more. He worked in a garage, was mad keen on cars, owned a second-hand Triumph Herald and offered to take her for a spin. Unfortunately she was late back at work and given a final warning, and she found she couldn't care less. It was a very bright and breezy Patricia that worked in that shop that afternoon, and the manager couldn't understand the transformation, for she worked like a Trojan, efficiently and competently, and was cheerful and pleasant with the customers.

At the end of the day the manager complimented her and said she was withdrawing the final warning if she could maintain her new standards. Patricia wanted to tell her exactly what to do with her final warning but desisted, not through wisdom but in the belief her day might yet come, a day of release, a day of real freedom, a day when she would laugh in her manager's face, laugh at all authority, laugh at life itself.

An hour or so with irresponsible Richard had brought this on, but more time spent with him was to prove her downfall.

*** 

### Micky and Rita

After Norman's demise, and his note of condolence, Micky had to repel thoughts of wanting to get in touch with Enid in the hope of seeing her. She wouldn't be able to write anyway as Rita would know he'd received a communication. He'd been honest about the brief correspondence he'd shared with Enid immediately she'd lost Norman, but knew Rita was now wary and concerned, and he would do nothing to upset her, least of all with the wedding coming. His love and his life was with Rita, full stop. Enid might've had a happy marriage and might want to keep her memories secure and not sully them. No, he must put such nonsense out of his mind for all time.

And gradually that is what he did. By the time of their May wedding he had no thoughts at all for his childhood sweetheart. They had a short honeymoon at a small hotel in Orford, Suffolk, and returned home to Mrs Grant who had been cared for by Iris Coffey who stayed for those few days. But Rita's mother was giving cause for concern with her health going rapidly downhill. They realised she'd put on a brave face and tried so very hard to be at her best so that they could have their honeymoon, but now they regretted leaving her.

It was the people they were. Mrs Grant wanted nothing more than her daughter's happiness and had resolved, come hell or high water, she'd make sure they went away, but Rita and Micky felt that they'd done the wrong thing going on holiday. They both cared for 'mum' so much.

Within a few months Mrs Grant was rushed to hospital one Friday evening and the following Wednesday passed from this life to the next, Micky and Rita holding her hands as she slipped slowly away. They returned to Malford Grove and just sat quietly in a loving embrace as the sadness took its merciless grip on their emotions.

Mrs Grant had been an essential element of their lives and without her they knew there would be a void that nothing could fill.

Micky made the funeral arrangements, but the day was dogged, not by anything going wrong but by dreadful weather, pouring rain and high winds and, as it was a burial, it more or less soaked them all.

"Poor love," Rita murmured for the umpteenth time back at Malford Grove where they were looking after the mourners who'd wished to take refreshments. As it happened it was an opportunity for them all to dry out. "I don't think mum deserved that." she added. Micky put his arm around her shoulder and squeezed gently. He could think of no words and concluded he was better saying nothing.

"Knowing my mum she's probably in heaven now having a good laugh. She'd say something silly like 'that's life' or say it was the next best thing to being buried at sea! She's always liked a good laugh with us, didn't she, darling?" Micky squeezed again. He knew only too well what she was going through and that her brave words were her defence against the grief in her heart.

"I love you Micky." she whispered. "Please don't ever leave me, I couldn't stand the pain." He squeezed once more, and in that second suddenly thought of Enid. He eradicated the thought instantly. What an appalling thing to let happen, he admonished himself. He hadn't thought of her for ages, but today wasn't going to be the only time she invaded thoughts as he was to discover.

"I love you too much to ever leave you, you know that. It's just us now, but we have many happy memories of our times as a threesome, and we must cherish those memories more than ever. Mum'll always be with us, y'know, and if she's looking down at us now she'll be saying 'cheer up, you can't get rid of me that easily'." Rita giggled, sniffed and went over to see Iris Coffey and her husband David while Micky chatted with Syd and Moira Berry.

If Rita had wanted to admit it she was still worried about Enid, although she knew she had nothing to bother herself with. Micky was *her* husband now, he loved her dearly, deeply, and would never stray, she was so certain.

\*\*\*

*Enid*

Following Norman's funeral Enid had swiftly come to terms with the fact she was unnecessarily mourning a man she loathed and who had made her life a misery, so there was no point wasting tears, it was time to move on.

With the resolve she had demonstrated throughout her marriage she started to build the future and was able to devote herself entirely, and safely, to her beautiful daughters. Patricia was now her main concern. Her emotions had been pulled this way and that, and it was Patricia who wanted to visit the memorial gardens to see 'daddy's rose bush' from time to time, whereas Lorna didn't and, curiously perhaps, neither did Louisa.

As a family they'd decided on the rose bush and a simple plaque giving the names and dates. Patricia would've liked to add something about 'daddy' but couldn't come to terms with anything suitable so the idea was abandoned much to silent approval of the other three.

"Daddy bought me my piano, and it wasn't his money. It's not my piano at all," she'd wailed, adding that she didn't want to touch it again. Over the weeks Enid brought her round and finally she played again, but without the joy she'd once experienced.

Her mother thought Daniel a nice young man and began to feel he could be her deliverance from her anguish, but was conscious of the fact her daughter kept pushing him away and was therefore quite sorry when she packed him in. Patricia had always felt her dad would've set them up in a home, but was now repelled by the idea knowing that, in her mind, it would be someone else's money paying for it. No doubt Daniel was believed to be guilty by association in a plan the girl saw today as being sordid and unthinkable.

The arrival of Richard Gregory presented Enid with a whole new cupboard full of problems. He blotted his copybook from the outset when he called the first time, being brash, looking unkempt, calling Enid 'ma' and generally displaying no manners or courtesy whatsoever. And she shivered as he set off in his car at pace, screeching the tyres on departure, while her beloved daughter waved frivolously out the open window.

So matters were not helped when he brought her home at eleven thirty, and it was as well for him that he didn't come in. Enid was shaking with concern and fear, and overcome with relief when she walked through the door. But how to handle the situation? She felt enraged but knew she had to quell that instantly. Patricia was not yet of age and was therefore regarded as still being under parental control. To tell her off, to warn her, to be angry with her, none of these actions could be considered. Even to say she'd been worried about her might produce a fierce reaction. Calming she approached the girl in the hall.

"Hello love, hope you've had a good evening." Patricia walked past and went straight upstairs.

"Yes mum," she offered up on her way past, "Yes. Now I'm tired. Night." And she was gone.

Enid would have to tackle this when the time was right, and if Patricia reacted badly, so be it. She'd been worried sick and her daughter needed to understand that. And she would have to

175

put her foot down and restrict her evening movements, and that was bound to lead to unpleasantness, but it had to be done. She was under twenty-one and she'd jolly well have to do as she was told.

As she thought it all through she realised she would create a wall between herself and the girl and could see no way out of it. Then she remembered Dorothy. She'd give her a call tomorrow and ask her advice. Yes, that's what she'd do.

\*\*\*

Unlike Micky, who had washed away constant thoughts of his lost love, Enid had often turned her own thoughts in his direction. She'd considered what might have been, suffered regrets and had frequently laid awake at night pondering the matter over and over, but had never once believed there was any reason for them to meet. She had been surprised to receive his condolences.

Having said that, she'd kept herself busy and had otherwise little time to concentrate on her loss. It was the night times. That was when Micky invaded her mind and occasionally rendered sleep impossible. She'd abandoned the Spirella work, joined the local Townswomen's Guild, and become active in charity work as a volunteer as well as devoting much time to her girls. She'd widened her circle of friends and socialised a great deal more than she'd ever done during her marriage. In truth she was happy and content with her lot, but that didn't stop her fretting over Patricia.

The family had been to stay with Dorothy in Shropshire a couple of times during the summer months when Dorothy was not at school, Lorna in particular loving the adventure, spending much of her time horse riding, whereas Patricia was inclined to mope. For all that their hostess manged to bring out the best in the younger daughter. One of her successful ventures was to take Patricia to a neighbour who had an electric organ and the girl became fascinated by it, especially as the neighbour, Ian Gordon, was happy to devote much time to helping her learn to play the contraption.

Enid thought she might ask for one of her own, but she didn't, the memory of her father's purchase of the piano probably weighing against her making such a request, and Enid wasn't going to offer.

They also spent plenty of time at the chalet but both girls were losing interest, even in taking a weekend away there, and it was on the cards it might be sold in the near future.

Louisa Belham knew which side her bread was buttered and mostly behaved in an amiable way, save one instance when she tried to exert herself. Alone with Enid one evening she spoke up.

"You know Enid, you should be more beholden to me. If it hadn't been for Norman, my son remember, you wouldn't have all this to lord over, and I don't think it's right that you should rule the roost. Should be something we share, y'know. I should be the matriarch, in charge, y'see."

"Well, you're not. Norman provided for you in his will, and I'm stuck with you, and that's as far as it goes. You've got a home for life, Louisa, me to look after you, and I will ensure you don't go short of anything. That's my promise. But as for anything else, forget it. Now, I'm prepared to be friendly, and will always consult you about things that concern you, and I'm willing to be pleasant at all times. Why don't you decide to be just the same?" And she returned to reading her book. Louisa looked up from her knitting with a scowl, but said nothing, and since then had been bearable, even good company on occasion. No further words had ever been spoken on the subject.

*   *   *

Enid had a secret she kept hidden away in her bedroom, somewhere even the crafty Louisa Belham would not find it. And her mother-in-law was known to go prying when alone in the house. Under the edge of the carpet was an envelope and in it a newspaper cutting taken from the local and featuring a photograph of Micky's wedding day. He and his bride Rita pictured outside the church in Wanstead.

It was a treasured possession, often brought out and looked at, especially late at night when she wanted to try and cope with any particular sadness that might be engaging her at the time. Just now and then she would kiss Micky and refer to him as her darling. The wedding day had brought with it a final acceptance that she had lost him for good. He wouldn't have wanted her now anyway, she'd concluded; she was soiled goods.

She'd destroyed all her own wedding photos after Norman's death and was pleased to see the back of them, but Louisa, perhaps all rather pointedly, kept a framed one in her lounge as if to annoy Enid whenever she went in there. Lorna detested the sight of it, but Patricia often glanced in its direction, maybe considering the times he'd been a good father and mixing her emotions up by remembering how it all turned out.

At Enid's suggestion Lorna invited Philip Cullen round and was quite delighted with him. What a stark contrast with Richard Gregory! Was this where her elder daughter's future lay? She longed for Lorna to find love, happiness, contentment and peace, and hoped Philip might be the answer. She dreaded Richard being any sort of answer to Patricia's future.

Dorothy had listened intently to Enid's lengthy discourse on the subject of young Mr Gregory and Patricia's bad behaviour when coming home late, and had offered simple advice.

"Sit her down, speak quietly, tell her she can have her say afterwards, but you are speaking first. Remind her she's a minor, tell her what time you want her in of an evening, advise her of the sort of horrible things that can happen to a girl late at night, and explain that when you get to know her boyfriend better you may feel like granting her more leeway. If she behaves in the meantime. She's got her own income so you can't exactly threaten to stop her pocket-money, can you? Best not to threaten at all. If she asks what you're going to do if she doesn't follow the rules just say you're worried about her safety, but that as her mother your rules are binding."

The meeting did not go well. Unsurprisingly her daughter did not want to sit and listen, employing a sulky expression when eventually conceding and advising her mum that she had only two minutes to spare. Enid ignored that. Patricia kept interrupting until Enid stressed she was speaking first, then Patricia could have her turn. Having concluded her speech her mother waited for comment and waited in vain. Her daughter then rose and walked out calling back as she went.

"Can't stop me. You might think you can but you can't. I'll do as I please."

Later there was another call to Dorothy.

"Don't worry," her friend comforted, "I think you've won. Time will tell. Mind you, listen to me talking. All I do is teach them, not had any kids myself yet."

But she hadn't won. A few nights later Richard brought Patricia back at nearly one in the morning. Enid flew out of the front door as the car drew up, grabbed hold of the driver's door, and shouted at Richard, making sure he understood he must bring her home no later than ten-thirty.

She slammed the door, went round and took hold of her daughter's arm and pulled her indoors. Once inside the trouble really started.

"You're getting violent, like dad. Fine pair of parents I've had. That's the only answer you've got. Violence, and I've had enough of it. Maybe you hit him as hard as he hit you. Maybe you two fought all the time. Perhaps that's it." She pouted her lips, crossed her arms in front of her in a show of defiance, and looked away from her mother. Enid sat in one of the kitchen chairs and decided, right or wrong, on her course of action. When she spoke it was with softness but firmness. At least the girl hadn't stomped off upstairs.

"Patricia, what I do I do because I love and care for you. I am always here for you, will help you in any way I can. This is our home, your home, but we all have to abide by some sort of rules out of consideration for each other. Because I love you I worry about you when you're out like that, and I don't want anything to happen to you. If you stayed out even later what time should I phone the police? You might be in dire need of help, don't you understand?"

"Mum, I'm out at work, old enough to run my own life. Richard's been with me all evening and brought me home. It's not as if I have to walk home in the dark all by myself." Enid chose not to ask where she'd been. Patricia continued. "I won't be dictated to, I won't," and she turned to look straight at her mother seeing, for the first time, the tears flowing down Enid's cheeks. "Oh mum, I'm sorry….." and she came round the table and hugged Enid. "Mum, I'm sorry, I'm sorry. I know you had a bad time with dad, and I don't want us to be rowing all the time. We'll just finish up saying rotten things to each other just to be nasty." At that moment Lorna appeared having been woken by the to-do, and asking what the hell was going on.

The upshot was that the three of them retired to the lounge where they sat together and spoke openly and freely about the situation for the next hour or so. The discussion unfortunately produced no agreeable outcome, Lorna siding with their mother, and her sister arguing every point with the verve and commitment of a teenager who believes she knows it all and is right. Enid was desperate to avoid the girls falling out, but knew she had to make her feelings clear, and almost wished Lorna would take issue with her on certain points in order to establish a rapport with her sister.

But it wasn't to work out like that. With reluctance Patricia accepted that which must be leaving Enid to hope it would come good, but dreading that it wouldn't. And in time, of course, it didn't.

# Chapter Eighteen

At the second attempt Lorna passed her driving test. Enid wanted to lend her the money for a car but realised that would create a tricky situation with Patricia, so let her take her own when she wanted to go out. Having sold both of the original vehicles she now had a two-tone Vauxhall Victor that looked elegant in its pleasant greens, and which was practical for the family, comfortable with space enough for four and with plenty of room in the boot.

Phillip Cullen had his own transport and he and Lorna went about in that, so Lorna's use of the Victor was actually rare. Patricia showed no signs of wanting to drive.

And then, over one Sunday dinner, Patricia managed to unintentionally sow seeds that swiftly grew in Enid's mind.

"Don't know why we've got to live here. I hate it. Everything seems so false now. It's like my childhood was false. Dad looked after me but he was bad. I hate everything about this house. All my memories here, all false. Why can't we move away? Let's go somewhere nice, somewhere different, leave all this behind us, leave all the lies here. We could move up to Buckhurst Hill. Richard lives there; it's really nice." Her last line may have revealed an ulterior motive, of course, but the suggestion struck a chord with her mother.

Enid had been considering a move, but primarily for financial reasons. She knew she would have to find work, even if only part-time, to boost her income, and there could be money to be made from leaving Broadwalk. After her husband's demise it had always been her intention to be away when the time was right. The money wouldn't last forever. Their home was in a sought-after location and would be in demand, without a doubt, although she questioned in her mind if the purchase of a property in Buckhurst Hill would yield much profit. Another classy area, she mused.

Nonetheless, the idea was worth exploring, especially as Louisa Belham voiced her dislike of the prospect, and Lorna approved of it. The matter made for a lengthy conversation after dinner, and appeared to gain much favour, although obviously not from Enid's mother-in-law.

\*\*\*

Micky and Rita were not a childless couple through choice, and it saddened them to think they might never share the joy of a family. It had also perplexed Micky that Rita remained at Williams and Co, not from the point of view that she would ever divulge closely guarded information about his business, but that it didn't seem right to him that she was employed by a firm he did business with. When he discussed it with her she'd dismissed it as a sign of being old-fashioned and that hurt. He was always very proud of keeping standards he regarded as becoming increasingly irrelevant if not lost altogether, and that included matters of courtesy, decency and plain good manners.

In a quiet moment he had deliberated the problems he felt society would be creating for itself in the years to come if those standards were allowed to slip, and they were on a slippery slope right now. His wife regarding him as old-fashioned, and doing so all too often, was becoming a sore point, despite her comments usually being light-hearted and otherwise inoffensive.

Right now Micky had a completely different problem to contend with, and one that was causing him embarrassment, with the likelihood he would not be able to attend to his business. He had developed extremely uncomfortable haemorrhoids and was going to need hospital treatment, possibly a stay of some days, and it worried him sick.

But help was at hand. He'd recently taken the lock-up garages at Loughton and now employed a man to help him there. Ray Farnham lived a stone's throw away and had proved himself a good asset being able to turn his hand easily to the various tasks, such as pulling the batteries and keeping everything in good order, leaving Micky free to expand the business successfully.

Ray was quite easy-going, pleasant, hard-working. He could follow instructions but lacked the imagination to be innovative and was, frankly, content with his lot. He did erect a cubby-hole, as he called it, in a corner of one of the garages that served as both an on-site office and his personal staff-room. Micky was happy for him to do so, and often joined him there for a morning or afternoon brew.

There was another side to Mr Farnham. He was a would-be jazz pianist, and played in a small band that secured few bookings, perhaps in consequence of being rather poor performers, but which nonetheless pressed on enjoying themselves even if their entertainment value was low. He also had a driving licence so would be able to make calls in Micky's van in his boss's absence.

Micky now had a one-ton Commer van which suited his business perfectly. He fretted about his enforced absence, for that was Micky all over, but he'd introduced Ray to Rita and knew the two of them would keep things going successfully. But he worried as that was his character. It was, after all, his own business, his baby, and he detested being called away from it.

He'd already avoided jury service by explaining that his business would collapse and, thankfully, they had more jurors than they needed that day so he was excused.

In time Micky was admitted to the Jubilee Hospital at Woodford Green and operated on. His recovery was assured, just as Rita and Ray ensured his business barely suffered.

*** 

Meanwhile Louisa Belham solved a difficulty for Enid by dying from a stroke, and doing so swiftly and without inconvenience to anyone. Her funeral was treated with respect but precious little sadness.

Enid then found a delightful house in Loughton, small but adequate, and in a lovely location, that appealed to all three of them and she put in an offer, instantly accepted. The house in Broadwalk looked like being snapped up and a substantial profit seemed set to be realised. The sale and purchase went ahead smoothly and at long last they were free of the past. And with an appreciable boost to the family's income assured.

Patricia was happy. She was close to Richard at neighbouring Buckhurst Hill. Lorna was happy, being able to use mum's car for work, although she could also take the train or bus with ease.

Enid was happy and her conscience was clear. This was now her home, her *own* home and she had left behind her dreadful past and could rebuild.

But it seemed that in Enid's world happiness was never allowed to remain uninterrupted for long, and sure enough Patricia's blossoming relationship with Richard re-emerged as a potential vehicle for trouble. The girl had given up her job when they moved and was now employed in a coffee bar in Loughton, and her life appeared to be going nowhere in particular, with Enid convinced her boyfriend was bad news. She'd had enough with Norman being into criminal activities and with their dire consequences, and she was blowed if her daughter was going to be caught up in anything underhand. Richard Gregory exuded 'underhand'.

Then came that dreadful Saturday evening when Patricia didn't come home at all. A phone call at about 11.45 p.m. did nothing to placate an irate and distressed mother, least of all when her daughter simply explained she'd be home some time Sunday, not to worry, and had then hung up just as Enid was ordering her home. Seething, livid with rage, stamping up and down the hall, Enid only calmed when Lorna used all her consoling powers to get her mother to control herself.

She knew where Richard lived. She'd met his parents once and they did not appeal to her in the slightest, his mother showing great insensitivity, perhaps deliberately, by referring to her being the widow of 'that criminal' who was drowned. Right. She knew what she'd do. Drive to Buckhurst Hill and confront them, indeed she would. Lorna declined to come and did her best to persuade her not to, but to no avail.

It was a largely wasted trip. The door wasn't opened to her and the wretched woman stuck her head out of an upstairs window to tell Enid she had no idea where Richard was, so didn't know where Patricia was either. But apparently Richard often stayed out, so what? Before Enid could tell her she'd closed the window. Enid drove home and sat in the lounge all night, angry and worried sick, and eventually fell asleep around seven in the morning. Lorna had waited up but gone to bed once she felt her mother was reasonably settled. Even she laid awake, dreading the bust-up that was sure to follow on Sunday, concerned equally for her mum and sister, and frustrated that she had no idea how to quell the storm.

It was as if her mother wanted to be over-protective and consequently picked holes in everything Patricia did, whereas her sister seemed determined to wind mum up to encourage the very violence that epitomised her father. It did appear that her sister harboured this concept that by making her mother out to be as unpleasant as her dad she could suppress some of the hatred she felt for Norman.

Their father had gone to great lengths to ingratiate himself with both daughters throughout their childhoods, and poor Patricia could still not reconcile her memories of him with the awful truth. Lorna knew this but could not talk to her sister about it. She'd tried. Tried several times but without success, for Patricia would cut her dead and walk away leaving her sister gasping with the sadness of it all and close to tears, tears of defeat, tears of dread.

Finally, that night, sleep overcame her until she was woken by Enid who thankfully looked much calmer this sunny, bright morning, and who was clearly more in control.

"What can we do, mum? Does there have to be a row? You're always on at her. Can't we find a better way of sorting this out?"

"Am I? Am I really always on at her?" Enid sounded as if she didn't believe it for one minute and was ready to deny it.

"That's the way it seems to her, mum, even if you're not or don't mean to be. I thought we'd all be so happy. Dad's gone, we've moved here ….."

"Yes, my pet but it's your sister who is spoiling it. And I admit I don't know how to talk her round. I've tried accepting the situation in the hope she sees me as supportive but perhaps that's only made matters worse. She doesn't seem to understand that I worry about her being out all night, especially when she's with Richard. He's bad news, Lorna, surely you can see that?"

"Yes mum, but she's rebelling. She's seeing how far she can push you. Every time she does something wrong you're much too firm, sometimes raising your voice, and I'm certain she sees her father in those moments, you know, that time he really hit her, and she thinks you'll turn out to be just the same.

"Dad pretended to be nice to us to get at you, you told me he did, so Patricia thinks when you're nice you're hiding your real self. Can't you see it mum?" With reluctance Enid could see some truth in those words, and could also see what a lovely person Lorna had become. So perceptive, so understanding, so intelligent. Such insight for one so young. And yet, of course, she was just shy of her twenty-first birthday. She was a woman in her own right. Lorna had grown up, faced the problems of her life and overcome them, and was ready for the future. Enid could be proud of her, and pleased that all her efforts had paid off. No, she didn't have a good, well-paid job with prospects, but she was happy with the horses and had formed an attachment with Philip who was a much better proposition than Richard Gregory.

"Yes," she sighed, "I think you're right. You have some of the common sense I've always credited Auntie Dorothy with, and she's been a great guide for me over the years." They both chuckled. "And you have wisdom ahead of your years….."

"Then I have inherited it from you, mum." They laughed together then hugged. "Whatever can we do about sis? I don't want to witness another row."

"And you shall not. I am quite resolved. But we'll have to play it by ear, not rehearse it. She'll be expecting an explosion when she gets here, but by the same token, you're quite right, if I am too kind she will see it as some kind of façade. Let's have some breakfast, come on." And she led the way downstairs to the kitchen.

*** 

Enid's father, Peter Campton, would be retiring soon and he and his wife, Maggie, had been contemplating moving away from London and finding an attractive bungalow for their autumn years. With their daughter now in Loughton the couple decided to seek something north of there, but out in the country, yet not remote, and had not been able to locate their ideal retirement home since it probably didn't exist other than in their dreams.

However, they found just what they wanted and did so by chance, for it bore no resemblance to those dreams being a delightful country cottage, not a bungalow, to start with. It was

186

just outside Coopersale which itself was just outside Epping, so it had many convenience factors in its favour, not least Epping having a rail connection to Loughton. It wasn't strictly rural but it was good enough and it was close to shops.

They were acquainted with Enid's problems but could offer little practical help from experience as Enid had been such a well-behaved and likeable child who did as she was told and rarely required much admonishment. The thought of a daughter who was disobedient and rude was anathema to them and they had to confess to each other that they might have been at a loss had Enid turned out that way.

Sale and purchase of properties agreed they were planning the move itself when Patricia's latest escapade came to light, Enid phoning them that Sunday morning before the recalcitrant girl arrived home. They could offer no advice, just comfort and support, and it was woefully short of value at that precise moment. Enid said her goodbyes and put the phone down with a long exhalation of air. Next on her list was Dorothy.

Dorothy had ideas but lacked the experience of her own children. Basically the only piece of sound advice was not to be aggressive, not to malign Richard, although such a measure was well called for, and to insist they have a brief discussion with open minds. Yes, it was Dorothy's much praised common sense but somehow it simply wasn't right in the circumstances, and Enid found herself no further down the road.

And then there was a screech from the road as Richard dropped Patricia outside and made good his own escape. He didn't actually help matters with his passing comment as she alighted.

"There's a naughty girl. Go and let mummy smack your bottom." It was intended as a light-hearted piece of sarcasm, but she was not in the mood to appreciate any humour it might have had, and was working herself up ready for the usual upbraiding with a great deal of additional scolding to match the occasion. She'd wanted him to come in and apologise and take all the blame but he was having none of it.

She'd had a great time at the party, dancing into the small hours, getting slightly inebriated, sharing fun and laughter with the crowd, Richard's friends, and being overtly passionate with her boyfriend when chance permitted. It was from an upstairs bedroom that she had phoned her mother. She'd never been to Theydon Bois before, and the house they were in seemed astonishingly palatial. It was all a very new and astonishing experience. After the party they walked, or rather staggered to another friend's house nearby where they went to bed together for the first time. She was not used to drinking alcohol and had too much so was largely beyond caring what happened, and was too tipsy to derive any pleasure from it.

As it was she was later sick over the bed and left to sleep on the floor while Richard cleared up. The morning brought her first ever hangover, and she was not happy to be shaken awake when all she wanted to do was die. He gave her some headache pills, saying he needed to collect his car from up the road and take her home, so she wasn't best pleased with him as what she assumed would be the day from hell started to unfurl. But by the time they arrived in Loughton the throbbing headache had disappeared although her head still hurt.

Letting herself in she was confronted by her sister.

"Patricia, it's okay. Mum's not angry or anything. We just want to sit quietly and chat. Put things right for all of us." It was all the girl needed to hear. Oh God, she thought, I can do without this. I just want to go to bed till I feel better. Then Lorna surprised her.

"If you're tired and want to rest, have some peace and quiet, whatever you want is okay. We can talk later." Patricia studied her through eyes that were not focusing properly while she weighed up this latest ruse, for such she considered it to be. Then she spoke.

"Okay. I'll go to bed then mum can have her two-penneth later, and you can add whatever you want, goody-two-shoes. Oh God, I'm sick of it all." She swayed slightly then slowly made her way upstairs to her bedroom, slamming the door and regretting it at once as the sound reverberated through her sore head.

Enid and Lorna said little, for there was little to say, and they idled their time away until Patricia came to join them early afternoon. They had no appetite so sustained themselves with hot drinks and biscuits, and occupied themselves by doing odd little jobs around the house when the mood took them. There were no thoughts for their Sunday roast and the meal remained unprepared. Lorna had been shocked by her sister's appearance but had said nothing to her mother who had diplomatically stayed out of the way.

And about half-past one they heard Patricia pay a short visit to the bathroom and then make her weary way downstairs.

\*\*\*

Micky was back home and recovering swiftly, being particularly well looked after by his wife, and was longing to get to work. How he'd missed it! There was no denying it; Rita and Ray had done magnificently, Rita also benefitting from Mrs Stevens help with the housework. It was a large property and Rita was starting to wonder if they ought to think about moving. The bungalow was ideal when her mother was alive and equally ideal for the family they seemed doomed not to have. But it had come to represent sadness in some strange way, its emptiness emphasising their feelings of loneliness now Mrs Grant and passed away and the longed-for children had not arrived.

They were not God-fearing people but did believe if they were not to be blessed with a family then there was nothing to be done, and so sought no medical advice, accepting their loss with a reasonably good grace. After all, they had each other, and that was a blessing of the highest order.

Micky had become aware, from the local paper, that Enid's house was for sale and had periodically passed by the estate agent until the word 'sold' had been appended to the picture in his window. And then he knew she was off, but had no idea where. It had been tempting to ask Mrs Stevens but of course he couldn't do that, so he was left to try and understand why, when he had a lovely, wonderful wife, and it was all such a long time ago, he was still interested. Sadly he didn't know.

Rita was unaware of all this, satisfied he was over Enid for good and had forgotten her completely. Strangely, perhaps, in all the time they had lived so close to each other, coincidence had never brought them face to face, not even the occasion when he saved Lorna's life and took her home. However, Enid living in

Loughton a stone's throw from Micky's garages was to be the medium by which a coincidental meeting would come about when the dying embers of fires would be re-ignited and potentially bring no happiness to anyone.

At Williams & Co Sybil Harris was now held in some esteem, especially by Rita and the boss, Mr Gaffney. Both felt circumstances had kept her in check. Perhaps her parents, particularly the garrulous Mrs Harris, had held her back in some way, and maybe she had rebelled at school and found herself in all sorts of trouble. Rita often recalled Micky's humorous telling of the tale of Sybil's slippering at the hands of the headmistress and wondered how the situation had reached the need for painful retribution. Was Sybil simply marked down as a bad lot at school? And was her mother actually to blame? Micky thought it all rather funny at the time, but Rita would nowadays look at the pleasant, efficient and caring Sybil and feel sorry for her dreadful past, knowing she might not have been as black as she'd been painted. Poor girl.

Right now Rita was delighted for her as Peter Collis had proposed, been accepted, and she looked set to enjoy a very bright future. Peter had even, in a lovely old-fashioned way, been to see her parents to seek permission to ask for her hand in marriage. Oh, how romantic, thought Rita, how very 'Jane Austen'. Just like Micky she mused.

Rita was one of life's romantics, but enough of a realist to know life didn't always work out quite like that. She had a sneaking admiration for the story of Micky and Enid and believed that in a romantic novel they would finish up together, and that belief always brought a pang of pain to her heart. She herself could not have dared hope for such a magnificent man as she thought him to be. Honest, hard-working, loving and true. Thoughtful, caring and considerate. And so right and proper. How had she landed this vision of perfection? She still felt unworthy, and was often disturbed to think that Enid was still out there, and now a widow and therefore a threat, although in her heart of hearts she knew she had no reason to think that.

But perhaps a sixth sense was niggling at her. Maybe it was.

\*\*\*

"I just want us to sit and talk about what each of us wants, our needs, things we dislike, what is important to us, anything like that, Patricia. Please just say whatever you want. Let's just come to an agreement. We're a family, we live together as a family, we love each other, let's look at the good and the bad, eh?" Patricia looked sulky. She wanted to lead her own life as she saw fit and didn't need a discussion about it. "And we're all adults now. I want to treat you as an adult, Patricia, but most of all I want to treat you the way you want to be treated. I only ask that you have some consideration for me and your sister." Patricia was pouting her lips and swinging the leg she had crossed over the other. There was silence for several minutes.

"Okay," she said. "Okay. Here it is. I'm grown up, and you treat me like a child. I hate it. I'm an adult. I want to come and go as I please and not be questioned about it, and certainly not have to have a silly inquest like this." Enid kept herself under control, but only just.

"Agreed. I'm sorry for my behaviour, Patricia. There, I can't say more than that, can I? You can do as you please." Lorna looked shocked. "All I ask is that I know where you are and when you are going to stay out all night. If you want to tell me who you're with that's up to you. Because I love you beyond words I worry about you and want nothing terrible to befall you. If I give you your freedom could you not have some consideration for my feelings please? That's all I ask." If Lorna was shocked Patricia had the appearance of someone who had seen a ghost and was horrified by the spectre. Regaining her composure she asked:

"Right, what's the catch?"

"None. I mean what I say. Your freedom but with consideration for a loving mother. That's give and take, isn't it? What loving relationships are all about?" Patricia pondered all this. There just had to be a catch, there just had to be.

"And what about goody-two-shoes over there? Is this an excuse to give her whatever *she* wants?" Enid answered at once, determined to keep the upper hand she'd gained.

"Lorna considers my feelings before she does anything. I don't do anything without consulting both of you, you both know that. Lorna, is there any way I can improve things for you?" This stunned her elder daughter who had to think quickly.

"Yes, I'd like you to lend me the money for a car. I'll pay you back what I can afford monthly."

"Alright, I'll do that. Patricia?"

"Want an electric organ. Dad bought me a piano. I want an organ as a present. Not a loan to buy one."

"Fine, I'll do that if Lorna agrees." Lorna agreed. "And it's only fair, then, that I give Lorna the money for the car, rather than make it a loan." The carpet was out from under Patricia's feet and she knew it, and also recognised it as, in her opinion, a set up job. Had her mum and sister been planning this? The more she thought about it the less it seemed likely. They weren't to know what her answers might have been. It was time to concede. Up to a point.

"Okay. Sounds like we have an agreement." Patricia was full of pomp and brimming with confidence. "I'd like to bring Richard here whenever I like, and if he stays he stays in my room." Patricia was committed to extracting all that she could from this new arrangement. She did not want her mum to celebrate victory.

"That's acceptable," Enid replied at once, despite the fact it was anything but. Nevertheless, she was resolute in her belief that she must win at all costs. Patricia smiled inwardly and decided to put this new freedom to the test as soon as possible. Presumably Lorna would be allowed to bring Philip home for the night whenever she wished, but then goody-two-shoes wouldn't upset mum like that. And at long last the first pangs of guilt washed through Patricia's mind. She was still a special mum and, deep down, Patricia loved her. It had to be true that mum had endured beatings to prevent the girls from suffering cruelty at dad's hands. She could hardly recall anytime when her mum had given her the slightest slap, and now she knew her mother had taken horrific beatings in her stead. Emotionally overcome Patricia, feeling some remorse, rose slowly and went to her mum's side and hugged her as the tears fell. Lorna just sat there looking relieved, and knowing a gulf had been crossed and all might yet be well. And so it proved to be.

Enid had one more task to perform. She'd told them about the 'birds and bees' at an earlier stage in their teen years and now she stressed the need for 'safety' and 'protection'. Patricia giggled and Lorna looked embarrassed. "And one more thing; I am not spending a fortune on either of you. Let's call it an early Christmas present. You can both make do with second-hand goods at the right price."

"That's alright, mum," Patricia interjected, "Richard can find sis a great car at a good price and he can service it and so on." Neither Enid nor Lorna looked impressed but both let the matter pass.

# Chapter Nineteen

*Lorna's 21$^{st}$ birthday*

Lorna did not want anything special by way of a party but Enid was not of the same mind so a number of relatives and friends were invited, despite the house being much smaller than their Broadwalk property, and therefore more cramped.

Although there had been some concerns Richard Gregory found Lorna a delightful second-hand Hillman Imp, which she adored and was quite proud of. Her mother bitterly resented paying Richard for it, but as it was actually being sold by the garage he worked at, and the formal receipt came from there, her conscience was eased as she believed it must all be above board. He did, however, bring discredit to himself by telling Patricia he'd earned commission on the sale and offering her the proceeds which she readily refused. That was her mum's money. It didn't mean much more at the time, but it did later on.

Patricia herself was becoming proficient at her electric organ. From the outset she'd marvelled at the idea of having pedals you could play, to say nothing of the many switches that brought about changes in sound so that you could imitate different instruments. Enid found her a local tutor, Edna Cammel, who had been advertising in a newsagent's window. By this medium they learned that Edna played in a jazz band, usually on trombone, and that her band was amateur by every definition, not least that it wasn't very good and consequently rarely secured a booking.

But they were an enthusiastic bunch. Edna herself was very accomplished on the organ and was an ideal teacher. She told them the band had a pianist, Ray Farnham, which was why she played trombone. And she demonstrated one day that she was very accomplished with that as well, the three Belham's applauding with gusto and appreciation.

Lorna and Philip's relationship was steady and blossoming gently, Lorna still harbouring wariness where any human being was involved. At long last she received her first ever Valentine's card, and it was a beautiful handmade creation containing the loveliest of words. Her friend Cathy now boasted no fewer than three boyfriends, very fickle, meaningless arrangements, leaving Lorna in no doubt whatsoever that her friend's definition of fidelity was at odds with her own.

Enid was looking for a suitable 21$^{st}$ birthday card in Loughton High Road when something quite extraordinary happened. She came face to face with Micky.

They recognised each other immediately and time stopped still. Nobody else existed. The sounds of the traffic, the people, all disappeared as they stood, almost open-mouthed, two feet from each other.

***

"Enid, it is you, isn't it?" All she could do was nod once. "You haven't changed." There were no more words as they stared at each other unable to move. Micky knew he wanted to embrace her, kiss her, and knew he could not. Enid wanted nothing more than to be held and knew no such thing would happen. Eventually she found the power of speech.

"Hello Micky. How are you? How is your wife?" The words she spoke brought pain to her heart, and she realised she was dreading the reply.

"I'm okay Enid, thanks for asking." He ignored the reference to his wife. "How are you? Sorry about your husband…. "

"Micky, I've never thanked you for saving Lorna's life," she blurted out. There was more silence as they both thought back to that day in South Woodford. Their eyes were locked together. Enid's words were gasped swiftly, nervously, for they were the only words she could think of. He had, after all, saved her precious daughter.

"Pleased I could help," he stuttered, "she's okay I assume?" Enid regained some composure.

"Yes … yes, and nearly twenty-one." Both were trembling, both had a lump in their throats, both were speaking shakily.

"Is she still as beautiful? As beautiful as her mother?" Enid knew the tears were welled up and knew she must not let the dam burst. Micky's words cut through her and tore her heart apart. In that moment she wished Lorna was their child. How happy they

195

would've been. If only she'd waited, if only. She could think of no words to reply, nothing she could speak, and Micky recognised the torture and acknowledged he was responsible and regretted his reckless, thoughtless question instantly.

"Enid, I'm sorry, it was a careless thing to ask. I'm sorry."

"No, no, no …. it wasn't. Lorna is as lovely as can be, her sister Patricia likewise." She was stumbling hopelessly through a minefield of words and getting it all wrong. "Do you have children Micky?" she almost squealed through the pain, the helplessness etched in her face.

"No, Enid. None. Here, what are you doing in Loughton anyway?" He wanted to change the subject.

"Oh, live here now, moved … you know …. from Broadwalk…."

"Right. I see." Then, after a pause, "I'm still at Malford Grove, don't know if you knew that, knew I was there, Enid."

"Yes …. yes, Lorna told me after …. well, after the incident near Gowan Lea, you know…."

"Yes. And she's doing okay?" It seemed like neutral territory and Micky hoped it was.

"Yes, works at the stables near Snaresbrook station. Do you know it?"

"I do, or at least I know there are stables there. Does she like horses then?"

"That's right. Loves them." More silence.

In time they abandoned their efforts at conversation and agreed there was nothing to be gained from further discourse and that they should part without detailed debate. And so they went their separate ways, saddened, unhappy and emotionally distraught.

Enid completely forgot about the birthday card and walked home in a dazed state, full of confusion. Micky walked back to his garages, his main worry being a matter of conscience and decency as he wrestled with the problem as to whether or not he should tell Rita.

\*\*\*

196

Patricia and Richard had been trying to dream up a special present for Lorna and had come to the conclusion that something horsey might be appropriate. There the thinking ran out for neither of them knew enough about horses. But auntie Dorothy did: time to phone her.

Auntie Dorothy was frivolous, first suggesting a horse itself, and then an engraved saddle.

"Oh auntie, can't you be serious?" pleaded Patricia.

"Yes, that's very naughty of me, but I am in a good mood and I must tell you my news. I am going to have a baby at long last. What d'you think of that? Do tell your mum and Lorna, won't you?"

"Wow, that's wonderful news. What does it feel like? I mean …. oh, I don't know what I mean, but congratulations anyway. That's brilliant. How does uncle Max feel?"

"He's a dog with two tails. We are so happy, you cannot imagine. A child at last. We're both deliriously happy."

"I'm so pleased for you auntie …."

"Now Patricia, you're grown up, so forget the auntie bit, just call me Dorothy, please."

"So, anyway Dorothy, what does it feel like?"

"Well, I'm just so happy. But I will have to be looked after, being pregnant at my age. I think I'm over the hill…. "

"No, of course you're not. I'm so happy for you, I really am. But do they think there's a problem, you know, the doctors?"

"Don't think so, just being cautious at my age. Anyway, how are you getting on with Richard? Any wedding bells on the horizon?"

"Dorothy! Really!" She heard Dorothy laugh. "No, no, not at all, and I don't think mum would approve."

"You might just be wrong there. All I ask is make sure he's right for you. And that's all your mum wants. She's simply worried about you and I expect most mothers are the same when it comes to daughters' boyfriends, you know, being a bit too critical, but she'll be alright, trust me. But please make sure he's the special one for you. Do you love him dearly?"

"Dorothy, of course I do, but we're not planning marriage or anything this early. But I know he loves me and he's not rushing me."

"Pleased to hear it. Now, back to Lorna. Let me sleep on it and I'll ring you tomorrow. By the way, how's the organ playing?"

"It's great, it really is, and Edna's brilliant. She can really play and she's teaching me well. I'm getting an interest in jazz too, so all going well, Dorothy." Their conversation ended soon after, leaving Patricia to muse on this new intelligence that her mother might actually approve of her marrying Richard. She still thought it unlikely. She was also bothered that someone who was old enough to be an aunt ought to be too old to have a baby, but then anyone over the age of thirty was considered to be old by her definitions, so a woman of over forty was ancient! Not that she thought her mum or Dorothy to be in that category. It was the way the young tended to look upon their elders, almost as if they believed they might never grow old themselves.

***

Philip Cullen had been thinking about many things, not just Lorna's coming of age, but about his true feelings for her and what the future might hold. Yes, he did think about wanting to be married to her, but nevertheless thought himself unworthy and incapable of ever asking her. It had taken him so long before he asked her out, frightened of rejection, afeared for her reaction, and the prospect of asking her to become his wife must therefore surely lie sufficiently far ahead that he might lose her to someone else in the meantime. It was a quandary.

He loved her quite passionately, cared for her and her feelings, and adored her, not just for her beauty, but for being the loveliest of people, and he treasured that. He cherished her but was aware her beauty was against him, for she must certainly attract other men, not that he'd any evidence of her interest in others. But didn't she have a face that would have any good artist reaching for the paint brushes? Any good poet waxing lyrical in a way he could never hope to replicate? Any good author similarly painting a picture with words? He would lose her, he knew he would.

In fact he had no chance of losing her. She loved him beyond words but was careful not to say too much for fear that he might slip through her fingers, and her one and only love be swept away forever, and she couldn't bear the thought of losing him. She wanted him desperately and longed for him to propose. But he was eternally shy and she was over-cautious. Both secretly harboured the hope that some event or other might force the matter to a head, little realising such a medium was now within touching distance. But it wasn't to be Lorna's birthday that did it.

\*\*\*

Ray had left early, as previously arranged, and now Micky sat in the cubby hole nursing a mug of coffee before tidying up and heading for home. He looked around at his stock in this particular garage and wondered how his business might fare in the future. Perhaps it was time to have a second string to his bow, another interest that could yield profit, even if a low income to start with. Competition in the metal trade was growing apace, and it attracted those whose who were less than scrupulous as well as those who were not averse to engaging in illegal or highly suspect practices.

He occasionally fell foul of them. Only recently he'd taken a drum of gunmetal borings to Williams & Co who'd discovered the gunmetal was a cover for iron waste which made up two-thirds of the content. He had to refund Williams the difference and he was concerned about how much the incident had damaged his own reputation, not that he needed to worry as Rita and Mr Gaffney had re-assured him, but that was Micky, utterly honest. The firm he'd bought the borings from had deceived him, used him. That didn't prevent Syd Berry having a good go at him, but that was Syd all over and nothing much to bother about.

Then there was his other little difficulty: Enid. He'd already decided on the truth, tell his wife he'd bumped into her in Loughton as that was, apparently, where she now lived, and say they shared the briefest of conversation before going their separate ways. The only problem he had with that perfectly honest recollection of the encounter was that Rita might think he took his garages in Loughton to be near her.

No, she wouldn't think like that. Would she? Of course not! But all kinds of doubts ran through his mind. Perhaps it might be best not to mention it at all. Maybe. Not disclosing it wasn't lying, was it? Puzzles, puzzles, puzzles, life's full of puzzles and problems he concluded as he washed his mug and started clearing up.

At Malford Grove he walked through the kitchen door to be greeted by one of Rita's most disarming smiles and a fabulous kiss to follow. That decided it. He wouldn't mention his meeting with Enid. Not necessary. But the deceit, as he felt it was, niggled at him for days. It would be hard to imagine that Enid could have been a better wife than the one in his arms, and in all probability Rita was the better of the two. Didn't he love her to the moon and back? Wasn't she the most wonderful thing that had ever happened to him? He couldn't have it both ways. If Rita was the best then Enid was to be forgotten at all costs. He'd shared such a happy and rewarding marriage with Rita, it had been quite sensational really, and he could not spoil it. Nobody would ever know how it might have worked out with Enid. He must forget her.

Back in Loughton Enid's daze remained in place most of the evening. She did silly things without thinking, served up their dinner without cooking the carrots at all, knocked over her coffee cup in the lounge afterwards, and appeared to Lorna to be on a completely different planet.

"Mum, whatever's the matter with you? For heaven's sake. "

"I'm okay, I'm okay, perhaps just a bit tired. Got a lot on my mind. Doing too much thinking and not concentrating on what I'm doing. Sorry, but I'm okay. I'll have an early night and try and get a good night's sleep." Lorna wondered if that was going to be the answer. Her mother was distant and seemed to be thinking about one thing in particular, an absolute distraction, whatever it was, and that was Lorna's interpretation of Enid's behaviour.

"You're going round the bend, mum," was Patricia's unhelpful assessment, but it brought grins to all three of them, even if only temporarily so. But Enid's thoughts were too flooded with her chance meeting to be easily washed clean, and she instantly relapsed into her weird state, looking vacantly across the room, tapping the arm of her chair with her fingers. Lorna knew that it was one matter that her mother was obsessed with but had no idea what it could be. She tried asking again later, when they were alone, mentioning her theory, but mum brushed the concept aside assuring her a good night's rest would do the trick.

"I'll be back to normal in time for breakfast," she'd added with a cheery but unconvincing smile.

***

Micky's evening, in contrast, was completely dissimilar. His own mind was at peace and he rarely recalled the meeting, enjoying a roast pork dinner and a very pleasant evening with Rita, reading, watching the television, having a game of cards, chatting about work, the garden, the state of the country (which they put to rights), and finally immersing themselves in a lovers' cuddle on the settee before bedtime.

With that they retired and fell asleep in each other's arms, happy and contented. It was past one in the morning that Enid drifted away. She had her early night but had been cuddling a pillow since then, eyes closed, and in a world of her own, a world where she and Micky had been wed and revelled in a trouble-free marriage, full of undying, unbounded love and devotion, blessed of course with two lovely daughters. She didn't want that aspect to be any different. It never occurred to her they might have had sons, or one daughter, one son. Or more than two children. It never occurred to her that it might not have been an ideal union in the end. Who would ever know? She was just intoxicated with a dream she'd had since he came back from Japan and surprised them all. Came back too late, that is.

What a hopeless, pointless dream it had all been, but she simply couldn't see it as such.

Come the morning she was indeed restored. She'd have to get that card she'd forgotten, and there were a hundred and one other things she needed to do, and she now applied herself to the real world, and her real life, Micky's memory safely returned to the special casket in her mind where it dwelled most of the time and where it was no trouble.

201

***

*The Party*

The celebration, when it finally arrived, went very well. The house was packed, with the weather, pouring rain, precluding use of the garden. They still managed to find room for a small dance-floor and although pop music throbbed most of the time Patricia played a melody of lively tunes the 'oldies' could dance to. And also accompanied a sing-song.

Philip was there, as was his mother. Richard also, but he upset Patricia by spending much of the time chatting to other people much to her annoyance. She rectified this in her own way by grabbing Philip for a dance and then sitting him down for a long conversation, thus keeping him from Lorna, not that her sister minded. She was occupied as the centre of attention.

Enid's plentiful buffet was well received and well devoured, as was the special cake she'd made. It was Saturday night, actually two days after Lorna's birthday, but the best time for a party. Fair to say everyone had a glorious time. And there was to be a further benefit in the days to come as Philip's chat with Patricia provided a vital insight into her feelings and behaviour.

The family had given their presents on her birthday, her mother's gift a small diamond brooch in the shape of a horse, Patricia and Richard (at Dorothy's suggestion) a large porcelain shire horse complete with appropriate bridle, and Peter and Maggie bought an engraved silver goblet. Philip, being unusually mysterious, waited until the party night.

Patricia made the speech during a break in proceedings, and did so nicely and with pleasant humour, toasting her sister at which point all present raised their glasses. Philip announced he had two gifts, which he slipped outside to bring in.

"Knowing Lorna's love of horses I decided to give her something relevant." And with that brought in a sack of horse manure, freshly gathered, so he said, that morning. There were fits of laughter all round. The bag was swiftly removed! He then handed her the second item which she unwrapped with some caution. It was a book about horses, autographed by the author, and inscribed with a printed message of love dedicated to his beloved Lorna. It reduced her to tears.

Then the party resumed at full swing and continued into the wee hours. The only cloud on Enid's horizon was that this was the night Richard stayed over, and did so in Patricia's room, deliberately in her mother's view.

Dorothy had not been able to attend having contracted flu three days earlier, her absence a great disappointment, but a necessary absence naturally. Enid had been privately horrified by the news of the pregnancy, disbelieving a woman of her age could still conceive, worried that there could be all sorts of terrors ahead. She'd so looked forward to seeing her friend and, of course, Max, who was due to drive her over for the weekend, but the pleasure was denied her. Lorna was saddened too, but realised she couldn't possibly come.

The next morning found them quite subdued, which was hardly surprising given the raucous partying they'd thrown themselves into the previous evening. Richard left almost as soon as he appeared, an event that brought Enid some relief. His '*bye ma*' as he vanished through the front door was not appreciated but then she'd never liked the way he addressed her or spoke to her at any time. An unpleasant young man. Why couldn't he have been like Philip and gone home after the festivities? Patricia must've invited him to stay knowing it would upset her mum.

Enid could not figure out why her younger daughter should be doing this to her. Was it really provocation? Did she really want her mother to lash out as her father did that time, that time when he shattered all her beliefs and revealed his bad side? Enid acknowledged it was a huge burden for a girl to carry, and one of great confusion and muddled thoughts and emotions, yet Patricia had resolutely refused to discuss anything much about it with her mum and sister.

Lorna now had time to study the multitude of gifts bestowed on her, and concluded that she'd been very lucky. How kind people had been. Once more she'd examined the inscription on her book. Words of love, pure and simple. The book, Philip's present, had been taken to bed with her and laid under her pillow, and she'd slipped into a deep sleep dreaming about her man and remembering, with a chuckle, the bag of manure!

Her sister was the most weary-looking of the three. She slumped in a chair, declined food and accepted coffee with reluctance, and made some comment or other about the weather, noticing there was now a thick mist where there had been incessant rain.

"Are you seeing Richard again today?" her mother asked, but not through interest.

"No. He's busy somewhere. Something to do with his precious cars. Often think they're more important than me." Yes, Enid felt, that may well be the case, young lady.

"Oh well," she said instead, "I expect you'll be with him again soon."

"Yeah, probably," Patricia moaned, "but don't know why you're asking, mum."

"No special reason. Just interested in you, my pet." Her daughter took a sip of coffee and rolled her eyes. "Just conversation really, Patricia." Enid left it at that. Lorna closed her eyes believing the fuse on a bust-up had been lit and hoped it would die out and not erupt. Indeed, it didn't erupt, so peace reigned for the time being.

"Your Philip's nice, sis, had a good old chat with him. No, don't worry, not about you or anything, he was good to talk to, that's all. Enjoyed it." Lorna looked across at her but decided against commenting choosing to finish off her bacon sandwich and cup of tea.

"Well girls, suppose we've got to clear up. If you've nothing planned I'd appreciate some help shortly. The place is in a right mess. No time last night of course, we were all far too tired, but it was a really lovely evening, wasn't it?"

"Yes, thanks mum. You did it so well, everyone had a good time, didn't they? I loved it, and I'm really very grateful, and thanks for the present. Thanks for yours as well, Patricia. And thanks to you both for making it so special. And it was special. Very."

# Chapter Twenty

"You were engrossed with Patricia at my party. She said she enjoyed talking to you but didn't say much more." Philip Cullen was taken aback, and for a moment he wondered if he had committed a terrible sin and that Lorna was about to end their relationship. "Good heavens, Philip, you're shaking, whatever's wrong?" He pulled himself together realising he was over-reacting.

"Mmm ... well ... she talked about herself mainly, you know, but ... well .... I did encourage her I suppose, but ............ well, she told me about what had happened to her, you know, with your dad and that, and I asked questions. I just got ... well ... interested in what she was saying and she seemed keen to tell me and I listened ....... that's all."

"Well, Mr Cullen, I'm fascinated because I can never get her to speak about the matter so perhaps you can enlighten me." He looked horrified. He'd told the truth and was now in hot water, or so it appeared. Thankfully, Lorna laughed. "Oh Philip, don't look so serious. I was curious, that's all, and there's no need to say any more I assure you, unless you want to of course." She was hoping and he didn't disappoint. He stopped brushing Ellie and looked right at Lorna. The horse looked at him as if to say 'excuse me, why have you stopped? I was enjoying that'.

"Lorna .... it's .... it's ..... well, let's say it didn't mean much at the time, just the two of us chatting, like you do at parties, not that I've been to many, but I've thought about it a great deal since. I'd like to talk to you about it, but I think you'll consider me impertinent talking about your sister and it's not my place, but .... but ...."

"How about Saturday afternoon when we're done here we walk up the Hollow Ponds. I'd like you to tell me all, Philip. And it's alright. I'm worried about Patricia. It'll just be between you and me, promise. Private, you know. I won't tell sis, and I won't tell anyone. Please." He hesitated and looked at the floor while Ellie the mare stared at him full of anticipation.

"Alright. Yes, I'd like that. I just don't want to say the wrong thing and lose you, Lorna…."

"Lose me? Lose me? And here am I bothered about losing you, you silly thing. You won't say the wrong thing, Philip, we're closer than that. Saturday then?"

"Yes please." She smiled so beautifully in response that he leaned forward and kissed her and then leaned back to revel in that angelic smile again, and at long last Ellie's patience was rewarded as he returned to grooming her while Lorna resumed her own duties amongst the animals she adored.

\*\*\*

Disaster struck one Thursday afternoon. Williams and Co was invaded by the police and the premises searched from top to bottom to reveal what they were looking for: stolen goods, in this case metal. Everyone was questioned at length, including a bemused and shocked Rita Bowen, and the owner, Des Gaffney, was taken to the police station for further interrogation, where he was later charged with Receiving.

Rita was so shocked she had nearly a week off and was prescribed some sort of tranquilisers by her doctor. Fortunately, Sybil stepped competently into the breach at the office. Des's son, Eric, a junior partner in the firm, was cleared of any offence and found himself having to run the business, ably assisted by a shaken Syd Berry and Sybil's fiancé, Peter Collis, similarly shaken. In fact, Syd and Peter were given a good grilling by the police, but were deemed innocent at the end of it all. They all agreed they were lucky only poor Rita needed tranquilisers.

There remained suspicions that somebody else at the company must've been involved, the police clearly lacking evidence, but it left a nasty taste in the mouth and gave rise to unpleasant incidents and angry words as worker accused worker. Gradually the tension eased and normality returned.

Micky was astounded, not only by the criminal activities and Des Gaffney's role in them, but by the extraordinary way Williams & Co didn't suffer, the industry, by and large, being sympathetic. In truth, the reputation was, if anything, enhanced, and Micky couldn't believe it. He was already of the opinion that

206

his trade was becoming littered with less-than legal operations, and this confirmed his view that he needed to work in other fields, for he could see the scrap metal business was going to be cut-throat and the money would dwindle.

Rita recovered but said to her husband that she'd really like to leave Williams, and if they moved away she'd have an excuse to do so. This was music to Micky's ears, not that he said anything, but it was a concept he'd have to gently encourage and he set about doing so. Rita repeatedly commented that things weren't quite the same at work. It was difficult to put her finger on it, but she realised a great deal of basic trust and the former sense of compelling teamwork had been lost, possibly forever. Life there wasn't the same.

Eventually Des Gaffney was tried, convicted and went to prison along with five other people who'd been involved in the thefts. Micky's world was changing and he knew it, and he wasn't persuaded he liked the way things were going.

He'd bought an Adana printing press, a small but useful device, and he'd started a side-line in printing letter-heads, business cards and so forth. He took an interest in antiques (he'd always been keen but not had the time) and joined the Pot-Lid Circle and started a small collection of the porcelain items. It was an investment, he decided, for the future. Some evenings were spent printing. He had drawers full of type, loved setting the jobs, one letter at a time, getting everything precisely right and then inking up, and printing the work. It was a new pleasure and it yielded small profits. A starting point.

The idea of moving was firmly planted in their minds. Their bungalow had been valued and they could move away to a cheaper, smaller property and reap a handsome figure which would be added to Rita's money, thus giving themselves financial security for a long, long time. And she could find a local job and say goodbye to Williams & Co.

\*\*\*

Lorna and Philip left the stables around two in the afternoon and set off for the Hollow Ponds. It was a blustery day, but not very cold despite the greyish clouds that were set right across the sky. The weather didn't bother them this Saturday for they were well wrapped up, never felt the cold anyway, and were usually too engrossed with each other to care about anything else.

Today was no different in that respect, but it was different without doubt. Lorna sensed that Philip had something vitally important to say about his chat with Patricia and she was dying to learn what it was, and was hoping she would not be disappointed. They reached the Hollow Ponds and went to their favourite spot where the remains of a fallen tree provided an excellent, if less than comfortable seat. It felt a little exposed, the wind being in their faces, and they sorted out that issue by the simple expedient of sitting the other side of the log.

Holding hands as they usually did here they gazed lovingly into each other's eyes while Lorna grew impatient waiting for Philip to start, and annoyingly he seemed reluctant to do so.

"Well?" she asked. He looked away for a moment.

"Well?" she tried again. His eyes returned to hers and his mouth made some movements suggesting words might be on their way.

"Well?" she added, her voice now full of frustration and agitation.

"Look love, it's not easy. I'm sorry. I've thought about it ever since. I've been trying to think what it all means. This isn't easy for me, so please forgive me if I go slowly. This is about your sister, about you and your mum, and I don't want to say the wrong thing. I just want to try and help but I'm afraid of getting it wrong." His eyes went back to the ground and he turned his head slightly away. Lorna was now quite desperate to hear his thoughts but knew she had to demonstrate a patience she didn't feel.

"It's alright, darling. It really is. In your own time and don't worry. I know it's about me and my family. It's alright. Don't worry. I think you have something important to say so please don't worry." It was all the encouragement she could offer and prayed it would be sufficient. He allowed himself more time for his thoughts as if he was composing his response, and studied the ground some more prior to taking a deep breath.

"Look, I'm sorry. I just got these feelings while I was talking to Patricia. It's my interpretation, that's all. Sorry. Well ... I ... I ... I felt she wanted me to ask questions, to try and understand, felt she wanted to tell me more than she was saying. Oh God, I'm no good explaining this..."

"Yes you are, darling. You're doing fine." She had to keep encouraging him. "Do it in your own time. In your own words. Don't worry. And don't bother about what you say. I'm really interested even if I don't come out of it well. She calls me goody-two-shoes anyway!"

"Yes, she told me. But she loves you, loves you so much. Look, I'll try and explain. The whole thing. Just give me a moment or two, precious."

***

"I think she rejects security. She doesn't like it because what she thought was security wasn't real and was torn away. She had ... well, had a secure childhood, but all that vanished as you know. She still loves Daniel, but he represents security, something that can be taken from her in an instant. She loves her mum, but it could go the same way as your dad, if you see what I mean."

"Yes, and presumably I'm in the same boat?"

"Afraid so. I don't think she cares that much for Richard but he doesn't represent security. But that gives us a clue to her innermost feelings. Or at least I think so. I'll explain."

"Hang on, Philip. You mean there's more than this security thing. I suppose that's an obvious and understandable explanation, you know, security not being what it should be, but you reckon it goes deeper?"

"Yes, very much so. But I'm not an expert. It was just the way I kind of got feelings listening to her. Those feelings encouraged the questions I asked, and they weren't questions I might've asked otherwise. Am I making any sense, darling?" He looked frustrated and rubbed his head as if seeking inspiration.

"Yes, you are. Funny really. I think I understand without understanding! But take your time and it'll come out right." She was anxious, impatient, yet couldn't push him any harder. Once again he sighed, took a deep breath and started once more.

"Daniel was special. First love, I suppose. She hates herself for repeatedly sending him packing and believes she will never find true love and happiness with anyone else. Richard is simply a medium for expressing her anxiety and anger at her own stupidity. Her reasoning is if my mind won't let me have the man I love I'll have somebody I could never love. I don't think she's with Richard to get at your mum at all. She doesn't use Richard for that purpose. That's purely incidental.

"She loves you like mad. But she's angry with you for the way you've coped with what your dad did and the way he betrayed you all. And that anger again is basically with herself. She's incensed that what you told her turned out to be true, and she's upset and kicking herself for not believing you, for that might've saved her so much pain later. Or at least that's what she thinks. She's actually livid she didn't see through your dad earlier so that, for example, she could've rebelled against the nice things he did for her. Like the piano.

"Your mum's the best, believe me, she loves her like there's no tomorrow and is so grateful for everything she's done, and she's furious with herself for not showing greater affection when she showed so much for your dad. See what I mean? The problem is that the anger is pent up inside her and she takes it out on the people she actually cares about and hates herself for it. Oh God, I'm not explaining this at all well. It must sound like gobbledegook. Sorry."

"No, you're doing fine. You are. Please go on."

"All that anger is in fact produced by an accumulation of all her tangled memories and emotions, or at least that's the way I see it. She can't cope with the past yet. She's not being rebellious. She's being angry, angry with herself. So much of what she does is kind of meaningless if you see what I mean. It's frivolous so it doesn't matter to her way of thinking. Fighting with your mum she sees as being of no consequence because your mum will always love her and forgive her. Do you see what I'm driving at?"

"Yes, yes, I think I do. And Daniel? Where does he fit in?"

"Much the same I should think. She reckons he'll always be there for her, that he loves her, so why worry, treat him rough! He'll come back. Her friendship with Richard gives her an outlet for doing what she pleases; she can have fun but she knows it's not really fun at all. It's all meaningless….."

"And she told you all this?"

"No, not at all, it's the way I see it reading between the lines. I could be talking nonsense for all I know, wasting your time, trying to be clever and being stupid instead …."

"Not a bit of it, Philip. In amongst all that I can see sound reasoning. Perhaps mum and me are too close. Sometimes a fresh pair of eyes can see things we can't."

They sat and chatted some more, then rose and walked off slowly, hand in hand, with no particular direction to follow, just responding to the need to walk, and maybe also because the log was increasingly uncomfortable.

That evening Lorna was lying on her bed contemplating the situation and wondering how on earth she was going to explain this to her mother without sounding like a know-all child talking drivel. Later she joined Enid in the lounge and set about her task having decided not to mention Philip's role, and found it easier than she'd anticipated. She may have been helped by Patricia's decision to spend the night away at Richard's place, an event that had their mum on tenterhooks, a bag of nerves, and very cross.

Enid was really in no mood to hear Lorna's discourse, much less try and understand it, but her daughter was speaking with such eloquence, lucidity and emotional warmth that she found herself listening intently. She had previously sensed Patricia was successfully combining the trait of being a typical troublesome teenager with the role of one who has been damaged by sad and dreadful events in her family, and hoped that with the passage of time she would grow out of the first and come to terms with the second.

Now she was hearing Lorna expound the theory that Patricia was angry with herself, effectively blaming herself for what happened, and was naturally shying away from anything that was good as that could be snatched from her, so she believed, in a split second. She actually wanted all the love she was given but was indulging in the bad things because she thought they didn't matter. In truth she needed professional help, not just someone to talk to. Time for Enid to have a word with their doctor.

They were at a new practice now, having moved from South Woodford, and she decided she would contact them first thing Monday morning.

***

In due course Patricia was referred to the right person who slowly but surely started to make a difference. The girl was set fair on the path to recovery when suddenly it all looked like falling apart. And then, when help was needed most, it came from an unexpected source and proved to be Patricia's salvation.

Meanwhile Lorna's romance blossomed and both Enid and Rosemary Cullen, Philip's widowed mother, were hoping wedding bells were not far in the distance. Enid and Rosemary had become firm friends since Lorna's 21st party and by this route Enid discovered that Mrs Cullen intended to sell the stables and move away from London, ideally setting her son up in his own riding school business out in the country. Obviously she hoped Lorna would be part of the plan and this appealed to Enid greatly. It was very good news indeed.

But how to get this shy pair to the altar? Happily no parental encouragement was required thanks to an accident where there was fortunately no injury other than hurt pride and a few minor bruises.

They had been out with a group of young novice riders who seemed to thoroughly enjoy themselves. Upon their return Lorna and Philip decided to set off to the Forest for a brief ride together, as was often their wont, and as a trot became a canter Lorna entangled herself in an overhanging piece of foliage and was thrown from the saddle. She was getting to her feet when a breathless, worried Philip arrived at her side.

"Are you hurt, are you okay?" he enquired, gasping his words at a frantic speed.

"Just hurts a bit. Landed on my seat. That's a bit sore, but I'm sure I'm alright. Bit shaken up."

"I am a qualified first-aider," he ventured.

"You're not going to give me first-aid where I'm hurt," she swiftly replied with a grin.

"Aw, go on. At least let me rub it better ….."

"Philip, you rascal. I tell you, you'd have to be married to me to get to rub my bottom better."

"Okay, let's get married, then I can practice my first-aid now…."

"No you can't. Whatever next!" Her eyes were full of mischief. "But if that's a proposal I accept." He blushed to the roots, mumbled something and then looked as if he'd come to a dramatic conclusion.

"Yes. Yes. Yes it is." And he went down on one knee. "Lorna Belham, I love you with all my heart, please be my bride." She roared with laughter and knelt down in front of him.

"And I accept. And if you're a good boy I might just let you try out your first-aid when we're back at the stables. Now, how about the kiss of life?" Fortunately, being good horsemen, both had kept hold of their horses' reins, but both animals were busy chewing the grass having lost all interest in their human companions and weren't about to run off anyway.

*** 

After her short course of tranquilisers Rita, at Micky's suggestion, had taken to enjoying a small bottle of Guinness every night. Micky had explained:

"My great aunt Emmie, gawd bless 'er, used to have a glass each evening and she lived to be a hundred and one." Rita had giggled. "Good tonic, give you strength. Just what the doctor ordered."

"No darling, not what the doctor ordered, but I'll take your advice. Never tried Guinness. 'spose I might actually like it!"

And Rita discovered she did like it. So Guinness was taken every evening, usually around nine, in the hope she might live to be a centurion!

213

# Chapter Twenty One

News of the betrothal spread far and wide. Enid and Rosemary were overjoyed, Lorna and Philip embarrassed, Enid's parents ecstatic, Cathy beside herself with happiness. The engagement was announced in the local paper and noticed by Micky who hoped she had chosen wisely and would not be let down.

Rosemary had sat Lorna and Philip down together and detailed her plans. She said she was going to sell her South Woodford home, move somewhere cheaper, and live in a granny-annexe next to the house the couple would share, and from there they could run their own riding school and stables. She promised not to interfere! Enid was so pleased; her daughter, from humble, very humble employment beginnings, was going to be a businesswoman in partnership with her new husband. Lorna had landed, and that meant everything.

Good news arrived from Shropshire. Dorothy gave birth to a baby son but not without complications. Thankfully mother and son survived when it was thought both might perish. Enid now had part-time work in a florist shop, Patricia's rehabilitation was going well, and the world seemed a good place despite her younger daughter still seeing the dreadful Richard Gregory.

It gave Enid small pleasure that Patricia no longer stayed away overnight or came home late. But she was changing for the good and her mother hoped the relationship might be doomed, little realising the unpleasant reason it was finally to become so.

Micky and Rita found a house they loved, not far from Ongar, made an offer, accepted, and put Malford Grove on the market. As it happened they would eventually be just a few miles from where Philip and Lorna would have their stables.

\*\*\*

Enid took Patricia to the doctor but not for the reason she had previously been. She dreaded the truth, the horrible truth, but within days it was all confirmed. Patricia was pregnant.

214

To make matters worse, to some degree, Richard dumped her at once, saying he wanted nothing to do with her, claiming it was another's child and that Patricia was not averse to spreading her charms around, an aspect hotly denied by the girl. No matter, thought Enid, at least she's free of the scoundrel.

Within days, and by absolute coincidence, Patricia received a letter from Daniel, a short missive saying that he hoped she was well and happy, and he would appreciate hearing from her. Her reply was equally brief, but stating that she was going to have a baby and had been deserted and had brought shame on the family. She wrote that it was all she deserved, perhaps a punishment for her wickedness, and left it at that. Daniel replied asking if he could call. Having asked her mother's advice she wrote that he'd be welcome. It was a Thursday evening when he came round, and after some general conversation in the lounge Enid and Lorna left them alone for what they assumed would be a fleeting chat and a final farewell.

"Patricia, I've never stopped loving you. I found a lovely girl, Amanda, and we've got on really well, but I couldn't get you out of my mind or out of my heart, so sadly we decided by mutual consent to call it a day. I don't think I'll ever stop loving you which means I'll never marry and settle down. I found my one and only, and I'll never find anyone to replace you. You were, you *are*, my whole world.

"So I just thought I'd say that I'd marry you now and we can raise your child as our own, if you wanted to. Just thought I'd ask, just in case, you know.... "

"Dan, I don't know what to say. I've treated you badly and yet you still say you love me. How could you love another man's child, I don't know."

"Because I love *you*. That's all. I love you, Patricia, and I'll love our child. Our child." Tears were in her eyes. How could this be so? How could it be true? How could he marry her now, let alone love her child?

"Dan, this is impossible. I'm a wretched whore, a filthy slut.... "

"No, you're not, you're the lady I love, yes the *lady* I love, and I'll love our child. Please at least think about it." She leaped

215

to her feet and threw herself at him. He looked startled as she landed in his lap but he quickly regained his composure.

"Oh Dan I love you, but you can't do this…." she cried through the tears now flooding down her cheeks.

"You're my whole world, Patricia. Please consider my offer. I'll make you and our child the happiest people in the world, I will." She felt she could do no more than consider what he had said and replied she would think about it if he would give her time. He departed soon after having accepted the situation and Patricia sat down with her mother to tell her what had happened.

"Mum, how can love be like that? How can he still love me after all I've done to him?" Enid sat quietly for a moment and then spoke.

"Patricia, let me tell you a story about me, and then perhaps it will help you understand Daniel and help you make the right decision."

With that Enid leaned back and related the whole tale about her and her childhood sweetheart, about her regrets, about her special love for Lorna and Patricia, and about her recent meeting with Micky, and Patricia sat there wide-eyed listening intently. Her mother told her about their meeting after the war, when she was married to Norman and there was no way out. She told her, as she had done before, about her dedication to her daughters. She related how painful it was to learn that Micky was married. She recalled her feelings when she heard how Micky had saved Lorna's life and brought her home.

The tears never stopped pouring down Patricia's face. Here was a mum in a million, and what sadness she'd known having lost her great love and been married to an absolute shocker.

"What would you do mum?" she cried at the end, "Tell me what you'd do? Please tell me."

"Do you love Daniel, really love Daniel?"

"Yes I do."

"Then don't throw that love away. Don't lose something so beautiful as I did."

\*\*\*

Suddenly family Belham had much to celebrate. Two engagements! And Rosemary and Philip Cullen had also found the ideal location for the new stables, much to the delight of Lorna who loved the spot.

Daniel and Patricia's wedding was, quite essentially, arranged quickly and preceded Lorna's, but that didn't seem to matter one jot. Time was of the essence!

Importantly Daniel had a good job with excellent career prospects. His parents were far from wealthy but the lad was earning enough to realise a fair mortgage, with Enid providing the deposit, and they settled on a terraced two-up, two-down house in Loughton. The wedding was quiet and attended by just a few invited guests including Dorothy who left baby son William in her husband's care. Patricia and Daniel Grainger had a modest honeymoon, spending a few days at a London hotel, paid by Enid as a wedding gift, and engaged in sightseeing, a theatre and a cinema visit, as well as a river trip on the Thames.

\*\*\*

It was a glorious Sunday in May, wall-to-wall sunshine abounding, temperatures rising sharply, that at about three in the afternoon Patricia gave birth to a daughter they decided to call Anna-Maria.

The following month Lorna and Philip married, a rather more elaborate affair it had to be said, but one very well attended and thoroughly enjoyed, with an evening party primarily for the young ones. After their wedding night at her mother's, Enid away with her parents by arrangement, they set off in his car for a fortnight in Scotland, where they had a fabulous holiday only occasionally marred by shocking weather, but made all the more special by the gorgeous scenery and the simple fact they were so in love their affection enhanced every view they took in. The infamous midges ignored them, which was just as well.

Enid returned home the day after the wedding and momentarily found the house very empty, but she fought back the tears just as she resisted the desire to visit each girls' room for a wallow. Then it was to work. There was a Sunday roast to prepare as Daniel, Patricia and Anna-Maria were coming over, and suddenly it all felt particularly good again. She mused, with considerable satisfaction, that it had all worked out well for her precious daughters in the end, just as she had hoped those many years ago, just as she had striven for in the meantime. Not that it was the end, of course, for in some ways it was barely the start, but her girls were married to loving men and both seemed to have secure futures.

She had her own security, she had money in the bank, a job, and owned her house outright. But she was fated to have another chance meeting with Micky in Loughton, and that meeting would be very soon.

***

Micky and Rita had sold up and moved and Rita left Williams and Co. She started part-time work in a shop in Ongar, sad to have left the firm but pleased to be away and be enjoying this fresh beginning. Micky appeared quite happy and settled and that made Rita joyous and thankful, and added to the pleasure of her new life. And into their world they welcomed Bonnie, a cairn terrier, who kept her mistress busy especially when a playful puppy. The pair of them loved their walks in the adjacent countryside although they didn't go that far, Bonnie only having little legs!

The weddings of the Belham girls had been noted by Micky who thought them the most beautiful of ladies, which was hardly surprising since they were bound to have their mother's loveliness, and once again he spent too much time thinking of Enid but no longer with any regrets. Rita was his love and life as she had been for many years and he kept the relationship exquisite and vital. He would do nothing to hurt her. But a challenge to this state of affairs was on the near horizon.

For the time being the Bowens fell in love with the corner of Essex they now called home, not far from Greensted with its famous wooden church and Blake Hall station on the Epping-Ongar branch of the Central Line. By common consent the station was the most remote on the London Underground system, seemingly miles from civilisation, or so it might have appeared even if erroneously so!

Rita had a short drive to Ongar for her work, although there were days of pleasant, warm weather that encouraged her to walk. And it wasn't far for Micky to drive to Loughton. He'd shied away from visiting the shops there since his chance encounter with Enid, but that incident was now consigned to distant memory where it never bothered him.

During one afternoon, with everything in his business that needed to be done having been executed satisfactorily, he decided to call it a day and head home and get his accounts up to date. Ray was happy to clear up and secure the premises. Before driving away Micky remembered something he wanted to buy and walked briskly down to the shops where once again he found himself face-to-face with Enid.

"Hello Enid," he stammered having been taken totally by surprise, shocked out of any reverie he might've been in.

"Micky, yes hello," she responded, her voice as shaky as his. Their eyes were locked, their faces a vision of disbelief. They quickly recovered. "Hello, how are you Micky? And your wife?"

"We're both well, thanks. And you?"

"Yes, fine thanks."

"I saw the wedding photos in the paper. The girls looked simply gorgeous. Are they alright?"

"Yes, they're both fine, Micky. In fact I'm a grandmother. Daniel and Patricia have a baby girl."

"Oh that's lovely. What's her name?"

"Anna-Maria, and she's a little darling."

"Has she got her grandmother's good looks?" Enid blushed. "Sorry, Enid, that was a bit forward of me. Sorry."

"No, no, not at all. I'm not averse to compliments especially at my age." Micky's mind was now flooded with a host of compliments that he knew he couldn't utter, yet he yearned to do so. Instead he changed the subject.

"I've moved. That is, we have. We're not far from Ongar ..."

"Oh, that's a coincidence. Lorna and Philip live that way now. They're starting their own riding stables. She's mad keen on horses, well, they both are." She couldn't resist any longer. Her feelings were overpowering her and she blurted out her invitation without cautious thought. "Look, Micky, I'm not far away. Fancy popping in for a cuppa? Just a few minutes chat between old friends. If you can spare the time. I expect you're busy." She thought she was behaving like a love-sick teenager, and was hoping, praying he'd say yes. Her heart was throbbing.

"Well, I was actually just about to go home. Got the book-keeping to do. But a few minutes wouldn't make any difference. I won't be expected until later." His own feelings were running amok and making a fool of his mind. He was already trying to kid himself that it was truly only two friends talking old times over a cup of tea, when he knew he would not be able to tell Rita and was therefore going to be being deceitful. "Yes, like to see where you live, Enid, if that's okay." Her heart missed several beats. She warned herself silently that she must be controlled and realised it was going to be immensely difficult.

She waited while he collected his van, picked her up and followed her directions. Once indoors she put the kettle on, prepared the cups and saucers and chatted about matters of no consequence such as the weather, knowing she was straining at the leash. Micky moved slowly round until he was standing in front of her. His heart was on fire, ablaze with passion.

"Dear me, Micky, that kettle's taking a long time to boil"…. But she was lost and knew it. Suddenly they flew into each other's arms and their lips met for the first time since before the war. It was an astonishing reunion. Passion overwhelmed them, Enid losing all the control she'd tried to persuade herself to employ, Micky utterly engrossed in the fiery feelings engulfing him and sweeping across his childhood sweetheart. Awash with such raging desire they caressed each other furiously as their kisses took their emotions on an incredible, spectacular and magical journey round the stars.

They were saved by the bell, if the word 'saved' was appropriate. The phone rang and brought them to their senses. Disentangling themselves, Enid went to answer the call and heard Dorothy's voice on the line. Normally that would've been a pleasurable occurrence but today it was agony, and as she attempted to chat normally to her friend she tried to think of an excuse to call her back later, settling on having to dash and pay the window cleaner who was waiting outside.

This time she and Micky did make the tea, and they went and sat in the lounge feeling a mixture of shame, excitement and sadness as they came to terms with what had happened. But gripped by such imperious emotional fervour it was only a few minutes before they were embracing again, and were lost in the splendour of their burning, vital kisses.

When they drew apart, but still in each other's arms, Enid was the first to speak, her voice soft, breathless, as she gazed helplessly into his eyes, eyes that spoke volumes, eyes full of love and which gave her the impression he was saying 'I want you'.

"Micky, Micky, this cannot be. This cannot be. This can go no further." Micky was not so much puzzling what he might say to Rita as whether or not he could go home at all.

"I know my darling. I know."

"Micky, I've never stopped loving you," her words urgent and pleading, "and I'll always love you, but you're married and that's all there is to it." Just as all those years ago, when they met when he returned from Japan after her marriage to Norman, she was dying for him to say the right thing, say he would leave Rita, say he would rush to her side and never leave, but it was hopeless and she was only too aware that it was.

"Enid, in my heart of hearts I suppose I have always loved you, but no good can come of this."

"Yes it can," she squealed, her mind now beyond her control and all good reason.

"I want it too, but it's out of the question. We've got carried away today, that's all." The last thing Enid wanted was an outbreak of common sense and the tears came instantly. He hugged her to him, holding back his own tears.

In time the tempest abated, and they kissed with renewed vigour, silently accepting the truth and wishing they did not have to. After the kissing came the realisation and, with pain etched in their faces, they talked quietly about that truth and what it meant to them. Finally Micky said he must go and Enid beseeched him to visit her again. He knew he must say no, be firm and really mean it, but what he said was that, yes, he would call again.

"Give me your number and I'll ring to make sure it's convenient." He wanted desperately to add that he would never leave Rita, nor break her heart, but he couldn't do it. Not this time, anyway. Enid jotted down the number, and they shared the briefest of kisses as he prepared to leave.

"Come again soon, darling. Promise me." She was imploring him and he couldn't withstand it, even though he thought that he wanted to.

"Yes my love. Very soon, Promise."

"Promise," she said as he made his way down the path and back to his van.

"Promise," he shouted back.

"Bless you Micky," she called. He waved, climbed in, started up and was gone. She waited at the door some time before closing it, and then returned to the lounge and, clutching his tea cup to her bosom, collapsed in the armchair, eyes closed, and smiled and smiled and sighed with pleasure.

***

Micky's mind was awash with a nasty series of dilemmas. He'd made a promise he knew he shouldn't keep. He wouldn't tell Rita where he'd been and acknowledged his deceit would hammer away at him like an incurable pain. He recalled that time, all those years ago, when he was training with the army in Scotland pre-war, that he kissed that girl and cried himself to sleep because he thought he'd been unfaithful to Enid. Now he'd done the same to his beloved wife. How could he say he loved her and crave the lips of another woman?

He was wide awake to the fact he had to end this business with Enid, once and for all, and make sure it did not affect his glorious marriage, and yet he could not work out why, when he was so content at home, he should seek out a lost love and want her in his arms so much.

He drove home carefully, as that was Micky all over, concentrating on the road and what he was doing, keeping his emotions in check and not letting the situation run wild in his brain. He received a very warm welcome from Rita and Bonnie, was treated to a delicious dinner, and went to his office to do his books, and that is where his problems overtook him.

In contrast, Enid rallied swiftly, free from mental and emotional anguish, and called Dorothy. Having established

Dorothy had the time to listen Enid related what had happened, detailing her feelings in some depth and saying she had no qualms in looking forward to his next visit. He would come. He'd promised. It was a good job she could not see her friend's face for Dorothy simply could not believe what she was hearing, her concern worsening the more she thought about Enid's apparent disregard for Micky's marriage and his poor wife.

Enid justified her positive approach by saying she was a widow and her lover would only call when he could, and when he was certain of not arousing suspicion, as if that made it right and acceptable. Once she could get a word in Dorothy disillusioned her, gave her chapter and verse on all the faults of the scheme leaving her in no doubt what a wicked woman she was, and these were not the words or opinions Enid wanted to hear.

There was no chance of them falling out over it, but it became a heated discussion before Enid began to accept some of the views her friend was expounding and calmed accordingly.

"Enid," Dorothy proclaimed firmly, "don't you dare have him back there, but if you do, make sure you confess to me. Do you understand?"

Having abandoned his accounts Micky sat quietly and contemplated his next move. He was conscious that he would definitely return but had attempted to kid himself it would be to bring a cessation to the arrangement before it could get a grip on his life. All the time his heart was rending knowing his was being unfaithful, and that was something his moral standards prohibited especially as Rita would be the one to be hurt the most should the affair ever come to light. At this juncture he had to pull himself together and pretend everything was as right as right can be to ensure his wife would have no inkling that anything was wrong. Thus he made his way downstairs to partake of a normal, pleasant evening with Rita, little realising that her feminine instincts would notice that he wasn't quite the usual Micky, and that it would bother her for days to come.

\*\*\*

About a week later Micky honoured his promise and returned to Enid late one afternoon. Since his phone call she'd been like a cat on a hot tin roof, whereas he'd been remorseful and had determined that nothing further should come of it. Enid saw it as a beginning and was excited, dressing to kill, wearing a perfume she hoped would be intoxicating, applying just a little make-up to enhance her natural beauty, which she was convinced was not fading, and waited with great impatience.

As soon as he walked in the door all Micky's resolve was thrust from him and tossed to the winds. Once again they embraced and kissed, gently and with greater tenderness than previously, leaving Micky's conscience in tatters and Enid's heart beating fit to bust. They enjoyed half-an-hour together, managed to chat about her daughters and their prospects, about Micky's new-found interest in printing and antiques, and kissed passionately quite often.

"All I ask, Micky, is that we have some time together like this when the chance permits. I know it will be painful for both of us, but neither of us wants to risk hurting Rita and I won't let it happen, I assure you. But half-an-hour or so, now and then, would be so lovely, wouldn't it?" Micky knew that would never prove satisfactory and that their affair would grow to the point where it would most certainly threaten his marriage, but he was powerless against the forces of nature and the allure of the woman he'd loved and desired from childhood. What will be, will be, he decided, knowing only despair and agony lay ahead. He spoke:

"Thank you, darling. But I think we both understand that as we re-kindle our undying love that a few minutes grabbed when opportunity comes knocking will just be too painful, and if we let it get out of hand we'll be in trouble."

"What are you saying, Micky?" She looked almost angry. This situation was putting him to the test and he was floundering.

"We have to keep it under control, darling, that's all. We will want to spend more time together, that's inevitable, and there's nothing I'd like more …. "

"We can't control the strong feelings we have for each other, Micky. We can't deny them. We will just have to find a way for more time, simple as that. And make sure we don't ruin your marriage and injure Rita. It's about being careful, and we can achieve that, surely?" He was lost, lost because he wanted her more than ever before, lost because he had turned out to be less than half the man he thought he was. Where were his morals now? Trampled underfoot, that was the answer.

With the passage of time they somehow managed to restrict their meetings to the same brief interludes while, if truth be told, they both wanted to run away together, or at the very least spend days and days and days and days in each other's embrace. After every meeting came the anxiety, the guilt, the shame; came the logic, the good reason, the sound common sense that hurt them so. And also came the pain and emptiness. Whatever they longed for they were always left bereft, saddened by the unsatisfactory arrangement they had forged and agreed out of necessity, whereas they coveted the concept of breaking out of their chains and letting love rule their lives despite the troubles it would bring. Half-an-hour or so of passionate kisses every two or three weeks was a poor substitute for a life shared together.

Dorothy was livid. She could not get through to Enid, try as she might. Then something unexpected happened.

It was a Tuesday afternoon and Micky had not been at Enid's five minutes before Lorna turned up out of the blue, leaving her mother fully flustered.

"Oh Lorna, my pet, this is Micky Bowen." She felt as if she was gasping for air. "You must remember him. He brought you home after your near miss ....."

"Yes I do, mum," she interrupted, "hello Mr Bowen. Thanks for rescuing me that day. Fancy you being here." Enid was too upset to find any suitable words but Micky stepped in quickly.

"Hello Lorna. Met your mum in Loughton as I have my works there and she asked me to stop by for a cuppa and a chat." But Lorna was wide awake.

"How do you know my mum, Mr Bowen? Didn't think you'd ever met." This was all too much for her mother to bear. She let the words fly at any speed they wished and without giving the matter any consideration whatsoever.

"Lorna, Micky was my childhood sweetheart. I've told you all about it. You cannot imagine how I felt that day you came home and told me he'd saved your life.... "

225

"And you recognised each other after all these years, y'know, since the end of the war?"

"Why are you questioning me so, Lorna? Whatever's the matter?" Anger now decorated her every word. Lorna appeared to calm.

"Sorry mum, didn't mean it. Sorry Mr Bowen. Just surprised, that's all."

"I'm going to make Micky a cup of tea, hope you'll join us love," Enid explained hoping a piece of normality might save the day. They took tea together in a strained and uneasy atmosphere, Micky taking the opportunity to mention that he lived with his wife, Rita, near Ongar, and asking about Lorna's work after she told him what she now did and where. And then Micky was gone, but Lorna wasn't letting go.

"Mum, the truth. That's what you always wanted from me, what you always expected. Now I'm asking you to be honest. You two have met before. You weren't talking like people who haven't met for dozens of years. And I saw the way you were looking at each other." Enid went to interrupt but was stopped in her tracks. "And he's got a wife at home, lives near me. Oh mum, how *could* you? How *could* you?"

"Look pet, its harmless innocent fun, two old friends chatting about our lives. He's interested in what you and Philip are doing. It would've been a different matter if you'd caught us in bed…"

"No it wouldn't. I don't know how long he's been here, how long he'd planned to stay, but he wasn't here just for old times sake, for God's *sake* mum. Mum, what are you up to? You may be free but he isn't. Now, about the truth mum." They were staring hard at each other. There was only one choice. The truth itself.

"Let's sit down, love. And I'll tell you." There was resignation and defeat in her softly spoken discourse. They sat and Enid told her whole truth, the whole story, while wide-eyed Lorna looked on full of incredulity and dismay, and some degree of anger.

"You're having an affair with a married man. My mother. Oh how *could* you, mum. That's shocking, beyond belief. Pack it up now, for heaven's sake. Tell me, *promise* me you'll end it, for God's sake end it." And Enid saw small droplets of tears slide slowly down her daughter's cheeks. Before she could speak Lorna rose and headed for the door. "I'm going now mum, but ring me when you're ready to promise." And the front door slammed behind her. Enid was shaking but with rage, sheer fury.

\*\*\*

Without knowing it Lorna had achieved in a few words what Dorothy Hawcress had been unable to do in countless phone calls. Enid had finally recognised her folly for what it was. Her temper was coming under control and eased further as the truth bit home relentlessly. Of course they were right, Lorna and Dorothy, she was going out of her mind trying to re-kindle an old flame almost as if she hoped to obliterate all those years and start afresh with Micky as if nothing else had happened. Madness, sheer madness.

Yes, she was a widow and free, but that didn't mean she could have a relationship with just any man, least of all a married man, and most definitely not Micky Bowen. It had to stop, this dreadful and appalling imprudence, before she wrecked his marriage and brought the wrath of the gods down on her head. If she loved him she surely could not ruin his life now. Moreover, she did not want a rift with her eldest daughter. She needed to pull herself together, act her age, and accept her responsibilities.

Micky had arrived home to a fish and chip dinner he struggled to eat. He had to try when really he'd have preferred no food at all.

"What is it love?" Rita's voice was full of concern and worry, but sounded drained. As he looked at her he wanted to tell her the sordid truth, speak up and confess, clear his conscience and take the consequences, be a man, but he was convinced he never would. That settled it. The affair had to end. For the time being he would agree a course of lies and deceit, and to a man like Micky Bowen that was equivalent to the end of the world, for it meant forsaking all his principles, standards by which he had lived his whole life.

How had his heart over-ruled his head and allowed him to be sucked into this sad business where there could be no happy ending, but probably plenty of pain?

227

"Sorry Rita. Look love, haven't wanted to say anything, but, well, business is going downhill. I'm having to cut my profits to the bone, the competition's fierce and there are some right cowboys out there, and some of them are not much short of being criminals. I didn't want to alarm you. Didn't want you thinking I couldn't do the job anymore. But it's a fact. I give it a few more years if that. Probably have to let Ray go soon and that's breaking my heart, you know me. Just didn't want to upset you. We've got plenty of money, we'll be alright ....."

Rita leaped to her feet and dashed round the table to hug her man.

"Darling, darling, we'll be absolutely fine, of course we will. I've got all mum's money as well. But my pet angel I'd live in poverty as long as I had you and your love. Bless you for telling me. I knew something was wrong and you've palmed me off every time I've asked. But I'm your wife, and we share it all, Micky. Never hesitate to tell me the bad things ever again, promise me that. Let me share your problems and your sadness."

As they hugged tightly Micky pondered how easy it was to tell lies and be believed, and in that few seconds he became nothing, a weak excuse for a man, a weak excuse for a husband, a pitiful wreck of a human being, not worth a light. He felt as if he'd abandoned himself to the dogs. Here was this marvellous, loving woman, and he had cheated on her in every sense, even now spouting rubbish to save his miserable skin. The only comfort he was able to take was that there was an element of truth about his business, but nothing so bad as he'd painted it.

\*\*\*

Bonnie was scampering around the lawn, letting out an occasional yap, while her mistress was tending the vegetable patch as they'd termed it. Rita was sorry for Micky because he'd worked hard all his life, particularly after his return from Japan, and was facing a strange world where so many things had altered and his efforts alone were no longer adequate. His treasured business, his honesty and integrity, now stood for so little in a commercial arena littered with a different sort of hunger, the lure of wealth at all costs.

If anything they had become closer still since he'd told her about the state of things and that had gladdened her heart, and he was finding more time to spend with her which warmed her feelings. There had been days when he'd been trying hopelessly to drum up new business but he couldn't match the prices others were offering, and even Williams & Co were now giving him rock-bottom rates on the metals he did buy. Market-driven rates now affected every aspect of the trade more than they had ever done. Certain metals became virtually unsaleable.

He'd given it all the hours he could spare, but for all his hard work his profits dipped, and it was likely that Ray Farnham might have to go, a situation Micky would hate. He was not like some employers who thought only of themselves and would put staff out of work at the drop of a hat.

Micky had one more meeting with Enid and thankfully, since both had decided the affair had to end, it was a more comfortable appointment than either of them dared hope. The kiss of greeting and the kiss of farewell were ephemeral moments of intimacy, in between which, and accompanied by cups of tea, they had discussed the position rationally, logically and with as much sense as their overflowing emotions would allow in the circumstances. Enid did not watch him drive away. She had repaired the damage with Lorna and sworn she would see him this one last time, end the matter, and never see or contact him again. Lorna would've preferred her not to meet him at all but conceded the point on the basis of her mother's promise.

Enid resolved that, in any case, having a larger property than she needed, she would move to a smaller home once Patricia, Daniel and her grandchild were more fully established in life. Right now she adored her role as granny, often looking after little Anna-Maria, and wouldn't dream of moving away.

Without children the Bowens were making the most of Bonnie who was cossetted, loved, easily-forgiven, cuddled and fussed over, being taken for frequent walks and allowed the freedom of the back garden, and who was making the most of this worship as she progressed from puppy to full-sized dog. Bonnie helped re-cement their marriage. She was part of a common bond that now seemed stronger than ever. Micky shared home with Rita and Bonnie, whereas Enid, when not baby-sitting, was alone in her abode and all too often lonely.

This was despite entertaining frequent visits from family including her own mother and father, as well as friends, and doing her part-time job and making calls herself. There hadn't been room for Patricia's electric organ in their home so a musical session at Enid's was another pleasure to luxuriate in. So in time the pain and emptiness slipped away, just as it did for Micky. But the hand of fate hadn't quite done with them, although the next episode was some way off.

# Chapter Twenty Two

*The mid-Seventies*

Enid has another grandchild, a brother for Anna-Maria, named Matthew, which has given her another joy, another reason for living on top of the many good reasons she already possesses. Philip and Lorna, under Rosemary's guidance, have a thriving business running a riding school which they have named after their mothers, the Enid-Rose Stables. Both mothers are excessively proud.

Daniel prospers with his career and has made a number of rapid steps up the promotion chain, is clearly well-thought of and able, and is now at lower management level with his salary boosted accordingly. Much to Patricia's chagrin he has had to take up golf, this being a process of necessity if he is to go further, and seeing him go off at the crack of dawn on a Sunday morning is slightly annoying. She feels she is merely fulfilling a wife's role as baby producer and nanny and housekeeper and it rankles just a bit. But she knows better times are ahead.

For one thing they are looking for a new house, a much larger and more modern affair, and Daniel has promised they can have a cleaner, which is just as well from Patricia's point of view. But they remain totally in love and committed being constantly swamped with the beauty of that love in all its guises. Add in the welcome baby-sitting available not just from Enid but from Peter and Maggie Campton, and from Daniel's parents as well and the loveliness of their position is fully appreciated.

Micky has had to make a number of adjustments to his business simply to keep up with developments in the scrap metal trade, and it pleases him not. With great sadness he has had to release Ray Farnham, at least giving him a very decent pay-off, and his work is now centred around the needs of a handful of customers, and this still does not yield good profits. However, having improved his knowledge he is now buying and selling antiques but is keeping a good stock of the pot-lids as an investment, and has a collection of walking sticks, pride of place being reserved for a shepherd's crook which often goes for walks with Bonnie! As yet they have no sheep…..

The small printing operation brings in a few bob and can keep him occupied of an evening. He has not adapted well to decimalisation, coping with the weights aspect as you might expect, but still having some small difficulty with money, and a whole lot of trouble with measurements. One day he came home with a small bar of chocolate.

"I ask you, Rita. Forty-five pee for this. Nine bob for a bar of chocolate! *Nine bloody bob!*" When carrying out any DIY he would routinely confuse centimetres with inches correcting himself before any lasting mistakes could be made. Rita could not help laughing at him, but that only served to make him happy. They had widened their circle of friends so were not solitary people by any means, and were well liked in their local community.

The only cloud in their sky is that his health is not as good as it should be, possibly a throw-back to his time spent as a maltreated prisoner of war, and he is often short of breath. Neither he nor Rita have ever been smokers.

Patricia and Daniel have, but have now managed to give up for the sake of their children. It was a struggle, but they reckoned it was worth it. Enid had always warned them it was an unnecessary expense when they were starting out on life's highway together and money was tight.

*** 

Sadness arrived in the shape of a heart attack. Peter Campton was rushed to hospital having suffered one, and survived for nine days before another took him from them. Maggie was surprisingly philosophical but it had hit her harder than she was letting on, and only days after the funeral did Enid come to realise how badly she was affected.

"Look mum, come and live with me. Tell you what, I was thinking of getting a smaller place, let's choose somewhere together in time to come. Can't do it now, but you can always

232

come and stay, and we've got the little ones to look after. Do you the power of good." Maggie patted her arm.

"You could come and live with me at Coopersale, you know. When looking after Anna-Maria and Matthew isn't as vital as it is now." Thus were the seeds sown. "Besides, Coopersale isn't so far from Loughton and Patricia's looking to stay in the area."

"Yes, you're right, mum. Loughton's ideal for Daniel going up to the city, no time at all on the Central Line, and I'm sure they'll stay local for that reason."

"He's doing well for himself, isn't he? She's so lucky. Not many men would take on another's child. But she's learned what real love is all about, hasn't she pet?"

"I'm happy for them both, and for the children. You know, mum, I still like to think me telling her all about me and Micky helped. Advising her not to throw real love away, as I did, provided she truly loved Daniel, and she did."

"You didn't throw it away. Norman deceived you, and you thought Micky was dead. Don't keep reproaching yourself, pet." But Enid's thoughts had inevitably swept to Micky. She just could not, try as she might, get him out of her mind, or for that matter out of her heart.

"No. Thanks mum. You're right." She sighed and then smiled at Maggie. "I know you're right. Yes, we can look at all this moving lark when the time's right."

*** 

The chalet at East Mersea was long gone and since her daughters had left home Enid had stayed with Dorothy when she fancied a holiday, but always travelled by train, the roads no longer what they used to be. She was adored by William, the Hawcress's young son who was destined to be an only child, both parents deciding not to try for another given the problems of birth that had nearly cost mother and baby their lives, and Enid was pleased and relieved to hear of the decision.

Micky and Rita had taken a number of short-breaks, mainly long weekends, but they did once have a fortnight in the Yorkshire Dales which they found to their liking, and now had another week's holiday to Torquay although Micky fretted about work continuously. They took Bonnie to Devon and she was more than happy and paid no heed to her master's concerns.

Lorna and Philip had a winter holiday to Madeira, just a few days, leaving Rosemary in charge at the stables, an occupation she was, of course, fully qualified to handle. But they were conscious of the need for hard work, and that, having built an excellent reputation, they were most needed in their business, so holidays were set aside for the time being. Needless to say Daniel and Patricia never had more than a night or two away, leaving the children in Enid's capable hands, as they respected that there would be more opportunity when their lot improved.

And as Daniel's ability as a golfer improved by sheer coincidence his promotions came through, and they moved to a three-bedroom house in another part of Loughton where they were joined by Patricia's electric organ.

Micky received some sad news: Ray Farnham was convicted of drink-driving and given a ban, and a few months later took his own life leaving Micky mortified and hoping his actions had played no part in it. But apparently Ray had not worked again since losing his post, and for a man like Micky it was a burden that he could well do without, constantly worrying himself that he started the rot. Rita consoled him but to little effect. Ray had no immediate family which in a peculiar way only made it worse for her husband. He contacted the band-leader, Edna Cammel, who said that she thought Ray had suffered a drink problem for years following a disappointment in love and that she'd observed him going downhill long before his employment was terminated.

Love has much to answer for, he considered. What a potent force, an irresistible force, a dangerous force he concluded, inevitably thinking about Enid in the same context. Enid, for her part, was full of regrets. Regrets about the wretched war and how it had destroyed her hopes for marital bliss, regrets that Micky had not run away with her when they met after his return from Japan, regrets they had not continued and developed their affair of more recent times. She even found herself thinking she regretted not pulling him away from Rita, for she was sure she could've done it and would've done it wilfully given the chance. Would she really have wrecked his marriage, ruined Rita's life?

No, of course not! And she chided herself for letting such thoughts hurtle through her mind.

Micky's only regrets were lying to Rita and deceiving her.

\*\*\*

And as planet Earth turned time and again the years rolled by, and the players in this drama went about their daily lives as so many people did and awaited whatever life had in store for them.

Mobile phones lay in the next decade and even then they would be nothing like the slimline versions of later years, and the advent of smartphones was further into the distant future. The concept of holidays was changing rapidly with more and more people able to afford trips abroad, especially those bargains to the popular Mediterranean islands and resorts, and long distance travel was shortening the distances to destinations such as the USA, the Far East, West Africa and so on, thanks to the new breeds of airliner.

It was a new era. Computer technology was coming to the fore, there were startling new developments in science and medicine, not least heart transplants pioneered in the last decade and hip-replacement surgery which was becoming common-place.

But nothing could be done for poor Rita Bowen.

Breast cancer flew at her in a blind rage, and carried her towards oblivion. Just four months passed from diagnosis to conclusion, the last few weeks spent in agony in hospital, her last days leaving her barely alive but suffering dreadfully. Micky was at her bedside when merciful relief came and he later wept bitter tears, angry at a God he'd never believed in, overcome with terrible grief, furious that her final days should've been so appalling, so sorrowful, when she deserved much more than that, so much more than that.

He returned home alone and wept some more with only Bonnie to hear of his heartbreak and pain, and the dog did not understand.

"Bonnie, Bonnie, bless you, but she's not coming home, ever," he wailed as Bonnie wagged her tail, panted furiously and looked at him full of hope.

He told Bonnie all about his beautiful wife, how much he loved her, about how they met and how he wooed her, about their engagement and their wedding, and about their life together, and all Bonnie wanted to do was play. But Bonnie was his present saviour for there was nobody else. A neighbour, Gladys Bradley, had looked after the dog many times during these fateful weeks and had done so while Micky was at the hospital as his darling slipped from his earthly grasp.

The nurse had been the other side of the bed as he clung to Rita's right hand, all the comfort he could offer in his despair, and he stared at her face as if he was willing her to suddenly be cured and rise up and smile at him as she had smiled so many times. The nurse's voice was sylvan and tender, soft and peaceful.

"I think she's gone, Micky." He knew it, he'd sensed it. He rose slowly and kissed his beloved wife one last time and left the room. The nurse appeared behind him.

"Thank you, Kathy," he said as she took his arm, "thank you so much for all you did. She's at peace now, no more suffering," Kathy nodded, "I am relieved she won't suffer any more. She didn't deserve it, you know, not to suffer like that. Thank you again." He held on to his tears as he'd done many times in his life. Grown men don't cry, not in his generation that is. He saved them for Bonnie and cried all over her as he told her his story and caressed her and cuddled her, and she licked him heartily and longed for him to throw her ball that she might chase it.

In the days ahead they were almost inseparable. She was taken out in the van and loved it. Micky had to carry on working. Apart from anything else it kept his mind from the sadness and horrors and his tragic loss.

So many people came to the funeral at the City of London. At Micky's request Syd Berry made a short speech in the crematorium and managed to inject a little appropriate humour into a completely moving account of Rita's life, mentioning the happiness she brought to so many, himself included, her cheerfulness which was infectious, and her love for her husband whom she regarded as the best man that ever lived.

"She told me that, many times. Best man ever." At the end Micky looked up and saw the tears down Syd's cheeks and saw a very different man from the one he'd always assumed Syd to be. There was an 'afterwards at' for those that wanted refreshments, the hire of a small hall at a hotel paid for at the insistence of everyone at Williams & Co. A lovely gesture, Micky thought.

He tried to be a good host but he just longed for it to be all over. Mrs Bradley was watching over Bonnie back at Ongar and he wanted to be with his dog, the pet he had shared with Rita and which had given them so much fun, and which was now his only real link with his married life. Eventually Syd and Moira drove him home, the couple declining to come in knowing he needed to be alone. He thanked Gladys on arrival, gave her a brief account of the occasion, and let her set off. She too realised he would need to be by himself, and he'd be alright with Bonnie for company.

The next few weeks were exceedingly difficult for him. Business was tough, there were no printing orders pending and there were things he wanted to do in the garden without having the heart to start them. He kept the housework up to date, for Rita's sake, but it was almost as if he wanted to leave the garden as she would remember it, despite common sense telling him she'd want him to tend it for her. In time he turned his hand to the garden.

There were plenty of friends who dropped by now and then, and sometimes invited him to their homes for an evening, or a meal, or just a cuppa. Gladys looked after Bonnie quite happily whenever he wanted, and he also enjoyed her friendship. Very gradually life took on a new meaning and he started to swim rather than sink. Rita would not want him to be unhappy, and the thought spurred him on and cheered him.

He inherited her money and resisted all attempts by the bank to help him with investments, leaving it mainly in his current account although he bought a few Premium Bonds just for the fun of it. At least his money was safe there.

Enid remained in complete ignorance of his loss and only occasionally permitted thoughts of her sweetheart to amble across her mind. Micky didn't really think about Enid very much and she only troubled him when nothing else much was occupying his mind, which was rare. All his attention was on his cherished memories of Rita and they sustained him through the dark days and out into the light at the end of that desolate tunnel.

Before long he was back to his old self yet still allowed himself the odd time when he would shed tears, chat to faithful Bonnie, and grieve privately. He also finished up the last few bottles of Guinness that his wife did not manage, and toasted her with each glass, saying that he hoped she was happy in her new home and was keeping an eye on him, criticising when necessary! That always brought a grin to his face.

# Chapter Twenty Three

*The Eighties*

Jacqueline sported the widest grin as she looked at her father and gurgled as infants are apt to do, her tiny arms and legs wriggling on Philip's lap. She didn't yet have her mother's supreme beauty but he didn't doubt she would do soon. Anyway, she made a delightful baby sister for Malcolm, born eighteen months before, named after Philip's father, and already growing into a very bonny lad.

There had been troubled waters to sail through between births as business at Enid-Rose Stables took a tumble, and there were times when Philip and Lorna seemed to do nothing but argue about even the smallest thing, on one occasion Philip acting right out of character and storming from the house to return a full two hours later.

Slowly trade picked up again and the pair patched up their differences, united by their love for Malcolm who took up much of their time, warmed by the knowledge they really could let nothing come between them. Jacqueline was the immediate result of their process of making up.

They had talked to Rosemary quite openly when there was a period of prolonged unpleasantness and she offered what wisdom she had, notably advising them gently that they would put the Stables in jeopardy if they carried on as they were. She also reminded them that Malcolm was the manifestation of the enchanting love they shared, and they should not risk him suffering during his earliest years.

Now the Stables was doing well again and they had brought sweet Jacqueline into their lives. It wasn't unusual for Patricia and her family to call, and Lorna and family often visited Loughton. Add in visits to and from Enid and it was truly a good and fulfilling life. The grandparents were expert babysitters, so both young families benefitted.

Rosemary Cullen gave them a bit of a scare: she was a keen whist and bridge player and had joined a club where a gentleman named Thomas Balford paid her a great deal of attention and actually took her to dinner one evening. Upon investigation Philip discovered the retired gentleman had previously wooed two wealthy women who had been quick to uncover his real desires and sent him packing. Philip had a lengthy chat with his mother and Mr Balford found himself undone for the third time.

"I'm just a silly old woman, Philip. I won't let anything like that happen again. Please understand that it's been ages since your dad passed away and I suppose I was easy prey. Perhaps I was too willing because it was nice to be embraced and kissed again, but I feel so foolish now. I ask you, a woman of my age." The meeting ended in the hugs and kisses of a mother and son, Philip breathing a silent sigh of relief.

Philip himself had always been wary of Cathy Northwood, feeling she was the epitome of a wild-child when she was most definitely not, and irritated by the affection Lorna showed her which he did not think was adequately returned. Cathy was still unwed and 'playing-the-field' with great frequency and enjoying notable variety in her efforts, with Philip disturbed by the fact Lorna valued her as her closest friend. He remained in ignorance of the knowledge that his wife had once been closer still and had adored Cathy beyond the bounds of normal friendship, and he would not have approved, which is probably why Lorna had never mentioned it.

Cathy had moved to Chelmsford when her job relocated there, had a pleasant first floor flat they had visited from time to time, and in her turn she called at the Stables, now and then staying the night. There was often a boyfriend in tow. Just recently she had shared a relationship with a man of fifty-seven who was married to someone else, and was currently with a lad of nineteen who described himself as an artist, a socialist and a guru, who despite having a job otherwise looked unemployable in Philip's opinion. Dressed in worn and torn clothing, an untidy mass of facial hair to match, he was given to propounding his political beliefs without any invitation or provocation to do so, much to Philip's annoyance.

They stayed at the Stables one Saturday night and didn't leave their bedroom until nearly eleven o'clock the next morning, believing everyone had a lie in on Sunday. Thankfully, from her husband's point of view, that was enough for Lorna, and she swore there would be no more overnights. Adding fuel to the fire Alain (for that was his name) gave Lorna a farewell kiss on the lips that was too lengthy for the purpose it should've been intended for. She looked disgusted, wiped her mouth contemptuously, and vowed to phone Cathy later to make one or two things crystal clear, which she did.

\*\*\*

Daniel had been learning more about golf, a game he professed to love yet usually cursed after every match. One important lesson learned was the ability to lose when wooing a potential client. It went against the grain, but had proved commercially successful so he managed to swallow his sporting pride for the sake of business and thus, in his view, sold his soul to the devil. Never mind, he was doing it for his family.

Patricia now had another interest: at Edna Cammel's suggestion she joined the jazz band as a part-time organist-pianist, and played at some of the rare gigs they did. She found that she really quite liked jazz now she came to think of it, but most of her enjoyment came from rehearsals which were rather more frequent than performances. They were an enthusiastic bunch and tried their best, but Edna and Patricia were the only quality musicians by a mile.

Anna-Maria and Matthew were boisterous youngsters with an endless supply of energy which Daniel and Patricia had channelled into all kinds of activities, most of which left the parents more tired than the children. But what a marvellous father Daniel was, as his wife so often mused, and what a lovely husband, a man capable of great love and passion, and of dedication and devotion. She shook her head when she thought of him, thinking how lucky she'd been when she might have thrown that irreplaceable love away.

And here he was, in a big multi-national company, a manager with executive prospects, thanks to which they had their fine home, a substantial income, a positive future, and so much to look forward to. She was determined to ensure her children would have the best chances in life, and in this she reflected her

241

own mother's commitment which she now acknowledged was full of strength and undying love, and for which she was grateful. How she loved her mum. Thank God for her mum, always there for her, always. True love, that, she reasoned.

Patricia was grateful for one other thing. The Pickled Hellebore Jazz Band, in which she was organist-pianist, was collecting a few more bookings these days adding to her unbridled enjoyment of their music making, which was always good fun if nothing else. It gave her a vital escape from the rigors of family life, a vital break from the challenges they presented and which she rose above so magnificently to achieve perfect happiness. Yes, alright, sometimes the children would play up, especially when over-tired, but she found she could control them easily just as Daniel could.

Neither had ever smacked the children; they didn't believe in it, Patricia for obvious reasons, and the threat of losing pocket-money was always successful. Daniel believed Patricia had something magical in her voice that automatically calmed their offspring! Her voice continued to beguile him as it had always done. They were a beautiful couple, part of a lovely family. But Daniel's work was about to apply a degree of pressure to that relationship and they would need all their love to overcome it.

*** 

As he approached retirement Micky Bowen was becoming a sorrowful character. Business was so very poor, and he now had a small van as that was all he needed, and he used that as his car as well. He had plenty of money, of course, but was not one for wasting it. He didn't need a separate car. His breathing was giving him trouble into the bargain and he'd been diagnosed with emphysema, a serious lung problem. He was still carrying out minor printing work but his great joy had been his ever-developing interest in antiques. Bonnie was his special and precious companion, no longer an enthusiastic over-active dog, but a chum, a mate, someone to chat to rather than play with.

The garden was a shrine to Rita and he devoted all his own enthusiasm to it, hoping his beloved wife would be looking down and nodding and smiling upon his efforts. He missed her but had not become a recluse in his misery. He revelled in the company of friends and neighbours and that kept his spirits up and prevented him wallowing in despair.

But she had been his everything. If only he could've let Enid go so much earlier he would've enjoyed his marriage more, and even now he regretted those meetings with his childhood sweetheart, for they had gone their separate ways, and that should've been that. But then he'd had a wonderful marriage. Rita was his true love and there never should've been any doubt about it. He found himself wondering if she was in heaven, looking down at him, and cross with him for lying to and deceiving her over those assignations. No, she'd forgive him, because he'd never left her and had always loved her, despite Enid.

He contented himself with such an opinion and took comfort from it. Nowadays he rarely gave more than a passing thought for Enid, for all his thoughts were given over to Rita and his love for her.

His sixty-fifth birthday drifted by almost unnoticed, celebrated by nobody, his only present a bone for Bonnie rather than a gift from her. No cards. Much as he liked it. And so Michael Reginald Bowen slipped into retirement and the benefits of the state pension and a private pension he'd been paying in to. Happily, he had plenty of money so no problems on that count.

Thus it was as it came to pass that he allowed more thoughts of Enid into his mind, for he now had more leisure time to permit such incursions. He wondered where she was, had she re-married, was she still alive, how were her daughters doing, what did she look like? She would always be a beauty, he assured himself of that!

Enid had never stopped thinking of him, but then she'd had a wretched marriage with a brute, a criminal. Now she had her family to think of and to put first, and since that was the greatest ecstasy her life was filled to capacity with pleasure and satisfaction.

Her daughters had done so well for themselves and both had secure futures with perfect partners. She loved her grandchildren and hoped they would grow up to be as successful as their parents. Her own life was busy and fully occupied, yet she could not help thinking about Micky, unaware his wife had died.

It was a chance meeting that changed things.

\*\*\*

Daniel's immediate manager, Sheila Paston, was a demanding woman, assured of her own competency, who required total commitment to the cause. Daniel was happy with this, respecting Sheila's ability and proven track-record. He also knew he needed her support to progress.

Out of the blue he was asked to travel to Hamburg with her on an important marketing mission and, having ascertained there were enough eager relatives to support Patricia and the children, he agreed, packed and took a taxi to the airport on the appropriate day. He'd only be gone three days but saw this as his big chance to impress.

Everything went well and a substantial deal was struck with the German company, leaving the backroom people such as the legal eagles, to tie up the contract. That night Sheila took Daniel for a celebratory evening out, a slap-up meal at a top restaurant, complete with cabaret and dancing, and it was in the early hours that they returned to their hotel where he was invited to her room for a nightcap.

"Just a personal thank you, Daniel. You were great. I knew you were the right person to bring, and you've done us proud." Daniel, although an ambitious and very clever young man, was also naïve in some respects, and thus walked unwittingly straight into the spider's web. Once in the bedroom he realised a drink was likely to be the least of his worries, but at the same time, thanks to a fair intake of alcohol and absorbed in the euphoria of the evening, he found himself thinking more about his career than his marriage. He was easily seduced believing if he resisted Sheila might well take it personally and hold him back in his ascent up the management ladder. After all, it was a one-off.

What he wasn't prepared for were the repercussions later in the morning, when he was over-run with guilt, overwhelmed with emotional agony, and distraught with the knowledge he'd been unfaithful to Patricia. He tried to console himself with the thought that she'd had a baby by another man which he had taken as his own when he married her, and found such consolation a poor companion. In truth, he felt wretched whichever way he examined his situation.

And there was the fearsome thought that Sheila might want a repeat performance if they ever went away again. Actually, there was no chance of that, but he wasn't to know it.

He wrestled with his conscience. Hadn't Patricia suffered enough? To be betrayed by the man she looked upon as her saviour, what havoc would that wreak in her heart and her mind? His problems cast a shadow over home life where there was tension, not helped by his inclination to be snappy and generally grumpy, and that wasn't the Daniel Patricia knew.

Within a few days he knew the answer: he must find another job. His announcement propelled the family into more stress and an air of uneasiness hung over everything. His excuses were flimsy to say the least but he was confident that a better post with greater chances of furtherment would be found, and he assured Patricia, and his mum and dad, that his skills would be much sought after.

None of them believed he should be leaving a secure position where he had already proved himself and won several promotions, but their protestations were to no effect. He was offered a job, but at a much lower salary and with very limited prospects of furtherance, and he was half-inclined to take it. But how to tell the family? A complete nightmare, all of his own making.

And, as if by divine providence, the difficulty resolved itself quite suddenly. Sheila gained promotion to another department, which meant relocating to Bristol, and Daniel was offered her position. He went home a changed man and spread his good news far and wide. Happiness abounded, but Patricia never ever quite understood why he had become so depressed about the job and then leaped at another step up the ladder. Well, it was all good enough, and the senior management post he now had gave him a sizeably increased income, so peace and love returned to family Grainger where the tensions evaporated, but he never forgot his infidelity and it hurt him for years to come.

***

Syd and Moira Berry were approaching their Golden Wedding anniversary and decided to have a substantial do, a real party night with fun for everyone, and chose a suitable venue, a large hotel and made their plans. On recommendation they hired a jazz band, a group known to be good entertainers who could provide variety when it came to dance music, good old sing-songs, and a jolly good knees-up, as well as entertain with their own brand of jazz.

And of course it was the Pickled Hellebores who were booked. And of course Micky Bowen was invited to the bash.

It proved a very lively evening, the band giving it their all and making a phenomenal success of it. The vital added ingredient was the fact everyone came to enjoy themselves, and this they achieved without anything getting out of hand. For Micky Bowen the evening had a further ingredient for Patricia Grainger was on piano and all Micky could see was Enid.

During a break he caught up with Edna Cammel, chatted about the late Ray Farnham which in turn brought the conversation round to his replacement, the direction Micky had wanted.

"I'm sure I recognise her, but don't know the name Grainger," he ventured full of hope and was rewarded by the response.

"Maiden name Belham, mean anything?"

"Yes indeed, I did know her mother, Enid, but from a long time ago."

"I'll call her over, hang on." Hanging on was apt as he was in a state of excited suspense.

"Patricia, this is Micky Bowen, says he knew your mum. Excuse me, must get another drink in," and away she dashed to the bar leaving the two face to face.

"Look, I'm sorry, I didn't mean …. well, what I mean is I didn't expect Edna to call you over. I thought, well, that is, I thought you looked like Enid and I know she had a daughter Patricia….."

"Micky Bowen. Wow, you're my mum's sweetheart from before the war, aren't you? She told me all about it. What a sad way to lose your love, I'm so sorry for you, but it was a hell of a long time ago." The lovely and cheerful way she spoke captivated him, for her naturally bouncy personality shone through, "And you saved my sister's life. Well, thanks for that Mr Bowen, thanks indeed."

"Please call me Micky. How is your mum, is she okay?"

"She is, she is. Lives in Loughton, by herself now, both of us, me and Lorna, married and away, but she loves being a grandparent and she's a wonderful babysitter, you know."

"May I ask, if you don't mind, how many children you have, if that's not personal?"

"No, of course it isn't, silly. Two, Anna-Maria, first born, and now Matthew."

"All well I trust, and your husband?"

"Yes indeed, Daniel's home now with mum looking after the kids. How about you, Micky, any children?"

"No I'm afraid not. Would've liked children but, well, it never happened for us."

"Oh, I'm so very sorry, I really am. Is your wife here tonight, Micky?"

"Sadly she passed away some time ago now, so there's just me." Patricia's faced dropped and she gasped her condolences, but before they could speak further Edna grabbed her as it was time for them to play again.

"I'll tell mum I've met you. Been a real pleasure ...." she called out as she vanished through the crowd. He stood quite stationary, gazing after her, enthralled but dazed, until Moira appeared at his side and took him away for a natter as she called it. Patricia had been so flippant about his association with Enid, almost as if she'd been talking about a romantic novel rather than a major event in her mother's life, and he realised he didn't mind a jot. Perhaps that had been the way Enid had told her tale. Maybe it was the way the younger generations viewed relationships.

He didn't know and he didn't care. He was happy for Enid at last. She was obviously in her element as a mother and grandparent and must be exceedingly blissful if Patricia's comments were anything to go by. Yes, she must've found contentment at last, just as he'd enjoyed a wonderful marriage and been a contented man. Yes, peace at last, freedom from

247

turmoil, acceptance of a good life as it now was, except in his case his beloved Rita was no longer by his side.

And here was dear Moira, droning on about all manner of things and he'd heard scarcely a word. Pulling himself together he made a better fist of being a friend, and made conversation with his hostess before the music started afresh, whereupon he accepted Moira's invitation for a dance. At the end of it all he took a taxi home thinking to himself that if Enid wanted to get in touch she'd have no means of doing so; she wouldn't know where he lived. No matter, he concluded, he would not write to her. Let sleeping dogs lie.

Talking of which Gladys had looked after Bonnie while Micky was out and would bring her back in the morning. His lovely dog, getting on a bit now, not so given to scampering after balls or very much scampering at all, but still his one true companion.

***

It was in the early hours that Patricia arrived home to find Daniel fast asleep in bed, their offspring likewise sleeping soundly, and her mother snoozing in an armchair in the lounge, still fully clothed. She smiled. That was mum, always ready, just in case! Awake as soon as her daughter came through the door Enid was keen to appraise Patricia that the evening had passed without any incident of note, but the girl was equally keen to escort her mother to bed, somewhere she too now longed to be, and so the two made their weary way upstairs. Tales of the evening had to remain untold till morning. They kissed on the landing and went into their bedrooms where they were soon in peaceful sleep.

Tomorrow, being Sunday, Daniel would not be going to work so he would have first shift with Anna-Maria and Matthew when they rose, which they did, bright and early! As the morning got itself into gear, there being rain first and a little sunshine later, Enid and Patricia arrived downstairs and made themselves a simple breakfast, and talked endlessly about their separate Saturday nights.

248

"Oh, and mum, I met Micky Bowen. You know, *that* Micky Bowen. Would you believe it?" To Patricia this was a matter of magic, an issue of excitement, and she was dying to hear her mum's reaction. "Lovely man. Can see why you liked him. Been married but his wife's dead now." She munched through a thick slice of white toast, butter and a generous helping of marmalade, while Enid's heart broke in front of her. Naturally, Enid could not show her emotions and had to bottle them up until she found a decent excuse to go to her bedroom.

"Ah, I'm sorry to hear about Rita, but I'm pleased to hear you liked him," was all she could say.

"Here mum, I didn't know her name," Patricia was looking puzzled as she tackled another mouthful, pausing to add, "How d'you know it was Rita?" Enid felt everything giving way, every single screen she'd erected around her emotions to keep them in check.

"I … I … I met him by chance in Loughton, oh, ages ago. It was only a quick chat. He must've told me then." She'd not told her younger daughter about Lorna's confrontation and, by agreement, Lorna had kept it from Patricia. The explanation seemed to work and Enid calmed.

During the morning she went to her bedroom to get her things together ready to return home, and there she broke down completely, smothering her head under a pillow lest her gentle wails be heard. Why was she reacting like this? She couldn't understand. Was it because Micky had lost the wife he loved and she was aching for his loss? Or was it because he was as free as she was? All was terrible confusion in her mind.

When she recovered she tried to cheer herself by remembering her age and that she was a grandmother. Good heavens above! What a way for an old woman to behave! But it did no good. She couldn't wait to get home, she couldn't stay a moment longer. And in her disorder she realised she didn't know where he lived. There was no way of getting in touch. But perhaps he still had her number? He might remember the address.

And so Enid went home in possession of hope and little else.

# Chapter Twenty Four

In the following days Micky, knowing Enid did not have his address, enquired of Bonnie what he should do and was answered with several good licks around his face which he took to mean, in canine terms, that he should write casually, and mention in passing that if she was ever near Ongar she could drop in and be welcome.

"What a clever girl you are, Bonnie. That's exactly what I shall do. Then she'll have my address and phone number as well. Good dog. Jump down and I'll get you a treat." He gave her a rub behind her ears, a practise she always loved as she did now, and he went and fetched a chew which she also loved. "If dogs could speak," he said to himself, "she'd say I was round the bend!"

His letter was well received. Enid chose a day a week hence and replied saying she would be visiting friends (actually Lorna, of course) in the area and would be delighted to call, say about 3p.m., if he would please confirm that was convenient. Two days later his confirmation arrived.

She was quite open with the girls, Patricia being excited by the news, Lorna wishing her mother would behave as befitting a widow of her age, and expressing her concerns on the day as Enid left the stables.

This time Enid did not worry too much about her appearance, not as she had done just a few years ago when they'd met at her home in Loughton and put the wind up her eldest daughter. The years had soothed the feisty yearnings of surreptitiously meeting one's illicit lover for a brief liaison, and she considered herself 'past it' in any case. She was also conscious that he was a widower as if that really made any difference, but perhaps she felt a little respect for Rita was due especially as she was going to Rita's home.

There were no missed heartbeats, no throbbing desire, as she made her way up the path to find the door opening in front of her. She was greeted by man and dog and made a fuss of the latter who seemed more pleased to see her than the former.

But she was shocked by Micky's appearance. He'd aged, and was very thin. At least he'd made an effort, putting on a shirt and tie and neatly ironed trousers for the occasion. That would be Micky all over. Right and proper. They shared a kiss which lacked the passion of those enjoyed during their Loughton affair, and he escorted her to the lounge and offered her a drink. Bonnie was intensely interested in the visitor, maybe believing here was a new playmate, or even someone who was prepared to stroke her, especially behind the ears, if play was undesirable.

The initial conversation was light as they settled back in their armchairs and enjoyed a cup of tea, Enid politely declining biscuits. They talked easily about each other's lives in recent times, and about Rita's demise and Micky's ill-health. Enid was careful not to be too enthusiastic about her ever-growing family, only too aware she usually showered listeners with far too much gleeful detail, and knowing Micky and Rita had not had the children they wanted.

She asked about his retirement and if he found giving up his business had been sad or even stressful, and learned that he had welcomed retirement as he had been struggling in his trade, now having little spare time being a keen gardener and an occasional printer! She was fascinated by that and eagerly accepted his invitation to see the Adana and all the print and other items that went with it.

Once in his office she immediately noticed the walking-sticks. "My goodness, you've got a shepherd's crook!"

"Treasured possession, but they're all worth something. A kind of back-up to sell if I ever fell on hard times. Just like my pot-lids."

"Pot lids?" He answered her surprised expression by explaining succinctly, so as not to bore her, and showing her a couple of drawers of the collection. "Well I never, Micky. That's incredible. And they are all worth something?"

"I have few valuable ones, but I might be able to sell them all in one go and get a good few bob in. It's been an interest, and an absorbing one, I can tell you." He showed her the press and some samples of printing work and she shook her head in amazement and wonder. "You have any hobbies or interests, Enid?"

"Mainly my family," she laughed, "but I like a good read and I'm into those sorts of romantic novels set in real places at real points in history, like the last couple of centuries. There's no end of books like that, so I'm well catered for! I like stories about women who are faced with astonishing struggles and come through okay, often in difficult circumstances, particularly if there's a happy ending. They're usually very well told stories, not really superficial romantic nonsense, very poignant if you know what I mean." Micky felt he understood, and also felt he could relate such matter to Enid's own past. Maybe that was where she had drawn her own strength of purpose, or possibly she was simply a strong woman who had battled it out anyway because that was the type of person she was. He wanted to believe that.

They returned to the lounge and jawed for another hour or so as the time flew past, but friendship had been re-established and they were clearly comfortable together again. Enid explained that she would be moving to her mother's home in Coopersale very soon and remarked how much closer she would be to Ongar, which Micky took to suggest such closeness could be advantageous in this new chapter in their lives.

"Time to sell up, put some more money in the bank, Micky. Rather like your pot-lids and walking sticks I suppose! No, no, the place is too big, too empty, and mum is getting on a little now and I think she'll need me more. Be good for both of us." Micky thought back to Rita and Mrs Grant and how they came to live under one roof in perfect harmony. Dare he hope it might happen again? No, of course not, not now, and he dismissed the idea before it could take hold.

All too soon it was time for Enid to go.

"Come any time Enid, and bring your mum. I remember her so well, a lovely lady."

"That's kind, Micky. I'll take you up on that. But in the meantime come and see me and let me entertain *you*. Come over next week and have dinner. I'll do you a nice roast if you like…."

"I'd love to come, but please don't go to any trouble …. "

"No trouble at all. I think I'm free Tuesday. How's that?"

"Tuesday would be fine, thanks. I'll give a ring on the day just to make sure."

"Good idea. Never know if I'm likely to get roped into baby-sitting or something." They shared a gentle laugh and then a tender kiss of farewell. "See you Tuesday then. Bring Bonnie if you want."

"Yes, I might do that."

"She's a lovely dog, ideal companion I expect."

"Yes, she's my mate, man's best friend and all that." They shared another peck on the doorstep and he watched Enid drive away while Bonnie sat at his feet and yapped, presumably sorry to see that nice lady disappear. "Yes, Bonnie. That was most pleasant, wasn't it? Don't know about you but I can't wait till Tuesday!"

\*\*\*

In the ensuing weeks the renewed relationship developed and the visits to each other's houses slowly increased in frequency. After an absence of dozens of years Micky met up with Maggie Campton again, this time at Enid's, and was gradually introduced in full to the whole family. Where Maggie had welcomed him with open arms (she had always adored him and thought he'd have made a perfect son-in-law) not everyone was so ecstatic about his reunion with Enid. Patricia was happy with the arrangement, having an intriguing slant on romance, but Daniel was distant and obviously not in favour, suspecting Micky's motives as he told his wife. Patricia could not draw him on the subject and so it remained a mystery. As she pointed out he was far wealthier than her mother so it couldn't be money he was after.

Lorna was wary, perhaps because of that occasion when he was caught at Enid's, a situation she disapproved of so heartily, and Philip seemed content to follow her example although he rather liked the man. The senior Graingers were merely polite without being over-friendly, but Rosemary Cullen, touched by the story no doubt in the same romantic way as Patricia, became a good and cheery friend at the rare times they met.

With the approach of the festive season Enid, without consulting anyone else, invited Micky to Christmas Day at Loughton where the whole family would be gathered, but he declined saying the occasion was for them and that he'd be perfectly alright by himself, nonetheless making it clear he fully appreciated the kindness of her offer. He knew he'd be the fly in the family's ointment, not that he said anything of the sort to Enid.

So Enid and Maggie came and had a Christmas dinner at Ongar a couple of days beforehand, and he and Bonnie thereafter had a quiet few days to themselves which, if truth be told, suited them down to the ground. The occasion was sacrosanct to the memory of the happier times he'd spent with Rita and her mother, later just him and Rita, and he couldn't bear the thought of going to what was, in effect, a large family party and keeping a stiff upper lip amidst some who weren't too keen on him.

A week into the new year brought heartbreak for Micky when poor Bonnie had to be put to sleep having become too seriously diabetic for cure or treatment. He decided he wouldn't have another dog. Bonnie would be his one and only.

***

The following spring, however, Micky fulfilled a dream. During his training at the start of the war he'd promised himself he'd take Enid to Scotland when they were wed, for he had found it such a spectacular country and then he knew he'd only seen part of it. When he suggested going now, also saying they should take Maggie of course, Enid almost jumped for joy. She recalled how excited Lorna and Philip had been and she often looked at the photos they'd given her after their honeymoon north of the border.

The situation was helped by the fact Micky's van was long gone and he now had a fairly new and very comfortable Vauxhall Astra, perfect for the three of them to travel in style along with their luggage.

And so they all set off for Scotland, up the Great North Road, the A1 and an overnight halt at Scotch Corner, thence across the Pennines on the A66 the next morning. Past Gretna Green, Annan, Thornhill, Ayr to Largs on the Clyde Coast which was to be their base. A delightful B & B that also provided evening meals had been booked and they found it entirely to their satisfaction, just as they enjoyed the resort itself.

During their stay they sailed over to the nearby island of Cumbrae, spent a night on the isle of Arran, visited the isle of Bute for a day, and travelled north to see Loch Lomond. They were lost in their enchantment, marvelling at all they could see.

The weather was fairly good, by and large, and they were as sad as could be when it was time to return home. Micky's only other sadness was that he could not take long walks with Enid as his breathing problems did not permit it, but she assured him the walks didn't matter. His health was of paramount importance to her.

All three concluded it had been the holiday of a lifetime, a truly refreshing, stimulating break amongst glorious almost unimaginably beautiful scenery. Good company completed the picture!

"Thanks for everything, Micky," the women chorused, "and thanks for doing all the driving," Enid added, "We've had a whale of a time. Absolutely perfect in every way."

"Well, thanks for your excellent company, of course. It it's been smashing, hasn't it?" Micky commented enthusiastically, smiling at the thought of the happy times just past, and the wealth of fabulous memories they'd created. He thought, too, of the love he shared with Enid, of her magical kisses and warm embrace, of the nights spent with her snuggled in his arms, cosy and content in their bed. Over fifty years since they first kissed and they had finally ended up together, and never more in love. Fate? Yes, it had to be written from the start it would be like this!

He pondered the question of Enid and Maggie moving in with him once Enid's home was put on the market but when he broached the subject Enid said that she thought they had an ideal arrangement as things were, better not to run the risk of spoiling something so lovely. He never really knew if she was thinking of Maggie, or even of him and his past with Rita. But he didn't give up on the notion.

In early July, the first weekend in fact, he was due at Enid's for Sunday lunch, and he went to bed Saturday night a very happy man. About five in the morning he visited the bathroom and on his return sat on the edge of the bed and spoke quietly to himself.

"Oh dear me, I feel ever so weak…." and with that slid to the floor. When he didn't arrive for dinner Enid rang several times and finally drove over, a worried woman. There was no reply so she let herself in with her key and received no answer to her calls. Something was wrong. She made her way upstairs gingerly, wandered into the bedroom, saw the unmade bed and realised something was very wrong indeed, and pain filled her whole being. And then she spotted a slipper, moved around the bed and saw him lying there.

Instinctively she knew, knew too well. Micky was gone, gone for good, gone forever.

She knelt down and kissed his forehead once, gazed at his beautiful face for as long as she felt she could, and then kissed his lips for the last time. She stood and prepared to go to the phone, whispering softly as the tiniest of tears left her eyes.

"Au revoir my lovely darling, my loveliest of men. Thank you for what we have shared these last months. Bless you my darling Micky. Bless you. Sleep in peace now my wonderful man. I love you as I have always done and will love you forever. Bless you, my sweetheart, bless you."

# Author's Afterthoughts

Love has much to answer for.

I wanted this to be a story of love in its many guises, about the pain and anguish as much as the joy and happiness, whether it be the love of two people, the love of the family, the love of friends, forbidden love, and so on. There are several angles woven into the tale. It is easy to understand Enid's yearning for her lost love given the dreadful marriage she endured, but not so easy to reconcile Micky's desires for her as he appears to love Rita dearly and enjoys a very rewarding marriage.

For a man who believes in 'doing what is right' and being honest his principles come to be easily challenged and defeated and all in the name of love. No doubt when Rita died, and in such a horrible fashion, his conscience may have been pricked in the years after. How much better might his life have been if he'd abandoned thoughts of Enid when he realised he loved Rita? But he is so engulfed in his former sweetheart he sees her in other women, notably Sybil, and his obsession overtakes him. Today we would probably say he had mental health issues brought about by such a preoccupation, and that he could've received professional counselling to help him. Perhaps. Possibly. Maybe not.

Enid and Dorothy became exceptionally close despite being socially poles apart. Without the war they would almost certainly never become friends in that day and age. Yet they found themselves united in adversity, love of a kind.

Lorna was clearly in love with Cathy and the views of this relationship stated in the text reflect how people generally felt about such matters at the time. I intended this passage to reflect the emotional turmoil Lorna felt when she had lost faith in loyalty and fidelity and was seeking a safe haven for her love. In the same way Patricia's first pregnancy, coming out of wedlock, is seen through the eyes of the time, an era when such an occurrence would often be considered by many to bring shame upon the girl and her family. Times soon changed!

Sibling love is examined. I worshipped my late sister but there were odd occasions in our childhood when I wanted to hate her! Lorna and Patricia went through these phases and challenges as many younger people do. Their sisterly relationship is tested on several fronts but in the end proves strong enough.

I have used several of my works to highlight the serious issue of those who are abused by their partners. Physical, mental, emotional, it makes no difference. Abuse can also be committed simply by a person's unacceptable behaviour. Where does love come into it? And in bygone times, such as when Enid was suffering, there was little or no help even if the abused had felt able to seek it and accept it. Abuse is not confined to one sex. And abuse of children is an unimaginable horror.

Loved ones can be taken from us by illness and misfortune, cancer being just one terrible killer, and such occurrences also crop up in my books, a reminder that emotional pain can come from any direction and be unbearable, made worse when the victim is blameless and undeserving of such fate.

***

I was born in Wanstead in 1949, brought up in South Woodford in the Fifties and Sixties, and have drawn on my memories of the area during the period in which this book is set. I have also incorporated to some degree experiences of members of my family although none of the characters reflects any particular person in my life.

My father was a prisoner of war in Japan and my mother served in the ATS. Their families lived in east London for the most part and endured the Blitz, with my father's mother being killed by a rocket bomb.

Mum came from East Ham, dad from Upton Park, and there were one or two real Eastenders amongst my relatives!

Schooling was undertaken at Churchfields, South Woodford, and for me later at Loughton, my sister attending Gowan Lea. Neither senior school exists today.

Normally I try to invent names for my characters but I must confess that in one or two cases this time I have adopted names from my past and hope that nobody will mind. It has been done with gentle affection and high regard.

For example Albert Coombes, my lovely maternal grandfather, has been type-cast as an avid gardener, just as I remember him!

Neither Enid nor Micky are based on my parents although my father was indeed a non-ferrous metal merchant and my mother spent a short period as a Spirella Corsetiere! We had a caravan, later a chalet, at Cooper's Beach, East Mersea, and enjoyed many holidays and weekends there, so I have incorporated it into the tale. My recollections of "Digby's" have found a way into the narrative, as have the ferry crossings to Bradwell on the 'Pedro'. They are very real memories.

Mersea Island is indeed an island when high tides cover the Strood, the sole roadway across the water, and we were often caught out in our early days.

There was (maybe still is) a stables near Snaresbrook station, but the stables in this story is fictitious (as is the owner) and is not intended to bear any resemblance whatsoever to the real one.

*** 

It is possible that my recollections of Woodford in the post-war years could be at some variance with those of other people, and I apologise for any unintentional inaccuracies. However, this is a work of fiction and I have adapted certain aspects to suit the story.

Cows did indeed graze freely in our part of Epping Forest and were inclined to wander up neighbouring streets and 'attack' unguarded front gardens! And yes, despite being in Epping Forest, it is High *Beach* and not beech!

My father rarely spoke of his time in Japan and never detailed the terrible things he witnessed, but he did keep a diary and it is poignant to see how the handwriting deteriorates with the passage of time to the point of being almost illegible. The diary does briefly mention the 'fried egg' incident so that has basis in fact, and he often talked about his journey home including the train ride across Canada and how he developed his buying-and-selling skills!

***

In Chapter Eight (Half Term) I have recalled my own memories regarding things such as the baker, the salesmen, the drain-cleaner, the dustman, and Arthur the milkman who was a real person often delayed on his round as explained! I have drawn on various events in my young life and used them as the basis for certain aspects of the story.

On Guy Fawkes night my lovely uncle Alan would appear and it was he who 'found' fireworks in his pocket just as we all came in!

Two pubs mentioned were real back in the day, but the Plough at Navestock no longer exists (as far as I know) and the Fir Trees (my favourite watering-hole) changed its name and identity as so many do.

Epping Forest is frequently mentioned. The Hollow Ponds, near Whipps Cross, were a short walk from where we lived and I remember one particular winter when they froze solid. Dad made me and my sister a wooden sledge and we had great fun sliding down inclines and across the ice. Our home-made device went faster and further than the bought ones other children had! The Eagle Pond, more of a small lake, stood in front of the grand buildings of the Royal Wanstead School, later Snaresbrook Crown Court, and was not far from the Hollow Ponds. High Beach is a renowned beauty spot further north, near Chingford, the name probably coming from the sand and gravel exposed on paths in the area.

## Explainers

'Pulling batteries' – back in the fifties car batteries were made up of several compartments. The process of 'steaming' meant heating the cases and slightly melting the bakelite so that each compartment could be 'pulled' out and the lead extracted. Both the lead and the case could be sold.

'Pot lids' – early pot lids dating back centuries were simple, plain and practical and nothing else. But in the mid 19$^{th}$ century technology was being applied to their manufacture and decoration. Felix Edward Pratt was the entrepreneur who employed a talented artist, Jesse Austin, to provide the artwork that could be transferred on to the lids. Others followed suit. In time some of the surviving examples became valuable collectors' items, especially those depicting famous paintings and special events. In Victorian times most pots would be used for snuff but there were other uses.

'Adana Printing Press' – still for sale, you can look them up online! A small, home printing press where you set up the jobs just as Micky (and my dad) did, all those years ago.

ATS – Auxiliary Territorial Service. Founded in 1938 it tasked women with an ever-increasing number of vital roles during the second world war. Those still in the service were transferred to the Women's Royal Army Corp in 1949 when the ATS was disbanded. By 1943 over 56,000 women were serving with anti-aircraft units, although none was allowed to fire the guns. My mother served in the Sheffield area and often cycled with friends into the Derbyshire Dales. Thankfully she didn't meet Norman Belham ....... !

Printed in Great Britain
by Amazon

19810899R00153